Praise for Anne Calhoun

"Uncommonly good storytelling."
—Beth Kery, *New York Times* bestselling author

"Scintillating sexual chemistry."
—Lauren Dane, *New York Times* bestselling author

"Anne Calhoun . . . tugs at your heart."
—Jill Shalvis, *New York Times* bestselling author

Also by Anne Calhoun

The SEAL's Secret Lover
The SEAL's Rebel Librarian
The SEAL's Second Chance

UNDER THE SURFACE

Anne Calhoun

St. Martin's Paperbacks

UNDER THE SURFACE

For information address St. Martin's Press, 175 Fifth Avenue, New York, NY 10010.

ISBN: 978-1-250-08460-6

Printed in the United States of America

St. Martin's Paperbacks edition / June 2016

St. Martin's Paperbacks are published by St. Martin's Press, 175 Fifth Avenue, New York, NY 10010.

10 9 8 7 6 5 4 3 2 1

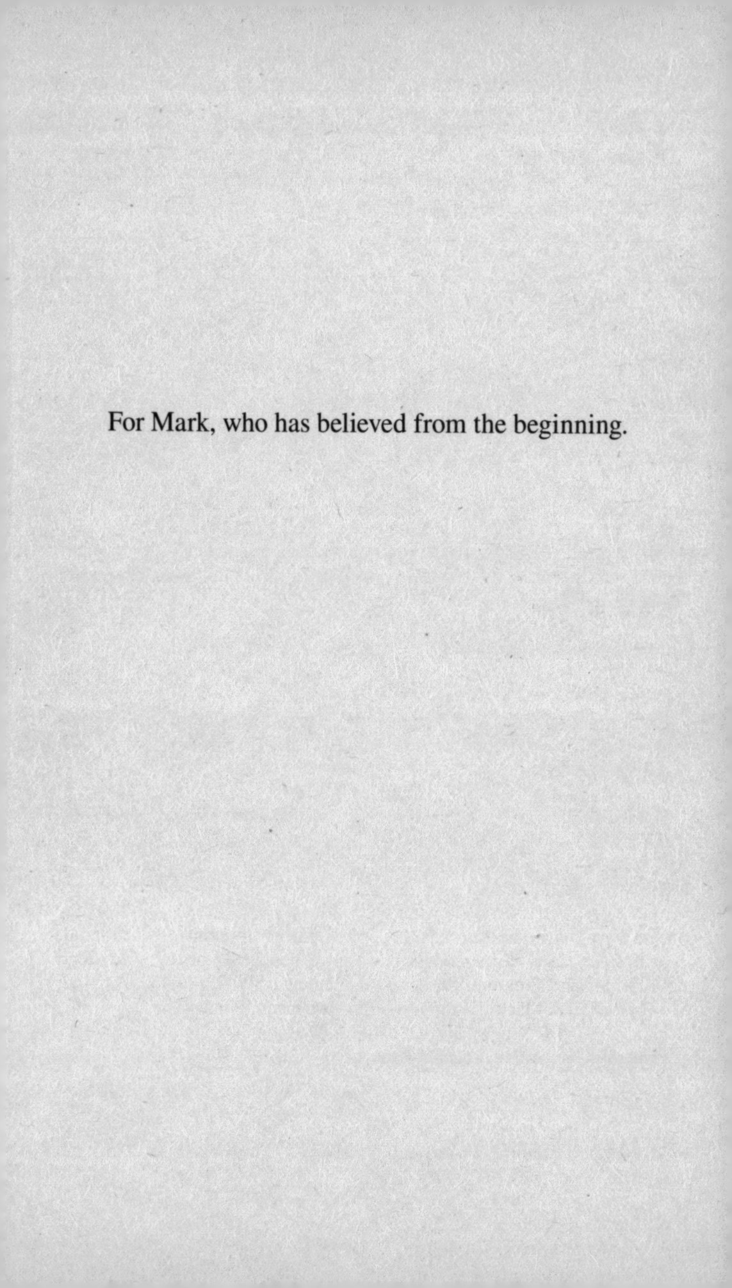

For Mark, who has believed from the beginning.

ACKNOWLEDGMENTS

I'm grateful for input and guidance from a number of people in the romance community. Special thanks go to Julie Miller and Kristin Gabriel, longtime members of the small but mighty Prairieland Romance Writers chapter, who both said (almost in unison), "Start when he walks into the bar." Thanks also to Jen, for smoothing out a rough section. Laura Bradford has loved this book almost as long as I have; thanks for your patience and persistent efforts on my behalf. Finally, my most heartfelt gratitude to Eileen Rothschild, the kind of insightful editor every writer dreams of. You read a manuscript I thought was the best it could be, and showed me how to make it even better. Thank you.

CHAPTER ONE

Sex on a stick, Lord, that's all I need . . . walking, talking sex on a stick. If he can mix a decent drink, so much the better.

Eve Webber shifted two boxes of limes to the far end of the bar and considered apologizing to the Almighty for making the risqué request. Not a single lesson in eighteen years of Sunday school covered petitioning the Lord for a good-looking man. But with a location on the edge of Lancaster's struggling East Side and nine people depending on her for their paychecks, Eye Candy's success depended heavily on gorgeous male bartenders who lived up to the bar's provocative name. She'd take all the help she could get.

"Drop-dead sexy, knowledgeable, with just a smidgen of honor. That's all I need," she muttered.

She picked up her iPhone and scanned for chatter on Facebook and Twitter. A couple of posts from women in her target market, young professionals, about meeting up at Eye Candy after work, which was very welcome news. She replied, tweeted her drink specials, then set the phone in the portable speaker unit for background music while she finished prepping the bar for the evening rush.

The heavy steel door swung open. She looked up from the limes and saw a lean figure silhouetted in a rectangle of thick August sunlight that cloaked his head and shoulders, shrouding his face.

"Chad Henderson?" she said, and if her voice was a little breathier than usual, well, he'd caught her off guard.

"Yes, ma'am."

The two words ran together, automatic yet without a hint of deference, not a drawled opening to flirtation. "Come on in," she called, consciously steadying her voice.

She moved out from behind the bar to meet him. He didn't offer any of the small talk applicants often used to connect with her, so she leaned against the end of the bar and watched him scrutinize Eye Candy's interior as he wove his way through the tables toward her. The walls were black-painted cinderblock, and tables and stools surrounded the oak parquet dance floor on three sides; her DJ's booth comprised the fourth side and backed one short wall of the rectangular room. The solid oak, custom-crafted bar she'd purchased for a pittance at a bankruptcy auction ran along the other short end of the room. The place was empty and echoing now, but in three hours couples would pack the dance floor and every table would be occupied.

Chad stopped in front of her and slid the earpiece of his Revo sunglasses into the V of his shirt, exposing surprisingly hard ridges of pectoral muscle, given his lean frame.

"Eve Webber. I own Eye Candy." She offered her hand and got a firm grip in return as she took inventory. Maybe six feet tall, because her heels brought her to five ten and their eyes were just level. He wore running shoes, faded jeans too loose to draw attention to anything underneath, and a dark green button-down with the top two buttons undone. Reddish-brown hair long enough to show finger-combing ridges curled at his ears and shirt collar, and hazel eyes met Eve's assessing look without a hint of expression.

"Thanks for the interview."

Definitely not anxious, or eager, or any of the other adjectives normally used to describe a job applicant in a tough economy. She liked the cool confidence. It made him very watchable. Some women liked to flirt openly with a sexy-yet-safe bad boy. Others wanted to watch, and wonder. He wasn't exactly sex on a stick, but if he had any skill behind a bar at all, Chad would round out the eye candy quite nicely.

"Make yourself comfortable," she said as she leaned against the bar and gestured to one of the bar stools.

He braced himself against the stool and crossed his legs at the ankle, effectively trapping her between his body and the bar. After another glance at her, one that seemed to take in every detail of her face and body, he folded his arms across his chest and scanned the room again. "Nice setup."

"Thanks. I've only been open a couple of months, but business is good so far." She'd made a high-stakes bet on a building on the edge of the proposed Riverside Business Park, an urban renewal project due for a vote in the city council in the next few weeks. If it passed, Eve's lifelong neighborhood on Lancaster's East Side would get a much-needed influx of money, jobs, and attention.

She wasn't going to think about what it would mean to her and the East Side if the vote failed. She'd poured her life savings and a hefty small business loan into the interior. Any hint of insolvency and her family would pounce on the excuse to send her back to a desk job.

The way Chad blocked her in left no other option than to use the heel of her boot to hitch herself onto the stool next to his. She crossed her legs, and his gaze flickered over their length, displayed to their best advantage in the short skirt slit to the top of her thigh. His gaze slowly returned to her face, and when that green-brown gaze met hers, she felt a heady charge flicker across her skin.

"Tell me about your experience," she said, trying to focus, because each second of silence amped up the current crackling between them.

"I'm at Gino's."

Not good. A neighborhood bar south of downtown, Gino's was a cop hangout, a laid-back, low-energy, peanut-shells-on-the-floor, ESPN-on-the-TV kind of place, where local law enforcement went to unwind, not raise hell. As bars went, it was about as far from Eye Candy's high-energy dance club vibe as possible.

"Why leave? Getting beers for cops is much easier than mixing hundreds of cocktails a night."

"I need full-time hours." He looked around again. "And better tips."

"This isn't Gino's. Not by a long shot," she said. "You'll work for your tips here."

She didn't mean to infuse a sexual overtone into that comment, but somehow the insinuation hung between them. His eyes darkened from hazel to mossy green, and a hint of color stained his cheekbones. Okay, they had chemistry, that heart-pounding, shallow-breathing feeling that meant the pheromones were surging.

Chemistry with me means chemistry with customers, she thought firmly. Watching him work would tell her all she needed to know. "Feel up to making me something?" she asked lightly.

"Mojito? Cosmo? Cum in a Hot Tub?"

He got points for naming her three most popular cocktails, in order no less, and major points for including the last one without a hint of innuendo in his face or voice. "Let's try a cosmo," she said.

He moved past her, close enough that she felt the soft denim of his jeans brush against her bare thigh, then strolled behind the bar, found the Absolut, the triple sec, and the juices, and measured all the ingredients over ice scooped into a metal shaker, his movements precise. A couple of deft twists of his wrist, then he poured the drink into a chilled glass snagged from the fridge under the bar.

"I haven't sliced the oranges yet," she said when he scanned the half-filled tubs of garnishes.

He set the drink on a napkin in front of her, offering it to her with the stem between his index and middle fingers to avoid leaving prints on the glass. She sipped as he splashed the shaker through the wash, rinse, and sanitize sinks, then set it on a towel to dry. His ease in his body boded well for someone who'd spend eight-plus hours a night on his feet, handling glass and premium liquor.

"Nice."

He nodded his thanks and reached for a bar towel.

"You'll have to pick up the pace, though. We've got a line out the door nearly every night."

"No problem," he said as he dried his hands, then looked at his abraded knuckles. Not a wince, or a comment.

"You don't talk much."

In the silence that followed, the door between her office and her apartment slammed closed. Chad looked up at the noise, then back at her, clearly expecting an explanation, but she held his gaze and waited. Finally he said, "Bartenders should be good listeners."

Based on that comment, she'd better set the tone now. "Eye Candy isn't just a bar. It's an experience. Women come for hot bartenders, dance music, great drinks, and a chance to unwind with girlfriends. The hookup quotient is high because the men come for what they call 'prime pussy.'" A small smile lifted the corners of his mouth and formed crinkles around his eyes, the flash of personality an appealing insight into an otherwise blank front. So she added, "My office is over the men's room and unfortunately voices carry up the ductwork.

"The ground rules are that you've got a smile for everyone, no matter if she's the prettiest girl in the room or her chunky, self-conscious best friend. No outrageous flirting, no requests for phone numbers or email addresses. No calling numbers if they come across the bar on a napkin or a twenty or a thong, which happened on Tuesday and led to one of my bartenders hooking up with a customer in the back of a pickup in my parking lot. I fired him before he had his jeans up. She went home alone, unsatisfied, and pissed off. That's not good for business and therefore pisses me off. Are we clear?"

A moment of silence, then, "Your bar, your rules."

Not many men could make that sound sexy, yet coming in Chad's whiskey rough voice, it sounded like temptation poured from a bottle. Eve thought for a moment, unable to put her finger on how he struck her, but the weekend was coming, he was clearly competent behind a bar, and her gut told her he wouldn't get caught bare-assed in the bed of a Dodge Ram.

"Take a shift tonight," she said. "If I like what I see, you're hired. If not, we go our separate ways."

"Fair enough," he said.

"Come back around just before five and I'll get you your shirt and introduce you to the rest of the crew."

This time all she got was a nod. She continued to study him, absently running her thumb and index finger up and down the glass stem. He met her eyes without reservation, as comfortable with her assessment as he was without it. The silence stretching between them took on an increasingly intemperate life of its own, and she broke eye contact first.

She handed him the glass. His fingers brushed hers as he took it from her, and the brief contact struck sparks along her fingers and halted her breath for a long second.

"Thanks for coming by. I'll lock up behind you."

He came around from behind the bar to follow her to the big steel door. She didn't peek over her shoulder at him. She didn't put any additional sass into her walk. Yet with each click of her heels against the cement floor, the tension hovering in the bar's dim, silent air ratcheted up another notch. She opened the door and waited while he slipped between her body and the edge, into the parking lot. Then it was her turn to watch him walk to his Jeep and climb in. The engine caught, revved, the back end of the Jeep skittered a little as the tires spun, then got enough traction to propel the car into traffic.

Startled into laughter, she leaned a shoulder against the doorframe and watched the Jeep zip away. "Not what I expected," she said. "Not what I expected at all."

She let the door swing shut, shot the bolt, and was halfway back to the bar when a knock on the door had her turning on her heel and retracing her steps. When she opened the door, her father stood blinking in the sunlight.

"Dad," she said, hearing delight and surprise in her voice.

"Hello, Eve."

She stepped back to let him in, then gave him a quick hug. "I didn't know you were coming. What can I get you? Juice? Soda?"

"Just water," he said.

Her father, a pastor for a small, vibrant church in the heart of the East Side, didn't drink. She scooped ice into a glass and dispensed water from the nozzle, then set the glass on the bar. Despite a grand opening that drew hundreds of Lancaster's young professionals, and an entertainment reporter and photographer from the *Times-Courier*, this was her father's first visit to Eye Candy. Her heart was pounding, so she picked up the knife and took refuge in the never-ending prep tasks. "What brings you by?"

"I was in the neighborhood," he said, and looked around. As he did, Eve knew he was seeing a sound system that cost more than the average East Side family spent on housing for a year and a wall of premium liquor that represented money that could have helped families facing shut-off notices or repaired the only vehicle available to get a breadwinner to a job.

The silence stretched. Eve swept the ends of the lemons into a trash bin, felt the juice sting a small paper cut on her index finger as much as the old argument stung her pride. Pastors' daughters didn't open nightclubs. They married sensible, stable men, got nine-to-five jobs with sensible, stable companies, and raised sensible, stable children. She'd tried "sensible and stable" on for size right after college, because her family deemed her dream of opening her own entertainment venue a frivolous waste of her time and education. So she'd dutifully gone to work in the marketing department of an insurance company, and spent two years gasping for air in a sea of gray-walled cubicles before "throwing her life away" to return to her position as an events coordinator for the Metropolitan Club. She'd saved her commissions, studied the market and the community needs, written business plan after business plan, and a year ago bought the building housing Eye Candy.

"I'm glad you came. Nat and I missed you at the soft opening," she said as she ripped open the top of a box of limes with a little more force than necessary. Getting her parents to the grand opening never would have happened.

"Your mother and I thought this was another one of your impulses." His normally deep, confident voice came with pauses between. The heart attack earlier in the summer had left him weakened, and he'd rushed his recovery to return to his vocation: taking care of the people in his congregation, and on the East Side. They'd fought over Eye Candy, and for a moment Eve considered closing her doors to ease her father's mind.

"It's two years of work, Dad," she said simply, "not an impulse."

The words fell flat in the empty bar, but her father said nothing about the folly of putting all her eggs in one basket. "This will help the East Side, Dad."

"I was out at the prison yesterday. Victor said Lyle showed up without warning during visiting hours last Friday," he said. "Victor says his son is full of big talk and improbable dreams, like always."

Her heart thudded against her breastbone, then stayed lodged in her throat. That's why she wouldn't shut down. Her family had a long history with the Murphys, from her father's lifelong friendship with Victor to her own unpredictable, complicated relationship with his ambitious son, Lyle. Lyle had paid her a visit, asking for some help with his own startup.

"A business associate of mine will bring you some

cash during the evening, when you're open. You deposit it with your nightly take, then transfer it into another company's online account. A trip to the bank and a couple of clicks of the mouse."

"You're starting a new business," she said, her brain whirring furiously away. "Selling . . . ?"

"I'm in recreation," Lyle said.

Which meant drugs. Lyle would be back only if the opportunity was worth his while, which meant something big, generating enough income that he'd need it laundered. A bar like hers that took in thousands of dollars a week in cash without providing a tangible product was the perfect front. "The bank will notice if my deposits jump suddenly."

"It won't be much," he said easily. "A little more on Fridays and Saturdays, a little less during the week. You're busy. Doing well. No one will notice."

"And you'd want me to transfer it to other accounts?"

He nodded.

"Business income must be accounted for and taxed," she said, as if she was worried about tax evasion. "Taxes pay for schools and roads and business development parks that provide jobs for local residents."

He leaned forward, all earnestness. "I don't mind funding local projects. Five percent ongoing for your trouble, to get you through the dry spells, or to help any community organization you want. Your dad's new program. The basketball court looks pretty beat up. He could buy new computers for the job training program."

He thought he could buy her. She pursed her lips, like she was considering the offer.

"You don't have to give me an answer now," he said. "I'll catch you later, see what you've decided."

She'd seen a once-in-a-lifetime opportunity to take apart a prominent pipeline of cocaine and heroin into

Lancaster, and gone to the police with the information. They'd asked her if she'd help them get the evidence they'd need to take out the biggest threat to the East Side's economic and social health.

She was the lynchpin, and she couldn't tell anyone. Lieutenant Ian Hawthorn, her contact, made two things abundantly clear: they needed hard-and-fast evidence of Lyle Murphy's intent to launder drug money through Eye Candy, and she couldn't tell a soul what she was doing. Not her father, who believed in salvation and second chances. Not her brother, a defense attorney who believed all cops were lying bullies with badges. Not her best friend and manager. No one. Which meant she couldn't say anything to her father about staying away from Victor, his best friend from childhood, because Victor might tip off Lyle.

"Nothing wrong with dreaming, Dad," she said finally.

"You'll be at dinner Monday night?"

Two years ago, before the rift over her job that kept her from the Webber Monday family nights for eighteen months, he wouldn't have asked. "I will," she said lightly. "Love to Mom."

The door closed behind him, and Eve went back to the cartons of fruit waiting for her, wielding the knife precisely, as if lemons sliced in quarter-inch increments would settle her nerves. But as she worked, the memory of the shuttered look in Chad's dark hazel eyes skittered across her skin to settle deep in her belly. While every owner and manager paid lip service to "appropriate relationships" and "professional work environments," the sexually charged atmosphere of bars and nightclubs was a breeding ground for quick, explosive, short-lived relationships based on chemistry—the kind of chemistry she'd felt in one ten-minute interview. With the bar finally launched to a promising whirlwind of buzz and a whole lot of chemistry with her newest bartender candidate, for the first time in a very long time she could look forward to mixing a little pleasure with business.

What her parents didn't know wouldn't hurt them. Everyone kept secrets, even a pastor's daughter.

Mistake number one: the "yes, ma'am" that came right after he opened the door and made eye contact with Eve Webber. The connection hit him like a blow to the sternum, dropping him twelve years into the past to boot camp, where *ma'am* and *sir* became spinal reflexes. While a bartender in need of a job might use *ma'am* out of respect, his tone would have been gentler, less authoritative.

Mistake number two: getting scratch on the way onto the street. Ideal employees didn't drive like a sixteen-year-old trying to impress a girl in the school parking lot. But the adrenaline contracted the muscles in his calf, and the next thing he knew the rear tires were spinning. Once again, instinct took over and he automatically corrected for the swerve. In an effort to slow his pulse he exhaled slow and deep, relaxed his grip on the wheel, and, most important, lifted the gas pedal from the Jeep's floor.

For Detective Matt Dorchester, one of the most treacherous parts of undercover work for the Lancaster Police Department was discovering exactly how deeply military and paramilitary organizations were carved into his bones. Twenty minutes into his newest role and he'd already made two dangerous mistakes, two more than he'd made in either of his previous, months-long undercover assignments.

Most men know how to steer out of a skid. It's not a dead giveaway that you've spent years behind the wheel of a Crown Vic with the Interceptor package. Most important, you're not clinging to your honor with your fingertips.

The sun hung low in the sky, the mid-afternoon heat index just over a hundred degrees. The humidity-saturated air lay thick and damp against his skin as he scrupulously obeyed the speed limit all the way from Eye Candy to the Eastern Precinct. Storefronts and chrome bumpers reflected the sun's glare as heat and shimmer, much like the thick layers of Eve Webber's black hair fell in her face as she talked, glinting against her jaw, her cheekbone. Intellectually he knew it would be cool to the touch, but that didn't stop his hand from tingling with the desire to slide through the strands.

Get a grip, Dorchester. That wasn't a job interview, let alone a date. You're a cop. She's an informant in danger.

At the stoplight before the turn into the Eastern Precinct he flexed his hand to short-circuit the sensation in his fingers, felt the scabs covering his knuckles tug at the healing skin. He'd stop tonight, get another bottle of ibuprofen for his brother, and pick up a tube of antibacterial ointment while he was at it. Battered knuckles wouldn't go over well in a bar like Eye Candy. Once inside the building, he sidestepped Officer Connor McCormick bringing in a handcuffed, viciously swearing man.

"Busy night?" Matt asked, taking in his arrest's prison-honed muscles and ink. Conn was a couple of inches taller than Matt and built like a tank. Conn had started working undercover in the last few months, mostly buy-and-busts. Matt knew him as a solid cop, usually first on a scene, and like Matt, he lived and breathed the job.

"Never a dull moment," Conn said, grinning.

"What'd he do?" Matt asked, nodding at Conn's detainee.

"Breaking and entering, assault, resisting arrest," Conn said. "For starters. Pattern matches a string of similar incidents."

"You got nothing, motherfucker," the guy snarled.

"What I've got is DNA from when you spit on me," Conn said, almost cheerful as the guy tried to wrench free. "Where do you think you're going? You're handcuffed and in the middle of the Block," he asked, using the name on the street for the Eastern. More usefully, he tightened his grip on the pressure point in the guy's elbow. "This dance is just getting started."

The guy snarled out a string of profanities describing his night with Conn's mother.

"Sounds about right," Conn said, but Matt didn't miss the glint in Conn's eye. "She's been dead for twenty years, but dead's probably the only way you get laid."

The guy checked for a second. "Respects, man," he said, "but you're still a pig motherfucker. Get your fucking hand off my fucking elbow! I can't feel my fucking fingers!"

"Need a hand?" Matt asked.

"Nah," Conn said. "He's a pussy . . . cat. Besides, Hawthorn's looking for you."

Great. Matt left him to it, and took the stairs two at a time to the undercover unit's bullpen. His partner, Detective Joanna Sorenson, sat at her desk. Another detective, Andy Carlucci, loomed over her shoulder, a blatant invasion of personal space guaranteed to drive Sorenson nuts.

"Jesus Christ, Dorchester, you're going undercover in a strip club? Who'd you piss off?" Carlucci said, mock-astonished. "No neo-Nazis? No domestic terrorists stockpiling explosives?"

Jealousy rode the edges of the words. Carlucci routinely petitioned Lieutenant Hawthorn for undercover assignments, and was just as routinely turned down. Volatile and far too quick to make assumptions or rush a situation, Carlucci lacked the qualities crucial for successful undercover work: an unflappable demeanor, bone-deep patience, wits, and finely tuned instincts. Matt's father drilled in unemotional patience. Nineteen months in Iraq and eight years on Lancaster's streets honed the wits and instincts.

Matt ignored Carlucci, sat down across from Sorenson, and powered up his laptop. Carlucci lingered at Sorenson's shoulder for a moment, then straightened and folded his arms across his chest. "Watch your back with the owner," he said. "A guy hiring all male bartenders . . ." He let the end of the sentence hang in the air. When he didn't get the expected protest, or any response at all, he linked his fingers across his belly and spoke to Sorenson. "Your last name's Sorenson. You're third generation LPD and your father shit gold bricks so you can write your own ticket with the lieutenant, but you're working with this stiff. He's got zero personality."

"He gets the job done," Sorenson said without looking up.

"Low standards, *Sorenson*," Carlucci said.

At the stress on Sorenson's last name Matt cut Andy a look, but Andy still focused on Sorenson, who was proofreading an arrest report. "Getting the job done is the only standard that matters, Carlucci," she replied with a lack of interest that would successfully drive *Carlucci* nuts. "How's your clearance rate?"

Carlucci turned back to his own desk. "Fuck you both."

"Black, two sugars, thanks," Sorenson said absently.

Same shit, different day. Matt dropped Carlucci from his awareness, started a new case file, and began composing the report describing his interview with Eve Webber.

At fifteen thirty hours I approached Ms. Webber in her place of business. Subject is female, Caucasian, approximately five feet six inches—

. . . mostly slim, toned legs. . . .

. . . *green eyes, black hair* . . .

. . . that kept falling in her eyes . . .

That memory halted his fingers on the keyboard. Touching hair was often a subconscious gesture expressing interest in a man. Eve Webber's just wouldn't stay out of her face, sliding free from its mooring behind her ear, shadowing an eye, but he didn't think she was coming on to him. A woman prepared to tell a potential bartender to keep his hands off the customers or face retribution akin to the wrath of God wouldn't bother to flirt. She'd name a time and place, and bring her best game.

And flirting didn't explain that strange humming connection that revved into the red zone when their fingers met.

"What's this all about anyway?" Carlucci asked.

The informant offered the job contingent on satisfactory performance tonight.

Delete.

Matt reached for the distancing language of a police report to describe the bar's interior, the possibility of alternate exits upstairs or in the back.

"The operation with the FBI and the DEA to get Lyle Murphy. He's moving home and bringing bad news with him," Sorenson said when it became apparent Matt wasn't going to bother answering Carlucci.

"What kind of bad news?"

"The Strykers."

As he reread the report, Matt heard Carlucci's faint whistle. Much better. Calm, logical, focused on the case at hand. No mention of hair or legs or eyes, as if describing features could sum up the sheer femininity radiating from Eve Webber during a simple job interview. Ten minutes with her and he'd felt something. Still felt it thirty minutes later. Not desire. He understood desire, dealt with it. This was different, more visceral, deeply buried, long forgotten, and leading him to make two mistakes when the acceptable error rate was zero point zero.

Lieutenant Ian Hawthorn walked down the aisle between the detectives' desks. "Well?" he said to Matt.

"I've got a trial shift tonight," Matt said. "If she's happy at the end of it, I've got the job."

Hawthorn folded his arms. "The FBI's been running this operation for over a year, and getting nowhere until a couple of weeks ago, when Ms. Webber walked in off the street and said Murphy approached her about using her bar to launder the money they're making in the region. She agreed to be an informant and help us get him. She's the connection the Feds needed to get the whole chain, from the buy-and-busts on street corners right up to the top guys."

Carlucci whistled again.

"That's the good news. The bad news is that somehow word got back to Murphy. McCormick was booking a Stryker when she walked in. Maybe he saw her, and reported back to Lyle Murphy. It doesn't matter," Hawthorn said. "She managed to talk her way out of the situation with Lyle but people who inform on the Strykers have a nasty habit of dying in a drive-by, or worse, disappearing off the face of the earth. So Detective Dorchester just got himself a job as Eye Candy's newest bartender."

"This is a big fucking deal. Shouldn't we put in plainclothes officers?" Carlucci asked. "Hang out in the bar, keep an eye on the situation?"

Sorenson shoved her keyboard tray under her desk and looked at Carlucci, her gaze flicking over the buzz cut, slacks, and suit jacket. "Even plainclothes cops look like cops. They walk and talk and think like cops, and a ten-year-old in that neighborhood can pick us out of a crowd. Matt, on the other hand, looks like the kind of guy who'd bounce from job to job, city to city. Just the right amount of bad boy," she said consideringly. "No offense."

"None taken," Matt said. He knew exactly how he looked, how to make it work for him, how to switch things up when it wasn't working. It worked for Eve Webber. Anyone with eyes could see that.

"She refused a police presence in her place of business," Hawthorn said. "Which works in our favor. If she knows Matt's a cop, she might make a mistake, tell someone, give the whole thing away before we even get started. Murphy would kill her without thinking twice about it. She doesn't know exactly how high we're aiming either. All she's thinking about is the East Side, not bringing down the whole Strykers' pipeline. If she makes a mistake, we lose the whole case and look like boneheads in front of the Feds."

Hawthorn wasn't telling them everything, which didn't surprise Matt. Hawthorn was the youngest member of the only LPD family with a longer history than Sorenson's. He'd learned discretion at his father's knee, grew up watching press conferences when his dad was the chief of police, and worked on his subsequent campaign for mayor. Hawthorn's detractors branded him a political animal, not human. Normally Matt didn't ask questions, but it was his ass on the line with Eve Webber.

"You don't trust her," Matt said. *That's emotion talking. Besides, you can't go back now and tell her who you really are, then ask her out.*

"I don't trust anyone," Hawthorn responded. "One, we offered her a police presence. She refused. Two, I know Eve from high school. She's impulsive, tends to act before she thinks."

"Great," Sorenson said.

"Three, she needs money. We ran her financials. Opening the bar has her in debt up to her eyeballs. People have been tempted for far less than what Murphy offered her. I'm not looking to get double-crossed. This way we keep our cards close to our chest, provide protection, and keep her on our side. Best-case scenario, nothing interesting happens and she never finds out. We get the evidence we need, Matt quits when this is over, and everyone goes away happy."

That was classic Hawthorn: get intel and trust no one, not even a high school friend. And the only thing Matt had to sacrifice was his honor. He was the expendable point man out in front, getting the most up-to-date, accurate information about a situation. Like walking point, undercover work was the department's riskiest assignment, requiring ice water for blood and an ability to juggle identities over long periods of time. But they were dead wrong about her. No way would she take money from a guy like Murphy. He knew an honorable person when he saw one. He just didn't see one in the mirror much anymore.

"Matt, what's your read?"

"The bar's right in that borderline neighborhood between the river and civilization. Two blocks north and you're shopping for high-end goods in SoMa. A block south and you're in those abandoned warehouses the city wants to knock down for the new business park.

The building's a basic cinderblock exterior with a very expensive, upscale interior and about as girl-oriented as you can get. Murphy's smart. We'd never look twice at this place."

"Did she ask for references?"

"I used Gino as my current employer. She knew the bar, so she might call him."

Gino was a retired cop now managing his family's bar. "I called him just after you left and explained the situation. He'll verify your cover."

"We're taking a risk with my undercover identity," Matt said. "She was carrying an iPhone like we'd have to pry it out of her cold, dead hands. I guarantee pictures from inside Eye Candy are all over the internet."

"Everyone has a cell phone with a camera these days. It's never bothered you before," Hawthorn said. "She doesn't hire women—"

"Thank God," Sorenson said under her breath. Matt huffed. He'd spent plenty of time on the other end of a mike feed listening to Sorenson banter with johns.

"—and you're our best."

Hawthorn's phone rang. Carlucci wandered off. Matt slumped in his chair and opened the top drawer of his desk, rummaging through the assortment of paper clips and pens in the pencil tray.

Across the desk, Sorenson was working her way through an arrest report. "What did you do to your knuckles?" she asked without looking up.

"Went at the speed bag a little too long last night."

That got him raised eyebrows, Sorenson's version of mother hen clucking and fussing.

"Luke didn't get the job. He's pretty frustrated."

His brother graduated from college in May and still

hadn't found a full-time job in his field of biology. Matt told him not to worry about it, but with each near miss Luke's temper frayed a little more. Tensions were high in the small house.

"And that sent you to the speed bag because . . . ?"

"Needed a workout," he said evenly.

Sorenson went back to the report. Matt returned his attention to his open desk drawer, pushed aside a jumble of small binder clips and rubber bands, and found a thin gold wedding ring He hooked it with his index finger, then used his opposing thumb and forefinger to set it spinning in a hypnotic, gleaming whirl on the surface of his desk.

Married? Not married? What's my angle here?

When the gold circle spun down and clattered to a stop, Sorenson asked, "You think this'll go down better if there's a Mrs. Chad Henderson?"

Sometimes a ring helped. He wore it when working prostitution busts because hookers were less wary of a "married man," as if wedding vows somehow explained trolling Craigslist for sex. The smart ones still made him strip to his skin before talking money because most cops wouldn't go that far to throw off suspicion.

He would.

"I wasn't wearing it for the interview," he said as he flicked the ring into a second spin.

"Left it at home?" Sorenson offered.

"Possible," he said absently.

If he wore the ring, she'd back off. No way would Eve start anything with a married man. But the stakes were too high to give her any excuse to put distance between them. Without her knowledge or consent, he had to get up in her business, in her personal life, in her head. He didn't like it at all.

Do your job. She's the most important informant in the biggest case in the department's history, and she's playing with fire. If the Strykers find out what she's doing . . .

Snapshots of brutalized bodies flared in his brain. To scatter them he flattened his palm over the ring, ending the spin with a thud, swept it back in the drawer, and got to his feet.

"Hold on and I'll wire you up," Sorenson said.

Standard protocol for undercover operations called for any officer involved to wear a wire, but Matt shook his head. "She had a concert-worthy sound system in there," he said. "And she said she'd get me my shirt later. No telling who will be around when I change." He'd have to ditch the nearly invisible Sig P239 inside his waistband before he reported for work. The Ka-bar and the Kahr PM9 would be fine on either ankle, hidden by his jeans.

Sorenson sat back in her chair. "So no radio either, in what could be a long-term operation," she said. "I don't like it."

He looked down at her. "You like working with someone who gets the job done."

"There's a fine line between 'results' and 'cowboy.' Grab a phone and give me the number," she said. "Check in when you leave too, so I don't lose my beauty sleep worrying about you."

"I'm late. Tell Hawthorn," he said, knowing his LT would be no happier with his unmonitored state than his partner was. Sorenson knew that too, because she flipped him off. He tossed her a half salute/half wave, signed out a cell phone he'd use as Chad Henderson's for the duration of the case, registered his call sign and location with dispatch, then headed out to protect the department's most valuable asset, who just happened to be the first woman in years he'd felt even a flicker of emotion for.

Lock it down, Dorchester. It's on.

CHAPTER TWO

Eve tapped the screen on her iPhone to disconnect a call and smiled at Chad. "You're early," she said.

He gestured to the fruit boxes stacked neatly to her left and the filled tubs waiting to be distributed along the bar. "Thought you might need a hand with prep."

"Prep isn't part of your job description." As the owner, however, no detail of Eye Candy's nightly operation was too small for her. Doing prep herself ensured her product met her rigorous standards and helped her gauge what drinks were selling each night, enabling her to adjust inventory accordingly.

A pointed glance at his watch, then back at the boxes. "You've got nothing better to do?"

Balancing her accounts, liquor inventory, plus another run through the social networking sites, but she also needed to keep her payroll costs down. "I like your initiative but I can't pay you, and I won't take advantage of you," she said before she thought about how it sounded.

His gaze went heavy-lidded, more green than hazel as he opened his hands. "I'm here."

The invitation simmered under his words, and a slow smile tugged at the corners of her mouth. "All yours," she said.

He came around the end of the bar, but rather than stepping back as she emerged, he turned sideways and brushed against her, chest to chest. From the firm set of his lips to the hard planes of his torso, there wasn't a hint of give to him.

The heat of his body, tangible in the cool, dimly lit space, must have softened her voice. "I'll be upstairs," she said, far more throatily than she intended.

"Your office up there?" he asked as he pulled out tubs and familiarized himself with the setup.

"Yes." And behind her office was her apartment, with another set of stairs leading down into the alley behind the bar. When he picked up a knife and said nothing else, she headed for the staircase.

Inside her office she collapsed into her desk chair, brought her laptop out of sleep mode, and pulled up her accounting software and a browser window. In between balancing the books, she accepted and left personal messages to friend requests. The local paper's Arts and Culture section had profiled Eye Candy a week earlier and the number of online connections quadrupled in that time, but online friends didn't necessarily translate into a line out the door.

Ten minutes later the front door slammed, then heavy boots clomped across the dance floor and up the stairs. The thud of boot sole against wrought iron punctuated off-key singing to 'NSync, audible clues that her best friend of twenty years and front manager, Natalie Gray, had arrived for work.

"Who's downstairs?" Natalie asked when she appeared in the doorway. Tugging white earbuds from one ear, then the other, she grimaced when she accidentally yanked on a section of her layered blonde hair. She wore black knee-high biker boots, a denim microskirt, and a white stretchy tank top with the Eye Candy logo straining across her chest, the outfit completed by thick mascara and baby blue eye shadow.

Eve got to her feet and closed the door on Natalie's piercing voice. "Chad Henderson. I got about a dozen emails in response to the online ad, but he was the only one who took the initiative to call for an interview. If he works out tonight, he's got the job."

Natalie slumped into one of the office chairs and gave Eve a shrewd look as she wound the earbud cord around her iPod. "He interviewed okay? We've been superbusy, with the warm weather."

"He mixed me a nice cosmo and doesn't seem likely to hook up with a customer. After what happened with Brent that was enough for me."

Nat pursed her lips and nodded. "I'm sure he'll be more than enough for you," she said slyly.

Eve ignored her. "Hand me my makeup bag, would you?"

Nat snagged the clear plastic bag from Eve's desk and held it over her shoulder. Eve uncapped her mascara to touch up the tips of her lashes. Just a hint of foundation, blush on her cheekbones, and smudged eye makeup in shades of cream and brown brought out her green eyes. The finishing touch was lipstick one shade of rose darker than her lips. The overall look said, "I'm hard to get but worth the effort" and needed minimal retouching, important when she wouldn't sit down between six and close.

She jabbed the mascara wand at the tube but missed, leaving a black smear on the back of her hand.

"You okay?" Natalie asked.

She'd told Natalie about Lyle's initial call, setting up

a "dinner date" to "catch up." Once she heard what Lyle wanted from her, she'd gone straight to the cops. Lieutenant Hawthorn, who she knew as "Ian" from when they were in high school, had suggested putting in officers to keep an eye on things, but Eve turned him down. Lyle was volatile, and violent. Trading on their history, she could manage Lyle if he thought she was loyal to him, but if word got back that she had cops hanging out in her bar, he was capable of anything if he thought his honor was damaged. The whole situation was dangerous enough without throwing a bunch of cops into the combustible mix that was Eye Candy, and there was no way she'd get Natalie involved in something so dangerous.

"I'm fine," Eve said. "Hand me a tissue?"

Natalie plucked one from the box on Eve's desk and handed it to her. "You haven't heard from Lyle again, have you?"

Her friend knew her far too well. "No," Eve said as she wiped off the mascara.

"He wasn't a bad person when we were growing up," Natalie said. "He just wasn't a good one either, you know? He had ambition. He hustled up a nice little business in high school selling steroids to football players and wrestlers."

"I know," Eve said.

Natalie tucked the iPod into her green tote. "Did you tell Caleb about Lyle?"

She gave Natalie a disbelieving snort, and Nat laughed. She knew the last thing Eve needed was her confrontational, brilliant older brother going head-to-head with Lyle. "Caleb hates all things Murphy. What he doesn't know won't hurt him."

"What did our favorite lawyer say about the building across the alley?"

Eye Candy backed to an abandoned building that faced a street with a front-row view on the empty warehouse district the city wanted to tear down to build the Riverside Business Park. The city was auctioning off the building in the hopes that someone would leap on the redevelopment opportunity and renovate it for shops or small businesses.

"Caleb's checking into it for me. Did you see yesterday's Business section?" When Natalie shook her head, Eve pulled the paper from under a stack of receipts and unfolded it on top of her desk. "The city planning commission reworked the plans for the East Side business park. It used to stop at Eighth Street, but in exchange for a big tax break they got Mobile Media to commit to building their regional operations center in the business park, which now expands to the opposite side of Twelfth Street."

"They're hiring nine hundred people?" Natalie exclaimed, leaning over her shoulder to skim the article.

"This location will do app development and cloud technology, plus all the back office work for regional ops, which means nine hundred young professionals freed from their dull, gray cubicle jobs every night, across the street from Eye Candy," Eve said. "I've got plans for that property . . . knock it down, pave over the lot, and put up a wrought iron fence that matches the decorative scrollwork along the park. I can think of a dozen uses for a space like that. Catered business lunches during the day, dancing at night. Put up fairy lights and greenery for private outdoor parties or wedding rentals when it's warm. Live music by local artists, maybe even get regional touring acts. I could even put up a tent and bring in heaters to do a winter wonderland ball thing like the Met used to do for Valentine's Day."

Thinking about the future helped take her mind off

the danger in the present. She loved the thrill of pulling off a major event, of searching for that right combination of music and atmosphere so everyone had a good time, and she was good at it. Unfortunately, it wasn't the kind of thing she was supposed to be good at. Church suppers and backyard barbecues, fine. Parties for two hundred, complete with ice sculptures, a rock band, dancing, drinks, and a bachelor auction, not so much.

Nat switched topics with her usual neck-snapping speed. "He's not really the bar's type," she said as she joined Eve at the full-length mirror hanging from her office door.

"Who, Lyle? You know how his mother felt about appearances. At dinner he wore a suit, tie, same cordovan wingtips Caleb wears, and he ordered a really nice Cabernet," Eve said as she checked her teeth for lipstick.

"You'll have to tell Caleb about the shoes." Eve laughed, and Natalie continued. "I meant Chad. You usually hire Tom Cruise in *Cocktail*. Gelled hair, perfect shave, lady-killer smile."

Eve considered this. "Which got me a bartender who treated the customers like his own private stock. There's something about Chad. He's different. Quiet. We could do with a little less hooking up and a little more Mr. Mysterious behind the bar."

"I knew you were going to say that," Natalie crowed. "He's not the bar's type, but he's definitely *your* type."

Eve tossed her makeup bag back in her desk. "How did you go from 'Can you mix a cosmo?' to 'Do you have a condom?' I just met him. Maybe he's married."

"Was he wearing a ring?"

His battered hands, the knuckles abraded, the tracery of veins on the backs, the collection of nicks and scars flashed into her memory. Those hands told a story she got the sense he'd never put into words, and he wasn't wearing a ring.

She cleared her throat and walked over to the full-length mirrored windows that overlooked the bar and dance floor, one story below. "No ring. Okay, engaged. Dating someone. Maybe he's not attracted to me at all."

Natalie gave an unlady-like snort. "So he's gay."

"Definitely not gay," she said, remembering the physical sizzle crackling along her nerves each time they got close. She thought about the way he didn't step back to give her room to walk out from behind the bar, instead holding his space and making her back up or brush against him, not to mention those sidelong glances that seemed to see everything about her, including the way she lit up when he talked.

But a look wasn't a proposition.

"You weren't going to date until the bar was open and running smoothly. We're two months in. No more excuses. Besides, it's fun to be the one closing the deal."

This was true. She liked the hunt as much as she liked being the prey.

Impulse drove her onto the small landing; Chad looked up at the movement. She beckoned him up the stairs. When he appeared in the doorway Eve introduced him to Natalie. He shook her hand while looking at her face, no mean feat given the D-cup breasts straining at Nat's ribbed tank top. Whether he knew it or not, this was the second round of the interview. If he couldn't handle casual banter with her and Natalie, she'd send him on his way before the first customer walked in the door.

"As Natalie's so capably demonstrating, my staff wears logo shirts," Eve said.

"I didn't notice," he deadpanned.

Natalie gave him a little finger wave. "What's your size, handsome?"

He shot her a narrow-eyed look, then spoke to Eve. "Large."

Eve turned to the battered credenza lining the short wall of her office. She selected a formfitting white T-shirt ringed with bands of black around the neck and arms, size medium, and tossed it at him across her desk. "Tighter's better, or so I hear," she said with a bright smile.

He checked the tag, gave her a look, then without a word he unbuttoned two more buttons on his shirt, pulled the tail free from his jeans and over his head with one swift movement, then dropped it. The action wiped the grin off Natalie's face, and Eve felt her mouth go dry.

Chad Henderson was cut, ripped, whatever the current slang was for not an ounce of fat visible from his collarbone to the low-slung waist of his jeans. Muscles, ligaments, tendons, and bone were sleekly delineated but without bodybuilder bulk. His was an endurance runner's body, a distance swimmer's body, leashed strength and power hidden under a bland button-down shirt.

Shoulders, knuckles, abdominals, shuttered eyes. Men were no more a sum of their physical parts than women, but in that moment Chad's sheer physical presence ignited deep in her belly.

A hint of color stained his cheekbones as he pushed his arms into the sleeves of the T-shirt and drew it over his head. The super-washed white cotton strained over his torso as the Eye Candy logo came to rest on his left pec and his hands went to his hips.

"Oh, the customers are so going to *love* him," Natalie breathed.

"I'm standing right here," he said, a hint of steel wrapped up in the velvet voice.

"I'm sorry," Nat said, her tone implying she was anything but. "The customers are so going to love *you*."

He opened his mouth, then looked like he'd thought the better of going toe to toe with Natalie and turned to Eve. "As long as my boss approves," he said silkily.

"Most definitely," she said, not bothering to hide her appreciation. "Doors open in ten."

"That's my cue," Natalie said as she ducked behind Chad to dump her tote in the corner then thundered down the stairs.

Chad picked up his discarded shirt. "Where should I leave this?"

"In here," she said with a wink. "You can get it after close."

He draped it over the back of a chair and crossed his arms over the soft cotton straining across his chest. "I'm not into games," he said.

"What just happened is pretty mild compared to what you'll hear from a woman with three mojitos in her. Nat's just playing with you," Eve said.

"I'm fine with what's coming from customers. And Nat may be playing, but you're not."

Her breath halted in her throat at the same time her pulse accelerated, leaving her light-headed. Suddenly he seemed bigger, broader, legs braced, arms across his chest, with that same challenge on his face.

"I work by your rules, but we play by mine. Don't start something you're not gonna finish."

The problem with giving in to an impulse was the way the slippery slope dropped out from under you. "I always finish what I start," she said.

His expression didn't change. "What exactly do I have to do to get this job?"

The insinuation made her laugh out loud. "Good work," she said. "Tell me you're not interested and I'm all business after that."

He said nothing. Downstairs, a piercing whistle shattered the charged moment. A muscle jumped in his jaw when he realized it was Natalie summoning her bartender to his station.

"Showtime, Chad," Eve said, copying Nat's bright smile and finger wave. "We'll *finish* this later."

He turned and jogged down the stairs, the T-shirt gleaming in the black lights. Her pulse was up, excitement skittering along her nerves as she sank into her chair. Round two went to her.

She couldn't wait for round three.

One of the most basic components of police work was learning to control a situation. In undercover work, situation control was tricky because it meant managing or manipulating rather than using a uniform, a weapon, and escalating force tactics. A good undercover cop adjusted his personality and attitude to manage the situation according to his objectives. Matt was as good as they came, and that bluff should have worked.

Except Eve Webber raised the stakes without blinking an eye, and suddenly white-hot, explicit images of exactly how they'd finish what she'd started flashed in his brain . . . the skirt that barely covered her upper thighs, her desk, and that sleek mass of black hair she kept tugging free from the glossy color on her mouth. Heat flashed through him, the sensation shockingly intense.

Your job is to keep her alive, not get her into bed.

To combat it he called up the picture of the alley behind the bar in the simmering afternoon sunlight, reconnoitered along with the rest of the bar after he finished prep. The back of the alley made a ninety-degree right turn into a tiny passageway leading to Twelfth Street. It was a rabbit's warren, a nightmare to capture and easy to defend, which made it a perfect drop spot for clandestine meetings and unnoticed deliveries. As Lyle Murphy no doubt knew. He'd done his research into Eye Candy, but he'd gotten Eve totally wrong.

"Ketel One and cranberry," a brunette said.

Matt snapped back to the present, then did a double take. His partner stood in front of him, wearing skin-tight jeans, a tight white top, and a sleek wig that rendered her nearly unrecognizable. She rested an elbow on the bar as she waited, which meant she wore platform heels that added five inches to her height. He mixed the drink, took her money, and stuffed the change in the tip jar when she sashayed away with a wink.

Eve emerged from her office around seven, iPhone in hand, and once she started working the room the vibe punched up several notches. Watching her smile and talk to the customers triggered something he couldn't put his finger on.

During a brief lull, he turned to Tom, the steroid-buffed player working the station next to his. "She looks familiar."

Tom hit the button on the blender to mix a raspberry daiquiri. "She won the newspaper's sexiest female bartender contest two years running before she switched over to events management at the Met." "Fucking moron" was implied at the end of that sentence.

A niggling memory surfaced of the newspaper's Arts and Culture section getting passed around before the shift briefing a couple of years ago, right before he made the leap to detective and started working long-term undercover assignments. The article's text meandered alongside a full-length picture of Eve, hair tumbled into her face, hands braced on the bar behind her, wearing a white blouse unbuttoned deep in her cleavage, a tight, short black skirt, black stockings, and heels. Her slim legs were crossed at the ankle, and the angle of the shot made them seem endless. He should have been focused on the briefing, but he'd given the photo a good thorough look before handing it to his partner, who'd looked even longer.

The provocative shot actually masked what won Eve the contest. In person she radiated vitality, a sheer visceral force that drew light, glances, attention. Even more surprising was the way she didn't hoard the energy but rather turned it back on whomever she was talking to. Like that person was the only person in the room. Like she heard what they were saying, and maybe even what they weren't saying.

Life flowed into this woman. She amplified it and sent it back out into the world, and he couldn't stop watching her.

She checked in with her bouncer, the size of the Hulk, with gang ink disappearing into the sleeves of his T-shirt.

"That's not an off-duty cop," he said.

"Friend of the family," Tom replied over the music. "Someone her dad knew."

"Bars this busy usually hire the pros," Matt said as he pulled out a fresh rack of glasses.

"You know what those assholes charge? They're fucking expensive," Tom said as he handed the drink across the bar. "And they're nosy. Hot Stuff doesn't like strangers in her business."

Matt would bet his Jeep that Eve wouldn't like being called Hot Stuff, but if Tom hadn't figured that out, Matt wasn't about to enlighten him. He watched as she cleared a couple of abandoned glasses off the bar in front of him and handed them to a passing busboy, then came around the corner of the bar, trailing her fingers along the polished wood. He handed the drink to a customer and gave her his full attention.

"How are you doing?" she asked, scanning his station.

"You tell me," he replied, and if he got a little closer than necessary to hear what she was saying over the thumping dance music, well, he was just doing his job. Given the heat in the bar, he expected perfume, something musky and sexy. Instead the faintest scent of mint and rosemary drifted into the air between them when she tucked her hair behind her ears.

"I'm satisfied," she said, not backing away. "The job's yours if you want it."

She was less than a breath away from him. A shift of his weight and a deep inhale, and they'd be breathing together like they were naked and horizontal. The heat sizzled and popped between them and it didn't take training in body language to read the signals. Eve Webber wanted him.

Chad Henderson. She wanted Chad Henderson. Not him.

No matter who he was today, neither he nor Chad could have her. He was supposed to keep her safe, make sure she didn't change her mind about working with the department, monitor any appearances Murphy made in Eye Candy.

He wanted her.

"I want the job," he said, not bothering to hide what he really meant. She looked at him through the layered, sweeping fall of hair he wanted to brush back so he could see her eyes, her mouth. "Hang around after close. I'll give you the paperwork to fill out and bring back with you tomorrow."

He leaned in, as if he needed to speak with her,

employee to employer, but didn't want to shout over the music. "See you later, *boss,*" he rasped.

She turned to look at him, her lips millimeters from his, and for one head-spinning moment Matt thought she was going to kiss him right there in front of the throngs crowding up to the bar. Something about the crush of humanity brought her to her senses. She spun on her heel and disappeared into the crowd.

At the other end of the bar Sorenson held his gaze for a second, just long enough to let him know she'd seen the whole interaction. Matt turned back to the crush of women waiting expectantly in front of his station. Mistake number three. Except he hadn't kissed her. Or let her kiss him. Or done anything except take the job he had to get in order to do his real job. But the look in her eyes cracked something inside him, exposing structural flaws in walls that used to be thick, seamless steel.

He was going to have to pretend to feel something in order to keep her safe, and at the same time he was going to have to keep it all under control.

CHAPTER THREE

Cesar bolted the door behind the last batch of laughing customers; seconds later the DJ pulled the plug on the sound system mid-song. Tom's lurid description of his pick for best in show rang out in the silence, then dropped to an undertone directed at Mario. Ignoring Tom entirely, Eve collected the night's take from the registers and climbed the stairs to her office. She locked the door, toed off her boots, and settled behind her desk to count cash, change, and credit card receipts, and fill out the deposit form. The faint sounds of chairs upended on tables and the joking and laughter filtered in.

A knock came at the door as she rubber-banded the bills into neat stacks. "It's me, sweets," Natalie called.

Eve zipped the bundled cash into a rubber-sided pouch, then unlocked the door. "Good night?" Nat asked, nodding at the deposit bag on Eve's desk.

"We're hanging in there," Eve said. She'd meet payroll this month, plus pay all the bills, a huge achievement for a brand-new business. Eating anything other than noodles and boxed mac and cheese was optional.

Natalie tucked her iPod into an inside pocket and clipped the earbuds to the strap of her bag. "Pauli and Cesar are working out okay."

Eve nodded. Both employees were placements from the Second Chance Center, her father's East Side non-profit that offered after-school and job-training programs. Pauli hustled dirty glasses through the dishwasher and stocked the bartenders' stations with clean ones, and did his homework during lulls. Cesar knew most of the local troublemakers by sight and kept them out of the bar. "Cesar's mother needs the help, with three kids still at home. Dad said he's missed a couple of his GED classes, though. I need to check in with him on that."

"What's your verdict on Chad? He was slow off the mark, but he hung in there. You could do worse."

Memories flashed through Eve's mind, of her body so close to his she could feel the heat pouring off him, of hearing not the music or the clink of glasses or laughter but only the low rumble of his voice in her ear.

See you later, boss . . .

Ever the voice of temptation, Natalie added, "And he's got yummy abs . . ."

Eve ignored that. "He took the job. Send him up when you leave. I need to get him the paperwork."

A few moments later a knock sounded at the open door. Even with her back turned as she put the deposit in the safe and spun the dial to lock it, Eve knew it was Chad because the firm rap of knuckles against wood made her heart speed up. "Just a second and I'll get you an application and a W-4," she said.

Seconds passed, then all the little hairs on the nape of her neck rose in unison. She peeked over her shoulder to find him staring at her. When she caught him looking, his gaze flicked around her office, pausing momentarily on the door leading to her apartment.

Then he looked back at her. A strange silence, thrumming with anticipation, stretched taut between them. In the wee hours of the morning the city was shrouded in a quiet that rang in her ears. Inside the brick bar, inside the cocoon of an office with no windows or doors to the outside world, she had a sudden, off-kilter sense they were the only two people awake, maybe even alive, in the world.

"Your paperwork," she said as she held out the W-4 and the job application. "Welcome to Eye Candy."

He closed the distance between them, took the paperwork and folded it lengthwise, slid it into his back pocket, and turned to go.

"Wait," she said, flattening her hand in the middle of a broad expanse of chest covered in soft, skin-hot cotton. "Don't forget your shirt."

He stopped moving, but not because she was holding him in place, or because she'd startled him into a reaction. His reserve and discipline went deep inside, a dark well of restraint that, in the vibrating, late-night silence of her office, she wondered if she could ever fathom. Her breath halted in her lungs when his fingers wrapped around her wrist.

"I'm officially your employee now?" he asked, doing nothing more than encircling her wrist with his fingers. When she nodded, he added, "Not worried about a sexual harassment lawsuit?"

A hint of seriousness lingered under the teasing, testing note in his voice, so she left her hand where it was, smack in the middle of his broad, hard chest. "First, I'm dead broke, so suing me will get you nothing. Second, like I said, tell me you're not interested and we're done. Third, you're harassing me. You ought to be illegal."

A startled smile flashed across his face, then disappeared when she pressed her fingertips against the firmly muscled wall of his chest. His heart thumped steadily through muscle, bone, and skin. The temperature around them shot up ten degrees, and he brushed his thumb over her pulse, then removed her hand from his chest, turning it palm up in his firm grip. Cool air licked against flesh warmed by his body heat.

"I won't lie," he said, quiet and firm. "I'm interested. But that doesn't mean we have to act on it immediately."

"We'll have to work on your up-selling techniques," she said.

Another smile quirked the corners of his mouth while he circled two fingers in the hollow of her palm. Nerves fired and came alive under his slow, steady touch, somehow both soothing and tantalizing. Her eyes slid closed as she exhaled the breath she'd been holding since the first touch of his fingers on her skin then drew in fresh oxygen.

When she opened her eyes, she saw he was studying her, his gaze intent, his mouth soft with arousal. "You get a lot of fast and furious."

"Comes with the territory," she said.

"Twenty minutes of conversation, then your place or mine."

He was still thinking? "Twenty's on the high side," she said, her voice breathy from the steady touch of his fingers.

"Let's try something different. Let's try slow."

"Slow," she repeated, as if he were speaking a foreign language. Which he was. The language not of impulse but of seduction.

"Conversations. Meals."

Eight years in bars and nightclubs left her jaded to all but the most inventive lines, but this one gave her pause.

"I work five nights a week. You want a meal, it's breakfast at one in the afternoon or dinner at three a.m."

"Any time," he said, the words rumbling deep in his throat.

Chad had snared her attention, something curious flickering behind her newest bartender's tall, dark, and mysterious surface. She let her hand slip free from his and put a couple of feet between them. "Good night, Chad."

"Sleep well." The words would have been friendly if not for the look in his heavy-lidded hazel eyes. Desire flashed through her like lightning, trapping her breath in the charged aftermath.

He stepped back and disappeared through the office door. Moments later she heard the front door open, then swing shut.

The office seemed bigger after he left. Eve turned back to her desk and gathered her laptop and a stack of invoices. Eye Candy straddled the line between red ink and black. Her family wanted to turn her into a corporate drone. Her new bartender turned what should have been an uncomplicated hookup into something she couldn't define, and she wanted to buy a building she flat out couldn't afford.

Oh, and she'd agreed to inform on Lyle Murphy for the cops. No pressure. None at all in what used to be a pretty typical small businesswoman's life.

Her palm still tingled from Chad's gentle, relentless touch. Stroking her finger over the same spot calmed her, anchored her. But sleep well?

Not likely.

When he woke up there was always a moment, never lasting more than a heartbeat or two, when he was no one, no alias or rank or even his name, just breath and heartbeat and usually an assortment of aches and pains. This morning the blank slate frame of mind ended when he saw the dog tags looped over the corner of the mirror over his dresser. He hadn't worn them in years, but the sight always grounded him: Matt Dorchester, former Army, now LPD.

A filter of identity settled into his brain: Chad Henderson, bartender.

A third facet of his current world took up residence in his awareness: Eve Webber, bar owner, informant.

Woman.

The woman he'd used the high-voltage chemistry with to sweet talk into getting to know him in a manner she would interpret as "date" when he meant "protect her without her consent or knowledge."

He shifted to his back, directly under the vent emitting a tepid flow of air. The AC unit was clunking away outside his bedroom window. He had to find the time to fix the air conditioner, maybe get the HVAC guy to add some coolant, try to postpone installing a new one until next summer, after he'd paid off the anesthesiologist.

Thinking about the state of the family finances didn't temper the uneasy pitch in his stomach.

He rolled out of bed, started the coffee, then stood under the shower until all the pieces of who he was today merged and the odd weight in his chest subsided. He was due at the precinct before his shift at Eye Candy, so he dressed in jeans and a polo before pulling the Eye Candy T-shirt from the dryer.

The damned thing had shrunk in the wash. "Fuck me *running,*" he muttered.

He gulped down half the pot of coffee while arming himself, then poured the rest into a travel mug. Before leaving, he stopped at his brother's room and knocked on the closed door.

"Luke," he said softly.

"It's open."

Matt turned the doorknob and watched his brother wince as he put his full weight on his arms to push himself up against his headboard. Luke's hair was even longer than Matt's and tousled from sleep. Jeans and an Oxford shirt were draped over the wheelchair next to the bed, meaning Luke had gone out last night. Matt inhaled, searching for the acrid odor of cigarette smoke. Luke had picked up recreational smoking in college, a vice Matt felt his brother couldn't afford physically or financially.

"I told you, I quit," Luke said, and Matt consciously relaxed his stance. "You got in late last night. Three a.m.?"

"Work. Could last a while," Matt answered. Noon, and neither of them were at work, very un-Dorchester. He scratched through his memory. Was this Luke's first day off this week, or second? "How many hours did you get this week?"

"Twenty-four," Luke said.

That meant three eight-hour days, and this was Luke's second day off. "Anything new on the career websites?"

"No," Luke said, rubbing his shoulder with slow, deep strokes that meant sore tendons and ligaments close to the joint.

"You seeing the physical therapist today?"

"This afternoon."

"No basketball."

Luke shot him a narrow-eyed glare, and Matt tried to soften his tone. "Your shoulder won't heal if you keep stressing it out on the court. I stopped on my way home last night and got a new bottle of ibuprofen. Ice, rest it, anti-inflammatories. Call if you need me."

He was halfway to the front door before he heard Luke behind him. "Thanks, Matt. You didn't have to do that."

Matt paused. "No big deal. CVS is on the way home."

"Thanks anyway. Hey, leave me the list of AC contractors and I'll call around, get prices."

"I'm going to do that before work today," Matt said.

"You're leaving for work right now."

"Stop trying to duck out of PT. I've got it," Matt said, and shut the door behind him. He climbed into his Jeep and drove on autopilot to the precinct, thinking about what he'd dreamed about all night: handling Eve Webber. He'd given her a simple choice in her office: back off the flirtatious little games or end up in bed with him. She went for option B with a delight that normally would have ended in the nearest decent hotel room, ASAP. Given that he was a cop charged with protecting her, her enthusiasm was a huge problem. He needed to find a new way to handle her.

Handle her. . . . Touch, however, softened her shoulders, made the corners of her wide, full mouth relax with pleasure.

His touch changed the quick wit into limpid desire.

His touch gave her bedroom eyes.

Last night he'd diverted her from hooking up by suggesting they "date". But even dating wouldn't stay at the hand-holding stage for long. She'd expect more. Kissing. Touching. Full body contact. Naked, sweating, rhythmic movement full body contact. "Whatever it takes" was the motto for most undercover cops, and Matt was the best there was, especially on long-term assignments. He'd do "whatever it takes" to blend in.

But while sleeping with her was a betrayal, pretending to date her was ten times the deception. He didn't need weeks in Eve's company to know he was trading a physical lie for an emotional one, or to know that she'd tolerate neither.

Rather than think about that, he focused on the way she interacted with customers. Women might come to Eye Candy for the bartenders and the dancing, but he'd bet they also came back to see Eve, who had a real knack for making everyone feel drawn into her inner circle. She circulated, moving from group to group, introducing people, getting clusters to merge and new friendships to form. After even a two-minute conversation with a customer, that person smiled more widely, laughed a little louder, looked just a little looser and more relaxed. She reflected light like the dozens of tiny, mirrored disco balls dangling above the dance floor, taking whatever energy radiated from an individual and multiplying it.

He strode into the squad room and nodded a greeting to Sorenson. Lieutenant Hawthorn emerged from his office and braced himself against Andy's desk. "Report."

Sorenson had scrounged up a whiteboard and a bulletin board, the latter of which was now decorated with photographs of the pertinent players: Lyle Murphy, Eve Webber, and Lyle's most frequent companion, a known offender from the East Side called Travis Jenkins. On the whiteboard Matt wrote out a list of employees, giving first names and last names when he'd been able to hear them, and drew a basic sketch of the bar's interior and exterior, including exits. "The staircase you can see in the bar goes into her office. There's a door here," he said, tapping the spot on the diagram, "and a staircase down to the alley you can see from the storeroom door. I'm guessing her apartment is behind the door in her office."

"I'll start pulling files," Sorenson said. "Does Lyle have anyone on the inside?"

"Cesar," Matt said. "Maybe. I don't recognize him, but the ink connects him to the Strykers at some point in time."

"Good work," Hawthorn said as he examined the building layout and the photographs. "Stay alert. We lose her, we lose the whole case."

The group dispersed, leaving Sorenson leaning against his desk, staring at the pictures on the bulletin boards. "She likes you," she said, noncommittal, just observing.

He didn't pretend to not know who she meant, but he did try to play it down. "She's flirting. It's a way of life for her."

"Is that a trained observer's read on Eve Webber?" Sorenson asked with a mocking look. "She doesn't strike me as the kind of woman who takes no for an answer."

I know exactly how to read Eve Webber. She's sexy as hell, secretive, whip-smart, and for the first time in a very long time, I want something. I want her.

I always finish what I start.

At the memory of Eve's husky voice, both flirtatious and flat-out serious, he flushed. He actually flushed, a very male, very human response—a very un-Dorchester response. Sorenson didn't miss it. Both blond eyebrows rose ever so slightly. He firmed up his voice and said, "I've got this."

"By the way, Hawthorn and I will be in the bar tonight. Hawthorn called in McCormick to handle exterior surveillance."

"Got it." He pushed away from the desk and headed back to Eye Candy.

Shortly after Eve found her chopping groove, Pauli ambled into the bar and disappeared down the hall. Every shift, he'd set himself up in the dish room with his homework and his iPod, emerging again at the end of the night soaked in sweat and smelling of industrial soap. A few minutes later the front door opened again, briefly silhouetting a now familiar, tall, muscular figure against the summer sky before closing.

Chad, who thought she deserved better than fast, back early again.

"You don't need to get here until closer to five," she said.

"I'm turning in my paperwork before you get busy, in case you had any questions." He slid the completed W-4 and application onto the bar.

She wiped her hands on a towel, then reached for the papers, neatly filled out in black ink with block printing. "No felonies or drug convictions, right?" she asked absently as she skimmed the application.

"No."

"It's not a deal-breaker," she said. "I just want to know up front."

"The answer's still no."

"Looking good," she said, eyeing his freshly washed and slightly smaller Eye Candy T-shirt. She tried to keep an amused smile off her face, and failed. "Laundry tip. Use the low heat dryer setting for cotton."

"Yeah, I got that." He came around the corner of the bar, clearly intending to help, but she stopped him at the end of the bar.

"As much as I'd like the help, I can't afford to pay you to come in a couple of hours early every night."

"It's three bucks an hour," he said. "I work for tips."

"Three dollars an hour times two hours a day times five days a week is really thirty bucks a week," she replied.

"On the house," he said as he came around the end of the bar.

"I'll pay you for today," she said, brushing past him to get upstairs before the office door opened. "Just show up when your shift starts from here on out."

She hurried past him but he caught her wrist in one hand, halting her forward progress while he looked her over. Even across the distance of their outstretched arms, his gaze struck sparks as it flickered against her curves. She wore one of her favorite bar outfits, a pair of black leather short-shorts, and a white, sheer, fitted long-sleeved T-shirt over a black silk camisole. Heavy beaten silver discs dangled from her ears, with a matching bracelet around her wrist. Black heeled shoes with an ankle strap lengthened her legs. And if Natalie asked, she'd forgotten she wore the outfit just last week. It had nothing to do with Chad.

"I told you to take advantage of me," he said, his deep voice a gravelly rumble in the silence of the bar.

She took a step back toward him, leaving only slowly heating air between their bodies, and decided to see if he'd keep his word. "You also told me we were taking things slow. If I can take advantage of you, the storeroom's quiet and dark this time of day."

One brief caress of his thumb across her wrist, then he let her go. In the silence that followed her heels sounded loud and sharp against the parquet dance floor. As she walked, she felt his gaze on her hips and the length of her legs.

"I bet guys walk into walls when you go out in that outfit," he said. He hadn't raised his voice but it still carried into the farthest corners of the echoing, empty room.

She'd always known it wasn't the outside that mattered, but who you were inside. What you did. She smiled, because unlike most men who complimented her, Chad meant it without expecting anything in return, then scrolled through her iPod. "Do you have a preference for music?"

"No club music, no boy bands, no disco, no punk, nothing from the fifties."

Amused, she raised an eyebrow at the decisive list. "Do you like anyone local?" she asked as she scrolled without much hope of a positive answer. Most people lapped up the pap distributed by nationally owned radio corporations.

"Yeah," he said without batting an eye. "Maud Ward, The Parakeets, Doe-Eyed Girl."

Three of her favorite bands. "Maud's great. Did you see the feature in the paper last week? She's going to be back in Lancaster this winter, recording her new album, which is great for us. When she's working on new material she shows up around town and does impromptu concerts to try out the new stuff. I've been trying to get her to do a show here, but she's been touring all summer," she said and found her name in the Artists list and slid the iPod into the Bose SoundDock she had on the bar. A low, melodic voice tumbled out into the bar, backed only by a single guitar, the sound of chatter and laughter running under the music.

"She's great," Matt said, half-focused on the song, unfamiliar but definitely Maud. "What's this?"

"I recorded it at the Rusty Nickel one Sunday night a couple of years ago, when she was working on material for her last album. This is an early version of 'Take Me Away.' "

He swept lime wedges into a plastic tub, then looked at her. "The Rusty Nickel, a couple of years ago. April, right?"

"It was warm, but raining cats and dogs," she said

in agreement as she found a second knife. "Were you there?"

"I was there," he said slowly. "How did you get in? I heard the cops had to turn away a couple hundred people."

"I know Maud. Back when she was busking on corners in SoMa and selling CDs from her guitar case, I helped her get some gigs at smaller venues so she could get the word out. She usually gives me a heads up when she's back in town."

"You hang out with Maud Ward."

"Not regularly or anything," she started, but stopped when he cocked an eyebrow. "Okay, yes, I hang out with Maud Ward."

"Her number's in your cell phone."

"Yes."

"Is there anyone in this town you don't know?"

"I don't know *you,*" she said, cocking her head and smiling at him. "Yet. Looks like we've already found something to talk about."

"I don't get to many concerts anymore. Working too many nights." He reduced another lime to wedges, his rhythm hypnotic, easy, automatic. She'd always been a sucker for hands. Not smooth, manicured, executive hands, but workingman's hands, the skin rough with scrapes and gouges and calluses. It made for such an erotic contrast, strong and tough, yet tightly controlled.

"Where did you get the idea to open Eye Candy?"

The question snapped her out of her fantasies. "I've wanted to own my own business for a long time," she said, giving him the short version of her views on business and community involvement. "As for opening a nightclub . . . my dad's a pastor, which is a labor of love, so my brother and I were on our own for college tuition." She scraped a dozen cut lemons into a tub and reached for more. "The summer before college I helped a girlfriend serve at a society wedding at the Metropolitan Club. The guy with the liquor contract for the Met also owned a club. He said he liked my work ethic, although in hindsight maybe my work ethic was icing on the cake."

Chad smiled like he knew where this was going.

"He told me I could make two hundred a night in tips, working for him. I knew my parents would go through the roof if I did, and when I saw the uniform I almost didn't take the shift because the skirt was straight out of a French maid costume and came with fishnet tights and four-inch heels. But I gave it a shot, and he was right. My first night three different men, all old enough to be my father, gave me a twenty for a buck-fifty beer and told me to keep the change. I told myself it was a fluke, that there was no way a man would tip me twenty dollars to watch me bring him a beer, but it happened the next night, and the next night, and the next . . ."

A huff of laughter as he worked. "Sheltered much?"

"Not after a week at Platinum. I put myself through college with those tips. Eventually I ended up running private parties, including networking events at the Met, and along the way I discovered that I'm good at this. That's when I first got the idea to open Eye Candy. The real money's in the liquor, not the tips."

"What did your parents think about that?"

It wasn't their first fight over her life choices. It wasn't the last either. "Imagine what you'd think a pastor and his wife would think of their daughter working as a cocktail waitress, then take that to a factor of ten."

Despite his careful attention to the garnishes he was prepping, he seemed to be listening with his entire body. "Tips that good must have come in handy when it came time to buy this place," he said, still focused on the rapidly diminishing pile of limes.

"They did." So did a degree in finance with a minor in math, and some savvy insider investment advice given along with a ten from some of Lancaster's leading investment bankers when she brought them a cognac with a smile. They thought she was cute, in her little skirts and frilly tights, asking questions about the stock market and investment strategies, like an East Side girl could make something of herself.

This East Side girl would, and she'd bring the East Side with her when she did.

"Done?" he asked when she set down her knife. At her nod he gathered the empty boxes and took them to the storeroom while she dumped the final lemon slices into the last plastic tub and distributed them to each section of the bar. A moment later Chad reappeared. He slid her a look under thick reddish lashes as he took in her casual position, braced against the bar. "Taking a break?" he asked as he washed his hands.

"Getting help with prep certainly frees up some time," she answered.

"Any time," he said.

She reached for an orange, rolled it between her palms, then dug her blunt-cut fingernails into the rind, peeling away chunks to expose the juicy fruit underneath. The tangy scent rose into the charged air between them, mixing with the musky heat rising from his skin while he washed fruit residue from his hands. Eve realized he'd cut the stinging lemons without a wince or a complaint.

"This is a tough neighborhood. How did you decide to buy this building?"

"A good friend offered me the building for the right

price. You know, usually I can't get a word in edgewise with guys. Tell me something about you."

"Nothing interesting about me, boss."

"You're working this tall, dark, and mysterious thing pretty hard," she said. "Conversation goes both ways. Why bartending?"

He shrugged. "Desk jobs expect you to be there at eight a.m., caffeinated and ready to work. I'm not a morning person," he said as he crossed the small distance between them and braced his hip on the counter.

"I'm not either," she said distractedly as she peeled apart another section of orange. "Mornings suck."

A thin trail of liquid escaped the rind and ran down her wrist; without thinking she lifted her inner arm to her mouth and licked off the juice. His eyes darkened, the pupils dilating into the hazel irises.

"Want some?" she asked innocently, offering him the orange.

"I'd say something about apples," he replied as he pulled off a couple of sections, "but you've heard that before."

"Eve gets the short end of the stick in that story," she said. "Adam could have said no. He didn't. Yeah, she was temping but take some responsibility."

His laugh seemed a little forced, and they both jumped when Natalie flung the door open. She tossed a casual wave to them, yodeling along to a song Eve vaguely recognized as a dance hit from the eighties.

"What the hell is she singing?" Chad asked, bracing one hand on the bar, the other on his hip.

"Pop, disco, hair bands, boy bands, punk, everything eighties," she said, breathless. "The music died when Backstreet Boys broke up. On the plus side, we don't have to fight over who gets nights off to go to concerts."

"She's gonna go deaf if she doesn't turn the volume down on those headphones."

Natalie stopped mid-yodel in the middle of the dance floor. "What's he doing here so early?" she yelled at Eve.

Eve motioned for her to remove the earbuds.

"What's *he* doing here so early?" Nat said again as she wrapped the earbud cord around the iPod.

"We heard you the first time," Eve said patiently. "He seems to think I need help with prep."

"Help with prep, huh? Flirting with the boss, I think."

"Just making myself useful," Chad said. Nat continued up the stairs, letting herself into the office.

Eve rolled her eyes at the choirboy tone in his voice. "You could be more useful," she said in a low undertone.

Another simmering hazel look through intriguingly reddish-brown lashes. "Slow, remember? Conversation. Getting to know you."

"What about getting to know *you*?"

"Next time."

"I'll hold you to it," she said.

CHAPTER FOUR

This wasn't going to be easy.

A couple of hours into a crazy Saturday night, Matt told himself the conversation with Eve before Eye Candy opened had netted good information and background details, but he knew already that his plan to take things slow wouldn't hold up for long. Eve was smart, determined, ran her show like the motherfucking boss she was. No way in hell would she wait around for him like some sweet young thing.

No way in hell would a woman like that give a second chance to a professional liar.

At seven forty-two his partner arrived. Her blonde hair was done up in a fancy arrangement of curls and combs with butterflies on them, and her eyes were transformed by contacts that this time turned her average blue irises into the color of the Caribbean in travel ads. She wore a shimmery, barely there neon-blue dress, cracked her gum at Tom and got an apple martini and a wink in return, then disappeared into the crowd.

At eight nineteen Conn McCormick walked into the

bar. Wearing jeans and a loose button-down, he steadfastly ignored the frank appraisals from the women at the bar and ordered a Rolling Rock from Matt. The anonymous exchange took seconds, then McCormick took up position against the railing surrounding the dance floor, giving himself a good view of both the door and the bar. As Matt watched, McCormick let himself get drawn into a conversation with a brunette Matt knew was half past toasted because he'd served her the last three of her four rum and Sprites. He almost wished he could listen in, just for the laughs.

At eight forty-seven Lyle Murphy, easily identifiable from surveillance photos, walked in. Matt barely managed to restrain a double take as Lyle smiled, said a few words, and patted Cesar on the shoulder. The two guys with Lyle, one matching the description of Travis, the other unfamiliar to Matt, also didn't bother to produce IDs. Lyle wore pleated slacks, a preppy sweater, and a hat straight off Justin Timberlake's head. Alone he would have blended right in with the crowd, but his two companions wore the latest in homeboy fashion—baggy jeans, and loose rapper shirts.

They stuck out like two East Side gangbangers in an upscale nightclub.

Murmurs rippled through the crowd as the trio made their way to the back of the dance floor. Natalie, in conversation with Mario at the far end of the bar, looked up as the shift in energy eddied to the far ends of the room. Lyle said something to a blonde woman that made her draw back, jaw open in shock, then headed straight for Eve.

Stuck behind the bar, Matt did his best to track Lyle's movements, but distance, demanding customers, and the shifting crowd on the dance floor made it impossible to get an accurate read on their interaction. McCormick discreetly worked his way closer to Sorenson at the far end of the dance floor, only one customer separating them from Lyle and Eve. The crowd closed again, blocking Matt's view.

Then Eve, Lyle, and the two sore thumbs rose above the crowd, up the winding staircase to her office, Eve smiling over her shoulder at Lyle, as if nothing was wrong.

Except for the white-knuckled grip on her iPhone.

Matt's every instinct was to abandon his station and find out what the hell was going on in her office. Three thugs and one slender female alone in a confined space usually meant brutal trouble.

The raspberry daiquiri Matt extended across the bar to a customer nearly slipped from his grasp and onto her expensive-looking white top. "Omigod," the woman gasped as the crushed ice and deep red juice sloshed to the rim of the glass.

"Sorry, sweetheart," he said, flashing all thousand watts at her as a distraction. Glass firmly in hand, she smiled back, mollified.

He looked up at the closed door and drawn curtains. No sign of movement, but the office was good-sized and in this noise no one would hear her scream. He'd give them another thirty seconds, then he was going up there. He'd think of a good reason to abandon his station on a busy Friday night and storm Eve's office, a place bartenders rarely went.

Then the mysterious door in Eve's office, the wooden staircase leading from the alley to a second-story door, and the best way to minimize the impact from the two out-of-place thugs clicked together in his brain. He caught McCormick's eye and tipped his head toward the front door. Sorenson and McCormick pushed through the crowd to the door as Matt brushed past

Tom and Mario to the end of the bar, then down the hall to the storeroom. He tugged open the door to hear Eve's voice above him, on the staircase's landing. She'd taken Lyle and his friends through the office and out the back door. Smart. Thinking on her feet.

"Look," she snapped, her voice sharp enough to slice through the brick walls lining the alley. "This isn't the strip club down by the warehouses you guys used back in the day, the one the cops raided the nights they weren't slipping dollar bills into thongs. If you want this to work, you have to fit in, and you have to treat my customers with some respect, or I'll go out of business and then we're all screwed. Understand?"

"Understood," Lyle said. "Looks nice in there. You done good, Evie. Not bad for an East Side girl. It'll be even better when you get rid of that thing."

Matt followed Lyle's glance to the brick wall behind Eye Candy. Get rid of what thing? The building?

"I have to get back to work," she said, her voice warming from arctic to almost-friendly. Matt could hear the effort it took. "I'll call you later."

But she didn't step back to let them in the building. There was a pause, then the sound of shuffling feet on wooden stairs, as Lyle and the two thugs trotted down the steps and turned the corner to the parking lot. Using the wooden stopper Matt wedged open the storeroom door, then followed them, sticking to the shadows, his running shoes making the slightest of scuffling noises in the dirt. He paused just outside the bright lights illuminating the crowded lot and watched Lyle get into the passenger seat of a Cadillac Escalade. The engine turned over and the SUV moved smoothly into traffic.

Avoiding Cesar's eye wasn't easy, but fortunately a party of scantily dressed women was fishing IDs out of tiny purses and bras. Matt scanned the parking lot until he saw Sorenson's pale hair and rhinestone combs winking in the lights at the back of the lot, then jogged over.

Sorenson sat on the trunk of Lieutenant Hawthorn's car, knees primly together, her bare feet resting on the bumper, her spike heels neatly lined up beside her. Hawthorn stood off to the side, elbows braced on the roof as he spoke into his cell phone: ". . . left the parking lot in a black Escalade." He rattled off the plate, waited a second, then disconnected the call. "McCormick just picked them up at the corner. He'll follow them, see where they go next. What happened?"

"She sent them out the back door," Matt said, his heart pounding. "There's a door from her office to her apartment that leads to the alley."

"I remember," Hawthorn said. "Did you hear them?"

"Through a crack in the storeroom door," Matt confirmed. "She handled it like a boss, LT. Ice in her veins. We need to tell her what's going on. She can handle it."

"Absolutely not," Hawthorn said, "because the more involved Murphy gets with Eye Candy, the better our case is. It's best for her if she doesn't know. The less she knows, the less she can accidentally give away, and the less danger she's in. Just do your job."

"We can't keep her in the dark," Matt objected.

"The hell we can't, Detective," Hawthorn said. "We do it all the time. *You* do it all the time. Sorenson's going back in. Get some sleep, get your head screwed on straight. I don't want to see you before noon."

Shoes in hand, Sorenson slid off the trunk of the car. They waited while Hawthorn left, then Sorenson looked at him. "I hate these shoes," she said conversationally, turning over the heels so the jeweled straps glittered in the lights. "My feet hurt, my back hurts, and my toes feel like they've been crammed in a sardine can. Next time you go undercover, do it at an old folks' home so I can wear comfortable shoes."

"I'm going back in through the storeroom," he said in response.

Matt jogged around the back of the bar and through the storeroom door, struggling to remain calm. Objective. Inside the bar the DJ was leading everyone in some arm-waving, swaying chant, the atmosphere was back to rockin' and rollin'. He needed to find Eve. Size and strength, not finesse, powered his progress through the room.

He found her down a short hallway, in front of the small alcove housing a relic from the twentieth century, a pay phone. Hands on her hips, her pursed lips and frown better suited a librarian, not the sexy woman dressed like a high-class call girl. A quick glance in the circular mirror high in the corner of the alcove revealed a brunette alternately shoving her skirt down her thighs and buttoning up her blouse behind a red-faced, tight-lipped man with his hands on his hips.

Try as he might, he hadn't been able to shake the cop's sense of humor, so he smiled as he came to parade rest behind Eve and folded his arms over his chest, giving Eve some consequence in case the guy got belligerent. "Need any help?"

"No, thank you, Chad," Eve replied, decorum dripping from her voice. "Our friends are either going to get another drink and enjoy the music, or continue their conversation outside."

The man nodded, taut frustration evident on his face, and the girl finally got her blouse buttoned. With the same gesture she'd used to send Lyle on his way, she extended her hand toward the main room, a wordless invitation to return to the bar, or leave. They scurried back into the wall of humanity and sound, leaving him alone with Eve.

To his surprise Eve spun around to face him and crossed her arms. The flirtatious bar owner was gone. "Where the hell were you?"

The brusque demand startled him. His job was to not react, keep situations calm, so words were the right answer in this situation, apologetic, explanatory words that smoothed over a rocky start to a relationship he needed to keep her safe, not let the department down. Instead, he used what he knew worked. He reached out and gripped the nape of her neck, holding her still as he searched her eyes.

His possessive move sparked a quick intake of breath, but she didn't shy away, never broke eye contact. His forearm lifted her hair so it slid forward, against the curve of her cheekbone, hiding her expression. With his other hand he impatiently brushed it back, saw awareness flare in her green eyes as his palm lingered along her jaw.

"Fine," she said, rising to his silent challenge, and stepped close enough for him to feel the rise and fall of her breasts with each quick breath. Her hands dropped to his hip bones then slipped under the hem of his T-shirt to brush against his lower abdomen, turning his efforts to control her into a challenge. The pulse at her throat leapt in response to the involuntary tightening of his grip; while she made no move to break his hold, she was anything but pliant under his hand. Color crept into her cheekbones, softening her lips, and her eyes went that shade of ocean green that made him think the wall in the alcove looked pretty good as a flat surface . . .

Get your head back in the game, Dorchester. Forget slow. He needed her trusting him, into him, safe with him, and he knew exactly how to go about getting what he needed.

Three giggling women emerged from the restroom and tottered down the hallway. The spell shattered, and Matt let his hand drop, his abused knuckles tingling from the silky slide of her hair against the back of his hand.

Eve stepped back, came up short against the wall. “That was fun,” she said, “but I asked you a question. Where were you?”

“I needed a break,” he said. But breaks were authorized by Eve or Natalie only, and only when things were slow.

“You better not have been in my parking lot,” she said, anger and just a hint of hurt vibrating under her skin.

He went rigid before his brain jerked into high gear and he remembered that to her, “parking lot” meant back-of-pickup-truck liaisons, not a rendezvous with two cops. “I saw a friend leaving, a *male* friend, someone I hadn’t seen in a long time,” he improvised.

She lifted one eyebrow, and her fingers lightly brushed just above the waistband of his jeans. “We’ll talk about this later, but if you leave your station for a break without permission from me or Natalie again, you’re fired. You’re hot as hell, but business comes first.”

She stalked down the hallway without a backward glance, as if she was the one who held all the cards, leaving him off-balance and uncertain. A Maud Ward ballad, the perfect slow dance song, emerged from the generic transition music, and Matt flashed back to the Rusty Nickel on that warm April night two years earlier. Rain had sheeted from a low, sullen sky, soaking him and his partner as they waded through the runoff streaming into the sewers and into the flash mob threatening to crush several women against the bar's closed front door. A little shouting, some backup arriving, and the crowd dispersed. He'd hung around as long as possible, listening to muffled guitar through the wood door before they caught another call.

He didn't remember seeing Eve. Maybe she was already inside. She knew every bouncer and bar owner in town, so she might have slipped in through the back door. Men did favors for women like Eve just to be near her. See her smile.

After her last interaction with him, she wasn't smiling. He took a deep breath and rolled his neck and shoulders to loosen up. Then he did the only thing he could to keep her safe. He went back to work.

CHAPTER FIVE

Just as the DJ cut the sound, Eve closed the front door behind the gum-smacking blonde with the spectacularly creative hairdo. The uncanny two a.m. quiet settled over the bar after closing, but rather than being soothing or seductive, tonight it jangled every one of Eve's nerves.

Her family accused her of acting on impulse. What they didn't realize was that the impulses came from a lifetime of family values. They just showed up bigger, brighter, flashier than getting married and having kids, like opening Eye Candy or going to the cops with Lyle's offer of much needed cash in exchange for fronting his illegal business. Ten years ago Lyle had treated her like his little sister, affectionate but without any of the teasing or bossing she endured from Caleb. What happened tonight was her first clue that Lyle Murphy would play rough.

Cesar was putting away his stool in the storeroom when she cornered him.

"What happened?" she asked, keeping her voice low and reassuring.

"He just kept coming," Cesar said. "I didn't think you'd want me to level him, so I let them in."

He had a point. He also had a ninth-grade education, no job skills, no legal work experience, and no future but the streets if she couldn't keep him employed while he worked on his GED. "It's okay," she said. "I can deal with Lyle. Let him in but anyone who doesn't meet our dress code has to wait outside. Keep them away from the queue." Baggy pants and hip hop shirts were one thing, but no woman should have to listen to what she'd heard from Lyle's bodyguards—"C'mon, drop it like it's hot"—in the thirty seconds it took to get them upstairs.

"I got it," he confirmed. As he stood up he slipped a battered paperback copy of *Moby Dick* into his shorts pocket.

"Good," she said, then looked down at the book. "What's this I hear about you skipping GED classes?"

"It's the math," he said, awkwardly shifting his shoulders. "History and English I got, but we started Algebra a couple weeks ago. *X*'s and *Y*'s. Balancing equations. It don't make sense to me."

She heaved a mental sigh of relief. He wasn't quitting, just having trouble with the work. Keeping her expression even, she said, "I'm pretty good at math, if you want some help."

"I dunno," he said, hitching up his jeans. "I got a lot of late work."

"Come by before your next class. We'll get you caught up. Walk Natalie to her car, then you're done." She handed him his share of the take for the night.

Tom winked and nudged her shoulder. She knew he'd like to add benefits to their friendship, but his shoulder nudge didn't register after Chad's out-of-the-blue dominant move in the hallway. "Hey, Hot Stuff, a couple of us are heading over to Mario's for drinks. You have plans?"

One hand on her hip, Eve lifted one eyebrow at Tom. He grinned at her, unrepentant, but didn't say anything else. She glanced at Chad. His eyes never left her face, but his personality had disappeared behind a brick wall. He looked distant, a little hard. Untouchable. Unapproachable. Maybe the reminder that she was his boss had put him off. So be it.

"Thanks, but I'm going to call it a night," she said.

Chad left with the rest of the guys without a backward glance. Let off their leash, the door slammed on a raucous discussion over the night's best . . . best tits, best ass, best legs, and best in show.

She switched off the lights in the dish room, the storeroom, and the bathrooms before powering down the overheads in the main bar and taking the stairs to the second floor. She gathered her laptop and the night's paperwork, then stepped across the threshold between work and personal life. As soon as she switched on the lamp next to the love seat, a knock came at the apartment door.

Outside stood Chad Henderson.

"Hey," he said as he slid his phone into his pocket.

"Hey," Eve said, a little off-balance. She'd expected Natalie, maybe Tom. Not Chad. "I thought you were getting drinks with the guys."

"I wanted to apologize. What I did tonight was unprofessional. It won't happen again."

Chad just delivered, without a hint of irritation or sullenness, the perfect apology to go with the perfect edgy, commanding demeanor from the hallway. Blunt, straightforward, no excuses, and the lingering irritation dissipated into the humid night air. "I'm all about second chances, Chad. Third chances, not so much."

"No third chance necessary," he said. "You said my choices for meals were breakfast at one or dinner at three a.m. How's dinner sound?"

He'd taken off the Eye Candy T-shirt and replaced it with a dark green polo. One half of the collar stood up while the other lay down against the curve where his shoulder met his neck. She reached out and smoothed it. He didn't move under her touch, simply watched her with that inscrutable expression on his face.

"Apology accepted. We're good. You don't have to take me out."

He gave her a crooked grin. "You're not going to eat? You had an orange at four."

"I had a yogurt for breakfast," she said defensively. "Look, this body doesn't maintain itself. I'm on the rock star diet."

Two lines appeared between his eyebrows. "Beer and cigarettes?"

"No," she said, straight-faced. "We all stay skinny 'cause we just don't eat."

A rusty chuckle, then, "Have dinner with me, Eve."

Simple words, voiced with low command that didn't quite cover an oddly intent need. "Okay," she said.

Something in him seemed to ease at her assent. "Get changed. I can't take you anywhere in that outfit without starting a riot," he said, the deep rasp of his voice settling into her skin.

"I can't take these heels for another minute anyway," she admitted. "Come in. I won't take long."

"You live back here?" he said as he stepped into the apartment and looked around. Faded cabinets and battered Formica countertops enclosed an area large enough for one person to work in. A bar stool sat under the counter facing the living room. The apartment was small and dim with windows in the kitchen and bedroom only, so she hadn't spent much on renovations, instead plowing all her seed money into the bar. But she'd painted the walls a soft yellow, and used bright red and orange throw pillows on her denim sofa to make the living room inviting. "It's not exactly the safest neighborhood."

"You must not be an Eastie," she said with a laugh, using the nickname for second-or third-generation residents. "I've lived here my whole life. The angels watch over me."

Chad gave her a sharp glance, then said, "You're a woman living alone in the roughest part of town."

Okay, so maybe it was a little naive, but this was her home turf, and anyway, the Riverside Business Park could change all of that. "This is an investment strategy. As soon as my cash flow stabilizes I'm going to rent it out and move," she said, bending over to undo the strap on her heels. She straightened and stepped out of the heels, sighing her pleasure as her cramped toes uncurled into the worn linoleum. "Want a drink?"

"I'm driving," he said, back to the door, arms crossed over his chest again. "Get changed, Eve," he said, remaining up against the wall as if he'd been nailed there. Something primordial in her liked how he used her name, the commanding way he said it, liked the way anticipation surged in her veins when she obeyed.

The anticipation fueled the impulse to leave the door open while she unzipped the side zipper on her black leather shorts, and pulled the cami and white T-shirt over her head. The tops went in the laundry basket; the shorts went back on a hanger. She pulled on a pair of jeans and a fitted thin T-shirt with faded butterflies curving over her chest and around to her shoulder blades, slid her feet into Birkenstocks, and ducked into the bathroom to wash her face.

When she reentered the kitchen, Chad was right where she left him, all hard-muscled man, leaning against the door with his hands shoved into his pockets. She saw his chest, rising and falling with his breath, stop mid-inhale, but he didn't move. Without her heels, he towered over her, and she couldn't look away from the heated light in his eyes.

Anticipation, the dark, silent night, and impulse crashed together and caught fire. She walked right up to him, pressed the whole length of her body against his, tilted her face up, and kissed him.

It was a simple kiss, chaste, close-mouthed, but he froze. A smile teasing at the corners of her mouth, she brushed her lips back and forth across his once, twice, waiting for his warm, firm lips to soften and open. Nerves popped and fired as one moment stretched, elongated into timelessness, then a soft groan rumbled in his chest.

"You'd think you'd never been kissed by a woman before," she whispered, then licked his lower lip.

"Not like this," he said.

Then his tongue slid against hers as he turned her so her back pressed against the door. Palms braced on either side of her head, he leaned into her, trapping her between the door and his hot, hard body. She ran her hands under his shirt, exploring the warm skin covering the muscles and ribs of his torso.

Any reluctance was gone. He melded his mouth with hers like slow was a distant memory. His tongue thrust deep into her mouth before he backed off, gently licking at the curve of her lower lip. He broke away to plant firm, hot kisses along her jaw and nuzzle her ear. One muscular thigh slid between hers and pressed hard against her desperately needy sex. Catching her breath, she buried her face in his neck, getting a little drunk on the musky smell of his skin. His hands slid up her torso to cup her breasts, his thumbs sliding back and forth across nipples that peaked at the attention, and she sagged further against his thigh, intensifying the pleasure building between her legs.

Forget slow. She wanted to go to bed with Chad Henderson right now.

"Chad," she whispered.

He froze again, then pulled away to look at her as if she were from another planet before his eyes cleared. He backed up a step into the kitchen, and clasped the back of his neck as he blew out his breath.

"I said your name, not *stop,*" she said, puzzled. "Want to work up an appetite?"

"No," he said. "We're going out. Now. I said slow, and I'm going to keep it that way." He opened the door and stepped out onto the landing.

She stayed where she was. "Are you trying to single-handedly prove chivalry isn't dead?"

"No," he said.

When it became clear he wasn't coming back inside, she picked up her purse and crossed the threshold. She locked the door and preceded him down the stairs to the parking lot. The Jeep had no doors, so she climbed in and buckled her seat belt while he did the same. "Do you mind the top down? I don't even have it in the Jeep right now. No rain for days."

"No problem," she said. Her hair waved naturally; to get it straight and styled required so much product it would take a hurricane to tangle it. Her mind jumped from tangled hair to *oh what a tangled web we weave* and from there to Chad's reluctance to get physical.

"Are you *married*?" She grabbed his left hand after he fastened his seat belt, feeling the skin just above the joint connecting the long, tanned finger to his palm. "If you're married, I'm getting out of this car right now, and God help you if you're lying to me."

No tan line, no dent from a wedding ring. Without a word he let her explore his fingers and healing knuckles. Seriously abraded skin drawn tight around scabs gave way to pink patches where the scabs had fallen off. "Good grief," she said.

He reclaimed his hand and ignored her quiet comment. "I'm not married, engaged, or anyone's significant other," he said, turning the key in the ignition and accelerating out of the parking lot. "I haven't been on a date in months, much less had a girlfriend."

Which made his reluctance to take the edge off what must be seriously frustrated desire all the more odd. The wind buffeted her hair around her face. She set her purse between her calf and the console, gathered her hair against the nape of her neck, and said, "You are a very strange man."

"Because I don't climb on top of you every chance I get?" he said. "Call it respect, boss. Or foreplay."

She looked at him. They were on city streets, moving at ten above the speed limit down the empty main drag, yellow lights turning red as they flew under them. The breeze tossed his hair around his battered features, blowing the reddish strands flat against his broad forehead, then back from his face, which had tuned again to unreadable as he drove. In the dark he looked like the kind of guy who'd take what he wanted without a care for her feelings. She wasn't above choosing a bed partner based solely on physical response. Her body rarely led her down the wrong path. But something about Chad's wavering resistance set off an alarm, a distant one.

Chad braked the Jeep to a halt in front of a twenty-four-hour diner near the interstate. Once inside, she slid into a booth and shook off her sandals, propping her tired feet up on his bench seat with a sigh. He reached for the laminated menus tucked behind the napkin dispenser, then shifted one bare foot into his lap and massaged it with his free hand as he scanned the menu. Eve slid further down in her seat and rested her head on the back of the booth, her eyes and brain completely unfocused by the deft, deep strokes.

"So here's what I want to know," Chad said without looking up from the menu. "Bust many couples in that alcove?"

Laughter pealed into the empty diner, the sound startling a curse from the fry cook in the kitchen window. Chad looked up, humor gleaming in his eyes.

"Oh, more than you'd suspect given that it's a completely public space right next to the bathrooms. That's why I installed the mirror, so Natalie or I see them before we're all really embarrassed."

The waitress arrived, pen poised above a blank notepad. Chad ordered four eggs, bacon, sausage, hash browns, and orange juice. Eve, her head back to its position on the back of the booth as he worked his magic on her other foot, ordered one egg, an English muffin, and a side of sausage.

"Coffee?" the waitress asked, stifling a yawn.

Eve shook her head. "I've got to get some sleep in a couple of hours." Chad declined as well.

"So here's what *I* want to know," she said when the waitress left. He stiffened, but she continued. "What did you do to your hands?"

He closed up, bricks layered and mortared before her eyes. The massage faltered, then resumed. "What do you think?"

"Boxing. Workouts, not fights. Not anymore," she amended.

"What makes you think that?"

"No marks on your face," she said, studying his eyes, the muscles in his cheeks, the tightness around his jaw. "Or on your ribs, but you've taken some hits in the past. Now the hits are all inside, hidden away. No weakness allowed. The workout's how you deal with it."

A muscle jumped in his jaw as he glanced at the pies in the glass case, then back at her. "You can tell all that from looking at me." It wasn't a question.

She shrugged. "You said bartenders should be good listeners. So are cocktail waitresses, but men don't talk with words. They talk with their bodies, and what they *don't* say during three hours of sports or stock market bullshitting. Am I right?"

He shrugged, neither confirming nor denying her assessment, then shifted his attention to her other foot. The pressure of his thumb against her arch made her jaw go slack and nearly had her purring when he said, "My turn. Here's what I want to know. Who's the guy you took upstairs tonight?"

Nice right cross. It was her turn to freeze. She sat up straighter and unintentionally tugged at the foot trapped in his strong grip. He tightened his hold, pushing one strong thumb against her arch in a move that made her entire body relax as he watched her with those all-seeing hazel eyes.

"Why?"

"No one goes upstairs except you and Nat. That's smart when you've got thousands of dollars in the bar at the end of the night. But he went right upstairs with you, like he belonged."

She hadn't told her family, her brother, her best friend about making herself the bait for a sting operation on Lyle Murphy, so she wasn't about to involve a near-stranger, no matter how well he could handle himself. "He's a friend. We went to high school together and he's looking for investment opportunities here in town."

"So I might have another boss besides you," he said, his finger lightly caressed her skin.

No way in hell. "More of a silent partner," she said. "I want to buy the building across the alley from Eye Candy, knock it down, and put up an outdoor seating area for live music and parties. I can't afford it without a loan, but my credit's maxed. He needs somewhere to put some cash. We'll see."

All of that was true. It would be so easy to take Lyle's money, go after her dreams, compromise herself and everything she believed in. She could tell herself that she'd use his money to improve the East Side and put him out of business, but she knew better. The East Side needed big, bold moves resulting in arrests and prison sentences to discourage the dealers and encourage people to force them out. Community activism started at home. It started with her.

The waitress slid platters of food in front of Chad, and a single plate in front of Eve. Relieved the conversation was over, she sat up straighter in the booth and reached for her silverware, her feet cooling against the scratched linoleum. He dug into his food with the focus of a big man coming off a twelve-hour fast.

She let him get half the sausage and eggs in his stomach before she said, "Here's what I want to know. Why are you still bartending? You have a degree from the U."

In reply he pushed the plate containing the hash browns across the table to her. At the shake of her head, he said, "Go ahead. You've been eyeing them since she brought out the plates. Something wrong with bartending?"

She took half the untouched fried potatoes and shook a glop of ketchup onto the side of the plate. "I'm the last person to tell someone to give up a dream for the day-to-day, but you don't seem like tending bar is your dream. What was your major?"

"Sociology," he said without looking up. "Not much of a job market for sociology majors. Never got out of bartending."

Fair enough. "What do you do when you're not working?"

"Sleep. Fix up my house. It needs a new AC."

She gave him paragraphs of answers and got monosyllabic responses to her questions, but before she could ask more questions the waitress cleared the plates and left the check. Eve dug in her bag for her wallet.

"I got it, boss." He tossed a couple of bills on the table. "Let's go."

Chad was even more closed off on the way back to Eye Candy, as if mulling over the exchange that had swung between friendly banter and intensely personal questions. He made a wide circle in the parking lot and backed into the alley with the speed and confidence of a racecar driver, braking to a halt in the narrow lane leading behind the bar. She got out and made her way around to his side of the Jeep, just a few feet from the stairway leading to her apartment door.

"I'll wait until you're inside," he said.

She was tired of waiting. He was mystery and intensity and muscular temptation personified. She wanted skin-to-skin contact and she wanted it now. "Here's what I want to know," she said softly. "Want to come up?"

"Not tonight, Eve."

She tucked her hair behind her ears, then laid a hand on his thigh. "You know, guys usually can't wait to get me flat on my back, yet you keep trying to make this mean something. I'm just looking for something simple. No strings. No promises. You're off the hook for a commitment."

"You deserve better than that, boss," he said.

He radiated desire, the potent masculine kind full of heat and promise, yet so tightly leashed he was almost vibrating. If anyone needed to succumb to an impulse, it was Chad Henderson. "That's sweet. Very sweet, but your timing sucks. I've got a lot on my mind, and I could use a fast . . . dammit, I left my purse in your car."

As she spoke, she stepped on the running board and leaned across his body, reaching for her bag resting on the floorboards by the passenger seat. The strap hooked on the stick shift, halting her irritated retreat. She braced one hand on the crease between his hip and thigh to yank free the strap and glared at him as she pulled back, intending to snap out something annoyed and cranky just short of "You're fired" because the last thing she needed was a sexual harassment lawsuit, but then his hand was under her hair, hot and firm against her nape, and his mouth was on hers, silencing everything. Thought, speech, memory. Everything in her went utterly quiet at the warm, drugging power of his mouth, and before she knew it she was in his lap, twisting on his lap to straddle his hips.

"Easy . . ." he muttered, holding his hands out to the sides until she settled herself.

Her eyes had adjusted to the darkness and she watched his pupils dilate, the iris almost disappearing. She opened her thighs wide and settled against him.

They were both breathing heavily when he growled, "This is a really bad idea."

"It's this, go upstairs, or we're done," she said. "You choose. Now."

Unease flashed in his eyes so quickly she thought she imagined it, but with a low curse he reached past her to switch off the engine and the headlights, plunging them into total darkness, a state that made the drift of his hands over her body that much more potent. His surrender was as abrupt and wholehearted as his resistance, nothing tentative in his kiss, or his touch. When his right hand slid up under the soft fabric of her T-shirt to cup her breast, she tore her mouth from his with a gasp that eased slowly from her mouth when his thumb rubbed slowly back and forth over the nipple.

His left hand still cupped her nape as he took her earlobe gently in his teeth and tugged. He pinched her nipple, rolling it between his fingers while she gasped into the hard muscle between his neck and his shoulder.

He pushed her shirt up to her collarbones. She caught the fabric between her arms and her torso when she reached for his belt to pull herself closer to that bulge she knew meant sweet release. The movement brought her swollen breasts closer to his mouth and he took advantage, flicking his tongue over each nipple in turn. In some dimly functioning corner of her mind Eve realized they were making out like high school kids, his hands everywhere, clothes disarranged, unwilling to stop despite the promise of nothing but frustration at the end.

Or perhaps not. The rhythmic motions of her hips pressed her clit against the seam of her jeans, and she found a hot, tight groove. He gripped her hips as if to halt the impromptu lap dance, then his rough, reluctant groan told her the dark, swirling tide of desire had pulled him under. Fingers flexing and releasing against the curves of her bottom, he let his head drop back against the headrest as he watched her move, his eyes heavy-lidded and moss dark.

Her mouth hovered over his, teasing him in gentle payback, her tongue dancing against his parted lips until he took control, one hand sliding up to cup her head and press her mouth to his. His tongue slid inside, mimicking the thrusts and retreats of their bodies. The other hand left her hip and unerringly found her nipple again. She rewarded his accuracy with a nip to his lower lip before luxuriating openmouthed in the stubble along his jawline.

He slid the hand on her hip around to the base of her spine. The pressure intensified, edging out all thoughts of modesty, all worries about getting caught on the edge of an orgasm in the front seat of an open vehicle. The delicious, blinding pleasure came at her in honey-thick waves now, pouring from her mouth, open against the sweat-damp skin of his neck to her nipples, as hard as diamonds between his fingers, down to her core.

"Oh God," she said as the sensations coalesced into one pounding crest that crashed through her. The rippling eddies left her slack-limbed and panting against his hard, warm body. She buried her face in his neck. His erection still strained against his jeans, a steel rod pressed to the swollen liquid heat of her body. "It's hot as hell out here. Want to come up and share a shower?" she whispered.

"Nope."

Feeling exceptionally relaxed and more than a little amused, she cupped his stubbled jaw, settled against him and said, "You're a liar and a tease, Chad Henderson."

"A consistent one," he replied. He leaned back in the seat and tucked one hand behind his head. "You're not satisfied?"

She cocked her head. Her hair fell in her eyes, and he lifted the other hand to tuck it behind her ear, then brushed his thumb over her mouth. She nipped at his thumb, then said, "Not as satisfied as I'll be when we're naked in bed and coming apart together."

Both hands dropped to her hips, tightening there as he rested his forehead on her collarbone and groaned, "Eve. Go upstairs. Please."

She ran her fingers into his hair and massaged the tight muscles at the base of his neck. He was strung tight, hard from his neck to his shoulders to his thighs to his cock, insistent between her legs. "Come on, Chad. Give in to the impulse. It'll be so good, I promise. Rat's-nest-hair-and-sore-muscles and maybe rug-burn-on-your-knees good. Your-friends-all-know-you-got-some good."

His even breaths halted for a moment, then he said, "I know, boss. I know how good it could be. But not tonight." Gently but inexorably he shifted her and her purse until they were both outside the Jeep. He looked up at her landing. "Go on. I'm not leaving until you're inside."

She climbed the stairs, gave him a little finger wave from the landing, opened the door, then locked all three bolts behind her. Only when she turned off the landing light did she hear the Jeep's engine crank over.

A kind, gentlemanly gesture from the man who wasn't keeping chivalry alive. So serious, so intense. Eve leaned back against the door, memories of his unyielding body against hers flickering in her skin. That much restraint hardened a man, in more ways than one. He needed a release besides the physically pounding adrenaline rush of boxing, something that would leave him soft and satiated, not bruised and scraped and sore.

She was just the woman to guide Chad down the impulsive path.

* * *

Well done, Detective Dorchester. You once again managed not to sleep with Eve Webber.

Air huffed from Matt's nostrils as he shot out of Eye Candy's alley and onto the street. Yeah, he deserved a medal for keeping his pants zipped. Just what he needed, more pieces of metal added to the jumble at the back of his dresser drawer.

Fuck. Telling himself he was just doing his job, that testing her to see if she betrayed the department's confidence to a near-stranger, made him feel worse, not better. He should have sat on his hands, not touched her like he had a right. She was savvy. Sharp. Playful. And she worked her ass off. Without makeup she looked like a girl he'd still do a double take at because the intelligence, humor, and kindness were easier to see. In jeans and a T-shirt, her face scrubbed bare of makeup, he wanted her more, not less.

He was lying to her. Bald-faced lying to her about who he was, why he was in her club, what he did. No one knew about Eve's plans to buy the building behind Eye Candy. She was smart to keep that close to her chest, because any interest would drive up the price. But she didn't have the money to buy the building, and almost no chance of getting a commercial mortgage.

To Hawthorn, this was going to make Eve look like a really bad risk. Hawthorn hated risks, managed them obsessively. In pursuit of his goal of shutting down the Strykers, he'd be as ruthless with Eve as Lyle was.

Impressions flashed through him as he drove. The way she ground against him was about as satisfying as a lap dance at a strip club, all teasing, simulated action, no release. The hot, sweet weight of her body against his, firm breasts against his chest, the pebbled tips of her nipples between his fingers, her hips rocking against him. Eve would take it slow for a little while, but it wouldn't be long before she'd expect more from him, details, stories, a connection. He'd give it to her. He'd done it before in undercover operations. He did what he had to do to build trust, without a thought of betraying it because what mattered was justice, the department, getting the bad guys. Hell, he'd used people on the periphery before, gotten dirt on someone he could flip for the prosecution, cozied up to women with information, walked away without a second thought. The simple fact was that he wasn't paid to be honorable. He was paid to solve cases by whatever legal means necessary.

This was different, because Eve was different. He'd known her for less than a week and already he didn't want to walk away.

That option had closed to him the moment he walked through Eye Candy's door with Chad Henderson's ID in his wallet. He needed to let it go, do the task in front of him, and move on, like he always did. That's what made him the best.

In the flat, inky stillness just before dawn he parked his Jeep on the street in front of the house to avoid blocking in his brother's modified SUV and sat in the car for a few minutes, letting that thought resonate through his consciousness. He'd forgotten what it was like to feel his heart jump when a woman walked in the door, butterflies flutter in his stomach when she smiled at him, brutal lust surge and sweep to the very edges of his skin. He'd almost forgotten what it was like to feel, period.

Across the street, his house, a ranch with dormers, three bedrooms, and a bath he'd enlarged and refitted himself to meet Luke's needs, sat dark and silent. Even from the Jeep he could hear the AC unit grinding away in the backyard. The neighbors now gave him pointed glances when he saw them. He'd inherited the house when his parents died, and the HVAC system was original, aging, and until this summer, far down on the list of renovations to make. A friend's father who worked in construction had recommended a guy who'd give Matt a fair deal for a new unit, even let him help install it to reduce the labor costs. He just didn't have time to call him.

A bitter sound huffed from his chest. He'd told some truth there. When he wasn't working he slept and fixed up the house. One truth among so many lies.

He eased out of the Jeep, crossed the street, and let himself in.

"I hope she was worth it." The raspy voice came from his brother's room.

"I'm on a case," he said. "Go back to sleep."

In his bedroom he stripped, tossing the sweat-soaked clothes into the laundry basket in the corner, and glanced at the clock. Almost four a.m. Time for bed. That's where Eve was, in her bed, all soft and loose-limbed. He, on the other hand, was strung tight and rock hard, exhausted deep down in his soul, but too wound up to sleep.

Hands on his hips, he bent his head and closed his eyes. Luke's faint whistling snores rumbled down the hall. He had to pare unnecessary, distracting emotions from duty and responsibility, lock them away. Resolute, he stepped into a pair of gray cotton shorts and laced up his shoes. The house had three bedrooms. He'd moved into his parents' room, the one with a window onto the backyard. For safety reasons Luke's was the first on the front side of the house; in case of fire, he wanted his brother closest to the front door. They'd turned his old room in the corner into a home gym with mirrored walls, a treadmill, a weight set, a heavy bag, and a speed bag. He started with the treadmill, knocking out five miles in half an hour before putting on the gel wrap gloves. Pounding the heavy bag held some appeal, but he wanted to shut down his mind, so he opted for the rhythm and endurance of the speed bag.

It worked. By the time dawn lightened the sky outside the window he'd exhausted his body and mind along with his soul. Dispassionate again, from the recesses of his now-silent mind he felt sweat trickle down the column of his back in time to the rapid thumps of his heart against his ribs. He unwrapped the gloves. Five hours of sleep, another pot of coffee, and he'd be back on his game. Shower first.

Want to share a shower?

He kept the shower cool, partially to dissipate heat before he got into bed, partially as a preventative measure, but at the memory of Eve's softly whispered words, despite the workout, the late hours, his physical and mental weariness, despite the cool water pelting his body, heat thumped strong and hard in his cock.

Without conscious thought his hand skated down his abdomen and gripped his shaft. He kept the steady, slow pace, riding the rush as his balls tightened and the pressure grew. He imagined her naked, in his bed, under him, spread for him, body quivering as he drove into her, taking his time, right there with him as the heat built, sucking them into the vortex. He slowed his strokes, and in his fantasy, she said his name, his real name when she came.

A low groan escaped, inaudible, he hoped, under the running water and behind the closed door, as he bent forward, shuddering as an orgasm pulsed through him. Exhaustion and something more elemental that felt far too much like fear slammed a rock-fist against his ribcage. He turned off the shower, toweled off, and went to bed.

Eventually he slept.

CHAPTER SIX

Normal. Look and act normal. Don't bring any suspicion on your family. Keep it together, Eve.

She took a deep breath of humid air saturated with late afternoon sunshine to steel herself for another Monday dinner with her parents, and opened the squeaky metal screen door. "Hello!" she called.

"In the kitchen, Evie, dear."

She walked into the tiny house she'd called home her entire life. A Bose SoundDock identical to the one she used to play music on during prep was hooked up to an iPod on top of the piano, Lionel Hampton, her father's favorite jazz artist, flying home at a low volume in the living room. She dropped her purse on the sofa, gave the knob on the window air conditioner a twist to cool the room for Caleb, and headed for the kitchen to find her mother.

"Hi, Mom," she said with a quick hug, then stood back to let her mother inspect her.

"Very nice, dear."

She wore a chocolate brown knee-length skirt, a

green blouse with three-quarter sleeves, and brown sandals, one of several outfits suitable for church, family dinners, and social occasions. "How can I help?"

"Set the table. Caleb called. He's preparing for trial and can't make it, so we're just three tonight."

"Dad didn't invite anyone?" From her earliest memories, the numbers at Monday night suppers ranged from the four Webbers to as many as eleven or twelve crowded around the dining room table. Homeless people, recovering addicts, someone newly released from jail in need of a home-cooked meal before a ride to the halfway house four blocks east, fellow pastors and childhood friends traveling through on their way to and from vacations or conferences, Eve and Caleb's friends, city council members. She'd learned the hospitality industry's Golden Rule—make everyone feel comfortable and welcome—at home, from her parents' example.

Her mother pulled a dented metal pan from the oven. "Not tonight," she said as she pulled back foil to reveal slabs of something edged in purple with seeds scattered in the middle green flesh simmered in red sauce.

"What's that?" Eve asked.

"Baked eggplant," her mother said in a harried voice. "Your father had another checkup with the cardiologist. His cholesterol is still too high. The doctor recommended a vegetarian diet."

Eve could imagine what her father thought about that, but since he was completely unable to boil water, he was at his wife's mercy when it came to eating. "I thought for sure he'd invite Cesar," Eve called from the dining room as she opened the drawers in the buffet to get the place mats.

"How is Cesar?"

"Struggling with algebra. Otherwise, fine." She

thought it best not to mention the altercation with Lyle Murphy, at least not until her mother had dinner on the table. The eggplant had reduced her normally unflappable mother to muttered almost-curses.

Eve set the table, including the serving dishes her mother set in the pass-through window. The transition from the casserole dish to the serving dish rendered the baked eggplant an almost unrecognizable glop, but the steamed broccoli doused in lemon looked okay, as did the rice. Her mother walked down the hall to her husband's office. As Eve took her seat, she heard her mother say, "Supper's ready."

She got a quick kiss from her father before he sat down. A quiet grace, they passed the food, and her mother led off the conversation. "How's business, Evie?"

Her mother's tone was polite, almost completely covering the tension underneath, but Eve knew what it cost her to even ask. "Steady," she replied as her fork sank into a slice of eggplant she could only describe as mush. The cheese sprinkled on top had the texture of oily paste. "Is this mozzarella?" she asked, distracted.

"Fat-free," her mother said, an edge to her voice.

Moving right along. "I hired another bartender," she said quickly. The eggplant needed something, anything, so she looked around for the saltshaker. It was missing from the table, so she settled for a generous sprinkling of pepper.

"I didn't know you planned to hire another bartender," her mother said.

"He's a replacement, not an add. I had to fire Brent," she said, using energetic motions to section off another tiny piece of eggplant. Maybe if she actively feigned eating motions she'd convince her mother some of the food had actually gone into her mouth.

"Not working out?"

"He was working out too well," Eve said. "I caught him in the back of a truck with a customer, so I fired him. The last thing I need is the bar getting a reputation as some kind of stud service."

Her mother's lips tightened, but for once Eve wasn't sure if her displeasure stemmed from Eve's irregular job or from the mushy main course. Her mother pointedly looked at her father. Her father mournfully considered his unpalatable dinner, and Eve steeled her spine for one of three possible discussion tracks: Lack of Husband Prospects, Late-Night Hours in an Unsafe Environment, or . . .

"I saw Lee McCullough last week at the SCC Board meeting. He said he'd be interested in seeing your resume for a position in their marketing department."

Lee McCullough was the VP of HR at Lancaster Life Insurance, so this was Door Number Three: Getting a Better Job. Eve kept her tone bright and positive. "Dad, that's really kind of him, but I don't need an interview, or career counseling, or a job. I have Eye Candy."

Her mother's face tightened. "This is a good job, with benefits, and a career track. Lancaster Life is growing. They're actually hiring, in this economy."

"They're hiring for jobs in a gray-walled cube, with people wearing business casual for tedious meetings, working over a computer all day. I'm not going back to that." She'd go back to the Met before chaining herself to a cube again.

"Why not, Eve?" her mother said gently. "You'd have a steady salary, regular hours, some security."

Her parents grew up in what was euphemistically described as extreme poverty. She understood her parents' drive for secure, stable lives for their children, knew where it came from. Benefits would be nice, but she was young and healthy, for now. "Mom, there is no security. Two years ago Lancaster Life laid off five percent of their work force, and the economy was better then."

"I'm sure Lee would protect you if that were to happen again."

"Lee would fire his own mother if the board of directors told him to."

True or not, this sharp statement earned her a quelling look from her father. "It can't hurt to talk to him."

This was true. He might need a location for a holiday party, or even think of Eye Candy for team gatherings, but she wouldn't deceive her father into thinking she was going for a job interview when she really intended to market her business to a member of the SCC board. When Eye Candy opened two months ago, Eve's efforts to help the East Side's most vulnerable workers became the weak spot in her parents' persistent determination to shift her from provocative to respectable. She played this card without hesitation.

"If I shut down Eye Candy now, I'm out five years of savings. My credit will need a decade to recover, and who would hire the people I currently employ?"

"With a proper job you'd be able to offer internships to SCC clients," he said.

"Maybe, Dad. *Maybe* if I'm in a management role, *maybe* one a year, probably unpaid, and they'd probably go to college students. Right now I employ people who support some, if not all, of their extended families on what I pay them."

"Eve, we never dreamed you'd make as much as you have out of working as a cocktail waitress," her mother started.

She committed one of the Webber cardinal sins and interrupted a parent. "*I* dreamed it, Mom. Ten years ago. *My* concept, *my* business, *my* building, *my* employees, funneling money into *our* neighborhood, all of it something I made real. We need small businesses on the East Side."

A sharp look from both parents, then a few moments of silence while her mother cut her bright green broccoli into tiny florets. "You had your fun when you were younger, Eve, but you're almost twenty-eight. It's time to think about something different than nightlife and fun."

Nothing new would come from this conversation, so she simply said, "I appreciate your concern, Mom," and changed the subject. "Dad, I talked to Cesar a couple of nights ago. He's having trouble with algebra, but he's going to come in for a little tutoring. I think he just needs a review on the order of operations and some one-on-one practice to boost his confidence."

"That's a relief," her father said, clearly as glad to change the subject as she was. "You're doing a good thing tutoring him."

"I'm happy to do it," Eve said.

There was a moment of silence while everyone bowed to the inevitable and forced down a mouthful of eggplant. "You could open a flower shop," her mother said.

"Two have gone under in the last five years," Eve replied, clinging to her patience with her fingernails.

"I heard East High is having trouble filling the two open math positions."

Students at Eve's alma mater had a reputation for breaking first-year teachers within a month or two. The graduation rate was the lowest in the tri-county area. Resigned, she gave up on the eggplant, angled her knife and fork together across her plate, and said, "One, I don't have a teaching certificate. Two, I need a major in math to teach it in this state. Three, I don't want to teach high school in any state."

"Then elementary school. You'd have summers off when babies came," her mother said.

"Let it go, Mom," she said, resigned. "Please."

They ate in silence for a few moments, then Eve cleared the table and loaded the dishwasher. Only when they sat down to frozen yogurt topped with strawberries did her mother circle back to Door Number One. "Are you seeing anyone?" she said brightly.

Just a tall, mysterious, newly hired bartender, and for the most part, in her dreams. "Not really," she equivocated. "No one serious anyway."

"Evie, dear, you don't really have time . . ."

The screen door squeaked, then the front door opened. "Hello?" Caleb called.

Thank God and all his archangels. "In here," Eve said as she jumped to her feet. "Have you eaten?" Normally she'd make Caleb get his own food, but escape, if only to the kitchen, seemed prudent at the moment. Her neck felt as tight as Chad's had in the Jeep.

Her brother skirted the dining room and came straight into the kitchen. Like her, Caleb had inherited their father's wavy black hair and green eyes, and he'd kept the muscular, rangy build from his college basketball days. "Hey, sis. Quinn and I split a pizza. What's for dessert?"

"Frozen yogurt and crushed strawberries."

He lifted his brows, then looked at the barely touched pan of eggplant congealing in the red sauce. "What the hell is that?" he asked incredulously.

"Language, Caleb!" Her mother's voice came from the dining room.

Eve lowered her voice. "Dad's cholesterol is still too high. Mom's gone vegetarian."

A longer look from her brother while she scooped frozen yogurt and spooned mashed strawberries into the bowl, then he said, "Based on the way you're attacking that tub of fake ice cream I'd say they had you roasted."

She slid him a glance. "Dad talked to Lee McCullough at Lancaster Life about a job for me."

"And?"

"And I don't want to develop communication strategies for a mutual insurance company," she said as she snapped the top on the container of strawberries.

Her mother's lowered voice filtered through the pass-through. ". . . should be watching out for Cesar, not dragging him into . . . admire her initiative, but . . . isn't going anywhere."

Caleb gave her a wry smile, then opened the fridge for her and said, "I've got your back, sister dear," then swung through the door to the dining room. Eve put the yogurt back in the freezer, then followed him. Her brother waited until she had a spoonful of strawberries in her mouth, then said, "So, Mom, who's pregnant?"

Eve glared at him, but the look slid right past their mother, who'd brightened right up. "Melissa Reyes just had her baby boy, and Trina Martin is due any day now. It's her first. Poor thing, she's so uncomfortable in this heat."

"That's wonderful," Caleb said, smiling right at her. "They must be so happy. Children are such a blessing, and the first one's really a special experience for the parents."

Goddammit, Caleb.

She made her escape an hour later but waited beside her brother's Mercedes until Caleb emerged, a plastic container of red sauce and purple goop in one hand.

"Thanks for all your help in there," she said.

He shrugged. "You're not going to change their minds,

Evie, so you might as well have a little fun with it." With complete disregard for the supple, tan leather, he tossed the container onto the passenger seat. "After the way they grew up, Mom and Dad have a finely honed sense of what's right and proper. I'm not saying you should spend your life trying to meet their expectations, but you have to understand where they're coming from."

"I know all about what *respectable people do,*" she said. "I grew up respectably. I am respectable!"

"Do you want their approval?"

"No," she said simply. "If I did I would have quit the Met ten years ago. I want their acceptance. The same acceptance they give you."

And, if she were honest, maybe their approval . . .

He gave her a slightly twisted, very un-Caleb smile. "Acceptance isn't all it's cracked up to be, Evie, because it usually means you're going up in flames on the pyre of expectations. You could get married. That might help."

"You're older. *You* get married."

He ignored her. "I missed the boyfriend discussion. You seeing anyone? Quinn asked about you again."

"I'm not going out with your partner, much less marrying him."

"He's a good guy," Caleb said mildly.

"Blond laid-back ex-surfer dudes are not my type."

"Eve, just define some parameters for me and I'll solve all your problems with Mom and Dad. Every unattached male at the firm's Christmas party last year asked me for your number, and a couple of the married ones too."

With Eye Candy's plans already set in motion, she'd served as her brother's hostess for the party to make connections, and would do so again this year. She rolled her eyes. "Men are dogs. Barking, rutting dogs."

He didn't deny it. "What are you looking for? An intellectual property attorney making half a million a year? A level-headed mediator leaving a trail of peace and calm wherever he goes? A public defender on a crusade against crooked cops?"

Completely unbidden, the image of Chad, his eyes dark and heavy-lidded as he watched her grind against him, bloomed in her mind. Tall, with boxer's hands and broad shoulders, and something dark lurking in his serious hazel eyes. The questions he asked about her, about Eye Candy, like he really saw her, really liked her.

"What he does for a living doesn't matter. When I do start looking seriously, I want someone who sees me for me, not as a piece of ass to bang for a few weeks, or a trophy wife to go with his car and his house and his big-screen TV."

"That's going to considerably limit my candidate pool," Caleb said wryly.

"I *have* met your colleagues," she said, then eased up a little. "Stop being such a big brother. You've got lots of time because I'm not looking for anyone now," she said, then pointed at the eggplant leftovers steaming up the Tupperware plastic interior. "You don't want to eat that."

"It's going down the disposal as soon as I get home," he agreed. "Take care, sis."

Caleb roared off in his Mercedes while she climbed into her Cherokee and headed toward Eye Candy. Once there, she got out of her car, her own plastic container of leftovers in hand, and stood in the empty parking lot. The heat clung oppressively to the blacktop, but as the sun went down the air became tolerable. Maybe she'd put on shorts and running shoes and go for a walk in the twilight, let humidity and exercise ease some of the kinks worked into her neck by her family's loving disapproval. Or their disapproving love. However she framed it, it clung to her much like the buildup of the day's heat, close, suffocating, yet life-giving as the air she breathed.

As she climbed the stairs to her apartment she tried to imagine Chad coming to a Monday night dinner with her parents, but somehow he didn't fit. Too quiet. Too constrained, especially on a night when Caleb and her father really got going on local politics and the East Side's pressing needs. Which was a shame because half of what attracted her to him was that solid quiet, listening, absorbing, processing.

For the next week, Chad continued to show up early. On Friday she tucked the cash for his extra hours helping her with prep into his tip jar, only to find it when she counted the night's take, neatly rubber-banded with a sticky note on top. NICE TRY, BOSS.

On Saturday she got downstairs before Chad knocked, which was unusual. She unlocked the door and found Travis Jenkins leaning against the wall. The second guy from Lyle's unwanted visit did his slouching thing against the black SUV.

"This okay?" Travis asked. He wore church clothes, black pants, a white shirt, and a tie. Eve would have smiled at the transformation if her stomach wasn't swelling like a bullfrog in her throat.

"That's fine," she said, surprised that her voice came out normal, not a croak. "Come in."

"Anyone else here?" Travis asked as he followed her into the dark room. Their footfalls echoed in the space, Eve's faster, more in time with her racing heart as she went for the light switches and turned on every light on the main floor. Normally she preferred to work by lights over the bar, especially when Chad stood beside her, but with Travis, she wanted as much light as she could get. At the same time, she turned on the video cameras, the ones she normally left off until the doors opened.

"Not yet," she said. Chad would show up in a while, Natalie shortly after. She needed to get Travis out of the bar before either of them appeared. "Where's Lyle?"

"Busy. How's your dad?"

"Fine," Eve said absently. Not good. Her contact at the police department, Lieutenant Hawthorn, made it very clear that they needed evidence of *Lyle's* involvement, not Travis's. She'd failed to get that evidence the night Lyle showed up, and she wasn't going to get it today either. She'd counted on seeing Lyle personally. If he started using a middleman to deal with her, this could take months, if not years.

Long haul, Eve. Stay calm, and focus on the long game.

"Your brother? What's he think of all this?"

Travis knew perfectly well how Caleb felt about Lyle. "Like I told him anything," Eve scoffed, then wondered if she was playing it too obviously. "What Caleb doesn't know won't hurt him."

Travis flicked a glance at the wall of liquor behind her. Eve realized he expected a drink. "What can I get you?"

"Vodka rocks," he said, nodding at the Ketel One.

Eve splashed a healthy amount over ice cubes and handed him the drink. This was precisely why clubs like hers were great for laundering money. Liquor ordered was easy to quantify coming in, but harder to quantify going out. As long as Lyle kept his deposits reasonable, she could explain the high take with a good client base and watered-down drinks.

Travis slid a slip of paper across the bar to her, followed by a black plastic bag wrapped in a rectangle and duct taped. "Account numbers and your first deposit."

She picked up the paper and looked at the account and routing numbers, then took the bag and used a knife to slit it open. Her eyes widened at the stack of bills, smoothed and neatly stacked. "Tell Lyle he's got to do this more frequently than once a week," she said. "I can't up my deposit by this much one day a week, even factoring in a Saturday night bump."

"He knows," Travis said, once again looking around the bar. "Spread that out over a couple days if you have to. We'll even things out next week."

Bank, routing, and account numbers were good, but Hawthorn had told her they needed more. "Any chance I'll see him again?" she asked, trying for casual as she shoved the dirty drug money under the counter.

Travis huffed air through his nostrils. "Miss him?"

"Of course," Eve said. "We were good friends. I want to catch up, you know. He got a girlfriend?"

Travis's smile shifted into an oily smirk. "Lots of girls. No girlfriend."

She almost choked on her next words, forcing them through her tight throat, because the last thing she wanted was to get personal with Lyle. They had been friends, when they were kids, back before Lyle made his choices. She hated everything he'd become, what he did to people and communities, knew the lies and betrayal were absolutely necessary, but it went against her grain to pretend she felt something she didn't. "Well, tell him I miss him and I'd like to see him one of these afternoons."

"What about you, Eve? Got yourself a man?"

His tone was silky, as intimate as the way his gaze slid over her. She was used to men looking at her like that; most of the time she ignored it, but right now, she didn't like it. But she bit back her automatic withering response. "Nothing serious," she said, trying for a coy smile, knowing she probably looked like a simpering idiot. God. The cops should give acting lessons. "Just a little something to tide me over until I find someone who's got the same interests I do."

"He said if you do a good job for him, he can do a good job for you," Travis said with an oblique nod at the back of the room.

It took a second for Eve to get it. The abandoned warehouse behind Eye Candy. Lyle must have friends at the county records office. "Oh," she said. "Oh! He could do that for me? That would be great!" The surprise was real, but the delight was totally fake. If Lyle bought that building and the operation worked, the land would be tied up with the court case, leaving her high and dry. More importantly, she got what she had on her own. She didn't want help from anyone. Not her family, who couldn't afford to help her. Not Caleb, who could. Especially not a drug dealer.

"I'll let him know you're keeping your options open," Travis said, then tossed back the rest of his drink. "All your options."

After he left, Eve snatched up the money and the accounts list, then called Lieutenant Hawthorn. No answer. She left a message for him to call her back as soon as possible, then went upstairs to get dressed for the night. After a quick stop in the office to stow the drug money and accounts in the safe, she hurried through the door to her apartment and stood in front of her tiny closet. Trying to pick out an appropriate outfit for the night wasn't easy, but she had to look and act completely normal. What she really wanted was to make sure Chad couldn't keep his eyes off her during the night, and his hands off her after close.

Black leather caught her eye. She shoved hangers aside, then smiled. Perfect.

The alarm on Matt's personal cell yanked him from REM sleep to full alert so quickly there was no time for his brain to layer identities. Shards of reality crashed into his consciousness in a huge, clattering jumble: Eve, cop, music, Luke, the prices of various AC units, and a recipe for a Soul Kiss an extremely persistent blonde had insisted on teaching him the night before. Her number was on a napkin in his tip jar at the end of the night.

Eve. Green-eyed, smiling, sexy Eve, who made the blonde look as appealing as a blowup doll.

The phone vibrated persistently on the bed beside him. He shut off the alarm. Eyes still closed, he fought free of the sheet then lay on his back and tried to piece identities together. No luck. The white napkin held an imprint of a reddish lipstick, not puckered in a kiss but in the stretched lips of a blowjob, with a phone number and a ridiculous, incongruous smiley face in the center. But Chad Henderson was falling for his boss, so he didn't want mindless, impersonal sex with the blonde.

Matt Dorchester didn't want to fuck her either, because for the last week, he'd continued to show up early, help with prep, talked to Eve every night.

The talking sucked.

When he could keep it purely physical, pretend it was just attraction and the lure of the forbidden, he'd hide behind his body's response to Eve, which started out sizzling and after a week of slow was on a steady boil. He treated her like a girl he was getting to know, a girl he liked, so he still got the smiles, the looks from under her sliding, gleaming hair. Every time he touched her, his brain stopped working for a second.

He swung his feet over the side of the bed and rubbed grit from his eyes before running his hands through his hair. It still surprised him every time he touched it, the length and wiry curl a distant memory from childhood, before his father took him for his first high and tight when he was seven. The hair went a long way toward masking cop/ex-military, and so did Eve's first choice of conversational topics.

Sometimes she talked about the Riverside Business Park but mostly she talked about music. Bands they'd heard live, bands they wanted to hear live, concert venues, their perfect concert lineup, tours they'd missed. He held up his end of the conversation there. Based on their conversations, she'd put together an ever-changing selection of music to liven up the repetitive prep work. He'd heard more music in the last week than he had in the last decade, and it was damned good music too—singer/songwriters who could articulate everything he felt but never found words for. Eve had an equally potent knack for stringing together playlists, and his stomach turned over at the thought of her sitting down in the early morning hours or early afternoon, drinking her coffee, poring over iTunes to find new music she thought he might like.

The serious cognitive dissonance between what his heart felt and what his brain knew meant two-hour workouts at three in the morning were now the norm. His body ached, so he needed extra time to pull on jeans and a polo, flexing his hands before buttoning his fly, stretching gingerly to see what popped, cracked, or flat-out broke. So far so good, but he needed coffee before operating a motor vehicle.

Half a pot of coffee steamed in the kitchen. He got down a travel mug and filled it, drained it black, poured out the rest of the old coffee, then measured out grounds and water for a second pot, and sat down at the dining room table next to his brother. Without a word Luke adjusted his ultra-lightweight wheelchair to give Matt some leg space under the table, then went back to clicking and tapping at his laptop.

"You look like shit warmed over," Luke said a few minutes later.

Matt grunted. "I'll take your word for it," he said. "Looking in the mirror this morning seemed like a bad idea."

"I heard you working out," Luke said. "You've been at it pretty hard this week."

"I've been busy," Matt said. "Sorry to keep you up."

Luke looked at him like he'd lost his mind. "You finish at six a.m. I'm up for PT at seven."

His brother hated physical therapy. In the months after the accident Matt had bullied, cajoled, enticed, and flat-out forced him to do the PT. Around eighteen, Luke grudgingly accepted that it was a fact of his life now, but he'd still rather do it first thing in the morning than dread it all day.

"You ate?" Matt asked as he mainlined coffee, then rummaged through the cupboards and pulled out a box of Pop-Tarts.

"Dude," Luke said. "Your diet sucks. If I have to quit smoking, you have to start eating something that grew in the ground or fell off a tree."

He shoved the box back in the cupboard. A bunch of bananas sat on the counter. He snagged one, peeled it, and after a couple of bites his stomach settled down.

"Fresh fruit," Luke said approvingly. "Good choice."

"How's the shoulder?" Matt asked around a mouthful of banana.

"Still sore. The therapist told me to lay off the basketball for a couple of weeks, rest it."

"Good advice. Do what she says."

This got him a grin. "You think it's good because it's the same advice you gave me. So what's the current case?"

The hottest woman he'd ever met and a growing moral dilemma. "Gangs. Guns. The usual seedy side of the city." He swallowed the last of the banana and used the coffee to clear the stickiness from his mouth. "Gotta go."

He'd brushed his teeth and was back in the kitchen checking his weapon and buckling on the ankle holster when Luke said, "Some frat brothers are planning a road trip to the drag races this weekend. I'm going."

Matt looked up. "Who's driving?"

"Me. It's easier to take my truck than it is to get me in and out of someone else's vehicle. Yes, they will be drinking, probably continuously, so I'm designated driver. The plan is to go to the races and the strip clubs. I'll be home Monday afternoon."

Matt looked at him. "You're not working Monday?"

"Sixteen hours next week," his brother said evenly. "Things are slow."

His brother had graduated at the top of his class, had great internships with two small biotech firms, what his frat buddies called the ace-in-the-hole of being handicapped, because yeah, that made Luke's life so much better than theirs, but a year into his job search still hadn't found full-time work.

"Call me on my cell or my work cell if you get into any trouble. No drinking and driving."

"Jesus, Matt, if we're telling each other the obvious, then cash the checks I've written you to help pay off the medical bills."

He sat back down because Luke hated it when he "loomed over him" and talked. Matt had unhesitatingly signed his name to any and all paperwork assuming responsibility to pay for Luke's treatment, but his brother had outmaneuvered him and gotten his student loans in his own name. "Send the money to Sallie Mae."

"I'm giving it to you. The government will just have to get in line."

"I don't need it."

Luke threw a pointed glance in the direction of the thrashing air conditioner. "Lying's getting a little too easy for you."

He ignored that. "I'm late. Text me when you get there. Don't make me worry."

Something about that made Luke press his lips together, but Matt was already late. Travel mug in hand, he was halfway down the driveway, headed for his Jeep parked across the street when his phone rang. Sorenson. He tapped the screen and said, "Yeah."

"Travis Jenkins just showed up at Eye Candy."

He cut the call and sprinted for his Jeep.

CHAPTER SEVEN

Thirty minutes before open, Eve took the spiral staircase to the main floor. Natalie and Chad stood behind the bar. They must have achieved some level of détente about the music because while Natalie's iPod was plugged into the sound dock, rather than her usual boy band extended playlist, the lead singer for Whitesnake wondered if it was love he was feeling. At least it wasn't New Kids on the Block.

Nat turned down the music as Eve crossed the floor and climbed up onto a stool in front of Chad. Without being asked, he filled a glass with ice and water, then set it in front of her. She gave him a smile that matched the flashing, purposeful look through her lashes, then sipped at the cold water.

"Looks like you're ready to kick some ass on a Saturday night," Natalie complimented.

Eve had compensated for stress with attitude, choosing black knee-high boots, a knee-length black leather skirt that clung like a second skin to every curve of her hips and bottom, and a black leather bustier with hook-

and-eye closures. The stiff construction made the most of her average cleavage and left her midriff bare from rib cage to hip bone. She'd taken ten precious minutes to style her hair into a sexy, tousled mass that brushed her cheeks and lips and hung in her eyes.

"When the world hands you lemons, put on heavy boots to stomp them into lemonade. That's my motto," she replied. "How's prep coming?"

"We're almost done with twenty minutes to spare," Nat said. "Lover boy here is good with his hands."

Chad said nothing, just flicked Eve a look as he decimated the last of the limes and swept them into the plastic storage tubs.

"We could use a couple more cases of the pinot, though," Nat said.

"I've got it," Eve said, shifting off the bar stool and down the hall, her boots thudding against the cement floor.

Chad was right on her heels, wearing the ubiquitous running shoes, jeans, and Eye Candy T-shirt. His wiry reddish hair looked a little more rumpled today, the faint lines around his eyes telling her he hadn't slept much more than she had and maybe he'd had a hard morning too. He followed her into the storeroom and closed the door behind him.

"Something up, boss?"

"Why?" she asked, stacking empty boxes by the door to clear a path to the wine. "Break those down, would you?"

"You seem a little stressed," he said as he ripped apart the bottom of a box and dropped the flattened cardboard on the floor.

So much for a bold, sexy outfit. She hefted a case of wine, and said, "It's just new business stress." She was getting far too good at this half-truths/half-lies thing.

He took the box from her and set it on the crates stacked by the door. "Hey. Talk to me."

"It's no big deal. It's just . . . things aren't going so well for the East Side right now. That upsets me." It was the strain of single-handedly running a new business, and dealing with Lyle and her family's well-meaning concern for her reputation and her future. Her liquor costs were going up as gas prices rose, and if the business park initiative failed, her odds of survival plummeted. Maybe she was wrong about her methodology for helping the East Side. Maybe she needed to apply for that job in marketing, and start volunteering at the SCC. Lots of kids needed help with math. She could run basic financial-management classes for teens and adults, help keep them out of the vicious cycle of check cashing and rent-to-own. "Could you see me working at an insurance company?"

"What?" he asked, clearly startled.

"Never mind. I'm fine. Once we open the doors and this place is rocking, I'll be better than fine."

"Why don't you tell me what's going on? Maybe I can help," he said.

Her heart lifted at the offer, because deep down inside he felt rock-solid, trustworthy. But if he wouldn't open up to her, she couldn't afford to tell him any more secrets. "Thanks, Chad, but I think I'm going to keep this one close."

He folded his arms, looked at her. "Why?"

Edgy nerves made her stomach and pulse jump. She copied his stance, folding her arms and opting for flat honesty. "Because despite enough chemistry to turn lead into gold, you've given me no indication you want anything more than friendship. Tonight, I need more than a friend."

A muscle in his jaw jumped, and, as if he'd opened

the grate on a roaring furnace, the temperature in the room shot up ten degrees. The look he cut her, suddenly, shockingly full of edgy masculine demand, seared her skin and stopped her breath. "Fine, boss. If sex is what it takes to get you to talk to me, then let's do it." He stepped toward her, hands on the buckle of his belt.

She held up a hand. "*Now?*"

"Right now," he said as he jerked back the leather to release the prong.

"Are you insane?" She lowered her pitch and volume to avoid alerting Natalie. "Do you have any idea how much work goes into this hairstyle?"

He stopped close enough for her to feel heat radiating from his body against her upheld palm, then took another step, pressing her hand between his chest and her leather-clad breast, his hand to her bared abdomen. "I won't mess up your hair, Eve. I promise." His voice was low and rough, vibrating with need. The tension humming between them turned the air thick and syrupy.

"Okay, I was kidding about sex in the storeroom," she stage-whispered. "Natalie's right outside the door! I want complete privacy and a bed."

He bent his head, carefully not touching her hair, and murmured in her ear, "It's even hotter when you have to be quiet."

Heat flicked through her, weakened her knees. "Later," she said with a push completely contradicted by her soft, intimate voice, but he backed up a step and lifted his hand from his belt. "Later you can mess up my hair all you want."

She took a deep breath, put her hand to her hair, then checked to be sure the bustier was fastened all the way up. The mixture of male interest and genuine curiosity in his eyes as he watched sent another flare of heat deep into her belly.

"I can't figure you out," she said, studying him.

A shrug as he looked at the floor, then back at her. He folded his arms across his chest, his biceps straining at the sleeves of his Eye Candy T-shirt. The shirt hem lifted just enough to reveal the brown leather through the belt loops of his jeans. "I don't like to see you under so much pressure."

She'd gotten him to acknowledge their chemistry, but with some distance between them she remembered why she'd held back in the first place. "You want my secrets, you have to give me something, Chad. I want you, not some enigmatic half-stranger." When he turned away, started to object, she added, "That's how relationships work. I tell you my problems and you help, and you tell me your problems and I help."

At the word "problems" his gaze sharpened. "What do you want to know?"

"Family means everything to me, you know, and you never talk about yours. Tell me something, because right now I've got the impression you sprang fully formed from the help wanted ads, custom-made to work at my bar and dig into my secrets."

The tips of his ears went red in the long moment that passed before he answered. "I live with my younger brother. Our parents died in a car accident a few years ago and he was paralyzed. We didn't have any other family, so I've been raising him."

Outside the storeroom Natalie sang along to 'NSync's "Bye Bye Bye." Her back to the closed door, Eve blinked with astonishment. "Chad, I'm so sorry. How old were you? How long ago did this happen? "

"Eight years. I was twenty-two. Luke was fourteen."

Twenty-two. At that age she'd been searching for a proper job, hanging out with Natalie, concerned about nothing more than enduring another grilling from her parents at Monday night supper. She couldn't begin to imagine the care required for a paraplegic, let alone dealing with the psychological and emotional consequences for them both. The medical bills routinely sent even people with good jobs and health insurance into bankruptcy. Knowing Chad as little as she did, she could guess that he'd kept it all inside. Suddenly the boxing made sense.

"How's he doing?" she asked, a general question that covered physical and/or emotional concerns.

"Good," he said with a shrug. "Just graduated college. He started a year late, but took summer classes to make up for the time he spent in a hospital bed."

His attitude was too casual; she'd spent enough time with teenagers to know how wearing raising them could be. With a nod at his hands, she said, "Taking out some stress on the bag?"

He looked down. Denial crossed his face, then he said, "Maybe."

"Everyone needs a release. That's the premise of my business plan, so I hope that's the case," she said, flicking a glance over her shoulder toward the bar. "There are worse outlets than boxing."

"It's just to stay in shape," he said dismissively.

"Sure," she said. If she'd learned anything in eight years as a cocktail waitress it was that you could tempt a man, tease him, flirt with him, but you'd better not push too hard for emotions.

He shrugged, then offered her a slightly crooked grin. "How's that? You going to tell me what's on your mind?"

"Not yet," she said. Instead, she crooked her finger at him, and the air around them crackled to life with a potent mix of desire, restraint, and anticipation.

He shoved his hands deep into his pockets, shoulders hunching a little at the move, and looked at her. She didn't move, simply waited, her gaze locked with his, not bothering to hide anything she felt. Fear, confusion, longing, interest, attraction, they all flowed through her and therefore across her face until he pulled his hands from his pockets, closed the distance between them, and lowered his mouth to hers. The kiss didn't even pretend to be sweet. Something aching and desperate tinged the way his mouth melded to hers, and that emotion, hinted at by his restraint and his dark eyes, raced through her. She wrapped her fingers through his belt loops and pulled herself up into his muscled body. Plastered together from lips to knees, the leather of her outfit softened under his body heat and his erection pressed insistently into her mound. The ever-present charge between them flared up again, as bright and hot and tantalizing as always.

"Later," she said, her voice low.

He opened the door, lifted two cases of the pinot, and headed down the hall. She watched him go, his shoulders straining against the tight cotton, triceps taut with the weight of the crates, and wondered how he bore the daily strain without cracking.

Probably because he had to.

Originally she'd thought Chad needed to give in to an impulse every now and then, but she now understood why he'd be so careful with himself, his energy, his emotion. Taking care of a child or a sibling was a huge responsibility, but aside from the conversations about music, he'd given no hint of anything he did for himself. He didn't drink. He didn't smoke. He'd stopped listening to music, and he flat out refused to engage in casual sex with a woman who was all but throwing herself at him. He boxed. That was it.

They were going to have a long conversation about the value of a hobby or two.

But not tonight. Tonight she was going to finish what she started in her office.

The steel Matt used to lock away his own needs was buckling, rivets popping left and right. He was supposed to be testing Eve, making sure she had the mettle to stay strong through a dangerous undercover operation, but instead she was working away at not only his cover but his time-tested strategy for dealing with the demands of his life. She wanted to know the people she let into her life, understand them, share their burdens, not just take from them. Unfortunately, when he told her the basic facts of who he was, she'd never trust him again. There was nothing he could do to change the events set in motion days earlier when he walked into her bar and interviewed for the job. Maybe if he hadn't hit on her—but then he wouldn't have the information he'd obtained—he might have been able to come back and apologize—but . . . but . . .

He was going crazy, so he shut down his brain and focused on the work. Absolutely nothing unusual happened at Eye Candy that Saturday night. He recognized a couple of uniforms in plain clothes circulating in the bar. Eve kept a low profile, letting Natalie handle most of what came up. She emerged from the office at nine-thirty to join a large, shrill, and totally out-of-hand bachelorette party for a few minutes.

"They have a designated driver?" he asked when Eve came behind the bar to sip from the glass of water he kept cold and full for her.

"Limo," she replied. "Keep an eye on them, would you? It's almost time to cut them off, at least the bride"—easily distinguished by the sparkly tiara on her head, a veil trailing over her long blonde hair—"and the maid of honor."

"They're pretty raucous," he said.

"That's the point, remember? Blow off steam, have fun, relax, bond over shared experiences," she replied, checking his stock of garnishes and giving the ice tub a good shake. Bent over in the black leather dominatrix getup, her pale breasts nearly swelled out of the corset she wore. In a move as smooth and hot as the leather clinging to her body, she straightened, standing far too close to him for a public place, her leg brushing against his, one hand resting on his hip. "We're going to give that *shared experiences* thing a try later," she said, low and seductive, then walked away.

He turned to see Tom glaring at him. "You got something going with Eve?" he asked.

"Yeah." He added, "So step the fuck back," for his own satisfaction.

Tom's eyes widened slightly, but he edged back to his station. Matt took a deep breath and tried to stuff the bristling cop back inside the bartender suit that was starting to feel like a straitjacket.

Finally, last call came and Natalie worked her way through the bar, ushering the stragglers out into the parking lot, calling a cab for anyone too drunk to drive. Matt helped the limo driver get the loose-limbed, completely intoxicated bachelorette party into the backseat, an innuendo-filled process that brought back not-so-fond memories of his days on patrol. At least no one puked on him.

When he came back inside, Eve came around his end of the bar, leaned one hip against his station, and watched him work. It was rare for her to slow down even for a moment until the last employee left. He wiped down his section of the bar, then looked at her.

"Something wrong, boss?"

"I've been thinking," she said, her face serious.

Oh, thank you Jesus, she'd come to her senses and he was off the hook. He paused to wring out the bar towel, because this close he could smell the mint and rosemary in her hair, feel heat rising from her skin. "About . . . ?"

"My dad knows the VP of HR at Lancaster Life. They're hiring in the marketing department. Shocker, given the economy, but there you have it. I know you don't have a business degree, but sociology's pertinent to marketing, and I can vouch for your work ethic. Do you want me to see if I can get you an interview? It's probably entry level, but you'd have a career track, and benefits. You could keep some shifts here for the money."

Jesus. She was offering to help get him a job. A better job. The kind of job a bartender with a paraplegic brother and a stack of medical bills would want.

He gaped at her for a long moment, then pulled himself together. "Thanks," he said. "Let me think about it."

She blinked, and he knew he'd fucked up. A guy in his situation should have been all over that, and connections were the best track to a good job. "I'm not suggesting you need to be something other than a bartender," she said. "I just thought—"

He cut her off. "Not a problem, boss. I've got a couple of other options, that's all. I didn't want to say anything because it would mean quitting here."

"Oh," she said, her face clearing. "If you leave for a better job, not because I've had to fire you for public indecency, then I'm happy to see you go," she said. "Maybe I wouldn't even have to miss you too much."

She flashed him a smile and turned to the bar to collect the night's take. Under the bright lights, the pale skin of her shoulders gleamed, the taut muscles and line of her collarbone completely transfixing before she flashed him a smile and disappeared upstairs.

As soon as the door closed Natalie gave her two-fingered, piercing whistle. The DJ, eyes closed, swaying to a slow, relentless Euro-techno-groove, snapped to attention. Nat made a cut-it-off motion across her throat and the DJ pulled the plug. That strange, reverberating silence hung in the bar while everyone cleaned up. As the staff trailed out, Eve walked through the building, clicking off the lights and checking door locks. Tired to the point of incoherence, Matt braced a shoulder against the doorframe and watched her walk, mesmerized by the smooth shifts of her body in the leather. In that vibrating silence permeating the point of no return, his conscience battled duty.

His conscience won. "Eve. I can't."

She took a deep breath in through her nostrils as she looked around the bar. Mario and Tom were finishing cleanup. Natalie was upstairs getting her bag. Cesar sat by the open door, watching Eve.

"Then we have a problem, Chad," she said, quiet and even to put his instincts on full alert. "I like you. I like talking to you. I like listening to music with you. But I'm under a lot of stress right now. I need sex, and if you're not willing, then I'm going to make a couple of calls."

She wasn't threatening him, just being Eve. She knew what she wanted, and how to get it. "Don't do it," he said over the sick lurch of his stomach. He was her friend, and he knew it, even if she didn't, but that friendship he found himself hoping would hold through the inevitable betrayal hung in the balance right now. "It's not that bad, boss. Let's get dinner and we'll talk."

"Sure. After you bring all that intensity you're locking down inside to bed with me." She looked him straight in the eyes, and he felt the emotions sear along his nerves to the tips of his fingers, down his thighs, tightening him. Her gaze flicked to the hand resting on the bar, and he followed her glance.

The hand was clenched into a fist. Worse, one of the scabs had cracked open. Blood trickled from his first knuckle into the hollow of his hand.

He consciously relaxed it. When he looked back at her, those ocean-deep, ocean-dark, ocean-dangerous eyes had softened with understanding.

"I think we both need this," she said, very, very quietly. "You might eat what's bothering you, but I think it's eating you alive."

He felt he'd taken a leg to the backs of his knees, sweeping his feet out from under him and knocking him flat on his back. The thought of her walking over to Tom and with a few smiles and a choice comment or two, suggesting he hang around after close while Matt walked out the door and got in his Jeep made him sick to his stomach. Not just because he'd go home alone and nearly out of his head with lust but because he knew, he *knew* he'd driven her to that point. The last thing they needed was another man in the mix, when he could be that man.

Rationalize much?

"Say yes," she said, low, intent, thinking she understood exactly why he was hesitating, thinking he was a good guy, trying to do the right thing by her, not afraid to nudge him a little.

You can't. You can't say yes. You can't say no either.

There was no clear right thing to do here. She'd already hate him. Might as well eat something else and keep Tom out of it. She'd need a friend afterward.

Yeah, you're a saint.

"Yes."

Her gaze searched his, then she said, "Lock the front door for me."

For a brief moment the emptiness he felt when he woke settled into his mind. Chad crossed the dance floor, glanced out over the parking lot to make sure it was empty, then kicked up the stopper bracing the door open. Chad secured the bolt and repeated the movements on the second steel door. Chad watched Eve return from locking the storeroom door. Chad watched her cross the dance floor and hold out her hand.

But Matt Dorchester took Eve Webber's hand and followed her up the spiral staircase into her office.

CHAPTER EIGHT

Matt waited while Eve unlocked the door leading to her apartment. The air was dark and close, heating around them as she fumbled with the key. Goose bumps lifted on Eve's bare shoulders. Without thinking he put the tip of his index finger to her spine, tucked between her sharp-edged shoulder blades as she struggled with the sticky lock. A hitch in her breathing, then the bumps disappeared into smooth flesh.

"Cold or nervous?" he asked. *Find an angle. Make her stay dressed, make her rethink her determination to get you in bed.*

Christ. If he were anyone else, he'd find this hilarious. Alone in the dark with the sexiest cocktail waitress in Lancaster, and he was trying to make her put on more clothes and keep her hands off him.

"Neither, now," she replied, looking over her shoulder through the tumbled mass of black hair gleaming in the red light from the EXIT sign over the office door. Inside the apartment she shed her bag and laptop on a small table by the door and walked into the kitchen to turn on the light over the stove.

"Water? Soda?" she asked as she opened the fridge.

"I'm fine." He sat gingerly on the arm of her love seat, and refined his strategy as she poured herself a glass of red wine. He would not undress. He would not unfasten, unzip, unbutton, or unhook anything on her. He would keep her hands off him, focus entirely on her. He would not walk through the open bedroom door to his left. He would stay on the love seat that was too small for any real trouble.

Who was he kidding? He'd gotten into plenty of trouble in smaller spaces. Like the front seat of his Jeep.

Wine in hand, she strolled back into the living room to set her iPod in the sound dock and clicked through to a playlist. The sounds of Maud Ward's latest hit drifted into the air, the volume too low for him to make out the words but high enough for him to hear the melody and bass line. His brain peripherally occupied with filling in the words to the song, he savored the way she was put together. Under his gaze her body relaxed, a small smile lifting the corners of her mouth, disappearing, then reappearing as she looked over her shoulder at him. She looked happier, calmer, as if she wasn't carrying the weight of the world on her shoulders, and he hadn't even touched her yet.

She took another sip of wine, then set the glass down on the shelf next to the sound dock and walked over to stand in front of him. He reached out and set his hands on her hips, let his thumbs stroke the bare skin between the bottom edge of the corset and the waistband of her skirt. When he closed his eyes, he couldn't tell where the leather ended and her skin began except by the way her breathing stumbled.

He kept his eyes closed, because with him sitting

down, the smooth, pale tops of her breasts and the sharp line of her collarbone were right at eye level, but darkness only heightened the sensation in his fingertips and the scent of Eve, mint and rosemary and a delicate soap underneath it all, rising into his nostrils. She slid her hand into the hair at his nape and bent forward, resting her forehead on the top of his head. The limitless black space in his mind blasted wide open, the heat and scent of Eve dissolving through him, opening him.

I need this.

I can't want this, let alone need this.

She pushed at his shoulders as he looped his arm around her waist, and then he was on his back on the love seat, the sweet soft weight of Eve all along the length of his torso. Their legs tangled together as he shifted back to get as flat as possible, and she pressed her mouth to his. He took her at her word and wove his fingers into her hair, gripping her skull and holding her to him for kiss after kiss, the click of teeth and the wet slide of tongues audible as the song selection changed. He was delirious, losing himself in the music and Eve's mouth, now moving over the scruff on his jaw to the spot where his pulse pounded in his neck.

She was lying between his sprawled legs, which wasn't going to work for either one of them, so he left one hand in her hair and bodily shifted her so her legs clasped his. Then he curled his fingers in body-warm leather and hitched her skirt up until it barely covered her ass, allowing her knees to drop to either side of his. Mouth open against his, she gave a little gasp and pressed her mound against his hip bone, the movement grinding against his cock. Involuntarily he gripped the curve of her ass and pulled her closer. His shirt rode up just enough to press the soft skin of her belly against his abdomen, another tantalizing reminder of what he wanted and couldn't have.

She was slowly going up in flames in his arms, breathy kisses and a rhythmic grind against him, and for a moment he thought he was off the hook. Then she stopped and looked at him.

"We are not doing this again," she said, nearly kneeing him in the balls as she struggled upright in the tight space.

He braced his foot against the high arm of the love seat, hitching himself out of harm's way as he grasped for something to keep her there. "I like watching you like that," he said, but she wasn't listening. With a haste he would have found hot as hell under any other circumstances she gripped his right ankle to push herself upright.

Except she didn't get ankle. She wrapped her fingers right around the Kahr in his ankle holster.

The most fundamental component of who he'd been for the last twelve years triggered a harsh automatic response. His hand flashed out, fingers clamping around her wrist so tightly he felt tendons and ligaments grind against bone.

Too late.

Her eyes went huge, and in an instant he knew there was no hope he could pass it off as a leg brace for an old injury. She scrabbled backward, inadvertently kicking him in the ribs with her motorcycle boot. He grunted and released her hand, and she completed her backward crawl off the love seat to stand in the middle of the room.

"That's a gun," she accused, jabbing her index finger at his ankle.

He scrambled to his feet. "Eve, let me—"

"Have you been carrying that in my *bar*? There's a

big sign right on the front door that specifically prohibits concealed weapons on the premises, Chad!"

Fuckfuckfuck. Arms folded, aggressive stance, well on her way through righteous indignation, into fury. "I know, but—"

"So you saw the sign and wore a concealed weapon to work anyway? Who *does* that?"

Goddammit, those signs don't apply to me! trembled on the tip of his tongue as his brain jerked into overdrive, trying to find an explanation that wouldn't blow his cover.

"Explain yourself!" she demanded.

A shadow darkened the glass in the kitchen window, then *POP! POP POP!* The tinkle of glass shards splintering into the kitchen sink shattered the supercharged moment.

Instinct and training took over. He tackled her, slamming her to the floor behind the breakfast bar separating the kitchen from the living room while someone emptied half a clip into the apartment, taking out the sound dock in a shower of sparks and plastic. She cried out when her shoulder rammed into the bar stool neatly lined up under the counter. The gun was now in his right hand, so he used his left to cover her head and hunkered down beside her.

"Stay down!" he hissed.

No questions, no screaming. She rolled flat on her belly and covered her head with her arms. A scuffling noise on the landing, then more gunshots shattered the glass in the bedroom window. The clearest threat was outside, not in the bar, so he yanked Eve to a stumbling crouch and shoved her toward the windowless bathroom. "Lie flat in the tub and cover your head." When she obeyed, he spun and sprinted for the apartment door.

Too late. Before he was halfway down the stairs the sound of feet pounded toward the far end of the parking lot, a car door slammed, then tires squealed on a vehicle he'd bet didn't have plates. Cursing steadily under his breath, he trotted back into the apartment and took up position in the bathroom doorway between the black-leather-clad, chalk-white woman huddled in the far corner of the bathtub and whoever just tried to kill them both.

Gunfire changed everything. He dialed dispatch from his department-issued cell phone and blew his cover straight to hell.

"Dispatch, three Nova eighteen. Shots fired. 1497 East Monroe, corner of Lexington, second floor apartment accessed from the alley behind the bar. Repeat, shots fired. Unknown assailant. Request immediate backup."

"Copy three Nova eighteen." The voice on the other end of the line stayed calm, but the pitch jumped a notch or two as the dispatcher parroted back his call sign and the address. A cop under fire and asking for backup would trigger an immediate and formidable response.

"Who are you?" Eve asked, bewildered.

"Three Nova eighteen, advise responding units U/C on scene, repeat U/C on scene," Matt said, his gaze flickering from the apartment door to the office door to Eve's face. Best-case scenario, he'd hand her the phone to maintain contact with dispatch while he did any number of useful, situation-appropriate things, like search the apartment, the alley, or the bar. One look at Eve nixed that idea. She was putting together gun and questions, Lyle and radio jargon, and based on the twist to her mouth, the answer tasted like raw sewage.

In the distance he heard the faint wail of an approaching siren, then a second one, the rhythm slightly off from the first. Sorenson was monitoring the radio; she'd be racing for her car, right behind the first responders, along with Lieutenant Hawthorn.

"Tell me who you are," Eve said, but this time her voice was a cold and flat demand.

"Three Nova eighteen, responding units request your exact location."

Not getting shot by an adrenaline-jacked responding officer took priority over confessing to Eve, so he relayed his position. Then he tucked the phone away from his mouth and looked at her.

"Detective Matt Dorchester, LPD."

Her eyes narrowed. If looks could kill, he'd drop dead right there in the doorway, carotid artery sliced open by her ice-green gaze.

"Detective Dorchester," she said, and the acid dripping from the words seared right through his rib cage, into his heart, "you're fired."

He was an undercover cop. He'd been undercover in her bar. He wasn't a bartender. He was a cop.

At some functioning level Eve knew her thoughts circled in a truly dimwitted fashion, but she forgave herself for being a little on the slow side. One moment she's dropping through arousal to hot need and seconds later she's manhandled into her bathtub while someone shoots out her windows.

Then her bartender calls 911 and transforms before her eyes into a cop. A detective, no less.

When she felt straps encircling his calf and the distinctive shape of a gun under the leg of his jeans, all the heat froze into an icy fear. In her experience, only two groups of people carried concealed weapons: criminals and cops. Both appalling possibilities warred in her brain for the split second she had before she heard the popping noises, then found herself flattened between about two hundred pounds of muscle and bone and the equally unyielding floor.

Under a cop. An undercover cop. She'd been a breath and a heartbeat away from going to bed with an undercover cop. She felt his eyes on her but refused to look at him. Matt. Not Chad. Matt Dorchester. Matt sounded a little like Chad, but . . .

"I guess that explains why you look at me so strangely when I call you Chad."

All activity in the room halted as two detectives, a lieutenant, three uniformed members of the Lancaster Police Department, and the CSI team stared at her. Had the words actually come out of her mouth? Oh God, she hoped only the last sentence and not her entire bewildered train of thought had been audible.

He said nothing.

Moments after she fired her newest bartender uniformed police officers had arrived in a flurry of shouting, the calls of "Clear! Clear!" creating a dizzying montage of television medical and police dramas. Chad . . . Detective Dorchester stayed in the middle of the doorway, blocking most of the curious glances as he directed the new arrivals to do a complete search. They'd stomped through every nook and cranny of her apartment, the bar, and the alley before Chad . . . *he* let her get out of her bathtub and go into the bedroom to change. Now dressed in jeans and a T-shirt, iPhone in hand like a security blanket, Eve huddled on the love seat in the middle of all the commotion. The sound dock was a total loss. The iPod looked okay, but she didn't trust her knees to hold her if she got up to check. Without glass in the windows the ninety-degree, humid outside air rapidly heated her apartment, but she couldn't stop shaking.

Out of the corner of her eye she saw Dorchester murmur in Sorenson's ear. The blonde detective crossed the room to crouch down by Eve. "Do you want a sweater, Ms. Webber?" she asked gently.

"Yes, please," Eve responded automatically.

Dressed in jeans, a T-shirt, and a tailored blazer, her gun and badge clipped to her waistband, Sorenson disappeared into the bedroom and returned with a cashmere V-neck in a deep green. Eve tugged it over her head and wrapped her arms around her torso. The shaking stopped, replaced with hot fury.

And all the while, *he* watched her. He had a low, terse conversation with Lieutenant Hawthorn. He conferred with Sorenson. He watched her with a frighteningly alert, focused gaze. She stared back, not bothering to hide her rage. The Lancaster Police Department had been lying to her, which, to be honest, she'd somewhat expected. Ian Hawthorn trusted no one but his tightly knit circle, and she wasn't in it. But she'd never expected Chad . . . Matt . . . to lie to her the way he had. With his body.

With hers.

Raised voices, scuffling outside on her landing, then Detective Sorenson quashed the commotion with a quiet "Let him in."

Caleb pushed his way through the crowd and into her apartment. He wore jeans and a loose button-down, his unruly black hair tousled from sleep. He shouldered aside a flat-footed uniformed officer, sat beside her on the love seat and pulled her into the circle of his arm. "My God, Eve. Are you okay?"

"I'm pissed as hell," she snapped. "Someone tried to kill me!"

Caleb's gaze sharpened, and he scanned the room. Apparently Dorchester's Eye Candy T-shirt hadn't registered with her brother. She'd woken him out of a sound sleep, and even with an adrenaline rush spurred by her shaky words, it would take Caleb a few minutes to put all the pieces together. Eve dreaded the explosion coming when Caleb's excellent brain became fully functional. For the moment, ignorance was bliss.

"Ian, what the actual fuck?" Caleb said to Hawthorn, going for the only familiar face in the room.

"We need to talk," Ian said, voice even. Eve was once again reminded of how different Ian was from the boy she'd passed in the halls in high school. His expression was wary when it wasn't entirely closed off.

Caleb looked around at the uniforms and the CSI team. "Somewhere quiet."

"Use my office," Eve said, and eased up out of the love seat she would sell at the earliest opportunity. She shoved through the officers and waited while Caleb, Sorenson, Hawthorn, and Detective Matt Dorchester, LPD, filed into the room after her. Caleb stood across from her, his eyes flickering between her and the police officers. Dorchester leaned against the back wall, as far away from her as he could get. No one else sat down, so Eve stayed on her feet too. Sorenson closed the door on the activity in the apartment, and for a minute, everyone looked at everyone else.

She felt Detective Dorchester's eyes boring into her. He stood with his back to the wall, arms crossed over his chest. The gun, that damn gun, was back in his ankle holster. Knowing it was there made the Eye Candy T-shirt look ridiculous on him. No wonder he had such physical presence. How could she have mistaken him for a bartender?

Because he was an undercover cop.

Oh dear God. She'd offered to help him get a job.

A dark flush of humiliation crawled into her cheeks,

blending with the anger simmering in the middle of her chest. She brushed her hair back out of her face and focused.

"Goddammit, someone start talking!" Caleb snapped.

"Lyle Murphy asked me to launder money for him," Eve said, too angry to care about what the cops wanted kept quiet. "I told him I would, then went to the cops. They asked me to be an informant. Ian is my contact." She looked at Detective Dorchester as she spoke, the implication clear. *And who the fuck are you?*

The cops looked at each other, engaging in some kind of unspoken communication. Still unusually silent, Caleb also waited, but Eve could see his shoulders tense as the puzzle pieces clicked together in his head.

Caleb knew Eye Candy well because he acted as Eve's attorney. Sorenson and Hawthorn were in street clothes.

Detective Dorchester wore the Eye Candy T-shirt reserved for bartenders.

He'd been in her apartment when the shots came through the windows.

At two thirty in the morning.

Caleb leapt to the worst possible conclusion in a split second. His gaze went dull agate green. "You son of a bitch," he said and surged toward Matt.

"Caleb, for God's sake," Eve said resignedly.

Lieutenant Hawthorn interceded, muscles bulging in his arms as he held Caleb in place. "Settle down, Caleb."

Dorchester didn't move, didn't step into the scuffle or back away. Nothing in his expression or stance changed as Caleb shook off Hawthorn but held his ground.

Sorenson, the shortest, slightest person in the room, stepped up. "Settle down, Counselor," she said, using the same words Hawthorn had, but in a much quieter, much less confrontational tone. Caleb looked at her for a long moment, then favored all three LPD officers with a venomous look, but stepped away, hands on hips.

Dorchester remained unmoving through the entire altercation, but Eve knew it wasn't from fear. Even across the room, even without looking at him she felt energy seething under his skin, his muscles tensed in restraint. All that tightly leashed sexual energy would mix combustibly with adrenaline from the gunfire. Fear and shock eddied across her back, roiled in her gut, but deep underneath those reactions something inherently female inside her responded to Dorchester's energy.

What would happen when the fear and shock wore off, and the desire surged to the surface again?

Caleb didn't miss a beat. "How the fuck long has this been going on?"

"A couple of months," Eve said.

"You didn't tell me."

"He said not to tell anyone," she said, nodding at Ian.

He swung to face Ian. "You put my sister in danger? Did you not trust her to finish what she started? Or is this some fucked-up idea of police protection? Either way, the lawsuit's going to be spectacular. Lengthy. Public."

"Caleb," she said resignedly. "I'm not suing anyone. That won't help. The point is to *help*."

"They're helping themselves, Eve. It's what cops do." The words, fueled by Caleb's short, bitter experience with criminal law, were directed at Hawthorn. "Jesus fucking Christ, Ian! What kinds of games are you playing with Eve's life?"

"No games, Caleb. There's a hit out on her life."

"Why didn't you tell her? Or me?"

Hawthorn lifted one eyebrow, taking in Eye Candy,

reminding without words of Eve's impulsive reputation, Caleb's temper. "Because I knew her. And you."

"Mother*fucker*," Caleb spat. "No way is all of this effort for a chickenshit East Side drug ring. Hooked yourself a bigger fish?"

Eve looked around. The cops had all gone suspiciously blank.

"Tell them," Dorchester said quietly.

"We're not just after Murphy for the East Side," Ian said. "The FBI and the DEA hope he'll roll on the people above him. If he does, we'll take out an entire distribution arm for one of the worst gangs in the country."

"We have a winner," Caleb said, and pointed at Hawthorn. Eve saw him run through all the shit he could sling at Ian—son of the former chief of police, brother to a Navy SEAL, looking to make his mark in his little corner of the world—then think better of it. Eve breathed a silent sigh of relief. One of these days Caleb's mouth would get him into trouble his brains and fists couldn't get him out of. "You didn't want to run the risk that she'd screw up your precious operation," Caleb spit. His finger swung to Dorchester. "He's using any means possible to keep an eye on your best witness. *Any means possible,* right?"

"We believe one of Murphy's men saw Eve walk into the East Precinct. That could mean more pressure on you, or you just flat-out disappearing. She needs protection," Dorchester said, not rising to Caleb's bait. "Getting shot at only proves that. Eve wasn't supposed to know who I am. Ever."

His voice sounded emotionless, as flat and still as a puddle after a rainstorm, but Eve knew better. She took a deep breath to restrain herself from picking up the stapler on her desk and hurling it at him, doing anything to shatter the invisible suit of armor he wore. "What I need," Eve said precisely, then paused when a knock came at the door.

"Come in," Eve and Ian said at the same time. She narrowed her eyes at Ian, who shrugged and turned to see who was at the door.

A vaguely familiar uniformed officer with shoulders like a steer and an uncompromisingly hard face peered around the doorframe. Eve mentally swapped the uniform for street clothes and came up with one of the customers from the night she saw Sorenson. "I picked up the car a couple of blocks from here, threw down the tire strips but he took off on foot. I chased him as far as the alleys but he disappeared into one of the warehouses by the river. I could have had him, LT. Let me go back and—"

A muscle jumped in Dorchester's jaw. "No way were you searching those warehouses by yourself, McCormick. You could have been walking into an ambush."

McCormick's flat expression somehow managed to convey exactly what he thought of this valid concern. "The K9 Unit is here."

"Send them through."

McCormick stepped back and let a gorgeous dog and his nondescript handler into Eve's office. The evening just took a left turn into the surreal. Eve took a couple of steps closer to Caleb. For a long, ridiculous moment, everyone in the room silently watched the dog sniff in every nook and cranny, going up on his hind legs to nose at Eve's laptop and phone, then again at the safe, before turning for the door down the spiral stairs to the club. "Nothing yet," he said, then shut the door behind him.

In sync, Caleb and Eve turned to look at Ian. "Are you seriously searching my club for drugs?"

"Murphy has had access," Ian said. "If he's storing

the drugs here without your knowledge, you take the fall in more ways than one. It's better if we know up front that there's nothing here."

A muscle popped in Caleb's jaw. To forestall the imminent explosion, Eve said, "What I need is for everyone to leave. All of you. It's been a very long night, and I'm exhausted. Take your crime scene techs and your uniforms and your dog and your undercover detectives and get out of my bar."

Caleb looked at her if she'd lost her mind. "Evie, you can't stay here," he said gently. "Someone tried to kill you here. You don't have any glass in your windows."

She'd forgotten. In the adrenaline rush and the argument between Caleb and the cops, she'd actually forgotten what triggered all of this. It would take a while to adjust to the new normal.

"I'm taking you to my house," he said firmly.

Not an option. "Caleb, I'm not endangering anyone else. Not you, not Mom and Dad. They can't know anything about this." She tried to remember the extremely small number in her petty cash account. Eye Candy's success depending on her living rent-free in the apartment, but given the circumstances, dying in her rent-free apartment was a very real possibility. "I can swing a hotel for a few nights," she started.

"I'll pay for the room," Caleb said impatiently, "but you can't be alone. I'm in court on Monday. Quinn can stay with you for a while—"

"Quinn's an intellectual property attorney. I've got better streetfighting moves than he does. I'm safer on my own."

"Come home with me," Dorchester interrupted.

Dead silence greeted this statement. Eve stared at him. She couldn't *go home with him*. She *didn't know him*.

Except, two weeks ago—an hour ago—she would have quite cheerfully gone home with him. Slept with him, in fact, then be-bopped on her merry way. And he was surely more qualified to protect her from whomever was trying to kill her—Lyle, a rival gang member, some random East Side kid making trouble—than an ex-surfer white-collar defense attorney.

"Is Luke real or did you make him up?" she asked, because right now she trusted nothing Matt Dorchester had ever said to her.

"Real."

Matt Dorchester spoke no more than Chad Henderson did. "No," she said flatly. "I'm not putting my family or yours in danger."

"He's out of town this weekend. After that we'll figure it out."

Initially flabbergasted into silence, Caleb rose to his feet and found his voice. "No way in hell," he said, biting off each word.

"It's not your decision to make, Counselor," Detective Dorchester said, his voice even as he looked at Caleb. "She needs protection and I can give her that. I'm already undercover in the bar and people think we're a couple.

"It's possible that my presence triggered this," he said to Eve. Matter-of-fact. Maybe he was used to people shooting at him. She wasn't.

"All the more reason for the two of you to never see each other again," Caleb said triumphantly.

"Your sister's a target. Leaving her unprotected isn't an option," Dorchester replied.

Detective Sorenson spoke. "Ms. Webber, if you're not comfortable with this, we will make other arrangements."

Eve was beginning to appreciate Sorenson as the voice

of reason. She thought about it for long moments, her eyes locked with her former bartender's. During the entire discussion he hadn't moved from his original position at the back of the room. He looked as impenetrable as a steel door, his entire demeanor subtly different. The way he held his shoulders, his stance, the way he not so much retreated as walled off, leaving only a shell.

The considerable physical presence couldn't mask flashes of emotion flickering deep in those hazel eyes, as if someone she might know was locked away inside. One thing was clear. Anyone willing to go as far as he had for information took his job seriously. And if he wasn't going to back down from this, then she wasn't either. She'd come too far to do anything that would jeopardize her role in the operation.

"I'm not committing to anything other than a safe place to stay until I get the glass replaced," she said, mostly to appease Caleb, then added, "I assume you have a spare room."

"You can have Luke's."

"I'd sell my soul for a bed right now." She looked at Detective Dorchester. "I can handle it if you can."

He nodded. "Pack a bag."

CHAPTER NINE

Caleb turned to Sorenson and looked her over from head to toe. Matt's partner was dressed in jeans, sneakers, and a fitted zip-front running pullover, with her hair back in a messy ponytail and her gun on her hip. She returned Caleb's stare without a hint of expression. "What about me?" Caleb said. "Is there a two-for-one special on this particular brand of police protection?"

"Caleb, for the love of—" Eve said, then grabbed Caleb's arm and hustled him out of her office. Matt heard "Stand there and keep your mouth shut," then the sounds of drawers opening and closing.

"That went well," Ian said.

"I take it you know him," Matt said.

"We went to high school together," Ian said. "And if you think he's an obnoxious, mouthy motherfucker now, you should have seen him then."

Sorenson just rolled her eyes. It would take more than a snarky come-on from a defense attorney to ruffle her feathers, but Matt had a bad feeling he hadn't heard the last from Caleb on this subject.

Twenty minutes later Matt watched from beside his Jeep as Eve walked down the stairs from her apartment, her brother at her side, and got into the backseat of a Crown Vic. Hawthorn and Sorenson waited until she was inside, then got in the front seat. Caleb leaned in to say something to Eve, then closed her door. The maroon car reversed out of the alley, executed a tight circle in the empty parking lot, and pulled out onto the empty street. A plain black suitcase was tucked in with the equipment bags brought by the crime scene investigators; someone would drop it off at Matt's house in an hour or two. To all appearances it looked like Eve was going to the station to make a statement; her bartender/boyfriend, Chad, accidentally caught up in all the excitement, would get in his black Jeep and drive off in the opposite direction, giving both of them some protection in case anyone was watching.

Caleb didn't slide into his Mercedes. Instead he strode across the parking lot toward the Jeep. Matt straightened and squared up for the coming battle.

"Eve told me she's practically been throwing herself at you, but I think that's bullshit," Caleb said in a flat, featureless voice that was more unnerving than emphatic posturing. Matt used that voice himself on a fairly regular basis. "She hasn't had to throw herself at a man since she was fifteen years old, although why she'd protect such an unethical bastard, I can't figure out. If she gives me the slightest indication anything, and I mean *anything,* happened that makes her even sniffle with regret, I will make so much noise you'll never get another job in law enforcement again."

"Think twice about that," Matt said evenly. "I did my *job,* and this is bigger than what went on between me and your sister. Smart money's on Lyle Murphy behind two attempted murders, one of a police officer, and the

Feds have him pegged for some very bad shit. This isn't going away. Right now I can still finesse the reports and downplay the personal side of the relationship. You go after me and I lose control over what becomes public and when."

Caleb didn't step back, but his energy switched from confrontational to calculating before he said, "Detective, I suggest you pray our paths never cross in a courtroom. I'll make you wish you'd never been born, let alone met my sister."

He spun on his heel and strode to his Mercedes. The most direct path to his car was straight through a cluster of uniforms, minus McCormick, who had zero patience for standing around bullshitting and was probably back on the street, heading for his next call. Tall and moving with a purpose, Caleb didn't say a word, break stride, or turn to avoid them.

The group parted for him without a word.

It had already been a long fucking night, and it wasn't over yet. Matt took a circuitous route home, the almost nonexistent traffic making it clear no one was following him, then rendezvoused with the Crown Vic idling outside his dark house. Luke was gone, so he parked his Jeep in the driveway, got out, and closed the door.

Hawthorn and Sorenson were waiting outside the car. Matt crossed the lawn and quickly looked in the back window. Eve sat staring straight ahead, her hair a gleaming black curtain against her cheeks. Hawthorn's gaze was trained down the street, his jaw set. Sorenson, facing the opposite direction until Matt approached, looked at the bent figure in the car, then at Matt, lifting one eyebrow as she did.

This was his problem, his mistake. He'd fix it, because the department's reputation and her life depended on it.

He held out his keys to Sorenson. “Change Luke’s bed for me, would you?”

Without a word she took them, then crossed the grass to the front door. “She needs a minute, sir,” he said to his lieutenant. Hawthorn gave him a level look, but walked over to the driveway, giving them some privacy.

Matt scanned the street again, then opened the door and crouched down to put himself on her level. “Eve. Come inside,” he said, keeping his voice low.

She met his gaze, her eyes red-rimmed and shiny with tears but the same flat agate green as Caleb’s. “We can talk about this—”

“Don’t say another word,” she said. “I’m in no mood to talk about any of this. Detective Dorchester.”

His rank and name hit him like a slap. She wasn’t wounded, or destroyed. She was furious.

He shut his mouth and stepped back.

She unfastened the seat belt and got out of the car, her gaze taking in the one-story house, Matt’s Jeep in the driveway, the ramp covered in all-weather green turf. She looked at him, arms around her torso, iPhone in hand, shoulders hunched. “The accident . . . that was all true?”

He said nothing, just nodded. Without another word she walked past him, up the ramp, through his front door, everything from the ramrod straight spine to the controlled, even steps saying she’d never trust him again.

Inside the house Sorenson was adjusting the comforter on Luke’s bed. Eve waited in the foyer, as close to the door as she could stand without being outside. When Sorenson came out, the old sheets bundled in her arms, Eve turned sideways to slide between them, into the room. Then she closed the door in their faces.

Sorenson gave him a wry, eloquent shrug of her shoulders. Matt took the sheets from her and tossed them to the bottom of the basement stairs. They convened with Hawthorn in the kitchen.

"Strategy?" Hawthorn asked.

"We'd better not do anything until we've discussed the situation with her," Sorenson said.

"Excellent point, Detective Sorenson," Hawthorn said, and Matt braced himself. The LT used name and rank primarily when he wanted to make himself crystal clear. Hawthorn fixed his unblinking, all-seeing gaze on him. "I can see you're exhausted, Detective Dorchester, so we're not going to discuss this now, but I expect a complete, detailed, written accounting of your actions from the moment you set foot in Eye Candy up to and including the shooting. Because, as your partner so logically pointed out, right now the odds of Ms. Webber continuing to assist this investigation land somewhere between 'Fuck, no' and 'I'm going to watch while my brother escorts every news outlet in town up the department's ass with a grappling hook and a Maglite.' "

In that tone, statements required a response. "Yes, sir."

"We've got her. We need to use her. She's still our only link to Murphy, Detective. Fix this."

Direct orders always demanded a response, even if he didn't have the slightest fucking clue how he'd fix any of this. "Yes, sir."

"We'll meet here tomorrow," Hawthorn said, and looked at his watch. "Christ, later today. Eighteen hundred hours."

Matt locked up behind them, checked all the windows, then walked back down the hallway to brace his arm on the wall next to Luke's closed door and listen for . . . he didn't know what for. Some sign of her mental state. Some sign of life. For all he knew she'd crawled out the window and started walking.

Silence inside. He put his free hand on the knob because while Eve's style was to march out the front door hurling grenades as she left, she might never want to see him again. The air was thick with thwarted emotions, and the sexual tension that had been simmering away between them since the moment he walked through Eye Candy's front door.

Situational awareness smacked him like the shock wave from a bomb blast. From that moment his standard operating mode of *don't react* had begun to fail, strands popping, tension cables buckling under the pressure. With the evening's events, the last cable lashing down everything he didn't want to feel and didn't want to know about himself snapped.

He'd fallen for Eve Webber. He'd fallen for the woman who'd fallen for his lies, the woman who made him remember all kinds of things he didn't want to remember.

Who he'd wanted to be.

How far he was from that man.

How thoroughly fucked the whole situation was.

Back to the wall, he slipped down until he was sitting on the floor outside her room, rested his forearms on his knees, and let out a soundless exhalation. Then he made himself sit there in the dark, listening to her sit in the silent darkness, until he heard a rustle of sheets and creaking bedsprings. He still didn't move. The doors were hollow core, not solid wood, so he could hear her breathing, short, tense inhales, all but inaudible exhales. All this frustration and anger and treachery had to go somewhere. He knew that from long experience, from losing his parents, watching Luke's childhood disappear into surgeries, physical therapy, a constant stream of adjustments to a world not made for disabled teens. He had to find a way to help her deal with what he'd done.

In her office she'd been moments away from hurling the stapler at his head. He could work with that. Plates. He'd pick up some secondhand dishes and let her go to town on them.

Only when the breathing evened out and deepened did he push himself to his feet and walk the rest of the short hallway and into his room. He pulled off the Eye Candy T-shirt, took his service weapon from his gun safe and put it on the nightstand with the rest of his arsenal, and eased onto the bed. Every muscle in his body ached, and the backs of his eyes prickled. From exhaustion, or so he told himself.

He should have been out cold in seconds. Instead, sleep was a long time coming.

Eve opened her eyes not to pale blue cinderblock walls and blackout shades but to posters of human anatomy and physiology renderings, and *Sports Illustrated* swimsuit models. A desk with a simple shelving unit above it sat in the corner. Standard-issue cream vinyl blinds covered the windows, and leaf-pattern shadows twitched and shimmied on the blinds.

This was not her room.

She closed her eyes, and opened them again. The room remained exactly as before, therefore she must not be dreaming. That meant that her skin-crawlingly humiliating memories of the night before were also real. She rubbed her eyes, then looked at her iPhone. Three forty-two p.m. Out of habit she scanned Facebook and Twitter. Nothing about the shooting. Thank God.

She had a pounding tension headache and her eyelids felt like they'd been abraded with sand. Emotion knotted into a ball in her gut, the strands of fear and anger and anxiety and agitation tightly wound with hunger and something equally primitive she didn't want to acknowledge in the hot light of day.

The whole day promised to be awkward as hell, so she got to her feet, wincing when her body told her exactly where she'd made contact with the linoleum in her kitchen. The shoulder that hit the bar stool throbbed dully. iPhone still in hand, she rubbed the shoulder and wondered if she had enough ibuprofen in her travel bag to get her through the weekend.

Standing up put her gaze level with a simple wooden shelf holding a college education's worth of textbooks and a framed family photo. A father, in suit and tie, hair cut brutally short. A mother in a green dress with a white collar, a smile on her face, tension in the lines around her eyes. A boy, a young man, really, standing rigidly behind his father, his expression an unconvincing copy of his father's. A younger boy, seated between his mother and his brother, and wearing the only exuberant smile in the group. Both boys had their mother's unruly chestnut hair. The younger boy must be Luke. Therefore the older boy was Matt, his expression already shuttered, dark.

She gazed at it until the voyeuristic feeling became too strong to bear, then set it down. Wedged deep between a stack of car magazines and another of biology and chemistry textbooks was another photo, visible only to the person who spent long hours at the desk.

The photograph was of a man dressed in fatigue pants, laced-up boots, and a khaki T-shirt. Forearms braced on his thighs, he sat on a cot in the middle of a large tent. The color scheme was an unrelenting khaki camouflage except for the wreckage of a package wrapped in red and green elf paper and the incongruous Santa hat on the man's head. He held one of the earliest iPod models up for the camera and a broad, delighted grin stretched his face. Eve mentally added unruly chestnut hair and wrinkles around the eyes, subtracted about twenty pounds of muscle from the broad shoulders, and recognized Matt, a decade younger.

"Who are you?" she asked the picture. It didn't talk back. If she wanted answers, she'd have to open the door and get them.

First she stepped across to the bathroom where she took care of basic necessities, washed her hands, then splashed some water on her face. She looked in the mirror after she dried her face and hands, saw anger still simmering just under her skin. Hiding in the bedroom in a sulk wasn't her style, and it also wouldn't solve any of the very large, very pressing problems they faced.

The house was a basic ranch, with living room, dining room, and kitchen at one end, bedrooms at the other. She was in the bedroom closest to the living area. At the end of the hallway she peeked into the two rooms at the end of the hall and found a complete home gym in one. The wall between the two bedrooms held a beautifully made shadowbox with some patches inside, stripes, rows of commendations, dog tags, service medals. While she couldn't identify what hung in front of her, she'd seen similar boxes before, in houses of parishioners who'd served in the military.

The other room held a straight-backed chair, a simple wood dresser, and a queen-sized bed on a frame. An Eye Candy T-shirt hung over the back of the chair. A clear jar two-thirds full of change sat on the dresser, along with some haphazardly folded receipts and a worn brown leather wallet. Another set of dog tags dangled from one corner of the mirror; from her position in the doorway Eve could see the stamped name

DORCHESTER MATTHEW R. and his date of birth. Seeing his full name like that, Matthew rather than Matt, gave him yet another identity, this one in a family life she knew nothing about. There was no quilt or blanket on the bed, and the rumpled sheets looked like they still held the warmth of the body that slept there.

His body.

She backed out of the doorway and turned resolutely to the living space. A navy plaid sofa and dark green recliner crowded around a large television on a self-assemble stand with an Xbox and some games underneath. Hundreds of CDs and a few paperbacks lined the shelves around the TV. Hardwood floors extended down the hall, through the living room, and disappeared into what Eve assumed was the dining room. More of the basic eggshell blinds hung in the windows, angled to let in a little late afternoon light without anyone being able to see in. To her left the living room opened into a tiny dining room with a nice maple drop-leaf table.

She came up short in her hesitant explorations, because the man she now knew was Detective Matthew R. Dorchester occupied the table's far end. He wore jeans and a chocolate brown polo, his damp, rumpled hair curling against the collar. Chestnut stubble covered his jaw, but the shadows visible under his eyes yesterday were gone. A cup of coffee steamed by one hand, the newspaper open to the Sudoku and crossword puzzles in front of him. He had a pen in the other hand. He tapped it against the table several times before setting it down.

The silence stretched out, thrumming with tension, anticipation, and something darker, raw. The house was small and warm, despite the air conditioner she heard grinding away from the backyard. Another truth. He did need a new AC.

Eve felt a hot flush ease up her neck to her cheeks as the red hot anger blended with something else: white hot lust. Daylight following a solid night of sleep hadn't lessened the sexual current flowing between them.

She stopped in the arch between the living and dining rooms, and folded her arms. "I can't decide if I should apologize for coming on to you or slap you for playing me."

He sat back. "Don't slap me. Looks great in the movies but it's ineffective as hell. If you want payback we'll go down the hall, tape up your hands, and I'll teach you how to light me up."

That's not how I want to light you up . . .

"Tempting," she said, "but I've never hit anyone before and I'm not about to start now."

More silence, then he got to his feet and shoved his hands into his pockets. "How are you?"

Telling him the truth was a point of pride now. "I'm sore," she said bluntly. "My whole right side hurts from getting tackled. My shoulder really hurts where it hit the bar stool. I'm scared. Terrified, actually. I haven't eaten anything in twenty-four hours, so I'm starving, or possibly sick to my stomach from fear. And I'm really, *really* angry at you."

He gave her a wry smile. "One thing at a time. A shower will help with the sore muscles. There's ibuprofen in the bathroom cabinet. Don't take it on an empty stomach. I'll make something to eat. Then we'll deal with the rest of it."

She blinked a couple of times, not expecting an eminently practical response to her tangle of emotions rocking in her stomach. "Okay," she said, because what else could she do?

"What fits in the rock star diet?" he asked.

"Fuck the rock star diet. I want comfort food," she

threw over her shoulder. After grabbing her bag from the hallway, she stopped in her room to plug in her iPhone to charge, then took her makeup bag into the bathroom. There were two dark blue towels and an economy-sized bottle of ibuprofen on the sink. She shook out four. The droplets spattering the walls and grab bars in the shower stall, the water temperature running hot immediately, and a damp towel hanging over the sliding doors all served to heighten the sense of intimacy she wasn't sure she wanted to feel. He'd showered before her.

Of course he did. He lives here.

Her stomach did a little flip-flop at the idea. She stayed under the hot water, rolling her shoulders and stretching until her muscles eased a little. The room was steamy when she got out, the foggy mirror hiding her face as she brushed her teeth. A towel wrapped around her body, she scuttled into Luke's room to change into a pair of jeans and a tank top.

She returned to the dining room to find a thick cheeseburger on a plate. His place was empty, and she gave a startled gasp when he materialized out of nowhere, a full plate in one hand and a bag of potato chips in the other.

"Sorry," he said.

"I'm jumpy," she answered, her voice shaky, rising.

"Eat," he commanded gently. "Food will settle your nerves."

He'd be lucky if she didn't hurl it back up on the wood floor. Just to be polite she sat down and bit into the burger, but when the food hit her tongue she ate with an almost embarrassing haste, slowing down only after she got half in her stomach. She reached for a handful of chips, then ate the rest of the meal at a more reasonable pace.

"Better?" he asked when she reached for a second round of chips.

She nodded.

"Took some ibuprofen?"

"Yes."

"That leaves terrified and angry," he said, business-like in his approach.

You may not like him very much right now, but don't underestimate him, she thought. Based on the picture in Luke's room, he'd dealt with worse than this. Despite the warm, cocoonlike air of his house, tiny tremors still rolled through her, but her brain wasn't thinking about fear anymore. Her body, thrumming under some basic delight at being alive, wasn't thinking at all. "I'm less frightened," she said slowly.

"Food and sleep go a long way to settling nerves after something like that," he said. "But you're still angry."

"Furious," she said, because that had to be what was slowly twining itself along her nerves, humming in her skin with an ever-increasing intensity. "Intellectually I can twist my brain around the argument that you were just doing your job. Emotionally . . ."

He didn't move, simply sat still and solid in the face of her reaction. In that moment she understood why Matt Dorchester ended up carrying the worst burdens of everyone around him. Because he could.

"I'm angry with whoever shot at both of us." Most definitely. She could easily separate that strand of emotion from the twisted knot inside her.

"We will get them." He said the words without inflection.

"I'm angry with you for lying to me. I'm angry with myself for falling for it."

He leaned forward, braced his elbows on his knees, hands loosely clasped, then looked at her. "Don't beat yourself up over it. You had no reason to suspect I was anyone other than Chad Henderson."

She looked at him. "That doesn't make me less angry, Matt," she said, testing his real name in her mouth. "You can make this all business, just doing your job, but to me it feels more personal than that. Were you faking everything?"

No movement. No reaction on his face, just a long silence during which she sensed more than saw him battling his emotions. "Protecting you was my only priority."

"You didn't answer my question."

"I wasn't faking anything."

His voice would be her undoing. She folded the paper towel he'd handed her to use as a napkin into halves, then quarters, smoothing down each fold. Avoiding his eyes, because looking at him only intensified whatever was simmering deep in the pit of her belly. Desire, electric and thrumming in the warm air of his house, was intensifying with every passing moment.

"So you were attracted to me and you used that attraction to keep me close."

"It was the best way to make sure you were safe. Later, I wanted . . ." He stopped, drew in breath. "I wanted something I shouldn't want. Something I can't have."

Of course. Explaining a sexual relationship to anyone from Caleb to Lieutenant Hawthorn to a prosecuting attorney to a jury would be unpleasant at best. But the dispassionate, observing part of her mind suggested that the key part of that confession wasn't "shouldn't" or "can't." The key part was "I wanted." Unpredictable, uncontrollable desires seemed to unnerve Matt Dorchester, and yet those desires were the most honest, most real part of what they shared. He wanted her.

With each heartbeat her skin felt more sensitized, the nerves anticipating his touch, his body against hers.

Swirling inside her was a dark mixture of desire and anger, potent, irresistible, and very, very tasty. The concoction flickered and skittered along her nerves, striking sparks before settling between her thighs.

It was just an impulse, a physical response to fear and fury in a situation so confined and unreal that anything could happen, then disappear in the bright light of ordinary life.

"Being angry doesn't seem to be putting the brakes on wanting you."

As motionless as he was, he went even more still, in a really interesting, intent way, jerking the feedback loop running between them into high gear. The body often wanted something the brain found incomprehensible, except wanting Matt didn't seem incomprehensible. It seemed inevitable. But he said nothing.

"If anything, it's making it worse," she continued.

Sex wasn't just about happy, cheerful emotions like love or affection. It was about darker things too. Hidden desires. Illogical attractions. Anger or fear or shock all could make people do something they wouldn't normally do. The shock was gone, the fear receded into the background of her mind, but the anger, the anger had turned up the intensity, making her blood simmer in her veins, making heat gather between her thighs, in her lips, in the pulse thudding against the skin of her throat.

He sat back, looked away, then back at her, and blew his breath out. "I thought about this," he said. "We've got a couple of options. You can go to town on the dishes."

She blinked. Looked at her plate. Tried to imagine shrieking and smashing things. "Not even remotely close to physical enough."

He nodded. "We can go down the hall, tape up your hands, and turn you loose on the heavy bag."

"Better," she said.

He held out his hand, the commanding move tempered by his watchful, wary eyes, as if the shift in territory from the fast-paced, sexy, loud nightclub brought out a softer side in him. Or maybe he was trying to find his way in all of this too.

She walked down the hall to the mirror-walled studio, and waited while he found wraps and tape. His fingers were businesslike as he wound the wraps around her knuckles, then fitted a pair of gloves over her hands.

"I don't know what I'm doing," she admitted as she took up position across from the heavy bag.

"Just hit it," he said.

She did, throwing a punch that barely shifted the bag on the chain.

"Drive from your shoulder, then from your hip," he said, demonstrating. She tried again, adrenaline searing her nerves, sending her heart rate bumping skyward, landed a punch with her right, then her left.

"Better," he said, watching her judiciously.

She kept at it for a few long moments, but it wasn't the full body contact she craved, the release she needed. "Still not enough," she said, breathing a little harder. "How could this possibly be enough, after what we went through?"

His hazel eyes darkened. Lust simmered in the room, flowing hot and sharp-sweet through her veins, bringing a rush of blood to his cheekbones. God, she needed this, needed to struggle under his heavier, stronger body, hands in hair and nails in skin, oh yes, she needed that. In the upside-down world that had become her life, *that* was perfectly acceptable.

Necessary, even.

Needs always bubble up in other places. They were

two consenting adults swimming in a pheromone-lit sea of sheer carnal need, and for the moment, all cards were on the table.

"Don't make a decision under duress," he said.

She laughed, but it was a sound so unlike her she would have sworn someone else made it. "Do you have that luxury?" she asked as he stripped off the tape securing the gloves to her hands. "I don't."

She stood, turned, and walked down the short hallway to lean against the wall by his bedroom door. Then she waited, emotions twining in her gut. Definitely desire. Fear that he wouldn't walk down the hallway.

Fear that he would.

Chair legs scraped against wood floor, but his approach, as always, was silent. He backed her into the wall and kissed her, the touch of his mouth soft and knowing. Sensation spilled through her veins like liquid fire. With a gasp she pushed him back.

Hands flung wide in a *take it easy, I'm harmless* gesture, his eyes assessed everything about her, her hands, her position against the wall, her eyes, her lips. His mouth was wet from hers, she noticed, before his gaze searched hers, intense, aware. Tightly leashed.

A man with that look in his eyes wasn't harmless. Good thing, because the last thing she wanted was polite, or politically correct.

"Don't be careful with me," she said.

He deliberately stepped back into her body, pinning her to the wall with chest and pelvis as he worked a thigh between hers. One hand fastened at her hip, the other at her throat, holding her jaw so he could ravage her mouth, and she felt something dark and very, very desirable flame to life inside her. She arched under his weight, ground her hip into the thick heat of his cock. He pushed back and angled his head to kiss her, mouths slippery, teeth clacking as the pent-up longing blew like a steam valve letting off pressure.

She fisted her hands in his shirt and pulled, more for the sensation of gripping something than an effort to move him. Still, he stepped back and yanked his shirt over his head, then shoved her back into the wall for another explicit kiss. This time her nails found skin, dug in as he worked his way along her jaw and down her neck, using teeth mostly, soothing the bites with licks until he reached her collarbone. With one hand he tugged her tank top strap off while the other hand slid under the shirt to cup her breast. The fierce, hot sensation of his thumb and forefinger on her nipple made her gasp before his mouth claimed hers again.

His body was hard and insistent through her clothes. He leaned into her, using his shoulders to pin her, his hand on her breast sending rivulets of need through her body, his hips grinding against hers in a slow, hot rhythm. If her nails stung his shoulders he gave no sign of it, but when Eve arched and whimpered he stepped back and directed her into his bedroom.

"Strip. Now."

They watched each other covertly as they undressed, her shirt tugged off and tossed aside, jeans unzipped and shoved down, familiar movements made abrupt by ferocious need.

Sunlight and shadows dappled his bed, and his body, as he watched her work off her jeans and panties. A light patina of sweat gleamed on his shoulders and ridged abdomen. His body was spectacular, all the hard-planed, shifting muscles she'd seen when he put on his Eye Candy T-shirt that first night, plus long, strong legs. His thick erection jutted out from a thatch of dark brown hair, visible proof that whatever else he'd said or done, he wanted her.

She crawled backward to the center of the bed, then he braced himself with an arm on either side of her shoulders and kissed her, sharp, commanding nips that trailed down her chin, along her neck, over her collarbone. When his teeth found her nipple she slid her fingers through his chestnut hair and gripped hard. This wasn't gentle, or careful. He was using hands, body, and mouth to pour gasoline on the fire burning inside as he gave the other nipple the same treatment, then moved down her abdomen to settle between her thighs.

She couldn't stand it. It was too intimate, too soon, and she gripped his hair again but then his clever tongue delved into her folds and circled her clit, and she was beyond caring. He held her thigh open with one hand and flattened the other against her belly and quickly learned what made her whimper, then moan. Pleasure tightened hard and fierce under his relentless mouth, and as the subtle, circling movements of his tongue set her on fire.

Sensation seared from her toes to the tips of her fingers, seeming to burn through her skin. She noted slats of late-afternoon sunlight lying across her belly and his hair, but closed her eyes at the image. He built the pleasure with an intensity that had her quivering in his hold, eyes closed, head thrown back, arching against him as her orgasm tore through her. When body and soul merged back together, he was braced over her, eyeing her with a heavy-lidded, predatory gaze.

"Damn," he said.

She refused to feel embarrassed. "More. Come on. More."

She lay limp on the bed while he yanked open the top drawer of his nightstand and grabbed a condom. He turned the package over twice before ripping it open and rolling the latex down his shaft. Without warning he shifted between her legs, and the fight or flight adrenaline was still there because her heart rate kicked into the red zone. Pinned between his body and the bed, all the vulnerability of the previous night rushed back. She gripped his taut biceps, felt her eyes widen, but he wasn't looking at her face. His breathing shallowed as he nudged into place.

His face was tight with desire, his jaw set when his gaze met hers. A bead of sweat trickled down the side of his face, into the stubble. The house was barely comfortable when they were sitting still. Movement, full body contact, made sweat slick their bodies. Reduced to the most primitive state of *female,* she forgot where she was, her name, or any of his several names as the impulse to *finish this* tightened her throat, swept through her limbs. She wound her legs around his, gripped his arms, and arched into his body.

He seated himself to the hilt inside her in one smooth, gliding stroke. Something—the sheer mass of his body against hers, the visceral punch of full-body, skin-to-skin contact—tore free the last of her restraints. She went wild under him as his mouth ravaged hers, bringing the copper taste of blood to her tongue, repaying him for her pleasure with the sting of her nails. The pressure of his cock inside her ignited the crackling mixture of fear and rage and shock. She cried out, curved her arms around his torso and held on. The pace wasn't the fast, frenetic battering she dimly expected, but rather firm, and utterly relentless. Her hips lifted to meet his, need fisting between her legs with each stroke. No escape, no relief from the emotional tidal wave cresting, driven by the pleasure building behind it, promising to obliterate everything in its path.

She couldn't hold out against his body, the pleasure, the emotions roiling inside her. She clung to him, lifted her head, and his big hand slid into her hair. When the wave hit she sank her teeth into his shoulder, felt more than heard a muffled curse rumble in his chest, but he didn't stop. He thrust through the spasms pulsing in her core, and this time, the waves swept her into blackness.

Awareness returned just as he dropped to his elbows, the shudders wracking his big body reverberating through hers. The tension ebbed from his muscles in slow stages, and as he relaxed against her she felt his heart pounding against his rib cage. He nuzzled into the spill of her hair, the oddest, most hesitant sigh fanning the still damp strands. When he got up to dispose of the condom she rolled onto her stomach and folded her arms, her face turned to the wall. The bed dipped as he lay down beside her, but didn't touch her.

Silence. Pleasure ebbed to the edge of her hot, damp skin. Very aware of him lying next to her, she did a quick sweep of her psyche. Not exactly calm, but the passion seemed to have burned away most of the anger, and she was too satiated to feel fear. For now. As for the desire . . . that lingered, ribbons braided with the pleasure.

Flashes of the encounter came back to her. "What was so fascinating about the condom package?" she asked, the words muffled in the crook of her arm.

A moment of silence, then, in an extremely reluctant tone he said, "The expiration date."

Even then he'd been thinking, protecting. Reaching over the side of the low bed she plucked the wrapper from the floor and peered at the date stamped into the edge, then dropped it without comment. She lifted her head to look at him. He stared at the ceiling, one hand tucked under his head, the other resting on his abdomen. A bruise the size of the toe of her boot marred the skin above his hip bone. This time he looked over at her, but while all the signs of ebbing passion were there—a dark flush fading from his cheekbones, full mouth—his gaze was unreadable. "What now?" she asked, the question purposefully vague.

Either he avoided the nuance or he opted for the most immediate answer. "Hawthorn and Sorenson are coming over at six. We need to talk about what happens next."

If Hawthorn was right, if Lyle was dead set on killing her, she had no option but to continue to cooperate with the LPD. "I don't really have a choice, do I?"

"People tell us to fuck off all the time, Eve. More often than not, they get scared, walk away. Your family has history with Murphy. If you want to make amends there and walk away, you probably could."

She could. She never, ever would. Death threat or no death threat, Lyle had to be stopped, and she was in the best place to do just that. But trusting Matt was a completely different story. "Did you sleep with me to keep me close? To make sure I'd take your protection?"

He smiled, but there was no real humor in the twist of his mouth. "Despite all evidence to the contrary, there is a limit to what I'll do for the LPD."

A hint of a smile curved her lips at the self-mocking words but she really didn't feel like liking him right now. "So why? Why give in to the impulse now, after weeks of no?"

"I wanted to," he said.

Oh.

His expression didn't change. She rested her head on her folded arms and closed her eyes. The vent emitted tepid air from the softly rattling air conditioner. She lay beside him and wondered how to handle a Matt Dorchester who was actually doing what he wanted to do.

CHAPTER TEN

He'd just made mistake number four. No, mistake number four was going upstairs with her, what was it, less than twenty-four hours ago? This was mistake number five. Making mistakes was becoming a habit, the kind of habit his father loathed, preached against, habits of weakness and emotion. Except this time his emotions weren't the only ones in the game, and it sure as hell didn't feel like a mistake.

He lay on his back beside Eve, one arm tucked under his head. She wasn't asleep, just stretched out on her belly, her ankle resting in the bend of her knee, arms folded under her head, her eyes closed. The pale skin of her back gleamed with sweat and her black hair tumbled around her shoulder and over the pillow.

For a moment he tried for the usual blankness when he could be nothing, no needs, no demands, no pressures, but there was no ignoring Eve in his bed. God knew she had every right to tell him to deliver meals to Luke's room for the next forty-eight hours, then go fuck himself, but he'd underestimated the unpredictable life force

Eve channeled. He'd tried to do this the right way, offering up the option that, until recently, had worked for him. It didn't work for her. Eve wasn't the kind of person to stuff everything down, or substitute exercise for emotion, or settle for anything less than what she wanted.

People did atypical things when they were angry. Physical things. They hit things, or each other. Ran. Stormed around, screamed obscenities, made accusations, went cold and hard and silent.

Sometimes, for all the wrong reasons, they had sex.

If he'd been able to pick the circumstances for his first time with Eve, anger-driven sex wouldn't have been on the list. Except she'd sat in his kitchen, looking like she was going to flare into flames from the inside out. Her tight, clipped sentences told the story as much as the edgy nerves she didn't even bother to hide. Then she said she still wanted him, despite the anger, or maybe because of it, throwing the words at him like a challenge. Just like every encounter with Eve for the last two weeks, he simply couldn't resist reaching out to touch that live wire.

It chapped his ass to hear her list any number of motives for sex, and burned like salt rubbed in the raw spots when she checked the condom wrapper for herself, but he'd earned that. There was more to come. But for now she was relaxed, breathing easily, soft and warm in his bed. It should have been purely physical, a way to ease her stress, scratch the itch and see if it went away. It hadn't. Instead, he felt sore inside, something similar to the ache left after he took a good pounding to his ribs. He couldn't name it, so he noted the feeling and set it aside.

He glanced at the clock on the nightstand. Less than an hour until Hawthorn and Sorenson arrived. "You want to shower again?"

"Yes," she said. "You go first. I'll take longer."

He eased himself away from her warm body, stood under a lukewarm shower, and repeated his new mantra: no more mistakes. He'd fucked up, but he could rescue this from the death spiral. All he had to do was keep it together, until they got Murphy.

He got out, toweled off, then went back into the bedroom to get dressed. As soon as he reappeared, Eve slid out of bed, gathered her clothes from the floor, and ducked into the bathroom.

She joined him in the kitchen ten minutes later, her combed hair lying wet against her neck. "Do you have any elastic bands?"

"Junk drawer," he said, pointing under the silverware drawer.

She found a rubber band formerly holding the ads in his Sunday paper, slicked her hair back and secured it with two quick movements. Lightning cracked through him, halting movement and breath for a heartbeat, then another as their eyes locked. He resumed breathing when she broke away to gather the dirty plates and silverware from the dining room table and slide them into the soapy water he'd run to do dishes.

"You don't have to do that," he said.

"I need to do something," she replied.

Framed that way, he was okay with it, so she washed, he dried and put away. While the sink drained, she went into Luke's room and returned with her iPhone. She swiped and tapped at the screen, then lifted the phone to her ear.

He raised an eyebrow in question.

"My contractor," she said. "I need him to replace the glass in my windows. I can't live here forever."

"East Side guy?"

"Of course," she said.

He cleared his throat. "A cop I know does renovation work on the side. I called him before you got up. He can install new glass Monday after work and he'll keep it quiet. I just need to call him back to give him your approval."

Slowly she lowered the phone and tapped the screen to end the call. "Because you don't want the whole East Side to know about the shooting."

"Until we have a better handle on the investigation, yes," he said quietly.

"How did you keep it out of the paper?" she asked. "Anybody with a police frequency app on their smartphone can monitor the radio."

"Do you have any idea how often we respond to a 'shots fired' call on the East Side? Multiple times a night," he said. "No one's going to pay any attention to what happened."

She rubbed her thumb across her iPhone as she considered his words. "And that's why I'm here, not at Caleb's office strategizing a lawsuit. Go ahead and call your friend."

He didn't push, just wrung out the dishcloth and draped it over the faucet, then made the quick call. When he turned to face her again, she was still staring at him, that assessing look in her eyes.

"You're handling this much better than I am."

"I've known from the beginning who I am," he said with a shrug.

"Somebody shot at us last night!"

Oh. That part of "this." "Not my first time at that rodeo," he said bluntly.

Eve narrowed her eyes and opened her mouth. "About that—" she started.

The doorbell rang. Eve looked at him. He waited, then his cell phone, clipped to his belt opposite his gun, buzzed. He flipped it open. "It's them," he said, but he still peered through the blinds before opening the door.

"McCormick said you live on the most boring street in all of Lancaster," Sorenson said as she slipped through the door, then nodded at Eve, hanging back by the dining room table. "I called in Carlucci to take over. He's great at sitting on his rear end, and McCormick would rather be back on the street anyway. Ms. Webber."

"Detective," Eve replied politely, then turned to Hawthorn. "Ian, you jerk. You are so on my shit list."

Her scathing glare slid right off the LT. "It was the right thing to do, Eve. We didn't know what you could handle, and we never thought it would turn out like this."

Eve opened her mouth to argue, but Sorenson stepped past Hawthorn and drew Eve into the living room, quietly asking how she was feeling, if she needed anything from her apartment. Hawthorn looked at her, then at Matt, shook his head, but said nothing.

Eve spoke from the dining room. "Ian, Detective Sorenson asked if I'd identify some people you've photographed with Lyle."

Matt recognized the technique. Start with something simple, giving names. Nothing incriminating or snitchy in that request, but it would make it harder for Eve to break the flow of the conversation if it took a more participatory turn.

"We'd appreciate it," Ian said gravely.

"Do you want your brother here for this conversation?" Matt said. Because it was the right thing to do.

Amusement flared in her eyes. "I think giving Caleb a couple of days to calm down is a good idea."

No one disagreed with that conclusion. Matt felt the vibe shift as Sorenson and Hawthorn incorporated this conversation into their judgment of Eve's shrewdness. Hawthorn headed for the dining room and Sorenson sent him a look that read *Damn, Dorchester.* His return look conveyed *See what I've been up against for the last two weeks?*

Hawthorn shifted a thick folder and a laptop to the table and began unwinding the power cord. "You're well connected to the East Side. We usually have to piece together networks and relationships after several arrests, and information from East Side informants is sporadic."

"No matter what we do it doesn't seem to improve," Sorenson added as they seated themselves around the table.

"Without backing from neighborhood leaders, you're wasting your time," Eve said. "The Eastern Precinct has a reputation for corruption. Why snitch when there's a good chance nothing will come of it, and an even better chance of retaliation?"

"Why did you come in?"

"Because if we don't work together, nothing will change," she said precisely. "And because I take it personally when a drug dealer thinks I'll be his shell company or whatever."

From the folder at his side Hawthorn pulled duplicates of the photographs decorating the bulletin board back at the precinct. "These are all individuals who've been seen with Murphy since he arrived. About half of them are in the system for one reason or another. We'd like your help with the other half."

She tucked her leg under her and sifted through the photos Hawthorn handed her. "Well, that's me," she said, pointing to the photograph of her with Lyle at Chat Noir.

"Pretty fancy for a dealer," Sorenson mused.

"Lyle's always been more uptown than East Side," Eve said. "His mother, Dolores, grew up poor. Good people who live in poverty often have very rigid definitions of respectable. They want better than they had for their children. She didn't want Lyle to have anything to do with Victor's business, and used Victor's money to make sure Lyle didn't look like a corner kid. Perfect grammar and elocution, nice clothes. None of it kept Lyle from worshipping his father."

"Why did he approach you?" Hawthorn asked.

"After what happened yesterday this seems impossible to understand, but we were friends. Caleb wouldn't have anything to do with Lyle, but Lyle and I, we had things in common." She stopped, as if she'd said something she regretted, or maybe just choosing her words.

Hawthorn typed. Sorenson preferred the old-fashioned method of pen to paper, although come trial prep half her notes were doodles and oddly drawn little caricatures. Eve looked at the photo, tilting it under the overhead light to reduce the glare before setting it aside.

"What did you have in common?" Matt asked in the silence.

The answer to that question came far less readily, and with a look through her lashes he couldn't read. She shifted in her chair, putting both feet flat on the floor, then crossing her legs as she chose her words. "Growing up with Caleb was difficult."

Sorenson gave an amused snort, and Eve cut her a glance.

"Impossible to understand, right? He's brilliant. You don't get a full ride to Yale Law without genius IQ brains. He could have played pro basketball, and he's a firstborn son in a family that's got some pretty defined gender roles. I wasn't him, which nobody expected of a girl, but I'm not my mother either. Lyle understood about not fitting in, especially after his father went to prison and his mother got even more religious and strict."

Her jaw tightened, then she shuffled through the stack of photographs again until she found pictures of a meeting deep in the East Side. "You probably have him in the system, but that's Travis Jenkins. He was Lyle's best friend back in the day, always ready to get dirty so Lyle could stay clean. He stayed around after Lyle left, but from what I hear he never made it to the Strykers' inner circle. He's a blabbermouth, always trying to look like he's on the inside by showing off what he knows. But . . . Travis's cousin Maria lives with one of the Stryker lieutenants, a guy who used to sing in my dad's youth choir. Beautiful baritone. Dad was crushed when he lost him to the Strykers but he still baptized both of Maria's kids eight, maybe ten years ago. Through Maria, Travis is probably Lyle's source of street information."

Eve's memory was nearly perfect, remembering names, relationships, connections forged in gangs or juvenile hall or after-school programs and church. Several hours later, Chinese takeout cartons and empty soda cans littered the table and the sun was setting. They'd identified most of the individuals not in the system, and Eve was sitting cross-legged on a dining room chair, picking through a carton of cashew chicken.

Sorenson sat back and dropped her pen on the legal pad brimming with notes. "It's a great cover," she said. "A business owned by a woman, targeting women, and highly visible on every social networking site. Bars don't take in or deliver a measurable product, so the money's hard to track."

"I'm practically perfect in every way," Eve said lightly. "Do you really think he meant to kill me last night?"

Matt shook his head. "Too amateurish. He meant to scare you. When a guy who's come up in the Strykers decides he wants you dead, he'll do it himself, and he'll do it in one of those empty warehouses by the river, where no one will find the body until it starts to stink. I think he planned on you being the same as you were in high school. Alienated from your family. Maybe he asked around before he approached you, heard about how your family felt about Eye Candy, maybe even heard you were estranged for a while. He thought you'd be alone, afraid, easy to persuade. He wants to own you."

"I am not for sale," Eve said precisely.

"Then he'll steal you," Matt said bluntly, trying to impress on her exactly how dangerous this was. "When I show up he thinks suddenly you've got someone in your life who doesn't care if you're a cocktail waitress or a bar owner, someone you can depend on."

"You," she said.

"Me," he agreed, then stopped, because talking about the soft, secret thing growing between them in front of Hawthorn and Sorenson made his stomach clench.

She knew it too. After another one of those unreadable looks through her lashes, she peered into the cashew chicken container, set it aside, and said, "What, exactly, are you proposing?"

Hawthorn spoke up. "We give Murphy what he wants. We pull Detective Dorchester out, and put someone else in undercover to protect you. Or we wire up the bar and set up a surveillance operation."

"Absolutely not," Eve said. "I'm not giving up that level of privacy."

"Natalie could take a long vacation," Sorenson mused. "I could step in."

"Nat's never taken more than a weekend off," Eve said doubtfully. "Her whole family lives in Lancaster, both sides, four generations."

"You could fire her."

Eve scoffed. "She's my best friend. If I fire her, everyone on the East Side will be talking about it. Look, if the point is for this to look totally natural, that's not going to work. We're working under the assumption Lyle is pissed that I'm dating 'Chad,' " she said.

"And?" Matt asked.

"If I thought someone shot at me because of my choice in men, the last thing I'd do is fire him or break up with him, and everyone on the East Side knows it," Eve said. "I'd get the biggest, gaudiest engagement ring I could find and set a wedding date."

Matt's heart stopped dead in his chest. Could he put on the gold band sitting in his desk drawer for a fake marriage? To Eve?

Jesus Christ. Caleb Webber would do his level best to slice off Matt's balls and feed them to rabid, flea-ridden dogs if Matt's crash-entry into Eve's life resulted in a sham marriage.

She gave him a glittery little smile. "Okay, maybe not a wedding date, but I wouldn't break it off. Webbers don't take intimidation well. We've had bricks thrown through the front window of the house and the church. When I was in the fifth grade Dad tossed two kids out of an after-school program. They stole our dog from the backyard, killed her, and left her body on the front porch. In honor of Goldie, we do not knuckle under to intimidation tactics. Lyle knows this. If I dump Chad because I'm spooked, he's going to think I've lost my nerve, and I'm not a good front for him."

"Maybe Chad got spooked and ditched you," Sorenson said dispassionately.

Fuck that, because in this case, Chad Henderson was basically Matt Dorchester, and Matt didn't spook. "If we keep going with this, then I stay undercover," Matt said.

"As my bartender or as my boyfriend?" Eve asked.

"Both," he said firmly, and hoped like hell he was doing the right thing.

"Detective Dorchester," Hawthorn began.

"Sir, something about this has Lyle spooked. Maybe he's getting pressure from higher up the food chain. We can't leave her protected only by surveillance gear. Keeping me there full-time is a hell of a lot cheaper than detailing six officers round the clock to watch the bar."

Hawthorn leveled a look at Matt that had Sorenson tilting back in her chair to examine the ceiling and a tiny grin dancing around Eve's mouth. "Your concern for the department's budget," he said, stressing the last word, "is duly noted, Detective. If Eve consents to your continued presence in her life, I agree."

Judging by the expression on Eve's face, that was by no means a given. She picked up the takeout carton again, dug through it for a tiny piece of chicken, considered it, then put the carton back on the table. She sat in silence for a while, shuffling the photos together and aligning the edges, the careful, precise movements buying time to think things through. Pale pink stole into her cheeks, then she said, "Congratulations, *Chad*. You've got your job back."

Her tone walked a fine line between playful and mocking, and he knew that no matter how wholeheartedly Eve committed to making a dent in the East Side's drug trade, getting manipulated into it didn't sit well.

After what happened earlier in the afternoon, getting called "Chad" didn't sit well with him.

"You fired him?" Sorenson asked.

"Right after he called 911," she said lightly.

A broad grin spread across Sorenson's face, marking the moment Eve went from *other* to *ally*. Even Hawthorn looked mildly amused as he said, "Thanks, Eve."

They could laugh at his expense, but this was no joke. His father's words echoed in his ears. *Emotion shows weakness, Matthew. Control your only strength, your only friend. You do the right thing for the people who trust and depend on you.*

On the East Side bad things happened to people who cooperated with the police. Especially bad, brutal things happened to women. He was now Eve's first line of defense against Lyle Murphy or the Strykers or whoever was after her.

Back to the bag. And cold showers.

"Okay," Hawthorn said, gathering up the photographs and closing his laptop. "For the time being, Matt stays undercover at Eye Candy. We wait for the next move and take it from there."

She stood to the side as Matt closed and locked the door, double-checking the locks and chain more than was actually necessary. When he turned around, he found her leaning against the wall not twelve inches from him. Her feet were bare, and wavy strands escaped from her ponytail, gently brushing her flushed cheeks. The skin of her throat and collarbone gleamed with a thin film of moisture, and he flashed back to watching pink infuse her face and neck as she tipped over the edge into orgasm.

He had to get new AC in this house.

CHAPTER ELEVEN

"Uh-oh," Eve said. "I've seen that look before."

"What look?" he replied. He'd learned to control his face from a very early age but controlling anything around Eve wasn't going well.

"It's Sunday night. We're here until Tuesday, alone in your house, with nothing to do except stay out of sight. It's the perfect setup for thirty-six hours of adult fun with chocolate syrup and whipped cream and whatever else you have at hand, but that look that says as much as you want to do this, you're not going to," she said dryly. "I'm very familiar with that look."

Shoulders square, hands loose at his sides, he looked her right in the eye. "You're right. I'm not," he said.

She absently tugged her hair loose from the rubber band, gently massaging her scalp and sending the now-dry strands tumbling into her face. "So you want to start pretending we don't send up sparks every time we look at each other?" she asked as she tamed the glimmering black mass and secured it with the rubber band.

For the first time in their relationship the circumstances were clearly defined, objectives identified. Protect her while they took down Murphy. Keep her physically and emotionally whole, so when this was over, she could walk away unscathed. People, especially women, got attached when they had sex. Denying what he wanted was best for her.

But he couldn't lie to her. When the job called for half-truths and misdirection, he'd done it; but not anymore, not with her cooperation, not with her in his house. "No," he said quietly. "That's not what I want."

"That's why you should do it. You want to."

"What about after?" he said as he shoved his keys into his pocket.

"Matt, I'm not thinking more than about thirty seconds ahead right now."

"One of us should."

She laughed, and again the sound was somewhere between playful and mocking. "Very mature of you," she said. "Very protective. But you're thinking too far ahead. Up until 2:30 a.m. Sunday morning we were the textbook example of sudden, explosive sexual chemistry. If we get very proper and formal with each other, it's going to look odd. To make this thing work we need to act like we can't get enough of each other, like the sex just gets better and better every time we do it, and we're doing it every chance we get."

In other words, like they were a new couple falling madly, totally, completely in love.

Her words spawned a whole medley of full-color, tantalizing images in his brain—sex in her bed, in the office, in the storeroom, all the time in the world to do everything he imagined and come up with a dozen new ideas—and the ache under his ribs intensified. His pulse sped up, sending adrenaline into his veins. With the sharpened senses came awareness. He felt vulnerable. Eve's crackling, live-wire energy exposed bruised places he'd kept hidden. He *felt,* and sex would only make it worse.

His father's shadowbox of medals and ribbons caught his eye, triggering his father's voice in his memory. *Emotions create weakness. Weakness puts you and your team at risk.* "So we keep acting." As he spoke he brushed past her, down the hallway and into his bedroom.

"We weren't acting," she pointed out, calm and logical.

He ignored her as best he could when she stood just ten feet away, shucking the jeans and polo for gray cotton shorts and his running shoes. When he emerged, she still stood at the end of the hallway, arms folded under her breasts, her face mildly amused and mildly inquisitive. "Time for a workout?"

He nodded. "Help yourself to whatever," he said with a glance at the shelving unit holding his outdated CD collection and a few books.

"Do you have speakers I can connect my iPod to?"

"No. Sorry."

"No stereo either."

That wasn't a question. "We moved it to make room for the Xbox." But the CDs still lined the shelves of the entertainment center.

"In Luke's room there's a picture of you holding an iPod."

His fingers tightened on his hips as memories flooded back, opening the Christmas package, seeing the little device awkwardly bubble-wrapped and taped to within an inch of its life, knowing Luke would have saved the money he earned mowing lawns and shoveling sidewalks for months to buy him the iPod so he'd have the music he missed so desperately. It was, hands down, the nicest thing anyone had ever done for him.

She was seeing things, and worse, making connections.

"That was a long time ago. Luke got it for me for Christmas during my first tour." His voice was emotionless, too much so. He forced out a breath, relaxed his hands. Sometimes you had to react a little to hide a lot.

"What happened to it?" Unlike his voice, hers was quiet, soft, and full of gentle curiosity.

He talked to the frame around Luke's door. "When my CO told me my parents were dead and Luke was paralyzed, I had ten minutes to sprint three quarters of a mile to the airstrip and catch the first transport to Germany. I left everything behind." He'd been wearing the sweat-stained, gritty cammies when he walked through Luke's hospital room door thirty-six hours later, covered in Iraqi dust and sand. "A buddy packed up my stuff and shipped it to me, but he couldn't find the iPod. Someone stole it out of my locker." He shrugged. "Guy needed it more than I did. Everyone has their music on their phones these days."

"But not you," she observed.

"I've been busy." When she didn't comment on this pathetic excuse, he turned to go into the bedroom that held the gym.

"Matt."

He stopped. "Yeah."

"I'll still be here when you come back."

No problem, because the workout was going to fix this. It always had, until he met Eve. He straddled the treadmill and punched up a hill course, waiting for the belt to pick up speed before he dropped into the workout. In seconds he ran at a pace that would have left her far behind if she hadn't been down the hall, in his living room.

Chest heaving, pulse well into the red zone, he drove himself through an eight-mile hill course in less than an hour but the emptiness never came. Fine. Going at the speed bag never failed. His fists fell into the regular five-count rhythm easily enough, but his brain would not shut down. He knew the heavy bag workout was useless before he even began, but drove punch after punch into the slowly twisting cylinder until he skidded on the sweat spattered on the wood flooring. With a low curse he tore off the gloves, fisted his hands on his hips, and bent his head.

This is not going to go away. For the foreseeable future she is in your house, in your life, and this is not going away. Face it, and deal.

Sweat dripped steadily from his jaw and temple to the floor. He grabbed a towel and dried off, then wiped the floor and walked down the hall to confront temptation. She was stretched out on the sofa, reading one of the few books shoved into the shelf next to his outdated CD collection. She'd turned on the lamp on the end table against the deepening summer twilight, and didn't look up from the book. In the kitchen he ran water into a glass and drank. When he had two full glasses in him, she spoke.

"Did it work?" she said absently.

He refilled the glass and walked out of the darkness of the kitchen to stand in the doorway to the living room, waiting until she looked up from the book. Her green eyes were somehow both languid and heated, her skin gleaming against the dark sofa. There weren't sparks flying between them. It was like an ambush, tracers arcing into the night sky, the shock and adrenaline of a firefight every time they were in the same room. "No."

At that her gaze sharpened. "Sometimes you can't shove down what you want," she said as she went back to the book.

He turned abruptly for the shower. Before he got the door closed she added, in a slightly louder tone, "Or ignore it."

To cool down, he let the tepid water stream over the top of his head before he soaped up. And while he couldn't ignore her, he could ignore the heat thumping in his groin. He could, and he would. He would ignore the ache building in his cock and the woman stretched out on his sofa by turning on *Sunday Night Football* and watching the game like any normal guy who'd had sex six hours earlier. He wasn't fifteen, for fuck's sake.

When he emerged from his bedroom, back in jeans and polo, he found his unexpected and highly unpredictable houseguest watching a public television special on the mating habits of baboons.

Don't react. The book lay on the couch beside her hip, her index finger functioning as a bookmark, the cover reflecting the light from the TV. After a contemplative pause, he said, "You watching this?"

"Yes. It's fascinating." In the dark her face was a pale blur relieved only by the sooty smears of eyelashes and eyebrows and a pink lush mouth.

Hands back on his hips, Matt watched a male baboon clamber up the back of another. After some howling and a few jerks of his furry hips, he scampered away. The victim of the hit-and-run looked over her shoulder and screeched at his disappearing back.

"Guess he didn't get the message about slow," Eve said brightly.

Do. Not. React. "The Bears are playing. Preseason game in Tokyo. Where's the remote?"

"Under my butt," she said.

Laughter surged in his chest, a startling sound he turned into a cough before bending his head for a couple of even breaths. Under control again, he looked up to find Eve watching him.

"You don't really want to watch football, Matt."

Looming over her felt weird, so he hunkered down beside the sofa and folded his arms on his knees. He knew what he had to do here. Say a simple, two-letter word, and this was all over, the humor, the banter, the sex. But just watching life eddy across her face turned off most of his higher neural functions.

She turned her head and looked at him, genuinely curious. "I looked through your CDs. Who still has CDs?"

"They're on my computer. I never got around to tossing them out," he said. A partial truth. His digital music library was maybe a tenth of what he had on CD. He'd stopped buying music. Didn't pirate it either. He just stopped listening to it. When she kept that clear, direct gaze focused on him, he added, "I came for prep at Eye Candy because it was a good way to get information, and because you liked the same kind of music I do."

This concession didn't get the response he'd hoped for, a reprieve in the unrelenting longing eddying in the room. She sat up a little straighter and tucked the book to her chest. "Aside from beating the living hell out of the heavy bag, what do you do that's for you?"

"I find my job very rewarding, and I love my brother."

"Admirable," she said quietly. "Noble, even, but you didn't answer the question. What do you have in your life that's just for you?"

His whole life was structured around duty and honor.

He didn't need anything else. "Give me the remote, Eve," he said with a beckoning motion.

She turned back to the book. "Come and get it, Matt."

A glance over his shoulder at the TV, where the announcer was detailing the signs of a female bonobo's readiness to mate. *Challenges the male . . . feigns disinterest . . . pretends to read legal thrillers . . .*

He could end this easily enough. He just had to say no. One simple word. End of discussion.

"We just got premium cable on Thursday," he said. "Two hundred channels. Any one of them could be ESPN HD. Finding the game's going to be easier if I use the menu button on the remote. If I can't . . . there will be consequences."

She licked her finger and turned another page. "Not your best tactic, Detective. You have no idea how much that turns me on. A deliciously firm lecture, or something more forceful? I'd prefer firm, but if my refusal to relinquish the remote drives you to forceful, then that's the price I'll pay."

He was not backing down from this. "Forceful? You want me to go get my cuffs?"

"You're really ripped, so the mirrors in the workout room interest me," she said without looking up, "but we can work something out."

On second thought, no banter. *No banter, no laughter, no chatter,* except her survival depended on looking like a couple so crazy for each other that she'd moved in with him. And while he'd forgotten exactly why, somehow watching football was critical to his sanity.

Just say no.

Desperation drove him to lean forward and press an open-mouthed kiss into her shoulder. A gentle touch of tongue, then he scraped his teeth over her skin, watched a tremor ripple across her nape as her breath halted.

No cuffs necessary. One kiss and she was immobilized. Interesting.

Air gently, almost inaudibly eased from her lungs as his mouth slowly followed the line of her exposed collarbone, tasting Eve and a hint of salt. Another nip, this time not as gentle, and she inhaled quickly. He used the distraction to slip his hand under her bottom and grip the remote.

Success.

Feeling triumphant and a little ridiculous, he lifted his head to look at her. She kissed him. With her head braced on the sofa arm she didn't even have to move much, just lean forward a little and brush her lips over his, a quick flick of her tongue, the caress just hot and slick enough to remind him how things could get so much hotter, so much slicker.

He froze, hand still wrapped around the remote under her ass. They remained absolutely immobile for a heated moment, then another before the mental cables restraining everything frayed and snapped. He yanked the remote from under her bottom, twisted to point it at the television, and pushed the power button. As the screen went black he clicked off the lamp above her head, plunging the living room into darkness broken only by what little streetlight filtered through the tall oaks and the blinds. The book dropped to the floor by the remote. The couch wasn't large, but after a few shifts he lay half beside her, half on top of her, much of his weight on one elbow while with the other hand he groped under her head to tug at the rubber band holding back her hair.

A few strands came free with the elastic. "Ow," she protested mildly.

"Sorry," he murmured, then he buried his face in her hair and breathed in the scent of mint and rosemary. The strands slipped through his fingers and snagged on the three-day stubble on his jaw. He had to restrain himself from gripping the silken mass in his fingers.

She angled toward him, her face tucked in the hollow of his throat, and put her hand on his hip, bared as his shirt rode up. "It's just sex, Matt. Responsible, protected, come-out-of-your-skin-with-pleasure sex between two consenting adults."

The words were completely casual, as if she truly expected nothing beyond the parameters of the case, felt nothing more than an itch she wanted him to scratch. The ache inside him eased a little. This was Eve, the sexiest cocktail waitress in Lancaster, who'd been willing to go to bed with Tom to settle her nerves. He might have to protect her from Murphy, but he didn't have to protect her from this. He leaned forward, into her body, felt a purely female little shudder roll through her. "So good everyone will know I got some, right?" he asked as he eased the Sig and the holster from its spot at the small of his back and set it on the end table.

She froze, then laughed as he echoed her words after the lap dance in the Jeep. "I don't feel the slightest bit sorry for you," she said.

"Cold, boss. Very cold."

"I offered to help you get a job!"

Her retaliatory pinch to the skin of his waist made him grip her hand. Something extremely basic inside him made him pull that hand above her head and grasp it with his left. His right hand now free, he inched up the hem of her tank top, exposing flat, pale belly between the low-slung waistband of her jeans and her rib cage. Using four fingers he stroked, his touch too purposeful to tickle, back and forth just above the button of her jeans. She just looked at him, her body completely vulnerable yet radiating strength and life force and enough energy to light him up. He wanted to sink into her sheer Eve-ness and disappear.

With a little shimmy she brought his attention firmly back to the physical, then flicked a glance at the now-dark television. "Channel 1606. If you hurry we can be done by the second quarter."

Pressing his body firmly against her, he nestled his thigh between hers and slid his hand just inside her waistband. Her breath caught as she softened, opened. Everything male in him growled with satisfaction.

"Don't bet on it, boss," he said as he unfastened her jeans. "I don't really want to watch football."

"You better hurry. It's almost five," Matt called down the hallway.

"Thirty seconds," Eve said on her way from the bathroom to his bedroom, where her small suitcase sat on the chair. "A minute, tops. I promise."

She'd said that five minutes ago, but at least now she was running around in a top and skirt, progress toward the eventual goal of dinner at her parents' house. The look on his face when she wore nothing but her white microfiber underthings suggested she get dressed or miss dinner entirely. She'd gotten dressed. In an adult lifetime of shocking, disillusioning, and downright disappointing her parents, missing dinner tonight of all nights was out of the question.

"You're sure we have to do this," he said.

"If the point of this whole exercise is to look like we've fallen for each other fast and hard, then yes." With a clatter, the bottle of foundation slipped from her fingers into the sink but didn't break. She muttered a curse, swiped her nose and chin with the makeup sponge, then said, "I have dinner with my parents every Monday night. We're dating, you work at my bar and have Mondays off, therefore you'd be coming over too. It will look strange if I miss it."

"Why Mondays?"

"Dad works Sundays, and between services, study groups, and appointments, he usually works all day. He takes Mondays as his Sabbath and the evenings were family time. I'm ready."

She emerged from the bathroom wearing a fitted pink blouse with short sleeves and about thirty pearly pink buttons running from the upright collar to the hem that hit just above her hip bone, an A line skirt the color of a green olive, and flat brown sandals. She'd straightened her hair, parted it on the side, tucked behind her ears, and she wore just a touch of makeup, foundation, mascara, lip gloss. He wore khakis and an Oxford, and standing in the hallway, looking at him, she had a disorienting moment where the world tilted just enough to leave her a little unsteady.

It was like the surface of reality cracked open for just a moment and a timeless truth flashed in the rip in the space-time continuum. Something she couldn't identify glinted in his hazel eyes.

"What?" she asked, as she smoothed her skirt over her hip bones. "Did I spill foundation?"

"Huh? No. You look nice," he said.

She cocked her head and considered him. "I don't look like we were in bed together thirty minutes ago, right?"

"No," he said seriously. "You don't look like you've ever thought about going to bed with a man."

"Perfect for family night," she said, and started down the hallway, only to come up short when he didn't move.

In her flat-heeled sandals she had to look up into his eyes.

"Your brother will be there," he said.

"Caleb comes and goes as he pleases," she said noncommittally. "Depending on how busy he is at work, he's there for the whole meal, or just dessert, or not at all." When he didn't respond, she stepped past him to rummage through her purse and come up with her sunglasses. "Come on, pokey. We're going to be late."

He locked the front door and followed her down the ramp. Beside his Jeep she raised an eyebrow at him. "You put the top on?"

"We may be flaunting this . . . this . . . all over the East Side, but I'm not driving you around in an open vehicle two days after someone tried to kill you," he said as he unlocked her door.

His hesitation, neatly avoided, summed up their current problem. What exactly *was* this besides a mirage?

She recoiled as hot air rolled out of the open door. "The AC works, right? It's been over a hundred degrees for three weeks straight."

"Yup." He braced a hip on the seat, started the Jeep, and turned on the air conditioning, then got back out and closed the door.

She shut her door and waited for the AC to work, watching him across the black hood as she did. "What would you call *this* if you were working with another cop?" she asked.

Hands on hips, he scanned the street, then the yard. "A flagrant violation of departmental rules governing conduct between officers."

Between the sex and the sense of humor, it was getting harder and harder to stop the shift from *deceptive asshole* to *okay guy*. "So you and Sorenson . . . ?"

"Never."

"Why not? She's very pretty. She's smart, which I think you like, and you work well together."

He cut her a look across the hood of the Jeep, already hot to the touch. "I like smart. Her father, mother, and grandfather were all LPD. I've learned more in the year I've worked with her than most detectives learn in a career. If I hit on her, which, for the record, I've never considered, I'd be dead to her. I'm not going to screw up a good working relationship by treating her like anything other than a law enforcement professional." He opened the door. "It's cooled down. Get in."

She buckled up and slipped on her sunglasses while he reversed out of the driveway. "So what would you call this, when people work as a team on something?" Halfway down the shady street they passed a nondescript sedan. Eve recognized the big, scary-looking cop, McCormick, in the driver's seat. "Was that . . . ?"

"Surveillance to make sure no one's tracked you down through me."

Paranoid much trembled on the tip of her tongue, but when he turned toward Eve's parents' neighborhood without prompting, a new light bulb went on. "You know where my parents live," she said. "You know where Caleb lives, what we drive, my dad's criminal record, all kinds of stuff about me and my family, things I'd have to tell a guy I was dating but I don't have to tell you."

"If you were another cop, we'd be partners within the chain of command," he said, ignoring her comment. "But you're not another cop. There is no partnership here. When we go back to the bar on the surface it will look like Eve Webber, Eye Candy's owner, getting hot and heavy with Chad Henderson, her newest employee. But you're now involved in an ongoing undercover operation run by the Lancaster Police Department.

That means you do exactly what I tell you to do, when I tell you to do it. Understand?"

"Don't forget who sat at your dining room table and gave you a lifetime's worth of information on the East Side players," she said, hackles lifting. "We're coming at this differently, and I may handle situations based on personal knowledge, not suspicion."

"Just be careful," he said as he turned off Thirteenth Street and back into the neighborhood.

Being careful meant she'd stop sleeping with him. She'd had her share of long-term relationships and hookups. This indefinable thing felt nothing like either of those, but that horse was out of the barn and in the next county. Out of curiosity she turned on the radio. "I'll do my best, but it's not my typical method of living life."

"Try," he said bluntly, and switched off static.

Her parents lived in a neighborhood comprised of elderly residents on fixed incomes and young couples building equity in starter homes. The cars lining the streets and driveways were solid, American brands. Her mother had been a member of the Lancaster Garden Club for thirty years, and her garden dominated the fenced front yard, a wisteria vine climbing the post holding the mailbox. Two Adirondack chairs sat on the front porch, and Caleb's Mercedes lounged in the driveway, the car somehow embodying his *fuck all y'all* attitude despite its luxury status.

He waited for her to join him in front of the Jeep. When they started to walk across the street she slipped her hand into his, gripped it, and gave it a flirty little swing. His eyebrows lifted as they crossed the street together.

"Hey, handsome," she said, putting a little extra show in her walk as she waved at the neighbors' grandkids.

"Don't overdo it," he said. "There's acting and then there's melodrama."

She batted her eyes at him as she led him through the impatiens and fleabane and up the front walk. "Who says I'm acting? Hello," Eve called as she opened the front door. "We're here."

She set her bag on the formal love seat in front of the picture window; behind her, Matt shoved his car keys into his pocket and looked around. To Eve's eye the most noticeable thing was that the living room furniture clustered around a piano, not a television. A trumpet rested on top of the piano, and sheet music was neatly arranged in the bookshelf between the love seat and the piano. A small curio cabinet held a few figurines and pictures.

"You play?" he asked with a glance at the piano.

"Caleb and Mom play the piano, and Caleb also plays the bass. I play tenor sax and clarinet. Dad plays the trumpet."

"A whole jazz band," he said.

"A long-time parishioner is our drummer, but yeah. Dad loves jazz."

Movement in her peripheral vision. Caleb stood in the doorway to the dining room, one shoulder braced against the opening, his arms folded across his chest. Her father, a head shorter yet no less arresting than Caleb, filled the rest of the doorframe.

Best to get this over with. "Hello, Dad," Eve said as she went to kiss his cheek, then Caleb's. "This is Detective Matt Dorchester from the Lancaster Police Department."

Her father stepped forward, hand extended. "Detective Dorchester," he said, his voice calm. Her father had learned control the hard way, in prison, and honed equanimity during thirty years as a pastor. It would take more than Eve bringing a cop to Monday dinner to faze him.

Her mother would be a different story, but she was nowhere in sight at the moment.

"It's Matt," he said as they shook hands.

Caleb said nothing. Judging from the look on his face, he knew something Eve didn't, but before she could pull him into the kitchen, her father spoke.

"Welcome. Supper's just about ready," he said, and stood back to let Matt and Eve precede him into the dining room.

She watched Matt take in the room's details—the polished mahogany furniture, the table covered with a lace cloth but set with everyday stoneware, a linen napkin wrapped around homemade biscuits, the open bottle of wine, a glass pitcher of water—and wondered what it was like to record details of your surroundings against a possible threat. Then the door to the kitchen opened and her mother came in with a covered casserole dish held between two oven-mitt-clad hands.

"What's that, Mom?" Caleb asked, eyeing the dish.

"Shepherd's pie," she said and set the CorningWare on a trivet.

"It doesn't smell like shepherd's pie," Caleb said. Eve shot him a glare as they arranged themselves around the table, her father in his customary place at the head, while Caleb staked claim to the seat at the foot, neatly trapping Matt and Eve along the side by the hutch.

"That's because it's made with lentils, not beef," her mother said, then whisked the lid off the dish. "Welcome, Detective Dorchester," she said in a harried voice.

"It's Matt," he said again, but her mother was out of earshot, clattering dishes in the kitchen.

"Dad had a heart attack last year," Eve said in a low voice as her mother reappeared to fuss with the arrangement of serving dishes, then take her seat. "Mom thinks a vegetarian diet will help lower his cholesterol."

He said nothing, just shifted the basket of rolls to make room for the asparagus, bowed his head through grace, declined the offer of wine in favor of cold water, and accepted generous helpings of everything available.

When her mother was distracted with spreading margarine on a roll, Eve leaned toward Matt and murmured, "You really don't have to eat that."

He glanced at his plate. "Why wouldn't I eat it?" he asked.

"I'd like to hear your perspective on what Lyle's return to Lancaster means to the East Side," her father said. The question, directed at Matt, ended Eve's warnings about the meal.

"FBI information indicates that Murphy's the leading edge of an expansion effort for the Strykers out of Philly," Matt said. "He's using his connections with the Strykers to take control of the meth and crack cocaine market on the East Side, possibly with an eye toward using this as a distribution base for the Midwest. They make more money here, and the local gangs aren't as organized. They've got a better product, a relatively open market, and weak competition in the local gangs."

From a purely disinterested business perspective, the strategy made sense, Eve thought, but kept her mouth shut.

"And his interest in my daughter's business?"

"Murphy identified Eye Candy as a possible front."

Her father's attention shifted to her, but he didn't say *I told you your club was bad for you, and the East Side*. "You're assisting the police department with this . . . investigation?"

She wasn't the only one struggling for a name to call what was happening. "Yes," she said.

"For how long?"

The only sound in the room was the clink of silverware against china. "A couple of months now."

"You didn't tell us."

"No," Eve said. "I didn't want to involve you in something this risky. Any surge in violence or drug sales on the East Side and the business park plans collapse, which will have a huge impact on the neighborhood's economy. I could help, so I did."

Silence around the table. Eve squished peas and carrots into the mashed potatoes, hoping that would help with the flavor. It didn't. The potatoes weren't her mother's home-cooked, whole-milk-and-butter-drenched version, but instead had the texture and taste of paste.

Her mother leapt into the lengthening silence. "How long have you been a police officer?"

"Six years," Matt said.

"And what led you to choose that particular career?"

She should have warned him about her mother's obsession with careers, but Matt seemed unruffled. Maybe cops were asked that question fairly frequently.

"I enlisted in the Army but my parents were killed in a car accident and my younger brother was paralyzed in the crash. I was discharged to take care of him. The best civilian option that would allow me to raise Luke and use the skills I'd learned in the service was the police department."

That was interesting. More than she knew. She should start asking questions of her own. Caleb had been quiet far too long, so Eve glanced past Matt at her brother. While his knife and fork were active, he'd taken fewer bites than she had. Her brother gave her a small smile she couldn't read, then said, "Detective Dorchester's being rather modest about his military career."

Matt went still for just a second before swallowing his mouthful of mashed potatoes. Eve glanced at him, but his face gave her no cue to work from, so she turned to her brother. "What do you mean?"

"You didn't put his name in a search engine?"

She'd put Chad Henderson's name into a search engine and come up with a bland Facebook page. "I've had a lot on my mind the last two days," Eve said.

Caleb slouched down in his chair, a sure sign he was about to get very serious about something. "Remember the pawn shop robbery six years ago when the police caught the thieves in the act?"

"I think so," Eve said slowly. "One officer was shot, and the two robbers were too. No one died, though."

"Then-Officer Dorchester was three weeks out of the Academy when he and his training officer responded to the silent alarm. The robbers came out shooting. His partner took a bullet through the neck. Officer Dorchester pulled him behind a case and managed to hit both of the robbers while calling in the officer down. He received the Medal of Valor before he was out of his probationary period as a Lancaster police officer."

Matt set his knife and fork on his plate, then said in an even voice, "It's not relevant to this situation."

"So neither is the Bronze Star for rescuing two wounded soldiers while under fire in Ramadi," Caleb said clinically.

Water plunked into the sink in the kitchen. Outside, the neighbors' grandkids squealed and splashed in a wading pool. Eve turned and looked at Matt. *Not my first time at that rodeo* . . . "It's not relevant," Matt repeated without a hint of emotion. "In both situations

I was doing my job, nothing more or less than anyone else with my training would have done."

Caleb looked up, his gaze intent. "It's relevant. It means I trust you to keep my sister safe. It also goes toward character."

Silence. Her brother and her lover were doing that male stare-down thing.

"Eve, I saw Lee McCullough yesterday," her father said. Matt went back to the nearly inedible shepherd's pie. Caleb continued to push vegetables around on his plate. Eve made a noncommittal noise, and her father continued. "He said he'd be happy to talk to you about any of the open positions at Lancaster Life."

Nothing, not rain nor sleet nor expansionist gang leaders shooting at Eve under dark of night would keep her parents from finding her another job. "Dad, please tell Lee thanks, but I'm not interested."

"After what happened Saturday night surely you'll reconsider, Eve," her mother said.

"No, I won't, Mom. After what happened on Saturday night I'm less likely to close down Eye Candy and disappear into a corporate cube farm. As long as my customers keep coming back, then I'm going to stay open. If small businesses take a stand, then maybe the larger ones like Mobile Media will step up to the plate too."

"Eve, the East Side's issues are a question of values and choices," her mother said.

"It's a question of jobs, Mom," she replied, but she felt heat climb in her cheeks as she said it. Normally her parents wouldn't air family dissent in front of a stranger, but apparently the threat of physical violence changed the rules. "Crime drops in strong economies because people are employed, not desperate. People with jobs have somewhere to go and something to do. They have paychecks to spend, and they buy houses and cars. They get vested in a life and a community. Since when do we cut and run at the first sign of trouble? Everything I know about community and family and faith I learned at this dinner table. What message do we send to the rest of the neighborhood if we back down when it gets personal?"

"Detective Dorchester, surely you have a professional opinion about all of this," Eve's mother said.

She waited for him to join the chorus of people suggesting she die a slow death in a gray-walled cubicle. Matt finished his mouthful of mashed potatoes, then said, "While there are a variety of security measures Eve could implement at Eye Candy, I believe Murphy singled her out because of their past history, not because she owns a nightclub. Any number of small businesses would have worked as a front. Ultimately, it's not my place to speak for her."

Caleb's gaze sharpened. Her mother covered her astonishment by guiding the conversation to mutual acquaintances, local politics, and the road construction snarling traffic into downtown. Promptly at six, her mother laid her napkin on her plate and got to her feet. "Excuse me," she said to Matt. "I'm one of the few people left in the world who gets her local news from the evening news broadcast."

"Pastor Webber, can I have a moment?" Matt asked.

CHAPTER TWELVE

In the kitchen Eve scraped the remnants of dinner into the garbage as water ran into the sink to wash the crystal, which was too delicate for the dishwasher. Caleb brought the last of the dishes from the dining room and leaned against the counter, his wineglass in one hand. "You've got a mark on your neck," he said, gesturing vaguely in the direction of his collarbone with his empty hand.

"The hell I do," Eve said matter-of-factly as she slid the leftover lentil casserole into the fridge.

"Evangeline!"

"Sorry, Mom," she called. The door to the den closed. Eve gave a resigned sigh. That had gone about as well as she'd expected. She wondered what Matt wanted with her father.

"Good to know," Caleb said with obvious relief.

"He's too skilled for that." Ruthlessly controlled, in fact, a master of the very fine line between not hard enough and too hard. She'd felt the edge of his teeth against her shoulder, her thigh, the power of his grip on her hip or her wrist, giving her resistance to arch and writhe against, making her nerves sing in anticipation and need, but not enough to leave a single mark.

She was rewarded for her noncommittal manner with Caleb choking on his wine. "I didn't need to know that," he muttered.

"Then mind your own business."

With a lift of his glass he acknowledged a point scored, but switched tactics in a lowered voice. "Jesus, Eve. You're sleeping with him?"

"Five seconds later and still none of your business, Caleb," she shot back.

"It *is* my business. You're my sister. And if you're being pressured in any way, then we call this off and the police department can figure out another way to get to Lyle. Are you okay working with him like this?"

"Trust me, I'm not being pressured." She thought about it for a moment. "We are so close, Caleb. So close to making the East Side redevelopment efforts a reality. Yes, I want that for Eye Candy, but I want it for the East Side too. If we don't stop Lyle now, the city council will pull backing again and give Mobile Media space for their location somewhere else. And if having him around for a few weeks will make that happen, then I'll deal with it."

"It's not the having him around I'm worried about. It's the consequences of living in close quarters in a difficult situation with someone you're clearly, although inexplicably, attracted to."

"It's no big deal, Caleb." It wasn't. It was purely physical. No emotions involved, just intense, visceral, feral desire sweeping through her body and shutting down her brain. She kind of liked him. Given the way they'd begun, kind of liking him wasn't a bad place to be.

"Eve," Caleb said, in his serious voice. "This is a violation of about fifteen different statutes on police conduct."

"Caleb," she replied, in her serious voice. "I know when I'm being used. And it's still none of your business."

He swallowed the rest of the red and set the glass on the counter, then picked up a tea towel. "Remember Steve Hollister?"

She handed him a dripping plate and said, "From the Christmas party? Vaguely. Why?"

"He's a mediator who specializes in troubled families in the court system for one reason or another. Never married. No kids. Volunteers with Habitat for Humanity when he's not working. I guarantee he won't treat you like a piece of ass, and anyone who drives a ten-year-old Honda Accord doesn't give a damn about whether your outfit matches his car."

No horrified shouts from the dining room. Mom must be out of earshot, she mused as she finished washing the crystal. "As much as you'd like to pretend we didn't have a cop sitting at the dinner table, he was there and he's not going anywhere. I can't possibly date right now."

"You never know. He might be into ménage."

"Caleb!" she yelped with a glance at the door.

"Evangeline," he said, his face completely serious as he dried the last glass, "medals aside, you don't know jack shit about this guy. Even if you did, this isn't real life."

It was hard to remember, given the immediacy, the sheer intensity of "now." "Now" meant she and Matt would go back to his house, and go back to bed, perhaps even to sleep for a while before returning to Eye Candy tomorrow. "Yes, I remember Steve Hollister," she conceded. *Barely.* "I'll think about it when this is over. I promise."

She collected Matt from the front room and kissed her parents as they moved through the front door.

Neither one of them said anything until they were back in the Jeep. "So . . . *not your first time at that rodeo*?" she asked as she jammed the buckle into her seat-belt clasp.

"It's what happens when you join the Army after nine eleven," he said, his voice tight as he shifted into first and accelerated down the street. "You're assigned to an infantry division in a war zone. People shoot at you and you shoot back. It happens less frequently as a cop, but it does happen."

Are you freaking kidding me? "Are those your medals hanging at the end of the hall?"

"My dad's," he said abruptly.

"Where are yours? The Bronze Star? You have dog tags hanging from your mirror."

"Framing medals wasn't high on my list of priorities when I got home." He consciously relaxed his grip on the wheel. "Your name's Evangeline? Your records all say Eve Marie Webber."

The topic switch and the white-knuckled grip on the steering wheel told her to go with the flow. "It's vaguely creepy that you've seen my records, Matt." His face didn't change, so she dialed down the sass. "They wanted to name me Evangeline, but I was three weeks early and Dad was away at his annual retreat. Mom was completely out of it when the nurse asked for my name, and Mom gave her the nickname. I'm Eve to everyone except my family, and then I'm Evangeline only when I'm screwing up."

"Or swearing."

She looked at him, dread in her heart. "How much of that conversation did you hear?" she asked.

"No ménage," he clarified.

She sank down in the seat, embarrassment heating her cheeks. "I'm going to kill him," she said.

"Unless the next time you get pissed at me, you decide that's how you want to work out your anger."

Her jaw dropped. "You're kidding, right?"

"Yes," he said. "No ménage."

Thank God.

"Caleb's hiding an honest-to-God big brother under that swagger," he said.

"Takes one to know one?" She sighed. "Sometimes he's such a jerk I forget he really cares."

Matt downshifted and coasted to a stop at a light. "What drives him? They teach argumentation in law school, but he takes combative to a whole new level."

She thought about how to answer that question for a long time before saying, "He made a mistake. Lives were ruined forever. He puts on a front because the world sees gold and Caleb knows better."

He nodded, as if that made perfect sense to him. Maybe it did. "What do you see?"

"My brother," she said simply. "He used to strap my Barbie dolls to bottle rockets, and light them while I screamed. He taught me to shoot free throws well enough that I won the school competition my senior year." She laughed. "Classic Caleb story. My sophomore year I wasn't allowed to date, but Nate Marshall asked me out. He was a senior starting wide receiver on the football team, teen idol movie star gorgeous, and he knew it. I was all angles, no curves, and he asked me out. So I snuck out to meet him. Nate drove me out to the reservoir north of town and said he wouldn't take me home until I—red light! Red light!"

The Jeep jerked to a halt halfway through the crosswalk, the seatbelt locking with the force of the stop. Matt cursed, shoved the gearshift into reverse, and backed up a few feet.

"You okay?" she asked.

"Fine," he ground out. "What happened?"

"I told him to go to hell and fuck himself when he got there. Then I got out of the car and started walking, and he took off, spraying me with dust and gravel from his nifty Camaro as he drove away. Caleb got wind of the whole thing, and found me a mile from home, walking along the highway. He got me inside without Mom and Dad finding out, and the next day, after school, he went after Nate. I didn't see it, you understand, so I'm just repeating what I heard, but apparently the entire offensive line was clustered around Nate's Camaro when Caleb waded through them, twisted Nate's arm up behind his back, grabbed his hair, and slammed his pretty face into the trunk of the car."

"I would have done the same thing."

"Two broken teeth, a broken nose, split lip, and Caleb hadn't hit him yet. Caleb took him apart. I was minding my own business, sitting on the front steps of the school with most of the drill squad, wondering where the hell Caleb was because he was my ride home, when Caleb shoved Nate in front of me and told him to impress us both with his eloquent apology."

Another one of those deep, unwilling laughs. "You have to respect his style."

"The school tried to suspend Caleb for fighting, but they couldn't get Nate to identify Caleb as the person who did it because Caleb said he'd make Nate tell the principal, the football coach, his parents, my parents, and most important of all, the football recruiter from Ohio State why Caleb beat him up."

"Nate believed him," Matt said, but it wasn't a question.

"Years and experience have reined in the temper, but Caleb takes personal offense when the strong take advantage of the weak." She watched the scenery shift from the small homes and small lots of the East Side to Matt's neighborhood. "He's just Caleb. That's all I see."

Matt said nothing for a few moments. "You were on the drill squad?"

"No. President of the Future Business Leaders of America. Nat was on the drill squad." Another memory surfaced, one that made her laugh at the irony. "I just remembered how Caleb found out what Nate had in mind for me. Lyle was at Aquinas High by this time, selling steroids to football players. He heard about it, and called Caleb." She looked out the window. "Maybe in the suburbs things are black and white, good and evil. It's harder to pin down the East Side. I know Lyle's bad news now, but to me he's still the kid who called my brother. Even then Caleb hated him, but Lyle still called him."

He pulled into his driveway and cut the engine, but didn't get out of the Jeep. "It's a gift, you know."

"What is? Forgiving Caleb for taking on the world and everyone in it?"

"Seeing people as they are and caring about them anyway."

Might get her in trouble, given how much slack she'd cut Lyle. "Guess I paid attention in church."

Another laugh, the noise tugged from somewhere deep inside, rusty and unused, but she liked it. She liked seeing his battered face morph into something filled with humor and personality. She liked being the woman who did that for him.

"They ride you pretty hard," he said quietly. "Why?"

Sitting in the now-warm Jeep, she smoothed the strap of her purse in her lap before answering. "Because at heart I'm selfish. I want what's best for the East Side, but I want something for me too. A good person, a good girl, wouldn't do what I do. I'd be teaching or in social work, volunteering at church and the SCC. I should be married by now. Raising babies."

"You'll be good with kids, but I can't see you at an insurance company, boss."

"You and I are the only ones with that particular deficit in our vision, Matt." When he didn't say anything else, she added, "It's Monday night."

"It is," he agreed.

"Football night, right?"

"Preseason game in New York," he said.

"Do you want to watch the game?" she asked. "We could order a pizza. My treat. Dinner was inedible. Mom's an amazing cook with unlimited quantities of butter and . . ."

Her voice trailed off. His eyes were heavy-lidded and intense. Despite the setting sun, the air in the Jeep was heating rapidly, twilight-dark, close.

"What do you want to do, Eve?"

Uncertainty shimmered in her stomach. Dinner with her family only brought back the realities she was ignoring, the troubles the East Side faced, her job, her lack of a steady boyfriend, and suddenly the fear was back, the threat from Lyle intensifying every worry she had about the present, let alone her future. Matt sat next to her, hands relaxed on his thighs. His only concession to the heat in the Jeep was the deep red flush on his cheekbones and the glimmer of sweat at his hairline. The scent of his skin, his sweat, was engraved on her memory, and oh, she wanted him. He could make her forget all her troubles, at least for now.

"I want to stop thinking for a while," she admitted.

Emotion flickered in his eyes, unreadable and almost imperceptible, and as the seconds passed she began to wonder if she'd seen it at all. "Stay there."

Following his order was good practice for that by-the-book officer/civilian thing he kept talking about, so she waited, marking time by the slow thump of her pulse in her wrists and throat as he walked around the Jeep and opened the door for her. He stayed close, protective or possessive, or both, as they walked up the ramp to the front door. She was hyperaware of his body, hot and substantial next to hers, as he guided her through the door and down the hall to the workout room. The light hung soft and heavy between late afternoon and twilight, light enough to see herself, six inches from the mirror, Matt visible behind her.

"Watch," he said.

She blushed so hard her cheeks were darker than the soft pink blouse. "I can't possibly," she said, even as her gaze skittered over the strangely demure woman in the mirror, feet primly together, knee-length skirt, shirt that skimmed her curves without drawing attention to them. She looked sweet, maybe even innocent.

His hands rose to the first tiny button on her soft pink blouse, unfastened it slowly, moved to the second. He gained deftness but scorned speed as he moved down, exposing her throat, then her collarbone. "What was all that about choosing mirrors over cuffs last night?"

They hadn't made it anywhere near the home gym. "You were supposed to watch," she said. "Not me."

He bent his head, the gesture at once both protective and authoritative, and murmured in her ear. "We're both going to watch."

Electricity cracked through her, igniting heat in her nipples and deep in her belly, and sending another flare of color into her face. He shifted focus from his big hands at the slowly parting edges of her blouse, and smiled. "I can't believe the sexiest cocktail waitress in Lancaster is blushing at having sex in front of a mirror."

"That's different," she said. "That's an act. I wear a costume, say lines. You get that."

"So you really are sweet and innocent?" he asked as he opened the last button.

"Shy," she murmured, because his fingertips were hot through the white microfiber bra, casually brushing her nipples as he tugged the fabric down her arms and off to puddle at her feet.

He said nothing, just drew the side of his little finger between her breasts and down the middle of her abdomen to the top of her skirt. She took in details as he slowly stripped her, noting the way her nipples hardened as he slipped the hook-and-eye free, slid the zipper down, gave the skirt the merest nudge to send it to the floor.

Then he cupped her breasts through the bra and brushed his thumbs back and forth over her nipples, the slow, measured movements rasping the fabric over nerve endings on full alert. When she gave an involuntary undulation Matt unhooked her bra, pulled it down and away to drop on the floor, leaving her in nothing but the sheer white panties and dusky twilight.

Her eyelids drooped, part response, part reluctance to take in the carnal image in the mirror. Her nipples were red, hard. The urge to look away overwhelmed her. She turned her head to the side, but Matt laid fingers along her jaw and turned her to face the mirror. "Watch," he said again, and this time the command held a hint of steel.

She met his eyes in the mirror. "Are you watching?"

"Hell, yes," he said. His gaze held hers for another

long, searing moment, the hazel gone dark and deep as his pupils expanded in the growing darkness. Then he deliberately looked at her mouth, then her breasts, then the shadow of dark curls covering her mound. She made an inarticulate sound and lifted her hands to cover something, her body, her breasts, maybe her eyes. He caught them, flattened her palms to the mirror at shoulder height.

That was easier, as if something to push against channeled the heat surging through her. She pressed her hands firmly against the glass, felt dampness slick the smooth surface. He slid his fingers over her hips and lowered her panties to the floor, leaving her naked in front of the mirror. She tipped her head forward enough for her hair to unmoor from behind her ear and slide into her face, hiding one eye.

"You've got nothing to hide," he murmured, low and rough.

Only how she felt about him.

The thought disappeared when he stepped into her back and braced his forearm on the mirror over her head while his right hand skimmed down her belly, between her legs. He knew her body now, dipped into the folds to trail moisture up to her clit. She gave an inarticulate little cry and strained into his unyielding body. Oh, that helped, the glass under her palms, the length of him against her back.

He didn't stop. They both focused on his hand, dark against her hip and thigh, touching her so intimately, so confidently. Another slow circle around her clit and she shuddered again, the fabric of his shirt and pants chafing her skin as she watched her mirror-self spread her legs. His finger circled her clit, sending darkly erotic pleasure in waves through her abdomen. Strung tight between her hands on the mirror, her feet on the floor, and her back and ass braced against his body, the tension climbed from her sex, seared along nerves connecting her nipples and clit. Her mouth dropped open, and a gasp shuddered into the air. The long muscles in her thighs began to tremble as the pleasure coiled dark and hard under his relentless touch. Then she shattered, waves of release pulsing out in time to the soft cries she stifled in her shoulder.

She sank to her knees on the floor, pushed her hair out of her face, and tried to catch her breath as she peered up at him in the mirror. He was fully dressed, hands on his hips, the tiniest of smiles lifting the corner of his mouth. "Still thinking?"

No. "Yes," she said. The vulnerability of kneeling naked on the gritty floor while he stood fully dressed behind her registered in her brain as slightly embarrassing and very arousing. She lifted her chin at him. "Take something off. Please."

With efficient movements he unbuttoned his shirt, tugged it free from his pants, shrugged it off. That was a little better, and yet wasn't *any* better. His lean, muscled torso distracted her until he dropped to his knees behind her and began to unbuckle his belt. Without a word he freed his cock from his pants and situated her with her hands against the mirror again, making her wait while he smoothed on a condom. Then he gripped her hips, positioned himself at her entrance, and pushed inside.

Climax made her sensitive, so he paused, lodged just inside her, and while he waited for her to stop trembling he leaned against the mirror and put his deft, knowing mouth to her neck. The sheer female submissiveness of the position coupled with the scrape of his teeth against her nape crashed over her in a wave of sensation. She tilted her head to give him better access, watched his hands smooth up her abdomen to cup her breasts, pinching the nipples firmly. The current running between her nape, her nipples, and the soft, aching walls of her pussy intensified.

Then he started to move, slowly but not gently, insistent demand in his rhythm and strokes. She took each thrust, balanced on the razor's edge of pleasure and pain, and arched her back for more. Her attention wavered between the interior sensations of his cock churning millions of nerve endings into screaming need and the image in the mirror, her widespread knees, the damp curls at the apex of her thighs, his tanned hands on her breasts, her parted lips. Fire licked through her, and she turned her head.

It was a mistake, because in the mirrors to their right she could see the finely honed length of his ass and back rippling as he thrust, felt the head of his cock drag against swollen inner tissues. The ache contracted tight and hard in her belly. "Oh, God," she gasped.

When he turned his gaze, dark and fierce with desire, and met hers, the jolt of recognition sent her over the edge. A second orgasm, deeper, more intense than the first, rocked through her, and she dimly heard soft cries echo in the room in time to the contractions. A growled curse, then he wrapped his arms around her torso, buried his cock inside her, and came.

"Was this payback for teasing you about the remote?"

A laugh ruffled the hair at her temple. "You looked too sweet to go after payback," he said, low and assured. Then he bit her earlobe, the pressure enough to sting, the sting enough to remind her that no matter how often they'd done this, the heat never entirely went away. "Next time you're wearing that leather outfit and you flip me that attitude, it's game on."

Sparks flew under her skin. "Promise?"

"Count on it," he said. "Still thinking?"

He'd very effectively shut down her brain. "Not anymore," she said with a smile.

"Good." He pulled out and walked out of the room.

Water ran in the bathroom as she looked in the mirror. Her eyes were a languid green, amused and satisfied all at once, but as the pleasure continued to ebb from her body, realization stole through her consciousness.

She could do more than like him. He'd handled dinner with her family under strained circumstances, and come out unfazed. Reality was tilted on its axis, and she could easily feel more than she should.

He appeared in the doorway, dressed in cotton shorts and nothing else, and just the sight of his torso made her want to fuel up and start all over again.

"What?" he asked when he saw her still on the floor.

"Nothing," she said. "Still up for pizza and the game?"

"Sure," he said as he helped her to her feet and picked up her skirt, "but it's a working dinner."

"A working dinner?" She clutched her clothes to her belly and turned for the bathroom.

He gave her a smile that managed to be both rueful and energized at the same time. "Playtime's over. We've got twenty-four hours to get you ready for a prolonged undercover operation."

And with that, reality began to seep into the fantasy. "Right," she said. "Just let me get dressed."

On Tuesday reality returned with a vengeance. While Eve washed the lunch dishes, Matt sat down at the dining room table and armed himself. He pulled the leg of his jeans over the knife and stood up to find Eve watching him with wide eyes.

"Were you wearing all of that every time you came to work?" she asked while she wrung out the dishcloth.

"Not the Sig," he said, trying to gauge her reaction.

Sometimes women found it sexy, which was a little on the weird side, and sometimes they thought he was paranoid, which was probably true. But the stakes were higher now. Eve was putting herself in danger to help them. They'd install a radio in her apartment, but most of the time it was just him and his wits against a deadly threat that appeared with no warning. There was no room for mistakes. Things were different now. She was his to protect, for real.

She pressed her lips together and draped the dishcloth over the faucet to dry.

"The concealed weapons law doesn't apply to law enforcement," he pointed out. "I need a longer T-shirt too."

"You can try a few of them on," she said doubtfully, "but they're designed to show off your body, not hide a gun in the back of your jeans."

When the dishes were done she packed up her few toiletries and her clothes, gathering her things from around Matt's bedroom and bathroom and zipping them into her overnight case. She was unusually silent as she worked, so he used the spare minutes for a pop quiz.

"My real cell."

She shot him a look as the bag's zipper caught on something inside, but recited the phone number.

"When do you call that?"

"It's my 'oh shit' phone," she said. "I use it only if I'm in trouble and you're not with me so there's no way to trace Matt Dorchester to Chad Henderson."

"And you'll never have to use it because from now on out, you're stuck with me. Chad's cell."

She jerked at the stuck zipper before calming down enough to slide the zip back, shove the fabric fully into the case, and close it, all while rattling off the number.

"Call that anytime. Sorenson's numbers. Cell, work, home."

She folded her arms across her chest, recited them, then added McCormick's, and dispatch in a flat tone.

He ignored the attitude. "Good. All of them backup "oh shit" phones. McCormick will get there faster than Sorenson; she's in court the next few weeks but he's assigned to patrol. Don't call Ian. He's in meetings most days."

He'd done his best to prepare her, drilling her on Chad Henderson's backstory, talking through what she should do when Lyle showed up, talking through a dozen other ways to respond to any kind of threat. She'd let him show her how a semiautomatic worked and, at his insistence, picked it up and showed him she could thumb off the safety and jack a round into the chamber, but she'd flatly refused to go to the firing range with him.

Everyone had boundaries they established to define who they were, and for Eve, handling a gun clearly crossed a line. They'd had a short argument about it at one in the morning. He'd lost, and he wasn't happy about it.

A car door slammed in the driveway. Matt moved through the living room to the window, one hand automatically moving to the small of his back while the other parted the slats of the blinds covering the front windows. He peered out, then let them close. "It's Luke," he said, and opened the door.

Shoulders and arm muscles bunching with effort, his brother rolled up the ramp and into the foyer. He stopped in the act of removing fingerless leather gloves when he saw Eve standing in the hallway.

Wide-eyed, he looked at Matt, then at Eve, then at Matt again. "I'm gone for three days and this is what I come home to?" A broad smile spread across his face as Eve held out her hand and looked to Matt for an introduction.

"Luke, Eve. Eve, my brother," he said, and went back down the hall to the bedroom.

Luke went back to removing his gloves. "Hi, Eve. Yes, I'm his brother, and you are . . . ?"

Matt brushed past both of them, Eve's case in one hand, his own duffle in the other. "She's a friend," he said as he walked down the ramp to his Jeep.

A *friend*? After the events of the last two weeks, specifically sex both frequent and hot enough to melt steel, if he were Eve he would have kicked his ass. But he couldn't think of any other way to describe "I pretended to be her bartender, nearly slept with her, saved her from gunfire, did sleep with her, then talked her into working on the investigation with us."

He tossed the bags into the backseat of the Jeep. When he walked back through the door, Eve gave him that glinting little smile again, then Luke spun to face him, his eyes dark. "She says she owns a bar and you're working for her. Goddammit Matt, you said things weren't that bad," he said, his voice rising.

One hand on his hip, Matt rubbed his forehead with his thumbnail, his keys under the curled fingers of his hand. "They're not. No worse than usual. She's part of a case I'm on. I'm staying with her for a while." Matt snagged the gym bag sitting on Luke's lap and brushed past Eve to toss it into Luke's room.

His brother was no fool. Luke lifted one eyebrow and opened his mouth, but Matt cut him off. "I've got my cell. If you need to talk, leave a message and I'll call back when I can. If it's an emergency, call Sorenson or the LT. They'll get in touch with me."

"How long are you going to be gone?" Luke asked.

"I'm not sure." He turned to go.

"Give me the number for the AC guy," his brother said. "I'll get an estimate, call around to comparison shop."

"I'll do it when I get back," he said.

"For fuck's sake, Matt," Luke said, resigned. "It's a couple of phone calls. I won't sign anything."

"I'll take care of it later," he said tightly. "We have to leave. I'll check in when I can."

Luke muttered something Matt pretended not to hear as he guided Eve down the ramp and into the Jeep.

"It sounds like he just wants to help you," she observed.

"He shouldn't have to help," Matt said. "His adolescence disappeared when he was fourteen years old. He deserves to have as normal a life as possible, and that means not worrying about mortgages or HVAC systems or medical bills when he can't find a full-time job."

Eve shifted her weight away from him and crossed her legs, and he regretted the way he barked at her. "I'm sorry," she said quietly. "It's none of my business."

"It's fine," he said. "It's just . . . complicated."

Silence reigned for the rest of the trip to Eye Candy. Noonday heat blistered the blacktop parking lot, the smell of fresh asphalt rising in shimmering waves. Eve reached for her small rolling suitcase and hefted it out of the back of the Jeep. Matt grabbed both her bag and his duffle in one hand and said, "Up the stairs. Now," scanning the parking lot then the rooftops, looking for slow-moving SUVs, hiding places, any threat, letting the sixth sense he'd honed over the years put out feelers into his surroundings.

She hurried up the stairs, him hard on her heels.

"Keys."

He unlocked her apartment door and entered first; at his okay she stepped inside. First things first. She hurried into the bathroom and turned on her curling iron. Then she looked around. New glass gleamed in her kitchen and bedroom windows. When Matt emerged from looking around her bedroom, she was picking up the pieces of her speakers.

"I'll play music on my computer for a while," she said, trying to make the best of it.

"That was a Bose SoundDock," he said. "You're going to notice the drop in sound quality."

She looked at him, eyebrows raised ever so slightly, then swept the fragments into the trash. "It'll have to do. I can't afford a new dock."

Her apartment was a shoebox, but she shoved clothes to one side to make space for his stuff in her crammed closet, and cleared a two-square-inch spot on the sink for his electric razor. While attempting to wedge his toothbrush into the caddy on her sink he burned his hand on her curling iron, and cursed under his breath as he ran cold water over the reddening strip of skin.

She grabbed the curling wand, intending to move it to the back of the toilet, except he'd put his shaving kit on the tank. "I'm sorry," she apologized, missing the knuckles of his other hand by millimeters as she set the hot iron down in its original position.

"Forget shaving. Women like the scruffy look," he said, then backed into the door. As the stopper twanged, he said, "Jesus. I'll be downstairs. I want to check the alley and interior."

He checked the storeroom and dish room, then opened the door to the alley. All quiet. Nothing suspicious. When he came back through the storeroom, Eve was making her way down the stairs from her office. She wore the black skirt she'd worn the day she interviewed him, a green silk blouse, and her boots.

"I need keys to all the doors and a list of who else has them."

"I've got a spare set locked in my desk. We can make copies while we're out this afternoon."

He looked at the rubber pouch on top of a three-inch stack of paperwork. "Deposit?"

"Including Lyle's first deposit," she said, wishing she'd worn gloves to handle the dirty money.

He put down the knife and wiped his hands on a wet towel. "I'll drive. The bathrooms are clean. I checked stock. You're low on gin and rye whiskey, and you're really low on vodka. When's your next liquor delivery?"

"Tomorrow," she said. "You really worked in a bar? You must have . . . you could mix drinks, or did you practice before applying?"

"My Academy class didn't start until almost a year after the accident," he said. "I worked private security, bartended, EMT shifts. Anything I could scrounge together with late afternoon or overnight hours. Doctors and physical therapists work nine to five," he said and dug his car keys from his front pocket.

She was giving him that look again, the look that looked right through him. Somehow, despite relaying what felt to him like bare-bones details about his life, every time he opened his mouth he gave something else away. But what? Nothing about his life was closed; the background check for the Academy took care of that. So what did Eve see that no one else saw?

They duped her keys at the corner hardware store, then doubled back down Thirteenth Street to get to the bank. "I know her," Eve said as they walked into the lobby and headed for the only available teller. The sound of her heels, staccato and sharp, rapid-fire against the floor, paused for a second.

"Close friend?" he asked, his hand shifting to the small of her back to urge her forward.

"She thinks so, but for our purposes, she's actually better than that," she said, regaining her stride. "She's the biggest gossip on the East Side."

Stella slid Matt a look through thickly mascaraed eyelashes, and took in his Eye Candy T-shirt, his hand at her back, and the possessive tilt of his body as Eve slid Saturday night's take through the window. "Who's your friend, Eve?"

"Stella, meet Chad," she said, giving Matt's arm a possessive little pat. Her every move screamed boyfriend, the way she leaned into his body, let the curve of her hip nestle into his, and Matt felt an odd shift in his consciousness, like one of those posters for sale at the mall, the kind that if you stared at long enough, you saw something else in the colors and shapes. Old woman, young woman. Undersea garden or dolphin. Eve as a community-oriented partner in the investigation or Eve as his lover.

Eve as *his*.

"Stella and I went to high school together," Eve said, snapping him back into reality. "Chad's working for me at Eye Candy."

Her gaze slid over Matt as she double-checked the deposit. "Must be nice to be the boss. You from around here, Chad?"

"L.A.," he said, neither discouraging, nor encouraging, just enough to answer the question.

Stella ran the money through the machines and slid Eve a deposit slip. "I keep meaning to come by, but getting George to watch the kids is like pulling teeth," she said as Eve picked up a pen. It spun from her fingers, the ball-chain slithering against the wooden counter.

"I'm clumsy today," Eve said with a bright, false laugh. Matt dropped a hand to her hip and stroked his thumb over the soft curve. Her shoulders relaxed. She picked up the pen again, signed the slip, the movements casual and precise. Normal.

She calms down when you touch her. Touch her a lot. To keep her calm.

"You won't believe what I heard. Guess who's back in town?"

"Who?"

Arms folded on the counter, Stella leaned into the window like she was sharing state secrets. "Lyle. Murphy. Can you believe it?"

"I saw him last week," Eve said like it was no big deal. *Good girl,* Matt thought. Calm, collected, laying the framework for any sightings with Lyle or his band of merry thugs and dealers.

"He had the total hots for you in high school," Stella recalled.

"We were friends! Just friends," Eve said. "My dad and Lyle's dad go way back."

"Honey, you are *so* blind," Stella said, then turned to Matt. "Every guy in the school wanted to go out with Eve, but after what happened to Nate, none of them dared. You know Caleb?"

"We've met," Matt said noncommittally, felt Eve swallow a laugh.

"I bet," Stella said as she retrieved the deposit slip from Eve. "Be good, you two."

"You think she'll talk?" Matt said as they left the bank. Part of the plan was to generate as much buzz as they could about Eve and her new boyfriend and hope the gossip got back to Lyle.

"She's probably group texting everyone we know from high school right now," Eve said. "Why L.A.?"

He guided her down the empty sidewalk leading to the bank's front door. "It's big enough that if someone says "Do you know my aunt Millie?" I can easily say no, but I was stationed at Fort Irwin, so I know the city well enough to handle most conversations," he said.

They rounded the railing protecting the landscaping from people cutting across the grass to the parking lot, and Eve reached for his hand as she scoped out the storefronts across the street. Lancaster Savings and Loan was located on a prime strip of the East Side, in the middle of local shops and restaurants. It was the middle of the afternoon, so gauging traffic from the lunch crowd wasn't easy, but a few people sat at tables at the front of the new sandwich and coffee shop across the street, and the lot on the corner that provided free parking for shops along Thirteenth Street was better than half full.

A blue Escalade emerged from the parking lot and pulled into an on-street parking space across from the bank. Lyle Murphy got out.

CHAPTER THIRTEEN

Matt felt Eve stiffen next to him. He clasped her hand, gave it a squeeze meant to both soothe and warn her to stay cool. "I see him," he said in an undertone. "Let's make sure he sees us. Look around. Talk to me about the businesses like I'm new in town and you're showing me around."

"Good lunch traffic," she said, only the slightest hint of a tremor in her voice. "Two Slices is a new soup and sandwich place. They've been open for a month and got a really good write-up in the paper so Henry's seeing quite a bit of downtown lunch traffic. I don't think Cindy's Cinful Sweets will last if the redevelopment effort collapses, but if we get the business park she might hold on. What's he doing?"

"He's staring at you."

Lyle Murphy was more than staring at Eve. Even half a block down and on the opposite side of the street Matt felt waves of animosity eddying across the pavement, lapping at their ankles. He scanned the storefronts, taking advantage of his mirrored sunglasses and peripheral vision to look like he was giving each window a thorough examination while he memorized the Escalade's plate and noted identifying dings.

And got his first up-close-and-in-person look at Lyle Murphy. He was tall, dressed in business casual, a long-sleeved golf shirt tucked into slacks, loafers on his feet. You could drop him into any office in Lancaster and he'd blend right in, except for his eyes. Light brown and fixed on Eve, Lyle had the eyes of a psychopath. Matt knew the look well from combat and years on the streets. It wasn't the homeless crazy, the off-my-meds crazy, or even the I-can't-take-it-anymore crazy. This was the subtle, evil psychopathology of a man who cared only about getting what he wanted. He'd watch Eve struggle and suffer for the sheer pleasure of it, then put a bullet in her brain when he got bored.

They'd been out of his house less than an hour, and already Eve was in the crosshairs. Every instinct Matt honed was screaming at him to get her away, to shove her behind a car like he'd shoved her into the bathtub, but that would effectively destroy everything they'd worked for so far. He fought down the emotion, forcing himself to slump his shoulders, keep his stance easy and relaxed, to play the role of Eve's new boyfriend, a man who knew nothing about Lyle, drugs, cops, guns, who cared only about banging his hot new boss. Eve had to take the lead here. She was walking a tightrope, and had to take each step on her own. All he could do was help her balance.

"You know," Eve said conversationally, pointing at an old-school barbershop, "if there's an uptick in gang violence and Mobile Media pulls out, all these businesses are going to go under. It makes me furious."

"You said he went to Aquinas, so he's smart, and unlike most of the people we went to school with, he had opportunities. Why is he so bent on selling drugs?"

"Oh, you know," she said lightly, and let her arm drop. "Fathers and sons."

Matt knew a thing about fathers and sons. The drumbeat under every move he took was the one his father taught him from childhood: control yourself, control the situation.

"This feels unnatural," Eve said. "I wouldn't ignore him." She turned, and her eyes widened like she'd just become aware of Lyle's existence. She lifted her hand and gave him a vaguely cheery wave, then wiggled under Matt's arm and looked up at him. Her smile was faked; Matt could see anger and nerves in her green eyes, but from a distance, her moves and body language were exactly that of a woman newly enthralled with a man.

Lyle never looked away.

She turned her back on Lyle and stepped in front of Matt, wove one leg between his and shifted a little to his left, keeping his right hand free. "He's watching us, right?"

"He's watching you," Matt said. "Eve, this is way more—"

She went up on tiptoes and kissed him. The first brush of lip on lip was perfunctory. Then she slid her hand up Matt's neck and kissed the corner of his mouth, his cheek, the edge of his jaw, and the spot below his ear. Each touch of her mouth left a hot spot smoldering on his skin, sent heat streaming down his spine.

She could have simply laid one on him, given Lyle a showy open-mouth kiss, a taunt, but she knew that the slow, seductive press of her mouth would show even more that she was completely preoccupied with Matt, that Lyle didn't have her under his thumb.

That rip in the universe again, the odd roaring

abruptly cut off as reality snapped back into place. Lyle was as still as stone, his mouth tight, the relaxed big-shot posture suddenly tense.

Matt gripped her waist and bent to her ear. "What the fuck are you doing?" he growled, his heart hammering away in his chest.

"I'm being me," she said. "The woman Lyle used to know wouldn't let him dictate terms, not in my bar, or in my personal life. I want him angry. He gets impulsive when he's angry."

"So do you," Matt said. He reached up and brushed her hair back from her face, hoping like hell the move came off as attentive new lover, not a tightly leashed impulse to fist his hand in her hair and kiss her into submission. "You're making yourself a target. Stop. Now."

"Better me than anyone else on the East Side. I'm already a target, remember? Hit on my life? I was from the moment I walked into the Eastern Precinct."

"You were a target the moment he asked you to front for him." Eve's eyes widened, but now wasn't the time to tell her exactly how dangerous Lyle was. "Get in the car." He locked his fingers with hers and led her around the back of the Jeep. When they were both inside, doors locked, he pulled out of the parking lot and drove past Lyle.

The moment they rounded the corner, stomach-churning fear swept through him, because for a second she'd made him forget everything that mattered, who he was, why they were on Thirteenth Street in the first place, his duty to protect her. "In fact, you were a target before he walked into Eye Candy and asked you to front for him," he said. "He's been thinking about this a long time, Eve. Thinking about you. This isn't just two old friends playing wrong-side-of-the-tracks games. Something's happened to him since he left town."

"Like what?" she asked, searching through her purse.

"I don't know, but you don't get expansion opportunities with the Strykers by playing nice with the other kids," he said, giving her the fit-for-civilian-ears version of the reports he'd read of beatings, torture, murders. They'd totally underestimated Lyle Murphy's ruthlessness, missed the madness seething behind his eyes. "It's in his eyes," Matt finished.

"I'll have to take a closer look," she said, her voice shaky as she fumbled with her wallet, sliding the deposit receipt into one of the expansion slots. "Next time I'll try a different approach. You weren't all that into it anyway."

He laughed, that unfamiliar noise she drew from him. "I couldn't really give it my full attention," he said, and looked at her. She was uncharacteristically pale, her eyes wide and unseeing. "You okay?"

"No."

"Put your head between your knees," he said.

She let her head drop forward and lifted her hair away from her neck. "What do you think?" she asked through the tumbled mass hiding her face. "Coincidence that he shows up in front of the bank while I'm there?"

"He's following you," Matt said, glancing in the rearview mirror as he drove. The Escalade was gone. "He wants to know what you're doing, who you're with, and why."

"How do you know?"

"I've seen his kind before. Psychopaths pop up pretty regularly in war zones."

Eve blinked, but they were pulling into Eye Candy's parking lot. There was no time to do anything but scramble through prep. Eve shook out her hands before picking up a knife; he watched for a few seconds to make sure muscle memory took over so she didn't slice off a finger.

She looked at the clock. "You're sure I can't tell Natalie?"

Matt kept up his rhythmic slicing and chopping. "The fewer people we involve, the better. It's too dangerous."

"So," she said, entirely too casually to be casual, "tell me about Ramadi."

She had a right to know. "Caleb had the basics," he said. "Two of our guys were injured and pinned down at the back of an alley. I got them out."

"Under fire."

Two words, three syllables to describe two mad dashes through a kill zone, just as likely to get hit by a ricocheting bullet from one of his fire team as from one of the snipers. All he could hear was his father's mantra: *Emotions make you weak. No fear. No failure.* "Under fire," he said, and swept the limes into a tub.

She considered this, then said, "How do you do it? How do you go back and forth between lives?"

Eve had one life—friends, family, people she connected with on a regular basis, people she'd regret lying to. He had compartments. He shrugged. "They're two distinct worlds. My life. My job."

"Oh," she said quietly.

Natalie hauled the door open and sashayed into the bar, wearing black leggings, knee-high boots, and a white sweater that clung to her breasts, hips, and thighs. The Eye Candy logo peeked out of the deep V of her sweater. "Well, well," she said, tugging iPod headphones from her ears. "Where were you all weekend?"

The first big test. "At Chad's house," Eve said. "Someone shot out my windows after close Saturday night. Chad was with me, so I went to his house."

Natalie exclaimed, made all the right noises, asked

all the right questions. He stood to the side, observing Eve and Natalie, as he sliced lemons and stocked glasses. Eve didn't quite seem like herself, her voice a little shaky, her gaze sliding to him every so often, for reassurance, but it was nothing that wouldn't reasonably be chalked up to nerves after gunfire.

"Why didn't you call me?"

"Until I know who did it and why, I didn't want to get you involved," Eve said. She looked at Matt. "Chad can take care of himself, and me. He's going to stay with me for a while."

"Do your parents know? Caleb?"

"Yes, and I'm worried about Dad," she said, hoping the effort to change the subject wasn't too obvious. "He's not feeling all that great these days. Mom's pretty spooked. Hey, can you make change in the registers for me? I'm really behind after being gone all weekend."

Nat hurried up the stairs and returned without her bag, a stack of bills in hand to distribute among the bartenders' registers.

Matt backed Eve into the bar, his hand automatically going to her hip while he eyed Natalie as she rounded the corner. "Not bad."

"Thanks." Her fingers found his, wove into them. Gripped hard. "I'm glad you're here. After seeing Lyle today I wouldn't feel safe doing this with two guys sitting in a car outside the bar."

He stroked the smooth skin of her cheek with the backs of his fingers. "Stay close. Don't do anything on impulse. Anyone asks you to step outside, male or female, act like I'm an overbearing asshole and check in with me."

Fists thudded against the heavy steel door, locked at the beginning of the night for the first time. Over the pounding Matt heard Tom's voice. "Hey, Hot Stuff! If you want us to work tonight you'd better open this fucking door!"

She gave a shakily relieved laugh. "There's reality."

He looked over his shoulder at the shuddering door, tried to ignore that her reality didn't include him. "Let's do this, boss."

Less than a week later Eve was going out of her mind.

Saturday afternoon she stood behind the bar, finishing prep with Matt. He'd figured out how to connect her computer to the DJ's sound system so they had tunes while they worked. The Goo Goo Dolls' "Iris" played in the background, a band she loved, but the melancholy, intense lyrics only heightened her mood. She'd accepted three more deposits from Travis or another of Lyle's flunkies, but without words exchanged or a visit from Lyle, they had nothing more than Eve's word connecting him to the money, or the drugs.

They worked in silence for a while. The days had fallen into a fairly predictable routine. Matt had cobbled together a fitness regime, jumping rope on the dance floor, a speed bag in the storeroom. He worked out while she handled the daily business tasks, then worked behind the bar. Eve handled the social networking and publicity shots with the parties booked into the club. Neither one of them bothered to hide the heat simmering under their every interaction from anyone, the bartenders, Natalie, the customers, people they saw on the street when they went to the bank. Woven into it all was a feeling she couldn't identify, something new, maybe unformed, but always there, just outside her mental and emotional range.

After hours Matt set about calming Eve's increasingly frayed nerves. Between the music, the crowds, and the constant fear of Lyle surprising her, she was brittle and on edge, and when they closed the club she went wild under him, against him, using teeth and nails like she was in a fight for her life. None of it fazed him. He just met her wildly emotional response with a slightly stronger level of force until the fear and need combusted.

"I hate waiting," she finally said. "I'm not good at it."

"Rushing a case means we get an arrest but not a conviction. Solid police work takes time and patience."

And the ability to push away instant gratification, she mused. After four years in the Army and eight as a cop, he was an expert at it. She wasn't.

She dropped a box of lemons on the counter with a little more force than she intended.

"You okay?" Matt asked.

Stop asking me that! trembled on the tip of her tongue, but she bit it back. She was *not* okay. She was in over her head personally and professionally, and with every passing day he seemed to grow calmer and calmer, going through the work at Eye Candy, staying connected to Sorenson and Hawthorn's street-level investigation, protecting her. His gaze slid over her much like his hand would over the silk wraparound dress she wore, pausing at all the right spots to admire, lingering on her eyes to assess her state of mind. She didn't like the way those two melded together.

"I'm fine. It slipped. Can you finish up for me? I need to finish the schedule, do some paperwork."

He nodded. She disconnected her laptop from the sound system and headed upstairs to do exactly what she'd said, plus make a purchase she'd been thinking about for days. The bar had been open for over an hour by the time she'd paid bills and gone downstairs to the storeroom to compile the liquor order for the next week. The rapid beat of a club remix thumped away at her nerves. She dropped the clipboard on a stack of boxes and resisted the urge to rub her tired eyes, instead pressing the heels of her hands into her eye sockets to smudge the makeup as little as possible.

Lady Gaga's lyrics crystallized when the door opened, went indistinct when it closed. Then the lock clicked shut. "Are you okay?"

Hands still pressed to her eyes, she said, "Stop asking me that, Matt. It's driving me crazy. I am as fine as I can be, given the circumstances."

When he didn't respond, she let her hands drop and turned to face him. His hair was a little longer and more tousled than when she hired him, she noticed, and a fine network of lines spread from the corners of his eyes. They were both tired, not sleeping well. Even after the sex. "Why aren't you out front?"

"It's slow tonight."

"Pink's in town," she said. "I think most of my customer base is at the concert."

"I hear the trapeze routine rocks."

She gave him the small smile he'd want to see after making a joke, maybe even felt it a little. "Me too."

"What's on your mind, Eve?"

"The usual," she said and turned to find her clipboard.

Not a flicker of emotion crossed his face now. Long hair aside, his expressionless demeanor could have been a recruiting poster for the Army. "We'll get him."

"Whatever it takes, right?"

A long moment stretched between them. Then he said, "That dress looks like someone poured smoke on you."

A by-now familiar diversion, but it worked. She wore a simple silvery-gray wrap dress with a deep V plunging between her breasts, lined with red silk that appeared as she moved. She'd bought it at an upscale consignment boutique and wore only silver earrings with it, as the dress was a sophisticated enticement all on its own. She smoothed her palms down her hips and looked at him through her tousled hair. "You like?"

Heat flared in his hazel eyes, moss over flecked stone. "I like how the red flashes when you walk."

"Hmmmm?" she said, closing the distance between them. She needed this. Whatever worked to keep her focused, strong. She needed him.

"Makes me wonder what you've got on underneath."

He stepped into her, wrapped an arm around her waist to hoist her against him, then carried her to the smooth metal shelf lining the wall by the door. She linked her arms around his neck and tossed her hair back from her face when he set her down and stepped between her legs. But when he reached for the tie holding the dress closed, she put her hand on his.

"This isn't a good idea," she cautioned.

He continued to tug at the thin gray cord, and the flap of her dress loosened. "I locked the door."

She tried to hold the gaping fabric closed. "I'm not exactly quiet," she said halfheartedly.

"It's really hot when you have to be quiet. Remember?" he said, and parted the flaps. His gaze flicked over her lace bra and thong. "Red. My favorite."

"I know," she said. Talking became impossible when he gripped the back of her head in one hand and her ass in the other, holding her to him for kiss after slick, hot kiss. He was notched between her spread legs, and she felt his cock thicken and grow hard as his tongue slid against hers. She hooked one heel behind his knee and reached for the button fly of his jeans, popping the first three buttons to reach inside and grip his erection.

"Jesus," he said, and broke free. She knew how he

felt. She was beginning to wonder if this would ever go away.

She skimmed her thong down and off while he opened his jeans and sheathed himself in latex, then, in one smooth, gliding stroke, in her. The thick shaft stretched her and she gasped, then whimpered as he pulled her to the edge of the counter. She wound her legs around his waist and her arms around his neck. Mindful of the foot traffic from the bar to the dish room, she buried her face in his shoulder to stifle her gasps. He stopped and pulled his Eye Candy T-shirt over his head and dropped it on the counter beside her.

"Makeup on my shoulder's a dead giveaway," he muttered.

As if glassy eyes, a flushed throat, swollen lips, and a languid hitch in her walk wouldn't tell everyone who worked at the bar, and maybe some of the customers, exactly what had happened. She didn't argue with him because running her palms over his shoulders and down his ridged abdomen ratcheted up the anticipation, and when it came right down to it, she didn't give a damn. She needed this. So badly.

She expected hard and fast, but he braced one hand against the wall behind her and wrapped the other around her hips, holding her in position as he moved. Slowly. Achingly slowly, letting her feel every single inch glide in, pause, then withdraw. The head of his shaft caressed nerve endings aroused and desperate for heat and pressure. Her eyes closed, she sank into her body, the tantalizing rasp of lace against her nipples as they brushed his chest, the warm metal under her ass. The backs of his thighs flexed and released as he moved, denim between her bare legs and his. One red patent leather heel clattered to the cement floor, then the other, as she tightened inside and out, clinging to him, mouth open against the muscled curve where his neck blended into his shoulder.

"Oh God, Matt. More. Please."

"Shhhhhh," he said. She could have smacked him for the male amusement under the husky words, but another slick stroke ended all thought of distracting him. "Like you like this, boss."

She couldn't hasten the pleasure building with slow deliberation inside her, like a fist tightening around her core. He was so hard, each stroke slick, unhurried, confident. She began to tremble, muscles quivering as molten pleasure coursed through her body, burning away muscle and bone. He took his time, drove her nearer and nearer the edge until she wasn't sure if she needed or feared the oncoming freight train of release.

She dug her nails into his shoulder, wound the other hand in the loose denim at his hips, and took it. Took him. Even with her face pressed to his damp skin, the cry that tore from her throat as the tight fist opened and flung her into oblivion echoed in the dark, still room. He gave an indistinct growl into her hair, thrust again, and again, then went rigid and jetted into her.

Moments passed. The thumping club rhythm seeped back into her consciousness as the tension eased from his shoulders and arms, then his back. The fingers gripping her hip twitched then went lax. Still deep inside her, he relaxed, letting her bear some of his weight. They were in the same position, her limbs entwined around the strong column of his body, but the attitude was completely different. He wasn't a figure carved from living granite but a man, sharing a stolen moment with her as the pleasure ebbed from their bodies.

And then she knew. Knew what she was feeling, the

thing at odds with the stress and fear and helplessness. She was falling for Matt Dorchester, a man completely capable of acting the role of a lover while feeling nothing at all. He was inside her, his sweat salty on her lips, his body under her hands, and she was falling for him.

Unlike the sex they'd just had, she was falling hard and fast.

As if she'd shouted the words aloud, something changed in the air. He cleared his throat, stepped back, and turned to the trash can. Cool air sidled up her torso, making her shiver. She slid off the counter, pulled on her panties, kicked her shoes upright so she could step into them, and rewrapped her dress.

A rattle of the doorknob, then a knock over Natalie's voice. "You naughty kids, I know you're both in there. Eve, an unexpected bachelorette party just arrived. We need you out front, sweets. You too, handsome. There's a blonde looking for her Chad special, whatever that is."

A distraction from her distraction. Eve looked at him, lifted an eyebrow and her hand to his mouth. "A Soul Kiss," he said after she wiped lipstick off his mouth and neck with her thumb.

"A little more subtle than asking for Sex on the Beach," Eve said as Matt unlocked the door and hauled it open.

"Well, hey, sugar," Nat said sweetly. "Make yourself useful?"

Matt ignored her, but Eve saw a muscle jump in his jaw before he disappeared into the bar.

"The things you put up with for your job," Eve called after his departing back, then stifled a hysterical giggle.

Natalie peeked in the door. "You decent?" she asked, then added, "You okay?"

No. She had to start thinking through her decisions. Helping the investigation wasn't an impulse. Tempting Matt into sleeping with her was, but she wasn't trained to work as an undercover agent. She didn't have an alter ego or a cover identity; she was just herself, mightily attracted to Matt Dorchester and acting on that attraction.

"I'm fine," she said. "But if people don't stop asking me that, I won't be. Let's go."

She walked into a nearly full house, music rolling through the crowd like waves after a storm. Natalie directed her to the bachelorette party. She smiled, complimented outfits, laughed, congratulated the bride-to-be, bought the first round, and took picture after picture as the maid of honor passed phone after phone from group members to Eve.

"Thanks for doing this," Miranda said, handing over another smartphone.

"My pleasure. Thanks for celebrating at Eye Candy." Eve shifted the lens so Matt's face wasn't included in the shot. She'd done her best, but a few pictures ended up on the web. It couldn't be helped. "On three. One, two, three." The flash went off.

"We booked a couple of tables at Miss Martini but the vibe sucked, so we left early," Miranda explained as she exchanged phones with Eve. "My cousin had a birthday party here last month, and my office is thinking about moving into the East Side business park. I wanted to check out the neighborhood."

"That's great," Eve said.

"Quite a few employees live across the river. The location's great, but there hasn't been the . . . infrastructure to justify the move. The business park would change all of that."

"You should try Cindy's cupcakes," Eve said. "They're sin in a small package. So good."

"As soon as I'm done dieting for this wedding. Fucking mermaid dress," she said conversationally.

Startled into laughter, Eve asked for one more for the Eye Candy Facebook page. iPhone in hand, she backed up to get a little more of the bar in the shot and bumped into a warm male body. She turned around to apologize.

Lyle stood right behind her.

"Oh my God!" she gasped. Her hand flew to her chest and she dropped her phone. The hard shell case cracked open and it and the phone itself skittered in different directions. One of the bridesmaids nearly put a stiletto heel through the phone.

"You okay?" Lyle asked.

She swallowed the hysterical laughter. "No. You scared me half to death!"

Miranda, the only remotely sober woman in the party, gave Lyle an appraising look, one he returned, with interest. Eve took advantage of Lyle's distraction to look for Travis. He seemed to be alone.

Helpful patrons found the shattered shell and handed it and the phone to Eve. The phone had a couple of new scratches but appeared functional. The case was a total loss.

"I need to talk to you."

It was the peak of a Saturday night. "I'm a little busy at the moment," she said. It took everything she had not to look in Matt's direction to see if he'd noticed Lyle. She was sure he would have. All she needed to do was act natural. "I'm a little busy . . . but I've always got time for you. Let me just take one more picture," she said to the party, and held up her phone. "Great. Thanks so much! I'll check in with you later. The next round's on me." Then she turned to Lyle. "What's up? I haven't seen you in a while."

"Let's talk upstairs."

She looked at him and saw a man who wasn't her friend, who wanted her dead, the reason why she was living with a cop and going out of her mind. "Fine. Give me a second," she said, and hurried toward Matt. She strolled around the end of the bar, stepped into his warm body.

"Get them whatever they want, sweetheart," she said as she laid her hand on Matt's hip, making sure to look over her shoulder as she spoke. Lyle's face tightened. Then she turned back to Matt. "He wants to talk in private," she murmured.

"He doesn't get what he wants," Matt said, and he didn't need volume to convey utter authority. The absorbed, attentive lover was gone, replaced by a cop. Had the lover ever really existed?

She slid her hand under the hem of his shirt and looked up into his face. "I'm checking in with you so he thinks you're a domineering asshole. Now I'm going upstairs."

"Goddammit, Eve!"

She slipped from his grip and hurried around the end of the bar, deep into the crowd. Lyle followed her up the staircase, into her office. Eve closed the door and pulled out her cell phone.

"You don't need your new boyfriend?"

"Who? Chad? Why would I? Just a second," she said, not giving him a chance to respond. "I need to post those pictures to Instagram." She swiped to the app she wanted, tapped it, then set the phone down and went on the offensive. "We've got a problem. Someone shot out my windows last week. Talk to whoever you have to and make that stop. It's bad for business."

Lyle settled into one end of her sofa and smiled that dark-eyed smile. Eve smiled back, studying his face. To her, he didn't look any different, but Matt had been closer, able to see Lyle over the roof of the Jeep. Or maybe her new "boyfriend" landed a little farther down the paranoid spectrum. "I didn't hear anything about it."

"Then I'm telling you now. Someone shot out the windows to my apartment last week. I wasn't hurt, thank God, and neither was Chad. It sure as hell killed the mood."

That got her a smile, the small one she remembered best. "I'm surprised, Eve. He's not your type."

"He'll do for now," she said, giving him her best sexy cocktail waitress glance to cover her pounding heart, her stomach's roller-coaster ride from her throat to her knees.

Lyle threw back his head and laughed, the sound unforced but with an edge she'd never heard before. It made the hair stand up on the back of her neck as some primitive part of her brain recognized the kind of threat that made animals everywhere go wide-eyed as they hunched in fear. "You haven't changed a bit, Evie."

She gave a nonchalant shrug. It was a struggle to confide in him as she would have when they were teenagers, to act like she hadn't caught on. "I needed something different from Caleb's lawyer friends."

He glanced out the floor-to-ceiling windows. "Your parents can't be happy about that."

She had to assume he knew she'd taken "Chad" to Monday dinner. "I didn't exactly ask for their permission," she said wryly. "They'll just have to get used to him."

The smile didn't change, a little smug, a little cold. "There's the bad girl I remember," he said. "And how's business? Your new man getting involved?"

She let out a laugh that trilled through the octaves,

and winced as she heard it. "Never mix business with pleasure. I need a ring and a prenup before that happens."

"You don't see him much on the Facebook page. I had to search to get a good look at the man who's captivated our little Evie. It's like you're hiding him."

Something like that. She looked at the iPhone. "He's not the best-looking guy behind the bar. I don't choose what customers post or tag. Look, Lyle, it's a Saturday night and I've got a full house. Did you want something?"

He kept that unreadable dark brown gaze fixed on her. "Have you heard anything from the city about the property behind you?" He looked over his shoulder to indicate the alley and the vacant building behind the apartment.

He had her attention now. The deadline for bids passed the prior . . . Wednesday? No, Thursday. She'd assumed the city assessor called Caleb with the news, and Caleb, in the middle of a trial, had forgotten to call her. "No."

"An associate of mine won the auction." He all but sprawled on her sofa, completely relaxed, at ease. "Told you I was interested in investing in the East Side."

Her blood turned to ice water in her veins. She'd lost the biggest space standing between Eve and SoMa, between Eye Candy and the rest of the existing East Side businesses and the East Side Business District. With the property in someone else's name, even if the police caught Lyle the forfeiture laws wouldn't apply.

The only way for her to get that property was to deal with Lyle.

"Wow," she managed, and cleared her throat. "Congratulations to him. What does he plan to do with it?"

Lyle smiled. "He's going to open a welding business. Or a strip club. He's not sure which." A laugh, then,

"Jesus, Evie. If you could have seen your face. I'm kidding. You bid for it, didn't you?"

She nodded. "Oh well. I couldn't really afford it." She couldn't afford not to have it either.

"Should have let me help you," he chastised. "I could see if he'd cut you a deal. He'd make a little money fast and you'd get the lot."

"Brokering," she said. "There's usually a fee involved."

"Just doing a friend a favor."

And there it was, the truth Matt had seen before she did. Lyle wanted to own her in every possible way. She let her eyes widen, like he'd just offered her the secret recipe for the hottest drink on the market, and tried not to gabble in fear. "That'd be . . . that would be great. I'll pay you back. I can't now, but I will."

He gave her a courteous, old-fashioned nod, and stood up. This time he let himself out, back into the bar. Eve paused at the bottom of the stairs and watched him walk through her building, her crowd, her business, like he owned it.

Matt materialized out of the crowd, gripped her upper arm, and all but yanked her into the phone alcove. He was white to his lips, his eyes hard. "What the fuck were you thinking?"

"He's not going to shoot me upstairs in my office with three hundred people in the building," she pointed out rationally, and jerked her arm loose.

A hand landed on either side of her head as he got right in her face. "There are a dozen other things he could do to you, Eve, starting with taking you out through your apartment door without anyone knowing," he said.

Her eyes widened. It was the most vivid display of emotion she'd ever seen from him. "I didn't think of that," she said.

Matt visibly got himself back under control. "What happened?"

"We can talk about it later," she said. "Two more parties are coming in."

CHAPTER FOURTEEN

After Eye Candy closed, Eve powered down the lights, and found a small task force assembled in her office: Matt, Sorenson, Carlucci, and Hawthorn.

"Murphy approached you?" Hawthorn said without preamble.

"In the middle of the rush," she said, rubbing her eyes without a care for her mascara. She was so tired. So wired, and she'd gotten them nothing they could use.

Sorenson got her notebook. "What exactly did he say?"

In response, Eve set her iPhone on her desk and opened the voice recorder. She pressed play, and the conversation broadcast into the office.

Matt stood beside her, arms folded, back to brick wall.

"I *was* listening when we talked at your house," she said in a low voice.

"I lost ten years off my life when you walked up those stairs alone," he said. His voice was equally low, his eyes focused on the iPhone as Sorenson replayed the conversation. "Do that again and I'll make 'forceful' look like riding the carousel at the zoo."

Certain he was joking, she stared at his unyielding profile, waiting for the tight line of his jaw to relax. Then he turned to look at her. For a moment of time measurable only by the atomic clock the real Matt Dorchester, the man locked away behind duty and honor and service, inhabited his hazel eyes, and she stopped breathing. He blinked, then disappeared.

Oxygen returned to the room, so she could speak. "I'm sorry," she said defensively. "It was the best option."

"The fuck it was. The best fucking option was to tell him that after some lowlife motherfucker nearly fucking killed you your domineering boyfriend won't let you do anything alone."

Lyle got stupid when he was angry. Eve got impulsive. Anger brought out Matt Dorchester's Army vocabulary and a glare that somehow managed to be both ice-cold and white-hot.

She opened her mouth.

"Later."

Her teeth clicked shut. "Yes," she said. "Later." She folded her arms across her chest and leaned against the wall. In the mirror on the back of the door, her jaw and Matt's looked identical, mulishly set.

Sorenson looked between the two of them as she took the phone from Eve and connected the phone to her computer, then transferred the recording to the laptop. "How did you get away with starting the recorder?" she asked, rummaging through a variety of cables in her bag.

"I said I was posting bachelorette party pictures online. Which I was. Then I started the app."

"That's a really tempting offer," Hawthorn said mildly.

Eve rubbed her forehead. "He's definitely got the upper hand. It's bad enough if that building doesn't come down, but if someone puts up a welding shop or a strip club, it sabotages the whole redevelopment effort."

"You're doing great, Eve," Hawthorn said. "We've got accounts, numbers, a history of transactions. We can track the outflows back into the Strykers. Just a little bit longer."

"I'm fine," Eve said. "I can do this. I can."

"And nice job with the voice recording," Sorenson said. "You were thinking on your feet."

"It was Matt's idea," Eve said without looking at him. "We talked about a variety of scenarios over the weekend."

Sorenson gestured for Eve to meet her by the door. "How are you holding up?" she asked quietly, her gaze holding Eve's.

Her voice was too low for either Hawthorn or Matt to hear her words, but she could tell Matt got the gist of the question by the way his jaw tightened.

"Fine," Eve lied.

"He's just doing his job," Sorenson said.

"I know."

The space between her and Matt seemed as wide as the ocean after Sorenson, Carlucci, and Hawthorn left. She closed her apartment door and turned to find him leaning against the door to her office. There couldn't have been more than ten feet between them, but the gulf seemed impossible to cross, and in that moment, Eve knew her whole life was crashing down around her ears. Lyle would win. She'd lose Eye Candy, and the East Side would lose support for the redevelopment bid. Worst of all, people were dying, and she . . .

She was if-you-don't-say-the-word-love-then-it's-not-real falling for a man so afraid of emotion he locked away everything he felt, everything he was, behind *layers* of fictional identity. Ten minutes earlier, for a split second, she'd seen the real Matt, the man suppressed under the bartender, the cop, the brother. The lover.

Now she knew. The sex, the laughter, the teasing banter, none of it was really him.

He leaned against the door, his fists jammed tight in his pockets, probably to keep from shaking her until her teeth rattled in her head, but she would have welcomed that, because it would have been real. Not this artificial, thrumming silence.

"I had to do it. He never would have given away so much if you were in the room. If we're going to end this anytime soon, we need that evidence."

"Fuck the evidence. You don't ever go anywhere alone with him again. Understand?"

She saw red. For the first time in a volatile, impulse-filled life, she actually saw red with anger. "I'm not your partner," she flung at him. "Or your girlfriend. You don't have any right to talk to me like that."

She'd just swung at a hot button with a sledgehammer, but for once it wasn't an impulse. Her reward was a second glimpse of the searing, wild emotion lighting up his eyes. The long muscles in his forearms, exposed by the short-sleeved Eye Candy T-shirt, tightened, standing out in stark relief under his skin. In the still darkness of her apartment emotion poured from him in waves. It was like standing in a lashing, pelting thunderstorm, the air crackling with electricity, sheer human feeling buffeting her like slaps of wind and rain.

The white-hot threat didn't disappear from his eyes this time. She lifted her chin defiantly and waited. *Bring it on.* For once, for just once in their ill-timed relationship riddled with lies and fictional identities, she wanted the man locked away in Matt Dorchester's soul.

She wanted the truth of him.

In the next instant, he was against her. He trapped her body between his and the door and kissed her. The pressure of his mouth on hers, demanding she open to him, was near enough to brutal to make her gasp in fierce delight. She kissed him back, hard enough to draw blood from her inner lip. He gripped her wrists in one hand and with the other held her jaw and throat for his demanding kiss.

His arm slid down around her waist, lifting her against his hard torso to walk into the bedroom and fall onto her bed with her underneath him. Air rushed out of her at the sudden impact. The old metal frame squawked in protest but held. Again he trapped her wrists over her head and with his free hand he yanked at the tie of her wrap dress and spread it open so she lay in a pool of red silk. His eyes were fierce and desolate as he straddled her, opened his jeans, rolled down a condom, and dealt with her panties with a swift yank of his fist.

She threw back her head in adulation. Then she couldn't talk because he'd shoved himself inside her, the impact of his thick shaft inside her and the pressure of his chest against her breasts forcing the air from her lungs. Her vocal cords turned the gasp into a whimper as the pressure sharpened to pain. She willed herself to stay open to him, and the edge softened into a swell of pleasure that rolled from her center into the pitch-blackness, where it melded with the tempestuous emotion emanating from Matt.

Every time they'd had sex, all she'd sensed from him was a firm grip on his control. Even in the most intense, heated, erotic moments when sheer masculine need seethed under his skin, he'd never let himself go. But now he was actually feeling—anger, fear, desire, a soul-deep longing she didn't dare put into words.

It was wildly, compellingly real.

She stripped his shirt over his head, leaving his carved torso bare to her hands. In response he shoved her bra to her collarbone and braced his elbows just above her shoulders to hold her in place. The searing touch of skin against skin brought a rough groan from his throat as he began to move.

There was no clawing at his back, no pitching and heaving under him, no sexy pleading. She gripped his biceps and lifted her hips to meet each thrust, every nerve ending in her soft channel screaming with heightened awareness. He pounded into her, a soft grunt huffing from his throat with each impact. It was raw, it was purely male dominance in search of release, and she loved every moment of it.

Emotion and sexual heat twined together and spiraled through her body, until, without warning, the tight fist at her core flew open and flung her into a star-spattered blackness. As if from a distance she heard her stuttering gasps of release. He buried himself deep inside her and shuddered, jaw clenched, to his own orgasm.

Long moments passed as he lay on top of her, sweat trickling from his ribs to hers, his breath gusting in her ear. Then he pulled away and went into the bathroom. She slipped her arms from the sleeves of her dress and curled up naked on her side, ribbons of pleasure fluttering against her nerves as she waited for him to return.

He didn't. Her stomach seized when she heard him pull on his Army running shorts, then lace up his shoes. "I'll be downstairs," he said abruptly from the doorway.

She pushed herself up on one elbow. "Matt, what's—"

"Not now," he said. Then he turned and left.

When the door closed with the faintest of clicks she understood. He might not be able to resist her, but giving in to her didn't feel like a respite from the staggering burdens he shouldered. Giving in to an impulse, giving in to *her* felt like a failure of character, a weakness. She might be his drug, but he hated the addiction as much as he craved the rush.

She loved him.

Being with her was tearing him apart.

He got as far as the top of the spiral staircase before his knees gave way. His palm slipped on the wrought iron banister, nearly pitching him down the stairs before he caught himself and sank down on the landing. The edges of the posts dug into his spine, and he latched onto the pain, welcomed it, braced his foot against the opposite railing and shoved. Hard.

What had he done? *What had he just done?*

You just made the worst mistake a man can make.

Cool air drifted over damp skin, triggering tiny flashpoints of memory—her soft mouth under his; the sharp, exhilarating tang of blood; the visceral, terrifying rush when he embedded himself deep inside her and everything disappeared, he disappeared, in an obliterating wave of infinite black energy. Into Eve.

So that's what it was like to feel.

He must have hurt her. No way he hadn't hurt her. He should go back and apologize. Except his mouth wasn't shaped around "I'm sorry" but rather words he could never speak, never take back.

The air conditioner thunked off, leaving only a ringing silence. No sound from the apartment. No sound from the bar below. Only the rush of breath and blood in his ears and that strange heaving in his chest, like a wild, caged thing gripped his ribs and rammed shoulder to breastbone like the bars of a prison, testing for weaknesses, seeking a way out.

He took a deep breath. Unfisted his hands. Consciously relaxed the muscles in his thigh until the pain grinding into his back eased. Control surfaced, familiar and comforting. He shaped his mind around it, felt the struggling thing inside him recede as iron gray steel reasserted itself under his skin, encasing his muscles and bones. His pulse slowed, and he got to his feet, found his shoulders squaring, his body once again under his command.

He took the first step, then the next. All systems go. She'd be asleep by now. They were both exhausted. Under duress. She needed sleep more than she needed to debrief what just happened. What he'd just done. In the morning he'd apologize for losing control and essentially brutalizing her.

The hell of it was, he knew walking out the door had hurt her more.

CHAPTER FIFTEEN

Noise. An intrusive, annoying clanging, too close to her head to be her alarm because her phone was charging in the kitchen. She'd have to get out of bed to turn off the alarm.

The bed shifted as the warm body beside her reached for the nightstand. Through the stupor of sleep she heard Matt fumbling for his iPhone in the mess on top, then a solid thunk as something hit the carpeted floor—the Sig or his department-issued Glock, probably. Maybe the knife. Possibly the economy-sized bottle of lotion she slathered on her hands before she went to bed. Most likely a gun.

"I'll take it," she said, her voice thick, trusting he'd hand her the shrill electronic device, not a semiautomatic.

He dropped the vibrating, buzzing phone on her abdomen and rolled onto his back. "Christ," he muttered.

She sat up, then paid the price for moving. He'd held her in place by gripping the hip that hit the linoleum the night someone shot out her windows, so when she sat up fresh twinges shot through the joint. Muscles in her thighs and calves protested vehemently when she moved.

None of that compared to the shredded ache she felt in her heart.

She swiped at the screen to shut off the alarm, then automatically checked various accounts without really seeing the comments and replies. It was something to buffer her against the turbulent emotions eddying in the air.

"Time is it?" he asked, his voice morning thick.

"Noon. Sorry. I should have set it back an hour, but I fell asleep instead." And she'd forgotten to charge the phone as well. She'd lain awake, unwilling to follow him down into the bar and badger him further but exhaustion finally won.

She felt like she would never be rested again.

"You okay?" he asked.

"I think that's my line," she said.

His arm covered his eyes, and his chest rose and fell evenly. Too evenly. In for a count of four, out for a count of four. Repeat. She looked at the hand loosely curled on his chest. The thin skin covering his knuckles looked like her heart felt.

He wasn't going to answer her. Finally she said, "I'm fine." Tears prickled at the backs of her eyes. She blinked hard, and after a few moments the sensation faded. "I'm sorry, Matt. I pushed when I shouldn't have."

I wanted something I shouldn't want . . . something I can't have.

"I'm sorry too." He lifted his arm from across his face, looked her right in the eye. "I was too rough."

"It was fine. You were fine." She could handle that. Handle more. "I won't break, Matt."

"I might."

She knew he'd meant to make a joke and defuse the

tension, but the words sounded like he'd forced them out through steel wool. A wave of mortified regret crawled up her throat. Ten seconds earlier she'd told herself she had to stop pushing, and here she was . . . pushing.

Give him some space, some time. "I'm going to get in the shower."

"Okay."

She untangled her legs from the light quilt and managed to walk to the bathroom without stumbling, then managed to shower without crying. Fifteen minutes later she stood in front of her tiny closet with her hair wrapped in a towel, wearing her bra and the short black skirt with the small front pocket for her iPhone. She pulled out a white sleeveless cashmere turtleneck, yanked off the towel, pulled the sweater over her head, and slid the phone into the pocket so she'd remember to charge it.

She looked over her shoulder at him. Matt was steadily going about his business, avoiding her eyes. "Make sure you charge that," he said.

"It'll be fine as long as I don't make a call," she replied. "I need makeup more."

She stood back to let him into the shower, the thin plastic curtain like a brick wall between them. She dried her hair and scrunched the waves into a simple style. She'd begun to dab concealer under her eyes when she heard a soft thump and a single knock at the door.

The UPS guy, delivering her latest shipment of boxed groceries she'd ordered online. She walked out of the bathroom, gently unchained and unbolted the door to the landing, and crouched down to grab the small white box.

She looked up into the barrel of a dull black gun. Lyle held it, staring down at her, expressionless. Staring at a gun looked just as unremarkable on television as getting shot at, but in real life Eve's entire body went numb.

Lyle took the box from her and shoved it onto the counter beside the door. "Downstairs. Now."

"I'm not going anywhere with you," she said, as her brain kicked into overdrive. In a split second she ran through the circumstances. Matt's small arsenal was in the bedroom on the nightstand. He was in the shower, defenseless. She was an idiot.

"Sure you are, Evie," he said gently. He gave her a smile so full of toothy malice the hair stood up on her arms. "Because if you don't I'll shoot you. And then I'll leave you here and go and shoot your father, your mother, your motherfucking brother. I'm sick of this fucking bar and all the trouble it's caused me. It ends now."

She went utterly still. Natalie, her best friend, or Cesar, supporting his family, or Pauli, who was just a kid. *Her family.*

The shower shut off. In a few seconds Matt would dry off and walk through the bathroom door, and maybe Lyle would shoot him too.

But he didn't know Matt was a cop.

Matt would find her.

She hurried past Lyle, out the door and onto the landing.

"Nice and quiet going down those stairs," he said, eyeing her four-inch heels. "Don't want lover boy getting alarmed."

No, they didn't want that, not until lover boy had gone and gotten all of his biggest friends with their semiautomatic pistols and concussion grenades. Lyle gripped her arm, hustled her across the parking lot, and shoved her into the backseat of the SUV. His cell rang. "Keep an eye on her," he snapped at Travis, sitting in the driver's seat, then slammed her door and took the call with a snarled "Yeah?"

Twisting sideways to fumble for the seat belt, she pulled her iPhone from the pocket of her skirt and slipped it between her thigh and the seat. After she fastened the belt she swiped her thumb across the screen to wake it, and tapped the phone button.

"Hey, Travis," she said as she lowered the volume. She bent over and pretended to adjust her heel, dialing a memorized phone number, praying adrenaline would make her fingers accurate.

Voice mail. The voice was faint, audible only to her ears as the relentlessly pleasant female operator asked the caller to leave a message. She hung up, waited a few seconds, pressed Call twice to redial the number.

Oh shit, Matt! Oh shit oh shit oh shit! Please answer your phone!

Travis wouldn't meet her eyes in the rearview mirror. She'd known him her whole life. He'd always worked to ingratiate himself into whatever circle was closest. The fact that he wasn't chatting her up, let alone looking her in the eye made her stomach lurch. Driven by the most basic impulse of all—survival—she reached for the door handle.

The locks clicked shut. She looked over the back of the driver's seat at Travis, who still wasn't looking at her.

"They'll meet us at the warehouse," Lyle said as he slid into the Escalade's leather seats. The truck pulled away from Eye Candy, into traffic.

After a firefight, routine mattered. Shower and dress. Jeans, polo, running shoes, gun at his right ankle, knife. Stick to the routine, the last stand against feelings, memories, images. Eve walking up the stairs with a sociopath. Eve taunting him, Eve trembling under him until he'd wrung every last drop of fight out of her and she turned to flame in his arms. The misery on her face this morning.

The silence in the living room triggered a mental alarm. Maybe she was in the office, doing paperwork. He walked into the living room and saw a package on the counter, but the office door was closed.

"Eve?" he called as he opened the door.

The office was dark, the door leading down the spiral staircase to Eye Candy's dance floor closed and deadbolted from the inside. No light shone through the curtains covering the floor-to-ceiling windows.

"Eve!" he called again. His voice tauntingly bounced around the cavernous space as he hauled open the door and launched himself at the stairs, his hands skidding down the curved railing. He jogged into the storeroom, the dish room, then behind the bar. Nothing.

"*Eve!*"

She'd vanished. He took the curving stairs three at a time and bolted through the office, back into her apartment. Her purse was still on the counter. The pegs by the back door held her car keys. On the landing he scanned the empty alley, then dashed down the wooden staircase and around the side of the building. The parking lot was empty but for his Jeep.

Cold certainty crawled up his spine and settled into the base of his brain. She was gone, taken from the apartment from under his nose, while he was in the shower.

He was drowning. He knew how it felt, a deceptive lack of feeling that marked the leading edge of a tsunami. Then the surge hit. He stood stock-still as the wave engulfed him—fear, anguish, terror, anger rising inside him, forcing their way up his chest, into his throat—then he was moving. He had to get away from this rampaging, acid-skinned, sharp-clawed thing inside him, threatening to gut him from the inside out.

He was headed for his Jeep, when his phone, slipped into his front pocket, buzzed. Chad's cell had a distinctive ringtone. Matt's was an old-fashioned bell-tone ring. He pulled it from his pocket. Eve's cell number appeared on the screen.

Oh shit.

He tapped Answer.

"—a little over the top back there, don't you think?"

He immediately muted the call, so he could hear her but nothing from his surroundings would be audible to Eve or anyone with her. Her voice sounded distant, melded with the radio, like the phone wasn't up to her mouth.

He could make out Lyle's voice, but his reply was too muffled to understand. But it sounded dismissive. As if Eve didn't matter anymore.

"Would you turn that off, please? I hear music so much at Eye Candy, I hate listening to it when I'm not at work."

That was bullshit, pure and simple. She must have gotten an assent, because the background noise shut off.

"Much better," she said. A pause, then, "Travis, I heard Maria's working at Two Slices. Is her mom watching the kids?"

Fight back the terror, the emotion that would get her killed. Phone to his ear, he sprinted to the sidewalk and pulled up a mental map of Thirteenth Street, running through the East Side, thirteen blocks from the river that formed the city's eastern boundary. The next mention will either be Spattered Ink or the crazy psychic doing business out of her house with about thirty cats for company.

"Can you believe Madame LaMoue is still in business? She gets a booth at the East Side street fair every year. Local color. That's how I describe her to people considering opening up shop on the East Side. Every community needs someone with *the eye*."

No response from Lyle, but Matt was in the Jeep, the gas pedal floored. He used Chad's cell to dial Sorenson.

"Lyle's got Eve," he said when she answered. "Took her out of the apartment while I was in the shower. They're moving south on Thirteenth Street. I'm on my way to the precinct."

"Shit is about to go down," Sorenson said. "Caleb Webber just came in. He got an anonymous call suggesting he track down his father. Pastor Webber made it to the men's breakfast at seven but not the volunteer lunch at noon. No one's seen him since eight a.m."

"Not answering his cell?"

"He doesn't carry one. Caleb checked the restaurant because sometimes his dad stays and works there, and his car's still in the parking lot, doors locked. No signs of his dad."

"It wouldn't take much to overpower him," Matt said. "I'm ninety seconds away."

He braked to a halt in the parking lot at the back of the building. Both phones in hand, he sprinted through the back door, shouldering aside officers in his haste to get to the team. Hawthorn, Sorenson, McCormick, and a couple more uniforms crowded into a conference room with Caleb Webber.

Caleb looked over Matt's shoulder. "Where's Eve?"

"Gone," Matt said, then set his phone down on the table.

"Jesus fucking Christ! You said you'd—" Caleb began, but the sound of Eve's voice echoing tinnily from Matt's phone cut him off mid-bellow.

"Where are we?" Matt could hear the fear running

under Eve's question. A car door slammed shut, then Eve said, "Is that the old Tyson plant?"

"Has she been relaying her position the whole time?" Lieutenant Hawthorn asked.

"Yes," Matt said. "She's dropping hints like bread crumbs, and there's long stretches of silence. Two Slices, Madame LaMoue, then a shooting that happened at Lassom Park." All heading toward the river, toward the maze of abandoned warehouses weighing down the East Side.

"Counselor, make a list of places your father could be," Hawthorn said. "We'll dispatch a squad car to check them out."

"Mom checked his appointment book. He wasn't due anywhere until this afternoon," Caleb said.

Sorenson stood in front of the large map of the East Side. "The Tyson plant is at Sixth and Harrison," she said as she tugged on a bulletproof vest.

"And before that, at First and Hancock," Caleb said, moving to stand beside her. He tapped an intersection an inch further north and east from Sorenson's. "Tyson moved operations in the nineties before they shut down. If they're deep in the alleys, Eve's not going to know exactly where she is. She's got a shit sense of direction."

Matt moved the phone to a safer location and searched for his size in the pile of gear on the table. Hawthorn and Sorenson were suiting up. McCormick and the other uniform were already in bulletproof vests, but McCormick was checking his equipment, patting his extra clip, turning down the volume on his radio.

"What's he doing down there?" Sorenson asked under her breath. "It's not near the projects."

Caleb surveyed this ratcheting up of firepower. "Isn't this the kind of situation for the SWAT team?"

"They're serving a warrant on a violent offender in north Lancaster," Hawthorn said.

McCormick woke up Hawthorn's laptop. "Is her phone GPS enabled?"

"Yes," Caleb said, still staring at Hawthorn. "You've only got one SWAT team?" he asked disbelievingly.

"Yes," Hawthorn said tersely, tuning his radio and staking claim to a channel. "A city this size barely justifies one team, and they all have other duties."

"What's her phone number?" McCormick asked.

Matt and Caleb rattled it off in unison. Caleb's eyes locked with his. "I'm coming with you."

"No, you're not," Hawthorn said.

"The hell I'm not. That's my *sister*," Caleb said, pointing at Matt's phone.

"I've got her," McCormick said, his gaze focused on the computer screen. "She's at First and Hancock."

"How accurate is the read?" Caleb asked.

"Depending on her phone and service, could be accurate to within inches, or it could be pinging off the nearest tower," Matt said.

"So she just as easily could be at Sixth and Harrison. That's a lot of territory in blind alleys. I grew up running those alleys. I know them better than anyone in this room," Caleb said.

"Regardless, you are not coming with us," Hawthorn said imperturbably.

Matt could see Caleb assessing his chances. There were six police officers in the room, and adrenaline was running high. "This won't help Eve," Matt said.

"She's my *sister*," he said again, helplessness twisting his features.

Sorenson looked over her shoulder. "How would you characterize your relationship with Murphy?" she asked.

Caleb blew out a deep breath and gave her a searing look. "What do you think, Detective? He hates my guts."

"Then you need to stay here," she said quietly. "Best-case scenario we resolve this quickly and without injury. Worst-case scenario, you can't help us deal with Murphy. Stay here. Please." And she turned back to the map.

"Which warehouse would Eve mean by 'the old Tyson plant'?" Matt asked Caleb.

He shook his head. "Either one."

Eve's voice rang out. "Where's Lyle, Travis?"

"Two targets," Hawthorn said, making eye contact with each of the officers to make sure they knew this. "Travis Jenkins and Lyle Murphy. Assume someone else was waiting for them at the warehouse, to make sure it was empty."

Caleb stared at the phone. "Travis's not answering. That's not good," he said. "He's an obsequious little suck and he'd lick Eve's boots if she'd let him. If he's gone silent, she doesn't matter anymore."

"Look, I don't know where I am, and I don't know where Lyle went. This is freaking me out a little." Matt could hear panic in Eve's voice. *Keep it together*, he thought, as much to himself as her. *You've got this.* "Is that the *Tribune*'s old production plant?"

"Sixth and Harrison," McCormick said. Two more uniformed officers had been rounded up after a trip to the city jail, briefed in low tones, and now focused intently on Matt's cell phone.

Still nothing from Travis.

Hawthorn and Caleb joined Matt and Sorenson in front of the map. "These are the old warehouses from the days when shipping along the river was as important as railroad, right?" Sorenson asked.

"Yes. They're all two-story warehouses," Caleb added,

obviously desperate to help. “Big. Lots of open space on the ground floor, maybe an office upstairs along one wall. They’ve been empty for years. If the redevelopment plan passes, they’re all razed for the business park.”

Matt tapped the corner of First and Hancock with his index finger. “I’m betting on this one,” he said. “The river.”

“Oh, that’s clever,” Sorenson breathed, eyes alight. “Old-school clever. You think they’re moving the drugs into the city via the river.”

“It’s a good strategy,” Matt said. “They drive the drugs to one of the state parks south of here, then move them upriver on fishing boats and unload into one of the warehouses at night, when no one’s around. We don’t patrol the river, so it’s less risky than driving through the city.”

“You don’t patrol the river?” Caleb said incredulously.

“Lost funding two years ago,” Hawthorn said without looking at him.

“I’m developing a strong opinion about the current bond issue,” Caleb muttered.

“Get out.”

The room went silent as everyone stared at Matt’s cell, relaying the drama unfolding in a back alley. There was a scuffling noise, then, “Ouch! Good grief, Lyle, take it easy!”

A rumble, slow then speeding up before clunking to a stop, obscured Eve’s next words. “Sounds like a garage door,” Hawthorn said.

“The loading docks down there all had big manual doors,” Caleb said. “We used to pop the locks off the doors and set up skateboard ramps inside until the cops ran us off.”

Matt shook his head in increasing frustration. "Still nothing that tells us which warehouse."

"She'd tell us if she could," Caleb bristled.

"I know she would," Matt snapped back, then took a deep breath. "But if we head to the wrong one—"

Caleb couldn't understand. Every second counted. Milliseconds counted. Sweeping the wrong warehouse would waste precious minutes, not to mention the possibility of losing the tactical advantage of surprise if someone saw them and called Lyle.

She could be beaten, raped, or killed on the filthy cement floor of an abandoned warehouse while he listened, unable to find her, helpless to stop it.

Hawthorn looked at Matt and Sorenson. "We go with Matt's instincts," Sorenson said. "First and Hancock."

"Dorchester, you're on the roof," Hawthorn said as he handed Matt a rifle, then pointed at the four uniformed officers. "You two take Harrison to the river and come up along the canal trail. You two, come around from the north," he said, pointing at the map to the alley running behind the warehouse at First and Harrison. "Let us know when that alley's secure. Sorenson, you're with Dorchester. McCormick, you're with me."

A logical division of duties, given that Matt achieved expert marksman status before he left the Army, and he'd kept up his skills. But he wasn't operating on logic. "Sir, put Sorenson on the roof," he said. "She's as good as I am, and I want point."

Caleb looked at Sorenson, both eyebrows raised. She met his eyes without flinching, then looked at Hawthorn. "I am," she confirmed.

"No," Hawthorn said.

"Sir." Matt fisted his hands on his hips, squared up, and looked his lieutenant right in the eye. "I want point."

Hawthorn heard Matt on multiple levels—Army, cop, man. His LT studied him for a moment, his gaze completely expressionless. "Sorenson, you're on the roof."

Matt swapped Sorenson the rifle for extra clips for his Glock and shoved them into his vest pocket.

"Lyle, who's that?" Fear made Eve's voice high, uncertain.

"Oh, no," Caleb said. His gaze locked with Matt's across the room. "No."

A laugh filtered into the room from Matt's cell phone, a low, derisive, mocking laugh, taking pleasure in her uncertainty and growing fear. Eve's voice rose, loud and panicked, and cut off his train of thought. "Oh my God!" she cried. "*Dad!*"

Eve stumbled across the cracked, dirty cement floor, twisting her heel on a loose chunk of concrete before falling to her knees at her father's side. The sun streamed through broken windows high above, light and shadow lying in jagged angles over him.

"Dad," she said again, reaching out to steady him. His face was waxy gray, the skin slack and shining with sweat. His arms trembled as he pushed himself up.

Lyle, circling the two of them, kicked and knocked her father's hand out from under his shoulder. He dropped heavily to the floor again, and this time made no move to get up.

"Stop it!" she screamed at Lyle over her shoulder. "Stop this right now! Do you hear me?"

Under the cover of hysterics, she slid her hand down her father's arm, the comforting move intended to cover transferring the cell phone to his palm. He pressed his palm to his chest, either to conceal the phone or assuage the pain.

"He had a heart attack last year," she continued, no need to fake the tremor or fear in her voice. "Please, let him go!"

In response Lyle spat on the floor by her father's head. "Ready to talk business, Evie?"

"First, let him go."

Lyle laughed. "You're in no position to negotiate, Evie. In fact, by the time we're done, you're going to be thinking of really creative ways to keep me happy. You think Mr. New Boyfriend's going to be okay with that?"

Her brain couldn't keep up, spinning wheels at seeing the terrifying emptiness in Lyle's eyes where a soul should be. It looked like something she should recognize, but she couldn't find the word. "Who?" she asked, distracted. Because she didn't have a new boyfriend. She had a cop.

He dropped to his heels beside her, and despite her tough façade she flinched back. "Not a good sign if you can't remember his name. Chad. He's in your bar, in your apartment. In your bed. So serious, so quickly," Lyle said, studying her face. "Are you in love with him?"

Evil. That was the word. Evil. After a lifetime of hearing about it in church, she was seeing it personified for the very first time. She controlled the impulse to look at the phone, still hidden in her father's palm. "Maybe," she said

"Maybe? The Eve I remember was either in love or not in love. So impetuous, all these whirlwind, passionate affairs. You were like something off a soap opera."

Heat rushed into her cheeks. "That was ten years ago. It was *high school,*" she snapped.

"Do you love him?" he said again.

The nearly inaudible words somehow drew Travis's attention from his position standing guard by the loading dock's door. Eve looked at him, wide-eyed and pleading. Maybe he wasn't having as much fun playing with the big boys as he thought he would. Maybe he'd help her.

Travis didn't move.

Dying in this warehouse was looking more and more likely. She didn't want the words to go unsaid. She knew the core of Matt Dorchester, and she loved that man. It didn't matter if he could love her back. She loved him. "Yes," she said quietly, "I love him, but he's got nothing to do with any of this."

Lyle dug his fingers into Eve's arm and dragged her to her feet. "You think Lancaster cops don't have something to do with this? Don't lie to me, Evangeline."

For the first time in her life, impulse compelled her to freeze. Still holding her, Lyle swung his gun, clenched in his fist, at her face. She screamed and ducked, heard her father's weak shout from the floor behind her. The blow glanced off the top of her skull. Lyle hauled her upright and stepped into his swing, this time with the full weight of his body behind his arm. When he connected, white-hot pain exploded under her eye, replacing her bones with a strange sense of weightlessness. Then the back of her head hit something hard and the world went black.

CHAPTER SIXTEEN

Matt hadn't driven so much as an unmarked police car in two years, had totally avoided driving anything that handled like a Crown Vic with the police package. He'd studied the way his fellow officers walked and talked, then trained himself to do the opposite. He'd crafted a smile, a stance, mannerisms and speech patterns that were as far from cop or ex-military as he could manage.

But when he heard the sound of something striking Eve Webber's flesh, heard her shocked cry of pain, an endless moment of silence, and then the scrape and thud of a body hitting cement, training took over. Lights and sirens switched to full wail, gas pedal floored, and within seconds he was doing eighty miles an hour down Thirteenth Street, Hawthorn and McCormick right behind him in another unmarked car, with the uniforms flanking them down Hancock, heading to cut off any escape at the river.

"What the *fuck* is going on?"

Hawthorn's furious question echoed in his ear, but Matt didn't bother to answer.

"Sounds like Murphy just hit Eve," Sorenson said into the radio. She had one foot braced against the floor, the other tucked under her as she loaded her vest with extra magazines, then ran the cord connecting her radio's handset under her arm and clipped it to her shoulder. She fitted her earpiece. Matt's earpiece was already in as he tracked the input from the car's radio, the earpiece, and Eve's voice all while maneuvering through traffic.

"Tell your partner to turn that fucking siren off when we hit the alleys."

"I heard him," Matt said. *Fuckfuckfuck!* Any more mistakes and Eve could pay with her life! He flicked the switch to cut the lights and sirens. When he swerved into the alley running perpendicular to the river and rolled to a halt at Second and Hancock, they hurled themselves out of the car.

Please God, let this be the right one. Let me be thinking clearly, logically. No emotion.

Hawthorn and McCormick pulled in behind them. Under a fire escape Matt laced his fingers together and braced himself. Sorenson put her foot in his cupped palms, her hands on his shoulders. On her count he boosted her to shoulder height. She pulled herself through the hole in the bottom of the fire escape, then reached down for the M4. With the carbine slung across her body she swarmed up the second flight of rusting iron stairs and disappeared onto the roof. Moving very lightly for such a bulky guy, McCormick jumped for the fire escape on the next building down, hauled himself through the opening, and took the stairs two at a time before hoisting himself over the wall, onto the roof.

Steadying his breathing, Matt waited with Hawthorn for Sorenson's voice over the radio.

"I'm in position," she said, low and calm. "Looks

like just Jenkins and Murphy. Pastor Webber's on the floor, Eve's about ten feet away from him, possibly unconscious."

"Weapons?"

Matt heard the click as Sorenson scanned the building through the high-powered scope. "Jenkins has a gun in his waistband. Murphy's holding a semiautomatic. No sign of anyone else."

"Confirmed," McCormick said.

"Do either of you have a shot?"

Through the connection to Eve's phone, Matt could hear footsteps. "No," Sorenson said, frustration obvious in her voice. "They just shifted position."

"Affirmative. I have the shot on Jenkins," McCormick said. "Murphy's pacing in and out of sight behind one of the big cement pillars in the middle of the floor."

Through the phone Matt heard Eve's sob as she achieved consciousness. Hawthorn pointed at himself and Matt, then at the front tires of the Escalade.

"You *bitch*! You were fucking a cop and lying to me!"

Anguish ate like acid at Matt's chest, but he used Lyle's raised voice as cover to dash behind the Escalade, Hawthorn close on his heels. They skidded to a halt on their knees in the dirt by the passenger-side wheel. The scent of heated rubber and grease seared into Matt's nostrils, the hot wheel burning his arm as he pressed against it.

"He's a cop?" Eve said in a dazed voice. "Wow. I didn't know. Good thing you found out when you did."

Matt had spent a fair share of his professional life crouching in the dust and dirt behind various impenetrable objects—vehicles, walls and berms, sandbag barricades—his mind usually empty except for awareness of the progress of sweat down the length of his spine and whatever snippet of song he had stuck in his head. In this moment, behind this particular tire, one completely out of context phrase from of all things, the Bible, floated to the top of his brain.

You reap what you sow. And he'd sowed nothing but dispassionate deception. He'd doomed any possibility of a real relationship with Eve Webber the moment he walked through the door to Eye Candy as Chad Henderson. For the first time since he met her, the right thing to do was clear.

Save her, then let her go.

"What?" Lyle yelled.

"I'd never work with a cop, Lyle. The Eastern Precinct's as dirty as the men's room floor. We all know that." Matt heard her gasp in pain. She must have sat up, moved her head, all while still trying to find a way to save their operation. They'd underestimated her from the very beginning. "The bastards. They didn't even ask. Just put someone in undercover. I can't believe it. Good thing I didn't let him come upstairs," she said, delaying, giving Matt time to get to her. Smart, tough woman.

"East Side girl like you? You should have known!"

"I'm new at this, Lyle," she said, bone-tired. "Cut me some slack, okay?"

Lyle laughed, the noise almost relieved, and for a second Matt thought she'd managed to talk her way out clear. Then his phone went silent for a second, leaving only the echoing noise of the laugh inside the warehouse.

"What happened?" Sorenson's low voice over the radio.

"McCormick, report," Hawthorn said soundlessly. "You have line of sight."

"What's that noise, Eve?" The audio was back, and Lyle's voice was menacing again. "Show me your—"

The audio went dead again, and with a sickening flash of clarity, Matt knew what was happening. The battery on Eve's phone, left uncharged the night before, was beeping the low battery signal. Each time it beeped, he lost audio for a second. Lyle heard the beeps.

"Her phone's dying," Matt murmured.

He got one foot under him to start around the end of the Escalade, but Hawthorn gripped his vest and held him back. "Not without the back door cleared!"

"Show me your hands, Eve."

"Why?"

"He's aiming at her," McCormick said urgently. "LT!"

"Where the fuck are they?" Matt growled at Hawthorn, referring to the uniformed officers they needed to secure the back alley, to make sure they didn't get caught in the crossfire.

"Show me your fucking *hands*!" A slap, then a cry from Eve, cut off as the audio went dead again.

Fuck this. Matt twisted, trying to shake off Hawthorn's grip on his flak vest.

"Are you in position?" Hawthorn snapped into the radio.

The excited voice of the young uniformed officer came over the radio in a high-pitched whisper. "We're by the side door at the back of the building. It's clear!"

"Where's your goddamn phone? That fucking thing you've always got with you! Where—do you have it?" The sound of scuffling, cries of pain from Pastor Webber and screams of sheer terror from Eve, then, "You stupid fucking cunt!" rang cold and bitter into Matt's ear as clear as if Murphy stood right next to him. A single gunshot rang out as Hawthorn shouted into the radio.

"Go!"

Sprawled on her back in the dirt, Eve saw a red mist balloon around Travis as he jerked a hundred and eighty degrees in place, then dropped to the floor. Then Matt and Hawthorn sprinted from around the Escalade's front end, shouting "Down! Down on the floor! Now! Get down!" at what must have been the top of their lungs but sounded like it was coming from across a crowded, noisy club. The back door flew open and two police officers swarmed down the stairs to the loading dock, onto the open floor, adding their voices to the increasingly distant cacophony.

She crawled to her father's side and rolled him onto his back. He was paper white, eyes closed, mouth lax. "Dad?" she asked, but the question transformed into a scream of pain as she was hauled to her feet by a fist in her hair. She twisted her ankle trying to get her footing in the heels.

"Looking for this?" he snarled, spinning her in a stumbling circle to face Matt and Hawthorn. He shook her by her hair like a dog shook a toy, sending pain spearing through her cheek and behind her eye before he pulled her tight against his body. "Back the fuck up."

"Let her go," Matt said, steely command in his voice.

"Fuck you," Lyle spat.

Matt and Hawthorn were slowly separating, flanking Lyle, giving him two targets, dividing his attention. He stepped back and jammed steel into her throat. Eve fought back a cry as her teeth clunked together and thick, hot waves of pain burst through her injured cheek.

"Let her go. Drop your weapon. Get down on the ground." This from Hawthorn, to her right. On her left Matt had gone silent, his face eerily calm.

Lyle jerked her around to face Matt. "Was she good? So smooth and pretty. A nice little bonus after a long day's work?"

A professional career in bars taught Eve the basics of getting out of a man's grip. She rammed her elbow into his gut and stomped on his instep with all the power she could put into the four-inch spike heel. It was amateurish but efficient; he yelped and released her hair, inadvertently sweeping her feet out from under her as he doubled over and lifted his injured foot. Eve thudded down hard on her bottom and hands, but she was free.

"Down! Get *down*!"

Male voices shouted, but not Matt's. Eve looked at him, but he was focused on Lyle, silent and deadly, gaze and aim never faltering. Eve scuttled away as Lyle swung around and pointed the gun at her, the face she knew completely disfigured by a twisted snarl. She kept moving but the gun tracked her as she scrambled backward, up against her father's body.

Then, as his finger tightened around the trigger, a sound ricocheted around the vast warehouse. The back of Lyle's head disappeared in a spray of brain, scalp, blood, and bone. He slumped to the ground in front of her.

A scream formed in her lungs, clawing at her throat, but emerged as the strangled whimper of a nightmare. Matt darted forward, his weapon trained on Lyle, while he kicked Lyle's gun to the corner of the warehouse. Then he dropped to his knees by Eve and holstered his weapon.

"Oh my God," she said. "Matt. Oh my God."

"Shhhh," he said. "It's okay." He was turning her father over as he said it, his fingers feeling for his pulse. "We need an ambulance!" he shouted.

"They're en route," Sorenson said. She knelt over Travis, fingers to his throat, holding his jacket over the bullet wound in his shoulder. Officer McCormick was directing the uniforms to kick open every door in the warehouse, searching for anyone hiding from the police.

"Dad." Her father's eyes were closed, his skin clammy and paste white against the dirty floor. Eve gripped his hand in both of hers and gave it a little shake. "Dad, it's over. Matt's here, with other police officers. You're safe. Just hold on a little longer."

He squeezed her hands. The ambulance lumbered down the alley behind yet another cruiser and braked to a halt next to the Escalade. Two EMTs leapt out of the cab and sprinted into the warehouse. Sorenson pointed to each body in turn. "Heart attack. Gunshot wound to the shoulder. Dead."

An EMT dropped to his heels by her father and snapped on gloves, then did a double take when he saw Eve. "I've got her," Matt said. He slid his arm under hers and helped her to her feet, guiding her out the warehouse door into the sun.

"But Dad—" she started.

"They've got him. They need space to work."

He gently helped her sit at the edge of the open ambulance door, then pulled a blanket off a shelf and wrapped it around her shoulders.

"I don't need a blanket. It's a hundred and five degrees," she said. The sun beat down on the alley and on her head. Maybe that was causing the blurry vision, the shimmering sense of unreality.

"When the adrenaline wears off you're going to be shivering," Matt explained.

"I remember," she said, fumbling at the blanket with shaking hands, then pulling it tight. "But I don't feel anything. For the first time in my life, I don't feel anything at all. Is that shock? I felt something after the first shooting. I was angry and scared. I felt *something*." She looked at him, heard her voice rising. "Do you live like this? How do you live with nothing inside you?"

Matt put his hands on her shoulders, his warm fingers curving around to squeeze gently as he peered into her eyes. "You're alive. Your father's alive. Murphy's dead. It's okay now."

With a shuddering sigh she subsided. Matt reached out and tucked her hair behind her ear. He laid gentle fingers along her jaw and exerted just enough pressure to turn her head so he could look at her face. The impact site throbbed, and in her peripheral vision Eve could see the reddened swelling skin. Matt pressed gentle thumbs to the edges of her swelling cheek, testing the bone, then found an ice pack and cracked it to activate it.

"Hold this," he said, his voice eerily quiet and calm.

"Okay," she said, and put the pack to her cheek.

"You'll need X-rays," he added as he dug through a kit and extracted a pair of tweezers. With gentle fingers he began to dislodge the bits of concrete embedded in her right knee.

"Okay," she said again, because what else could she say when he wasn't saying anything? "How are you?"

"That's my line," he said, but Eve couldn't laugh.

"You just killed someone," she said. His gaze flicked up, and she filled in the rest of the black, black comedy. "Not your first time at that rodeo either, is it?"

Oh, Matt. What do you do with it all, with the horror and terror and exhaustion, with the daily grind, with Iraq and Luke and undercover police work? Where does it go?

"What happened?" he asked.

"I was expecting a package. The UPS guy always drops it, knocks, then takes off. I heard the knock and opened the door. Lyle must have told the delivery driver he'd bring it up for him."

"So you went with him?"

"He had a gun! You were in the shower! You were *naked,*" she said, as if this was obvious.

He gave her a look, just a look.

"This is where you tell me you have a black belt in karate and are expert in hand-to-hand combat."

"I would have stopped him from taking you."

"Or died trying," she finished for him.

"Better me than you." *Because I'm already half dead.*

"That's not how I see it." Because half dead is half alive. "Half" meant room for hope, room for a second chance.

No response. She looked around the increasingly crowded open space between the alley and the warehouse as more police cruisers, unmarked cars, and a fire truck pulled up. Sorenson trotted over and gave Eve what was left of her iPhone. She clasped the pieces with shaking hands and watched Travis get loaded into the second ambulance. "You didn't . . . ?"

"Kill him? No. When Lyle aimed at you, Travis stepped toward you and McCormick got him in the shoulder, not the chest. I think he was trying to stop Lyle, and it saved his life."

Sorenson moved away to supervise Travis's trip to the hospital. Eve considered her ruined iPhone. "He shot my phone. I run my entire life through this phone and now it's got a bullet hole in it."

"I thought he shot you."

"I thought he was going to shoot me." She stared at the phone for a moment, then felt the hair on the nape of her neck lift. "You got my call." Obviously.

"Yes."

"That's how you knew where I was."

"Yes."

Keep going, as painful as it is . . . "You heard me tell Lyle I love you."

He bent over a particularly stubborn piece of grit. "You were under duress," he said evenly.

"Yes," she said. "That's happened to me quite a bit lately. But I know how I feel."

He said something she couldn't understand over the wail of another police cruiser pulling into the already cramped space. The ambulance driver leaned out his door, gave a piercing whistle even Natalie would envy and shouted, "Move! We gotta go!"

"This isn't real, Eve," he finished, picking bits of gravel out of her knees like each one was a tiny bomb requiring precision handling.

"Last night was as real as you've ever been with me, Matt," she said bluntly. "I can handle that. I can handle more."

"It's not real," he said, as if she hadn't spoken. "You can't trust your feelings in a situation like this. Close proximity, stressful circumstances, and sex all combine to create an unreal environment. You can't trust it."

"How do you know whether or not you can trust your feelings if you don't let yourself feel anything at all? You use protecting as a way to push people away. You wall us off, say you're keeping us safe, but you're really keeping yourself safe from the messy emotional reality of life and love." When he didn't respond she slapped his hands away from her abused knees. "Stop taking care of me! Stop hiding behind duty and honor and feel what's between us!"

At that urgent command he looked up and met her eyes. She saw the implacable wall going back up, shutting her out, then he said the word he'd never, ever used before.

"No."

She blinked at him, not believing her ears, but just

then Lieutenant Hawthorn and Officer McCormick strode up. "Jesus, Eve," Ian said. "Are you all right?"

"Ian," she replied, just as formal if a little more hysterical, "I'm fine."

"She's not fine. She needs x-rays and maybe an MRI," Matt said as he flung another bit of gravel to the side.

"And you, Detective Dorchester, need to go with Officer McCormick and report in to Captain Whitmore," Hawthorn said implacably.

Eve followed his glance to a group of uniformed officers, clustered around Sorenson and Carlucci, all watching Matt as he knelt in front of her. He dropped the tweezers on the ambulance floor and stood up. Her face throbbed as she tilted her head back to look up into his eyes. "Don't go to work for Lancaster Life. You are right where you're supposed to be. You are who you're supposed to be. Without you, Lyle sets up shop on the East Side, the neighborhood loses the business park, and the bad guys win. No one else could have done what you've done over the last few weeks. Don't let anyone tell you different, and don't let anyone guilt or bully or pressure you into becoming anyone else."

Then he turned and walked away.

Eve woke up in a hospital bed. A pair of sneaker-clad feet rested near her own, covered by a white sheet and blanket. Very, very carefully, because her head felt like it had been split in two, she turned and looked up the long, denim-clad legs to Caleb's solemn face.

"Hello, sister mine," he said, relief flashing in his green eyes.

"Hey," she said, but her throat was too dry and tight to get the words out. Caleb sat up and poured a glass of water, competently folding a bendy straw and dropping it in the glass, then offering it to her.

"Nice technique," she complimented after she drank. They'd spent more than their share of time in hospital rooms.

He leaned an elbow on the bed and considered her. "How are you feeling?"

"My cheek hurts," she said. The throbbing worsened as her attention found it, like a bad-tempered troll and his rough-hewn club had taken up residence, lumbering and grumbling under her eye.

"I'm not surprised," Caleb replied. "From what I gathered from Detective Sorenson's terse yet colorful description, Lyle hit you so hard you went airborne."

"I . . . I vaguely remember that." All she really remembered was the explosion of light and pain, then lying in the dirt next to her father. She listened to the silence in the corridor, looked at the old-fashioned clock, then the window. "It's the middle of the night. What are you doing here?"

"Sitting with the sick, comforting the afflicted," he said casually. "It's better than my other option, which is to find Ian Hawthorn and beat the shit out of him."

She laughed, then regretted it when the troll took a big swing at her cheekbone with his club. "It's not Ian's fault. I went into this with my eyes wide open."

Caleb was silent. Eve figured Ian could hold his own. "I have good news," he said.

"I could use some good news."

"Nobody showed up to make payment for the property behind Eye Candy. It's yours."

"That *is* good news," she said, but really, she couldn't feel much of anything. In a day or two she'd get excited about it. "How's Dad?"

"Down the hall and scheduled for bypass surgery," Caleb said.

"What?" she exclaimed, regretting it as the troll added a vicious kick.

"I guess one side benefit from all of this is that the doctors took a really good look at his arteries. They've been clogging faster than expected. You make an impact, no doubt about it."

She lay back and closed her eyes. "I work with the cops for three months and I get Dad and me kidnapped, and a man is dead, and now Dad has another heart attack."

"Don't forget Travis getting shot."

She'd never forget Travis's silence as he drove her through the East Side, to the warehouse. Forgiveness felt very far away. "How is Travis?" she asked, trying for Christian charity.

"Two doors down from Dad, recovering from a gunshot wound to the shoulder, with an extremely bored uniformed cop sitting outside his door."

She couldn't laugh, but she did muster a weak smile.

"Sorenson and Hawthorn were both here, but one cop, however, is conspicuous in his absence. Where's Dorchester? I figured he'd have to be pried from your side with a crowbar."

"He's gone." At Caleb's single raised eyebrow, she added, "Between the siren and the ice pack crackling I was a little distracted, but I put the pieces together in the ambulance. He said something about Stockholm, and this isn't real."

Clearly mystified, Caleb blinked, then gave a sharp bark of laughter that reverberated in Eve's cheek. "Stockholm syndrome, or a variation thereof. Under considerable emotional stress some hostages form attachments to their captors, although the analogy doesn't hold in your situation."

"He thinks what I feel for him isn't real."

Her brother sat forward, elbows on knees. "Maybe he's right."

The apocalypse must be on its way if Caleb was agreeing with a cop, even a cop who saved two members of his family from certain death. "Who are you, and what have you done with my brother?" she asked.

"He's right. It's not real, Eve, what happened over the last few weeks. It's a bizarre interlude in your life."

"I know that, Caleb, but that doesn't make the feelings any less real," she said evenly. "I love him. He feels something too, but he won't admit it. I think I scare him."

"You scare the hell out of me," her brother said, then the smile disappeared. "Oh, Eve."

Hot tears trickled into the bandage on her cheek, and her sinuses swelled and throbbed under her bruised cheek. "It hurts when I cry," she said shakily.

"I don't doubt it," he said. "You've got one hell of a shiner. The doctor said you're lucky you don't have a fractured eye socket."

"That's not what I mean," she said, and reached for the box of tissues on the nightstand.

Caleb shut his mouth, shifted onto the bed, and held her while she cried.

Matt stood in the basement, sunlight filtering through the dirty casement windows onto the dusty pile of stereo equipment. He had a decision to make. To do that he had to get very clear about who he was and what he wanted. Boxing no longer brought clarity, and only a fool continued to use ineffective tactics. So the first step was to bring speakers, tuner, and disc changer up from the basement.

It took two trips, but eventually the relics from an archeological dig into the late twentieth century sat on the floor in the corner by the entertainment center. The cables were still attached to the components. He plugged them in, pushed the main power button, inserted a disc at random, and pressed play. Nothing. He pulled all the cords out and licked them—a trick he'd learned wiring radios on patrol—plugged them in again. The slow guitar chords from Foreigner's "I Want to Know What Love Is" blasted out into the living room. Matt put his hands on his hips and let the music wash over muscle and bone held too tight for too long. When the song ended and the disc spun to the Violent Femmes he opened his laptop, grabbed a CD at random from the shelves behind the television, and inserted it into the disc drive to import. It would take a while, but he had time. He was on desk duty until the department cleared his role in the shooting death of Lyle Murphy, and he'd used the time wisely. A new AC unit would go in next week.

He was sitting with his back to the wall, watching the sun set and listening to Pearl Jam's "Given to Fly" when he saw Luke roll up the ramp. His brother opened the door and braked to a stop by the recliner, a pile of mail on his lap.

"I heard music when I pulled into the driveway and thought I had the wrong house," Luke said, looking around at the controlled chaos spread over the living and dining rooms. "Damn, Matt. I haven't seen you like this since you were in high school and Dad was riding your ass, and you'd shut yourself in your room for hours. Remember?"

One corner of his mouth lifted in a smile. Luke had been a scrawny little squirt, eight, maybe nine years old, completely unable to sit still for more than fifteen seconds at a stretch. He'd try to play it cool, study the album artwork or read the lyrics like Matt did, but after a while he'd just wriggle under Matt's arm and listen. There was no physical affection in the house; his father said it would weaken the boys, and his mother never disobeyed his father. Matt learned not to care, but Luke was wired differently. He'd been starving for cuddles, hugs, anything. Luke soaked up the simple comfort of sitting on the floor together as much as he'd soaked up Matt's taste in music.

"Yeah," Matt said. "You'd come in and we'd share the headphones. You'd pick a song, then I'd pick a song." Luke always picked songs he knew Matt liked.

"You always picked songs you knew I liked," Luke said, echoing Matt's thoughts. They'd been so close as kids, despite their age difference. "Those were my best memories from childhood. I've missed that, you know. You've been here every day, doing the right thing, but I've missed my brother."

At Luke's words, a boulder swelled in his rib cage, crushing heart, lungs, forcing rock into his throat. He breathed against it, waited it out, and slowly the weight rolled back.

Jesus. He'd survived eighteen months in a war zone and two shootouts in two weeks, and the intensity of the emotion swamping him might kill him.

"Yeah," he said. "I can see how you'd feel that way." He'd been so focused on being strong for everyone around him he'd never given people what they needed most. Emotion. Affection. Love.

"What brought this on?" Luke said, idly rubbing his shoulder.

"After what happened, I thought it would help," he said. This was true. Music was a way to express emotion, desire, and maybe if he let the music do his feeling for him, he'd find a way through the persistent, unrelenting ache in his heart.

The process was still somewhat automatic, his hands pulling out a CD he hadn't listened to in years, only to find that some song, even a phrase in a song, a guitar riff, something about the singer's breathing on a live recording, even, would ease some of the tightness in his chest.

He missed Eve. He'd counted on the memories associated with her receding by now, but instead he saw her everywhere, in the kitchen, on the sofa, at the dining room table.

In his bed.

"You mean the shootout?" Luke asked. His voice was tentative, flashing Matt back to childhood. Luke was using the same tone of voice they used with their father, hesitant, probing for the signs of a good day, a good conversation, a chance to be a normal family. Luke was using that voice on him.

"Among other things," Matt hedged. Early morning shadows on the pillows became a black spill of hair. The breeze in the trees in his peripheral vision transformed shifting contours into a soft, slender body, tantalizingly just out of sight. He no longer had to layer identities when he woke up, but now he would swear he felt her right beside him, heat and softness, breathing deep.

The music helped deal with the day-to-day strain of the job, but the wild creature still lurked inside the prison of his rib cage. Sometimes he put in a two-hour workout to wear out the frantic thing, but at least now he knew what he was fighting.

He was fighting loneliness. But the weakness of feeling lonely only jeopardized him. All the risk was his. No one else got hurt.

"Just get off work?" Matt asked absently, ejecting

Paul Simon's *Graceland* and sliding in *They Might Be Giants*. The disc spun, giving off a high-pitched whir as the tracks began to import.

"Yeah. My last day. I gave them my notice and told them to give my scheduled hours to the other tech." Matt must have looked completely sandbagged because Luke couldn't keep a smile from spreading across his face. "My chemistry professor left teaching at the end of the year for fulltime research with Genedac Pharmaceuticals. He needed a research assistant and asked me if I wanted the job. I did."

"In Chicago?" Matt asked.

"Their R&D facility in Austin. The pay's good. Really good. Good benefits and the temperature rarely drops below forty in Austin. After I get settled I'm going to help pay off the medical bills."

"No, you're not," Matt said automatically. "The accident wasn't your fault. There's no reason for you to pay off those bills."

"It wasn't your fault either, but you're paying them."

He looked at his brother. Really looked at him, for the first time in a very long time. "Fine. Send me a check every month."

"As they say, my brother didn't raise no fool. I'd do that if you deposited any of the checks I've written you up to this point. No, sir. I'm sending checks straight to the med center's billing department. Besides, you don't get a new AC unit in this house and Eve's never going to want to spend the night," Luke said.

"That's over."

"Let me get this straight. You had a relationship with her when it probably violated whole sections of the department's code of conduct, but when it's all over and you can be with her, you walk away?"

"I lied to her. She pretended to be my girlfriend so

we could trap a drug dealer, who then kidnapped and nearly killed her. None of it bears any resemblance to real life," he finished.

"Dad took us out to look at Christmas lights and a five-time DUI offender takes the curve on the Thirty-Sixth Street on-ramp too fast for the conditions and Mom and Dad die and I'm in this chair. That's life. It's unpredictable. Uncontrollable. You took a shower. She answered the door for the UPS guy. That's what people do, Matt. Shitstorms happen. It's what you do after the storm ends that matters." Luke waited a minute. "That's your specialty, so I thought you knew that."

"She doesn't need me. She's surrounded by family and friends and all the people who love Eye Candy. Her brother's got a mediator waiting in the wings when she's ready to date again."

"Let's think about that for a second," Luke said.

Let's not. "She doesn't need me to clean up after this."

"Yeah," his brother said, the sarcasm of youth dripping from his words. "A woman that involved in East Side community activism doesn't need to watch her back. Lightning won't strike twice in the same place. Probably she'll never get kidnapped or shot at again, but she'll be making waves until the day she dies—"

"Ninety years from now, in her bed, from extreme old age."

"—so there's no good reason for her to get involved with a cop. Except maybe she likes you. You can be likeable enough when you come out of that I'm-in-control-of-everything armor." His brother heaved a disgusted sigh. "Matt, has it ever occurred to you that maybe it's not only freaking annoying but unhealthy to frame every relationship in the context of service and duty? That was good for the Army and the department, but not for you?"

Matt kept his focus on the stacks of CDs.

"That maybe the people who love you want to take care of you as much as you want to take care of them? That maybe you hurt us a little more every day when you treat us like your responsibilities, but won't let us help you?"

Direct hit to the sternum. Breath and pulse halted as he locked eyes with Luke. Again, Matt broke first, looked away from the perceptiveness in his younger brother's eyes.

"You want her. You need her. And that spooks you."

He didn't just need her. He loved her. He didn't have a choice in the matter. He loved her. Going back to the way he used to be wasn't going to happen. Going forward terrified him. He balanced on the edge of a bottomless chasm, the gulf yawning at his feet, the ground crumbling behind him and no bridge in sight.

He gave a half-shrug, pretended to check on the import progress.

"What are you going to do once you've got all that on your computer?" Luke asked. "Which, for the record, is going to take days."

"Transfer it to my phone. Yes, I do know how to use iTunes," he said, when Luke opened his mouth.

"Mail call," Luke said, and handed him an envelope.

The envelope was postmarked in Lancaster. The return address was Eye Candy's. He slit the top of the package with his pocketknife and opened the envelope. Wrapped inside a sheet of stationery was a folded piece of paper, a CD case, and a section of newsprint.

He picked up the newsprint first. It was a column from the Metro section of the paper announcing the decision to go ahead with the redevelopment project, and

Mobile Media's commitment to the new business park. The sidebar announced the demolition of the building across the alley from Eve and welcomed the community to a demolition party to view the redevelopment plans and meet some of the business owners, politicians, and executives involved.

The picture of Eve showed a fading bruise on her cheekbone and a serious glint in her eye. Also pictured for the story were the East Side's city councilwoman, the deputy mayor, Eve's father, and the CEO of Mobile Media.

The city's sexiest cocktail waitress was gone, and in her place was a squared-up, dead-serious community activist.

"Let me see," Luke said.

He handed the clipping to his brother, and picked up the plastic case. The CD inside was neatly labeled PREP PLAYLIST.

"How did she know?" he muttered.

"Magic," Luke said knowingly.

Matt unfolded the sheets of paper, then scanned them, trying to make sense of the ads, the bar code, the name Maud Ward.

"They're concert tickets, doofus," Luke said.

"And backstage passes," Matt replied, still not believing his eyes. Two tickets to the upcoming Maud Ward concert. The sold-out homecoming concert. On the floor, six rows from the stage. He'd be close enough to watch her change chords.

"No fucking way," Luke said, leaning forward to snatch the paper from Matt's hand.

"Easy with that," Matt said, handing it over hastily.

"How did she get backstage passes to Maud Ward's homecoming concert?" Luke marveled, scanning every inch of the page.

"Eve knows her," Matt said casually, like it was no big deal. Like Eve's way of living, doing favors, big heart, paying it forward, wasn't everything he was missing, everything he'd ever wanted, and thought he couldn't have. "She got Maud some local gigs when she was just starting out."

"Dude. Two tickets. You have to take her."

"She's not like that. She wouldn't give me tickets in the hopes I'd take her. Besides, she can get her own tickets."

Luke just looked at him until Matt had to break eye contact. He opened the folded sheet of stationery last.

Dear Matt,

Music matters too much to do without it. I've gotten you started with the prep playlist, but as we both know, live music is the best. It's going to be an amazing concert. I hope you enjoy it.

Love, Eve

Sometimes you reap more than you sow. Sometimes, despite all efforts to the contrary, you reap love.

He'd walked away from her, believing it was the right thing for her, for him, for them. And she'd still sat down at her computer and made him an old-fashioned mix CD of all the songs they'd listened to while he'd fallen in love with the woman he thought he couldn't have. He ejected *They Might Be Giants,* inserted the CD into the drive, and watched the list of artists appear in iTunes. Blanket, Damien Rice, Anjulie, Maud Ward, 3 Doors Down, Alexi Murdoch.

Even now, weeks after he'd walked away from her at the warehouse, she was thinking about him. Giving him the joyful things in life—concerts, music, a chance to share good times with friends. A life of duty and honor was empty without music and laughter and love.

"Earth to Matt," Luke said.

A flash of black shifted at the edge of his vision. Intellectually he knew it was the wind in the big oak in the backyard dappling the shadows across the counters. Deep inside, he knew it was Eve.

And he knew what he had to do.

CHAPTER SEVENTEEN

"That's it for me," Hannah Rafferty said, closing her reporter's notes for a softer, follow-up piece on Eve and community leaders seizing the momentum to redevelop the East Side. She shut off the recorder on her phone, and looked at the photographer. "Got what you need?"

"The light's better over there," he said, gesturing to the setting sunlight pouring through the storeroom's open doorway. Eve straightened her suit jacket, then braced a shoulder against the doorframe and folded her arms, going for "determined" and "resourceful" despite Caleb hovering on the sidelines. He wore his best lawyer face, poker serious, protective. Eve found herself mirroring his look as the photographer took a few shots of her gazing at the camera, then a couple more from another angle that captured Eve studying the dust rising from the rubble behind Eye Candy. "Great. We're good now," he said, scanning through the images on his camera.

"Thanks so much for the interview," Eve said.

Hannah shouldered her bag. "It's important work," she answered.

"Where will this run?" Eve asked. "The last time you did a feature on me it was for the Arts and Culture section."

Hannah smiled. "Depends on the space available. If we have the inches, it'll run as a feature on the front page, more likely the Metro section due to the community activist angle. If not, you'll be back in Arts and Culture."

"Right," Eve said, trying to be grateful for any coverage at all. Despite being unable to reveal significant details thanks to the ongoing investigation, the sordid elements of guns, drugs, and two police shootings meant the basics of the story made the front page of the Lancaster *Times-Herald* for several days. Determined to milk the last possible drop of beneficial coverage from the incident, the politicians showed up for the photo op and spouted community-oriented quotes they hoped would be worked into the coverage.

"We've got to run," Hannah said. "Deadline's in two hours."

"Thanks again," Eve said, and showed them to the front door. When she returned to the storeroom, Caleb stood feet braced and hands in his pockets, admiring the ruins.

"When's all this cleared out?" he asked idly.

"Tomorrow," she said. Tomorrow the remains of the building would be hauled away, and in the spring, her dream of a patio would become a reality.

It was amazing what could happen when a community mobilized around a common goal. Her parents had attended the demolition ceremony, along with Caleb and Quinn, representatives from a number of community organizations, the VP of Community Engagement for Mobile Media, board members from the SCC, the East Side's city councilwoman, and the community relations liaison from the police department. An East Side landscaping company offered to do the brick patio at a steep discount in exchange for a tasteful banner mentioning their work and a few mentions on social networking sites. The city's last remaining ironwork shop offered the same deal for the railing. As word spread on Twitter and Facebook, every known band in the city contacted her for a gig next summer. Maud Ward agreed to open the summer concert series to kick off the tour for her new album. Eve's mother had not only volunteered to put her master gardener skills to use at Eye Candy to design and maintain the oversized flowering pots that would line the wrought iron fence, she also put together a team from the Lancaster Garden Club to mentor East Side teens and families interested in caring for a series of planters lining Thirteenth Street.

Not once did she mention Eve's job or single status.

But despite all the press for Eye Candy, Eve had seen neither hide nor hair of Matt Dorchester in the three weeks since she'd climbed into the ambulance transporting her father to the hospital, and she wouldn't push. She was a lifelong Eastie with a thriving business. He knew where to find her, if he wanted to.

The fall breeze caught Caleb's red silk tie. He smoothed it down. "Are you the first person on the East Side to organize a demolition party?"

She smiled. "Maybe," she said. "I hope I'm not the last."

He gave her a quick look. "Sleeping any better?"

"A little." Half her dreams were of the business end of a semiautomatic pistol, of the gun clenched in Lyle's fist and swinging at her head, of her father's pale, clammy face. Loud noises made her jump. The bruise on her face got double takes at the bank and the supermarket, concerned inquiries from customers, and when the whole story broke in the news, a flood of publicity that took days to handle, which was fine, because she wasn't sleeping much anyway.

For the first time in weeks, standing outside was a pleasant activity. Summer's heat and threat were both gone, replaced by fall's crisp air and deep blue skies, and a sense of possibility for the East Side's revitalization. Before the demolition ceremony she'd gone out to pick up the sandwiches donated by Henry from Two Slices, and cupcakes donated by Cindy's Cinful Cupcakes. According to Henry and Cindy, traffic was up at both locations, and optimism and purpose infused the East Side's main shopping district. For a moment, for just one moment in her afternoon, she let herself savor the victory.

Heels tapped briskly across the storeroom's cement floor, too brisk to be Natalie. Eve and Caleb turned in unison to find Sorenson behind them, wearing a navy suit the same shade as Caleb's.

"Hi," Eve said. "Thanks again for coming to the demo ceremony. It meant a lot to me."

"It was a good chance to get reacquainted with some of the community leaders," Sorenson said. "We're looking into the matter we discussed a few weeks ago."

The corruption festering in the Eastern Precinct. Caleb perked up, but Eve didn't give anything away. "I'm glad to hear it. I'll do what I can to help."

Sorenson's visit wasn't her first, or the only, from a member of the Lancaster Police Department. Lieutenant Hawthorn, Captain Whitmore, and several stone-faced officers from Internal Affairs had visited at other times, all asking the same questions about the shooting at the warehouse, and with the exception of Sorenson and Lieutenant Hawthorn, all carefully probing to see how she intended to portray the department in the upcoming media storm. Her responses to any and all questions followed the same basic script: "The Lancaster Police Department and the East Side citizens worked together in unprecedented and productive ways to stop a threat to our community. We hope that this is a sign of continued engagement and partnership."

"Care to clue me in?" Caleb said mildly, turning an inquisitive eye to Eve.

"That's up to Detective Sorenson," Eve said.

Caleb turned to Sorenson and lifted his eyebrows.

"I think not, Counselor," Sorenson said in a tone as smooth as silk. She shot Caleb a look obscured to Eve by the setting sun, but something about it made her brother go still. "Keep in touch, Eve."

"You too, Jo," Eve replied.

"How come you're 'Eve' and I'm 'Counselor'?" Caleb asked after she left.

"I didn't come on to her in front of her male lieutenant and colleagues," Eve answered. "Matt told me once that he'd never hit on her because if he did, he'd be dead to her. I'd say you're dead to her. Regretting your runaway mouth for once in your life?"

"There's no such thing as a lost cause," Caleb said, still staring at the doorway into the bar. "Speaking of Detective Dorchester . . ."

The name hung in the air for a second before Eve could breathe in and answer. "No, I haven't seen him," she said evenly.

"He's an idiot," Caleb said matter-of-factly.

"No, he isn't," Eve countered. "When he does something, when he commits, he commits forever, and with everything in him. He takes his responsibilities seriously. I love that about him." She paused but kept her gaze trained on the rubble filling her alley. "I love him. But I don't want to be an obligation. I want to be his partner, his lover, someone who helps him shoulder his burdens. If he can't let me in, then I'll just have to move on."

Caleb had no response to that, and she was grateful. She missed Matt so much she ached, and while the bruise was fading, her longing wasn't.

Her brother turned to go, then said, "I almost forgot. No dinner tonight. Mom caught me as they were getting in the car and said Dad's too tired from all the talking. He needs to rest. We should come over for lunch later in the week."

"Fine by me," she said. "I could use a night off."

He bent and kissed the top of her head. "Take care, sister mine."

Silence settled into the storeroom after Caleb left. The package with the concert tickets and the newspaper announcement should have arrived three days ago, but she hadn't expected him to come to the demolition. The gift was for her as much as for him. It was closure, or it would be, when she felt it.

Behind her she heard the *scritch-thump-scritch-thump* of hard-soled shoes. Natalie, who'd stayed behind on her day off to handle the cleanup process while Eve finished off the last of the interviews. She'd buy Nat tickets to the New Kids on the Block reunion concert as thanks, maybe even go with her.

"Check out that view, Nat," she said with a quick peek over her shoulder. "It's—"

"Beautiful" died on her tongue as a tall, broad-shouldered figure disappeared from the light of the bar into the storeroom's darkness. Her heart leapt in recognition, fierce joy surging inside her, but in a split second her brain discounted her body's visceral response.

Suit, tie, wingtips. Audible approach. Not Matt Dorchester.

Probably a reporter, or one of the city councilwoman's peach-fuzz assistants. She turned to face the newcomer and got the same electrifying jolt she felt every time their eyes made contact, sending her heart rate into the stratosphere and cutting off her breath.

Matt Dorchester.

In a suit and tie and wingtips, his badge clipped to his belt, his service weapon visible on his right hip. In his left hand he held a rectangular box wrapped in shimmery green paper. He stopped by the doorway, his gaze taking in her sleek hair and shadowed eyes, the fading bruise on her cheekbone, her conservative pantsuit and sensible heels, flicking over her as if afraid to linger.

Transfixed by one detail of his appearance, she didn't hesitate to stare. "Your hair," she said. It was cropped close to his head, gladiator-style.

"Regulations," he said. He ran a palm over it, crown to forehead, the move practiced and automatic, and for a split second the aura of uniform, helmet, and rifle hung around him like a mirage. Then it disappeared, and in its place stood a man. Just a man. An all-too-human cop, a brother. Maybe, just maybe, a lover. "I'm done undercover. My face was all over the internet and the news. They'll figure out what to do with me after IA clears me and McCormick for the shooting."

Jo had already told her as much, but despite the fact that their efforts to stop Lyle Murphy had cost him the work he loved, he didn't seem all that upset, or locked down, for that matter.

"How do you feel about that?" she asked cautiously.

He looked out over the rubble. "It's the right thing for the department." Another one of those quick, skating glances, then he added, "And for me."

Oh. "That's good, then," she said. Her heart thunked against her chest, and heat rose into her face, making the still-tender spot on her cheekbone throb a little more acutely.

"Nat's inside," he said nodding over his shoulder. "Want me to get her for you?"

"No! Ah, no," she said, striving for the same cool attitude he projected, as if seeing him walk back into the bar didn't fulfill the other half of her dreams.

"Good," he said. "She told me I was six kinds of asshole for lying to her and to you, and if I thought I could drink free because I was a cop, I had another thought coming."

"That sounds like Nat," she said wryly.

"What did you want her to see?" he asked with a nod at the gold-dipped skyline.

"The future," she said. "A long way off, but coming."

Matt surveyed the dust-covered rubble. "You did good, boss."

"So did you," she said. "We did this together."

"I know." He extended the box to her. "This is for you."

"You didn't have to get me a present," she demurred even as she automatically accepted the offered box.

"I wanted . . . I wanted to."

She gave him a startled glance, this time seeing the nerves under the calm. "You did?"

"I did." He nodded at the box. "Open it."

Turning so her back rested against the doorframe, she slid her finger under the tape securing the end of the carefully wrapped paper, then continued the motion across the top of the box. The paper dropped away to reveal a Bose SoundDock, the latest version of the one Lyle's flunky destroyed that fateful night.

Hope flickered to life. "Thank you," she said softly. "I missed this. I missed you."

A really sweet flush stood high on his cheekbones as

the cool façade melted even more. *He's nervous. Not under control. He feels nervous. He* feels.

"I . . . ah . . . haven't been around lately, so maybe you already replaced it. If you did, I hear the Backstreet Boys are touring again."

She threw back her head and laughed. "This is perfect, because I put a new sound dock on my Christmas list and spent the money on a wrecking ball."

That laugh seemed to rumble from his chest a little more easily now, and lingered as a smile on his mouth. He looked at the pile of concrete, shook his head, looked back at her. Then he pulled two sheets of folded paper from his inner suit pocket, unfolded them so she could see the bar codes. The concert tickets. She'd thought he would take Luke, never dared to hope he'd want to take her.

Matt straightened away from the door, squared his shoulders, and held out his hand. Alexi Murdoch's "Orange Sky" played quietly in the background. "I'm Matt Dorchester," he said. "I'm a detective with the Lancaster Police Department."

She'd heard a million lines in her time, but that one . . . that one took the cake.

She set the sound dock on the counter, slipped her hand into his. "Hi, Matt," she said and gave his hand a firm shake. "I'm Eve Webber and I'm not fronting for a psychopath drug dealer."

"Nice to meet you, Eve," he said, but he didn't let go of her hand. "I've got two tickets to the Maud Ward concert. Want to go with me?"

"I hoped you'd ask me," she said. "But really, you can take Luke, or—"

Still gripping her hand, he stepped right into her personal space, and stopped her babble with a soft, thorough kiss. "Go to the concert with me, Eve. Please."

"Okay," she said breathlessly, propriety forgotten in the desire hanging over them like the afternoon sky.

Matt's thumb stroked over the sensitive skin of her inner wrist. "It's Monday night. Are you having dinner with your parents?"

"Dad still gets tired easily, so Mom's taking him home to fuss over him. We're getting together later in the week."

"Do you want to go get dinner?"

"I'd love that," she replied. "If you want to."

"I want to," he said softly.

The words lingered in the air like the dust motes in the setting sun. She waited for him to release her hand, but he held onto it, his thumb now slowly stroking her palm. "You're going to have to let go of my hand."

"I don't want to let go," he said. In the background Alexi Murdoch sang about love and salvation. "I need to not let go."

Eve tilted her head and looked at him. Happiness, relief, reassurance lingered on the surface of his expression, while the depths held a possessiveness that was pure Matt Dorchester. Energy poured from him in waves, but the guarded look in his eyes, the sense of iron walls under muscle and skin, was gone.

"So don't," she said simply. "Don't let go."

He dropped her hand, wrapped that arm around her waist, and cupped the back of her head with his other hand to hold her close. "I missed you. God, I missed you."

Absolutely astonished, a heartbeat passed before a bubble of emotion—joy, surprise, tears—expanded in her throat, but joy rose to the top. She slid her arms into his suit coat, above all the gear on his belt, and curved them up to flatten against his shoulder blades and pull him closer.

When she rested her forehead at the hollow of his

throat, a long, slow sigh eased from him. He buried his face in her hair and drew in breath, exhaled again, and all that restless, tense, masculine energy prowled through her. Tension slipped from his muscles as he softened against her.

Let her hold him. He was utterly open to her. She threw open the doors of her soul and welcomed him in. She held him, he held her, and something clicked into place inside her. She turned her cheek to rest on the hard plane of his chest, breathed the simple, clean scent of him, and gently stroked his back.

The music played quietly in the background, and the setting sun filtered through the dust as they stood together under the orange sky.

"I really, really like it when you do what you want to do, Matt," she whispered, and felt a smile curve against the top of her head.

His hand slid through her hair to cup her cheek. He stroked his thumb over the fading bruise, then bent his head and kissed the mark, a soft, gentle, healing kiss. Nerves ignited under his mouth, sending sensation streaming to her lips, parted on a skittering inhale.

"You sure? Maybe we should experiment a little. Make sure you want what I want."

She traced his lower lip with her tongue, then he kissed her, just a gentle, open-mouthed kiss. It had never been this sweet. Never.

"For example, I wanted to do that. You?"

"I wanted you to do that," she replied. "How did it feel to you?"

"It felt right," he said against her uninjured cheekbone. "Really, really right."

The confidence in his tone made her smile. "Me too."

He did it again, then said, “This is definitely going to take weeks, because God knows we both have to work.”

“Months.”

“Years,” he said. The air flooded out of her when he tugged her out of the sunlight, into the cool dark of the storeroom, and backed her into the door, finally releasing her hand to slide his palm along her hip. “We’re talking about a lifetime commitment.”

She leaned back, and looked up into his face. “Are we?”

“I am.” His gaze searched hers. “I love you, Eve.”

A tremor ran through her at the words, but she continued to look into his eyes. “How do you know? We’ve been under duress.”

“I feel it,” he said simply, then brought her hand to rest flat on his chest. Through the white dress shirt she felt his heart beating. “Here. And here,” he added, moving her hand up to his throat. “Everywhere. You’re everywhere inside me, and I want you with me forever.”

She stroked the five o’clock shadow emerging on his jaw. “I want to be with you forever. We’ll make our own reality, you and me.”

“Sounds good, boss.”

Read on for an excerpt from Anne Calhoun's next book

GOING DEEP

Coming soon from St. Martin's Paperbacks

CHAPTER ONE

It was good to be home.

Cady Ward stood under the spotlight, the crowd's manic, vibrant energy rolling at her in waves, all but lifting her off her feet with the surging roar and applause. She smiled, lifted a hand in acknowledgment. The clapping and whistles ticked up again. Sweat trickled down her ribs and spine. Her silk tank top clung to her skin as she shifted her guitar to her back, put her hands together, and bowed her appreciation to the crowd. Some of them were still singing the refrain to *Love Crossed Stars*, her biggest hit, the final song of her encore set.

"Thank you," she murmured, not sure if the sound engineer had cut her mike feed or not. They echoed back into her earpiece, but the spoken words were lost in the din inside Lancaster's Field Energy Center.

Hometown crowds were always generous. By this time in the show, after two encores and several minutes of applause, people started to trickle out, maybe making one last stop at the merchandise table for a T-shirt or a magnet or a CD. But these folks showed no signs of dispersing. Just as reluctant to leave the high behind, Cady bent over and made her way along the edge of the stage, high-fiving and clasping hands with the people in the front rows. Her grandmother's bracelet, a cherished keepsake she always wore when she performed, nearly clonked a girl on the forehead as Cady swept by. "We love you, Maud!" she cried out, borderline hysterical as she waved her homemade poster.

Maud was her stage name, borrowed from her grandmother back when she needed a persona to work up the courage to put her voice out there, back when all she wanted was to be Beyonce, Sia, Adele, a one-name wonder with multiple hits, Grammys, platinum albums. But after eight months of touring as Maud, she was back in her hometown, able to spend a few weeks being herself. Ordinary Cady Ward.

"I love you, too!" she called back, vaguely aware that lurking behind the adrenaline rush of performing was the knowledge that tomorrow she'd feel like someone had taken a stick to her legs and back. Out of the corner of her eye she saw her manager, Chris Wellendorf, standing in the wings, tight shoulders and unsmiling face telegraphing his nervous tension. He didn't like it when she got too close to the fans without security personnel at hand. All it took was one crazy person to break a finger or stab her with something, one interaction gone wrong to spread all over social media.

She straightened and stepped back, automatically adjusting both bracelet and guitar again, then held up her hands. "Thanks for coming, everyone. Happy holidays. Drive safely, and good night!"

The wave of applause carried her offstage, and continued until the lighting engineer cut the stage lights and turned up the houselights. Breathing hard, Cady washed up against the wall. Around her, the band was efficiently packing away the instruments. Next, the road crew would take down the set, then the stage. By the end of the night, the auditorium would be empty, waiting silently for the next event. Given the time of year—early December—probably a Lancaster College basketball game.

"I can't sing it again." She turned to look at Chris. "I can't. If I have to sing *Love Crossed Stars* one more time, I will go out of my mind."

"That's the end of the tour talking. *Love Crossed Stars* will be your cash cow for the rest of your life. Besides, you think Paul Simon doesn't roll out *Sounds of Silence* or *Graceland* or *Mrs. Robinson* at every show?"

"Paul Simon has dozens of songs he can use for a final encore," Cady said. "Dozens. All of them brilliant. All of them telling profound stories about the human condition. Are any of them love songs? No."

"Paul Simon is Paul Simon, with fifty years of singing and songwriting behind him. You are just starting out. Be happy. It was a good show," Chris said.

"You always say that," Cady replied, looking around for her water bottle.

"And I always mean it," Chris said smoothly, producing a bottle from his jacket pocket and restoring the normally impeccable lines of his suit. In concession to the casual concert venue he'd stuffed his tie into his pocket and opened the top two buttons of his shirt. A single strand of his dishwater blond hair escaped from the gel slicking it back, giving him a vaguely rumpled look. "This time was different. Normally you're dialed up to eleven on the scale. Tonight you were around fifteen."

"These are my peeps," Cady said after she swallowed half the water. She hooked her thumb in her guitar strap and hoisted it over her head. "I'm home. I've been playing for them since I was fifteen, busking in SoMa."

"Usually without a permit," came a familiar voice next to her.

"Eve, hi!" She backed away a step when Eve reached for her. "No, you really don't want to hug me. I've sweated through my jeans."

"Don't be ridiculous," Eve said, and swept her up. "That was amazing! I loved the new take on *Summer Nights*. Where do you get your energy? You've been on the road for weeks now!"

Cady hugged her back, just as hard, so grateful for her friend's early and vocal support. Chris was checking Eve out, not all that covertly, either. Eve had that kind of impact on men, even in jeans, ankle boots, and a crisp white button-down. "I've been on the road for *months*. We did the state fair circuit over the summer, where I ate every kind of food on a stick you can eat."

"Including fried candy bars?" Eve asked.

"All the fried candy bars," Cady said. Performing burned so many calories she could eat whatever she wanted and stay in shape. "I drew the line at a Twinkie log on a stick, though," she added, then finished the rest of the water.

"You've got standards," Eve said, still smiling. "Oh, it's so good to see you!"

"You, too," Cady said. Absently, she introduced Chris and Eve, peering around the rapidly dismantling backstage, looking for her sister and mother. She heard Emily before she saw her, high-pitched voice, the clatter of heels as she rounded the corner and made straight for Cady.

"You're home!" Emily shrieked and launched herself at Cady.

"You're taller!" Cady laughed into Emily's hair as Emily wrapped her arms around Cady and pulled her close. "Great outfit," she said when Emily let go long enough for Cady to lean back and get a closer look.

"She tried on everything she owned," her mother said, coming in for a hug.

"Hi, Mom. Thanks for coming," Cady said over Emily's protesting *Mom.*

"Ah, good to see you again, Mrs. Ward," Chris said.

Her mother smiled at him and reached for Cady to give her a quick hug and kiss. "We need to get home soon," her mother said. "It's a school night."

"Mom," Emily groaned.

"It's a school night," she repeated firmly. Cady remembered this from her adolescence.

"It's Cady's homecoming concert! We talked about this. I'm going to drive Cady back to—"

Chris shot her a warning glance. Emily transitioned smoothly, "—home."

"You said you were going to do that, and I said I don't want you driving late at night."

"Mom," Emily started mulishly.

"It's fine," Cady said, snagging her guitar case from the roadie who'd appeared beside her. Best to head off a fight at the pass. "I'm coming home tonight, so Emily will get a good night's sleep. Right, Em?"

Emily had the good sense to be gracious in victory, giving their mother a big hug and standing demurely by Cady's side and holding the guitar case for her. "You really like the outfit?" Emily asked.

Her sister was five ten without the three-inch heels, slender as a wire coat hanger. She wore a black skirt with carwash pleats, a slim grey turtleneck, and grey suede over-the-knee boots that left a good four inches of thigh bare. The outfit would have been sleek New York professional except Emily had gone for broke with her makeup, layering in smoky eyes, a hint of blush, and dark lips. She looked far older and more sophisticated than the gawky girl Cady remembered from her last visit in February. Emily had been trying on styles for a couple of years now, trying to find who she was as a growing woman. "You look amazing," Cady said.

"I made the skirt," Emily started. "The sweater's from—"

A mic stand tipped into an equalizer before crashing to the floor just before a man stumbled out from behind a wall of boxed equipment. He untangled his feet, then tripped again as the mic stand rolled back in his direction. He got himself upright and looked around with the fierce concentration of the stupidly drunk. He caught sight of Cady and everyone stopped talking.

"Maud!" he yelled. He stretched a hand toward her. "Maud, I just want to talk to you!"

"Who's that?" Emily said.

"No idea." Cady quickly scanned the backstage area for an exit strategy. The last thing she wanted to do was bolt onto the stage, where a crowd still lingered, with their phones and cameras. Her back was literally to the wall, and her little sister stood beside her in heels that Cady would bet her favorite guitar Emily couldn't run in. As unobtrusively as she could, she stepped in front of her little sister.

"Security. *Security!*" Chris shouted, looking around wildly.

Great, Cady thought. *That's going to play well on TMZ.*

"Hey, big guy," she said easily as she swatted at Chris to make him shut up. "What's up?"

"Maud, I love you. I love you, and I want to be with you, and I've written some songs for us to sing together."

Once, just once, I want a man to confess his love for me using my real name. Not Maud "Really? I could use some new material," she said, because keeping him talking was obviously the right thing to do, and because behind the drunk, two men in police polos with badges and guns clipped to their belts had materialized. One had reddish brown hair and a lean build that would be easy to underestimate. The other man had a good six inches and fifty pounds of muscle on the other guy and shoulders as broad as a steer's that tapered to a narrow waist. His dark brown hair swooped back from his forehead, emphasizing a square face dominated by cheekbones and a fighter's chin.

"Hi, Matt," Eve said, lifting a hand in a casual wave. Her tone was totally relaxed, but Cady knew that Eve's Matt was a detective with the Lancaster Police Department. Her attention switched between the admirer, stumbling into boxes and amplifiers and lighting rigs, and the two men stalking him from behind. Cady was pretty sure Matt wasn't Shoulders, who'd drawn up silent as smoke just behind the drunk guy. She got a flash of slate blue eyes when he flicked a glance her way. *Distract him.*

"Um . . . what kind of songs?" she asked.

"A sequel to *Love Crossed Stars.* It's about our love. Because I love you."

Beside her, Chris snorted. "Uh-huh," she said. Shoulders was inches from his back, so she flashed her brightest smile, gave him a bobblehead nod, and lied through her teeth. "That's my favorite song. I'd love to sing a sequel."

When Shoulders' badge and gun registered in her admirer's alcohol-soaked brain, he swung out wildly. Shoulders ducked an ineptly aimed backhand and stepped right into the drunk's body, shoving him off balance, then caught his arm on the forward swing.

"Hey," Drunk Guy said, indignant, struggling. "Get the fuck off me, man. I just want to talk to her."

The taller cop got the guy's other arm in a firm grip, then locked eyes with Shoulders over the flailing drunk's head. "One . . . two . . . three."

Shoulders thrust his leg behind the drunk's knee. A neat twist of hips and shoulders, and they took the drunk down, face-first on the floor. A grunt, then a high-pitched yelp. "Ow! Maud!"

"Hey, Romeo," Shoulders said, snapping a cuff around the man's wrist. "You think this is your best move? Coming backstage where you don't belong, smelling like a frat party?"

"I just wanted to talk to her," the drunk slurred. "I love her. We're going to make music together."

Shoulders clicked the other cuff around the second wrist, then nodded at the taller cop. Together they hoisted the guy up and set him on his feet. It was an impressive display of strength, given that Drunk Guy had a significant beer-and-wings gut spilling over his belt. All Cady could think about was the way the band around the sleeve of his polo choked his biceps, the way the muscles in his forearms shifted as he easily controlled the prisoner. Just like that, her brain shifted from tour mode, when sex was easily forgotten, to rest mode, when it was all she could think about.

"How about you write her a nice letter from jail?" Shoulders said. "No, I've got this," he said to the other cop. "You stay with Eve. Come on, Romeo. You can serenade the rest of the drunk-and-disorderlies in the van."

Everyone watched him guide Drunk Guy through the maze of equipment, including Cady's suitcases. She cast them a loathing look. Tonight was the last night she'd live out of her suitcase. Tomorrow she would unpack in her own house, eat food from her own fridge, sleep in her own bed.

"Cady, darling, the only reason we let Evan go was you saying Lancaster was safe. That nothing ever happened here. That you were no big deal here," Chris muttered.

Evan had been her bodyguard on the tour. An obsessive workout that required two hours a day in the gym meant he had the strong half of strong silent type down, but he talked almost incessantly, a running commentary mostly on his workout and diet that, over the course of the tour, drove Cady nuts. "It is. It was," Cady replied, fingering the bracelet in a habitual nervous gesture before she caught herself. "And you know Evan had to go. I was ready to kill him in Topeka."

"Barbecued beef tongue is delicious," Chris said, back on his phone.

"It's tongue. It's gross. I didn't care that he ate it. I cared that he wouldn't freaking shut up about it."

The chestnut-haired cop strode over to the small, frozen group. "You all right, Ms. Ward?" he asked, his gaze skimming the group before settling on Eve.

"I'm fine," Cady said. Her voice sounded almost giddy. She wasn't sure if she was relieved the guy was gone, or that this was obviously Eve's Matt. "Thank you for handling that so quickly. Please tell the other officer . . . "

"McCormick."

"Please give Officer McCormick my thanks."

"I will," he said.

"Cady, this is Matt," Eve said, as if the smile on her face and the delight in her eyes didn't give it away. "Matt, meet Cady."

"Nice to officially meet you," Matt said with a nod. "I'm a big fan."

"Thank you. I've heard so much about you from Eve," she said.

"That's not good," Matt said easily.

"It wasn't all bad," Cady said, to laughter.

"He's been a fan almost as long as I have," Eve said. "Your first Maud concert was when?"

"The Slowdown, five, no, six years ago," Matt said.

"Wow, that is a long time," Cady agreed. She'd been nineteen, on her father's shit list for refusing to go to college, singing wherever she could get a gig and eating ramen noodles out of styrofoam cups. "I was still singing covers at that point."

"Yeah, but you had something," Eve said. "We all knew it."

"Thanks," Cady said again. She was too tired to think of something more creative to say, but with Eve she didn't have to. "I really need to get going. Emily has school tomorrow."

"Of course," Eve said. "Get some rest, then come see me. I'd love to have you at Eye Candy when you're ready."

"Ms. Ward won't be taking any engagements for the next few weeks," Chris said smoothly.

"It's not an engagement," Cady said. "It's a favor for a friend. A very dear friend."

He gave her a look reminding her that she needed to rest her voice. Only a few people knew about the upcoming album for which the label planned a surprise Beyonce-style drop around Valentine's Day, less than three months away. The thought made her stomach turn a slow loop. Chris chalked it up to nerves, to exhaustion, to creative fatigue, to anything but Cady's growing uncertainty that the album was the right thing to release now.

Chris broke the silence. "We can talk about it tomorrow, when you've had a chance to rest up. I've booked a car for you."

"Hello, remember me? I'm taking her home," Emily said.

"I remembered," Cady said. "Let's grab my suitcases and we can head out."

Cady, Eve, Matt, and Chris scuffled over who would carry the two enormous suitcases she'd lugged on tour buses and the occasional plane for the last eight months. Matt and Chris finally won, and followed Emily's runway catwalk stride through the backstage area to the arena door. Eve and Cady trailed behind them.

The cold air instantly froze the sweat still drying in her clothes. Cady shivered, and Chris immediately pulled her back inside. "No way are you going out there without a coat and a scarf," he said. "Emily, pull the car around for her."

He unzipped one suitcase and flung the lid back. The thick, spiral-bound notebook she used as a diary and scratch pad for songwriting slid out of the unzipped mesh pocket, onto the floor. Cady crouched down and gathered it up, tucking it back into the pocket along with an assortment of cocktail napkins and scraps of paper.

"Working on anything new?" Eve asked, helping her gather the loose paper. She'd been around Cady long enough to know that her process was firmly twentieth century.

"I am," she said, shooting a defiant glare at Chris across her suitcase. With a total disregard for her privacy he rummaged through a stack of underwear and her nightie, shifting heels and Converse, two of her favorite T-shirts, in search of her scarf and coat.

"She's always writing," Chris said, extracting the thick green scarf and her down jacket from the bottom of the bag. "Put these on. Hot water with honey. Bed."

"I know the routine," she said. She shoved her arms into the coat sleeves and wound the scarf around her face and throat.

"Part of the routine is me reminding you," Chris said.

Properly mummified, Eve opened the door again. Em's Corolla was idling by the arena's loading dock.

Matt and Chris stored the suitcases in the trunk while Cady slid into the passenger seat. Heat blasted from the vents, almost making up for the cold air billowing in the open door.

"I'll call you," Chris said, leaning over the frame. "We need to talk about your security."

"No we don't," Cady replied.

"My flight's at four," he said implacably. "I'll call around ten."

"Fine," she said absently. She wanted to ask Eve's Matt about Shoulders, but couldn't think of a way to do it that wouldn't set a bad example for Emily, so she called, "I'll see you soon!" to Eve and Matt, and closed the door on Chris's yelp about not raising her voice.

Emily zipped out of the parking lot and turned onto Tenth Street, then braked hard at the red light. Cady's shoulder harness jerked. She shot Emily a glance, but her sister stared straight ahead. In the streetlight her eye makeup was starting to smear. Cady couldn't even imagine what her face and hair looked like. After a show her face could resemble melting plastic as the lights and sweat worked away at enough makeup to animate her facial features.

"What's wrong?"

"You didn't introduce me."

"You know Chris," Cady said, bewildered. "You've met him a dozen times. And Eve."

"To the hot cop. Eve introduced you to him, but you didn't introduce me."

Cady blinked. "To Matt? He's Eve's boyfriend, and he barely noticed me. Eve's in a league of her own. No one notices me when she's in the room."

"Oh, he noticed you, Queen Maud of the Maud Squad," Emily said. "You could have introduced me to him."

"Things were happening so fast," she said. "Next time,

I promise. Thanks for getting the house ready for me. I'm so excited to see it. How about we plan on having you sleep over this weekend? You can help me decorate."

Emily's face lit up. "Ugh, I have to work both days and I've got homework, stupid finals coming up, papers due, but we can hang out when I'm off."

"I remember what December's like when you're in high school," Cady said with a laugh. "It'll be fun. Like old times."

The drive through the backstreets into one of Lancaster's older neighborhoods took Cady back in time. Her mother still lived in the house she'd bought after their dad left. It was small, but refurbished inside and out. The house was from the fifties but recently renovated top to bottom, three bedrooms, a full bathroom she'd shared with Emily, a three-quarters bath off her mom's bedroom, a kitchen with an eating area that overlooked the backyard and a den. Lights burned brightly over the front and side doors, but her mother's bedroom window was dark. "The other cop wasn't bad-looking. The really, really big one," Emily clarified.

"Emily, he's at least ten years older than you are," Cady said as Emily parked the car in front of the house. Her mother had the garage and left for work by seven, which meant Emily parked on the street if she didn't want to have to move her car at the crack of dawn.

"So? I'm legal," Emily said

Cady had spent too much time on the road with male musicians to be shocked by teenage girls lusting after an older man exuding power and confidence. "There's legal and then there's smart. Sometimes you have to be smart, for your own sake."

"And sometimes I hate being the youngest," Emily said. "You've done everything first. I can't even make my own mistakes."

"Sure you can," Cady said over the roof of the car. "You just can't complain when I say I told you so."

Her sister grabbed the bigger, heavier suitcase and started lugging it toward the door. "Boys my age are stupid."

"Grown men aren't always smart," Cady said as they hauled the bags through the front door.

"I'll make you some hot water," Emily said and strode into the kitchen.

Cady got her bags into what had been her room until Emily converted it into a studio after she left. Cady's single bed was pushed against the wall and covered with a big piece of plywood to turn it into a cutting board. Emily had moved the fabric scraps to the sewing station that took up most of the floor space. Cady stared at the tiny, crowded space and thought that there was no way she could fit herself and Shoulders, aka McCormick, into that bed.

That was depressing enough to make her leave the bags where they were and walk back down the hall to the kitchen, where Emily was drizzling honey into steaming water. A cup of cocoa steamed on the counter.

"Does that happen often?" Em asked.

"Does what?" she asked, still distracted by the memory of Shoulders' muscles flexing.

"Crazy drunk guys coming out of the shadows." Emily held out the mug.

"They're always out there," Cady said with a shrug. She clinked cups with Emily, then sipped the drink that was as much honey as water, and let out a sigh. She'd shed Chris, her stylist, her bodyguard, the band, and was finally alone and home. "It's so good to be home."

"Only if you leave," Emily muttered.